A LONE STAR CHRISTMAS

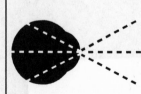

This Large Print Book carries the
Seal of Approval of N.A.V.H.

A LONE STAR CHRISTMAS

WILLIAM W. JOHNSTONE
WITH J. A. JOHNSTONE

WHEELER PUBLISHING
A part of Gale, Cengage Learning

GALE
CENGAGE Learning·

Detroit • New York • San Francisco • New Haven, Conn • Waterville, Maine • London

LIBRARY OF CONGRESS CATALOGING-IN-PUBLICATION DATA

Johnstone, William W.
    A lone star Christmas / William W. Johnstone with J.A. Johnstone. — Large print ed.
        p. cm. — (Wheeler Publishing large print Western)
    ISBN 978-1-4104-4608-4 (softcover) — ISBN 1-4104-4608-5 (softcover) 1. Jensen, Smoke (Fictitious character)—Fiction. 2. Cattle drives—Fiction. 3. Blizzards—Fiction. 4. Wilderness survival—Fiction. 5. Christmas stories. 6. Large type books. I. Johnstone, J. A. II. Title.
PS3560.O415L66 2012
813'.54—dc23   2012026935

Published in 2012 by arrangement with Pinnacle Books, an imprint of Kensington Publishing Corp.

Printed in the United States of America
1 2 3 4 5 6 7 16 15 14 13 12

A LONE STAR CHRISTMAS

CHAPTER ONE

Marshall, Texas, March 12, 1890

It was cold outside, but in the depot waiting room, a wood-burning, pot-bellied stove roared and popped and glowed red as it pumped out enough heat to make the waiting room comfortable, if one chose the right place to sit. Too close and it was too hot, too far away and it was too cold.

There were about nine people in the waiting room at the moment, though Rebecca knew that only four of them, including herself, were passengers. Two weeks earlier, Benjamin Conyers, better known as Big Ben, had taken his 21-year-old daughter into Fort Worth to catch the train. Now, after a two-week visit with Big Ben's sister in Marshall, Texas, it was time for Rebecca to return home. Her Aunt Mildred had come to the depot with her to see her off on the evening train.

Everyone agreed that Rebecca Conyers

was a beautiful young woman. She had delicate facial bones and a full mouth; she was slender, with long, rich, glowing auburn hair, green eyes, and a slim waist. She was sitting on a bench, the wood polished smooth by the many passengers who had sat in this same place over the last several years. Just outside the depot window, she could see the green glowing lamp of the electric railroad signal.

"Rebecca, I have so enjoyed your visit," Mildred said. "You simply must come again sometime soon."

"I would love to," Rebecca replied. "I enjoyed the visit as well."

"I wish Ben would come with you sometime. But I know he is busy."

"Yes," Rebecca said. "Pa always seems to be busy."

"Well, he is an important man," Mildred said. "And important men always seem to be busy." She laughed. "I don't know if he is busy because he is important, or he is important because he is busy. I imagine it is a little of both."

"Yes, I would think so as well," Rebecca said. "Aunt Mildred, did you know my mother?"

"Julia? Of course I know her, dear. Why would you ask such a thing?"

"I don't mean Julia," Rebecca said. "I mean my real mother. I think her name is Janie."

Mildred was quiet for a long moment. "Heavens, child, why would you ask such a thing now? The only mother you have ever known is Julia."

"I know, and she is my mother in every way," Rebecca said. "But I know too, that she wasn't my birth mother, and I would like to know something more about her."

Mildred sighed. "Well, I guess that is understandable," she said.

"Did you know her? Do you remember her?"

"I do remember her, yes," Rebecca's Aunt Mildred said. "I know that when Ben learned that she was pregnant, he brought her out to the house. You were born right there, on the ranch."

"Pa is my real father though, isn't he? I mean he is the one who got my real mother pregnant."

"Oh yes, there was never any question about that," Mildred replied.

"And yet he never married my mother," Rebecca said.

"Honey, don't blame Ben for that. He planned to marry her, but shortly after you were born Janie ran off."

"Janie was my birth mother?"

"Yes."

"What was her last name?"

"Garner, I believe it was. Yes, her name was Janie Garner. But, like I said, she ran off and left you behind. That's when Ben wrote me and asked me to come take care of you until he could find someone else to do it."

"That's when Mama, that is Julia, the woman I call Mama, came to live with us?"

"She did. You were only two months old when Julia came. She and Ben had known each other before, and everyone was sure they were going to get married. But after the war, Ben seemed — I don't know, restless, I guess you would say. Anyway, it took him a while to settle down, and by that time he had already met your real mother. I'll tell you true, she broke his heart when she left."

"Why did my real mother leave? Did she run away with another man?"

"Nobody knows for sure. All we know is that she left a note saying she wasn't good enough for you," Mildred said. "For heaven's sake, child, why are you asking so many questions about her now? Hasn't Julia been a good mother to you?"

"She has been a wonderful mother to me,"

Rebecca said. "I couldn't ask for anyone better, and I love her dearly. I've just been a little curious, that's all."

"You know what they say, honey. Curiosity killed the cat," Aunt Mildred said.

Hearing the whistle of the approaching train, they stood up and walked out onto the depot platform. It was six o'clock, and the sun was just going down in the west, spreading the clouds with long, glowing streaks of gold and red. To the east they could see the headlamp of the arriving train. It roared into the station, spewing steam and dropping glowing embers from the firebox. The train was so massive and heavy that it made Rebecca's stomach shake as it passed by, first the engine with its huge driver wheels, then the cars with the long lines of lighted windows on each one disclosing the passengers inside, some looking out in curiosity, others reading in jaded indifference to the Marshall depot which represented but one more stop on their trip.

"What time will you get to Fort Worth?" Aunt Mildred asked.

"The schedule says eleven o'clock tonight."

"Oh, heavens, will Ben have someone there to meet you?"

"No, I'll be staying at a hotel. Papa already

has a room booked for me. He'll send someone for me tomorrow."

"Board!" the conductor called, and Rebecca and her aunt shared a long goodbye hug before she hurried to get on the train.

Inside the first car behind the express car, Tom Whitman studied the passengers who would be boarding. He didn't know what town he was in. In fact, he wasn't even sure what state he was in. It wasn't too long ago that they'd left Shreveport. He knew that Shreveport was in Louisiana, and he knew it wasn't too far from Texas, so he wouldn't be surprised if they were in Texas now.

"We are on the threshold of the twentieth century, Tom," a friend had told him a couple of months ago. "Do you have any idea what a marvelous time this is? Think of all those people who went by wagon train to California. Their trip was arduous, dangerous, and months long. Today one can go by train, enjoying the luxury of a railroad car that protects them from rain, snow, beating sun, or bitter cold. They can dine sumptuously on meals served in a dining salon that rivals the world's finest restaurants. They can view the passing scenery while relaxing in an easy chair, and they can pass the nights in a comfortable bed with clean sheets."

At the time of that conversation, Tom had no idea that within a short time he would actually be taking that cross-country trip. Now he was in one more town of an almost countless number of towns he had been in over the last six days and ten states.

This town wasn't that large, and although there were at least ten people standing out on the platform, there were only four people boarding, as far as he could determine. One of those boarding was a very pretty young, auburn-haired woman, and he watched her share a goodbye hug with an older woman, who Tom took to be her mother.

One of the passengers who had just boarded was putting his coat in the overhead rack, just in front of Tom.

"Excuse me," Tom said to him. "What is the name of this town?"

"Marshall," the passenger answered.

"Louisiana, or Texas?"

"Texas, Mister. The great state of Texas," the man replied with inordinate pride.

"Thank you," Tom said.

"Been traveling long?" the man asked.

"Yes, this is my sixth day."

"Where are you headed?"

"I don't have any particular destination in mind."

"Ha, that's funny. I don't know as I've

ever met anyone who was travelin' and didn't even know where they was goin'."

"When I find a place that fits my fancy, I'll stop," Tom said.

"Well, Mister, I'll tell you true, you ain't goin' to fine any place better than Texas. And any place in Texas you decide to stop is better than any place else."

"Thank you," Tom said. "I'll keep that in mind."

In the week since he had left Boston, Tom had shared the train with hundreds of others, none of whom had continued their journey with him. He had managed to strike up a conversation with some of them, but in every case, they were only brief acquaintances, then they moved on. He thought of the passage from Longfellow.

Ships that pass in the night, and speak
    each other in passing,
Only a signal shown and a distant voice
    in the darkness;
So on the ocean of life we pass and
    speak one another,
Only a look and a voice, then darkness
    again and a silence.

With a series of jerks as the train took up the slack between the cars, it pulled away from the station, eventually smoothing out and picking up speed. Once the train settled in to its gentle rocking and rhythmic clacking forward progress, Tom leaned his head against the seat back and went to sleep.

Once Rebecca boarded, found her seat, and the train got underway, she reached into her purse to take out the letter. She had picked the letter up at the post office shortly before she left Fort Worth to come visit her Aunt Mildred. The letter, which was addressed to her and not to her father, had come as a complete surprise. Her father knew nothing about it, nor did she show it to her Aunt Mildred. The letter was from her real mother, and it was the first time in Rebecca's life that she had ever heard from her.

Her first instinct had been to tear it up and throw it away, unread. After all, if her mother cared so little about her that she could abandon her when Rebecca was still a baby, why should Rebecca care what she had to say now?

But curiosity got the best of her, so she read the letter. Now, sitting in the train going back home, Rebecca read the letter again.

Dear Becca,

This letter is going to come as a shock to you, but I am your real mother. I am very sorry that I left you when you were a baby, and I am even more sorry that I have never attempted to contact you. I want you to know, however, that my not contacting you is not because you mean nothing to me. I have kept up with your life as best I can, and I know that you have grown to be a very beautiful and very wonderful young woman.

That is exactly what I expected to happen when I left you with your father. I did that, and I have stayed out of your life because I thought that best. Certainly there was no way I could have given you the kind of life your father has been able to provide for you. But it would fulfill a lifetime desire if I could see you just once. If you can find it in your heart to forgive me, and to grant this wish, you will find me in Dodge City, Kansas. I am married to the owner of the Lucky Chance Saloon.

Your mother,
Janie Davenport

Rebecca knew about her mother; she had been told a long time ago that Julia was her stepmother. But she didn't know anything about her real mother, and on the few times she had asked, she had always been given the same answer.

"Your mother was a troubled soul, and things didn't work out for her. I'm sure that she believed, when she left you, that she was doing the right thing," Big Ben had said.

"Have you ever heard from her again?" Rebecca wanted to know.

"No, I haven't, and I don't expect that I will. To tell you the truth, darlin', I'm not even sure she is still alive."

That had satisfied Rebecca, and she had asked no more questions until, unexpectedly, she had received this letter.

From the moment Rebecca had received the letter, she had been debating with herself as to whether or not she should go to Dodge. And if so, should she ask her father for permission to go? Or should she just go? She was twenty-one years old, certainly old enough to make her own decision.

She just didn't know what that decision should be.

She read the letter one more time, then folded it, put it back in her reticule, and settled in for the three and one-half hour train trip.

17

Fort Worth, Texas

The train had arrived in the middle of the night, and when Tom Whitman got off, he wondered if he should stay here or get back on the train and keep going. Six and one-half days earlier he had boarded a train in Boston with no particular destination in mind. His only goal at the time was to be somewhere other than Boston.

Now, as he stood alongside the train, he became aware of a disturbance at the other end of the platform. A young woman was being bothered by two men. Looking in her direction, Tom saw that it was the same young woman he had seen board the train back in Marshall.

"Please," she was saying to the two men. "Leave me alone."

"Here now, you pretty little thing, you know you don't mean that," one of the two men said. "Why, you wouldn't be standin' out here all alone in the middle of the night, if you wasn't lookin' for a little fun, would you now? And me 'n Pete here are just the men to show you how to have some fun. Right, Pete?"

"You got that right," Pete said.

"What do you say, honey? Do you want to have a little fun with us?"

"No! Please, go away!" the young woman said.

"I know what it is, Dutch," Pete said. "We ain't offered her no money yet."

"Is that it?" Dutch asked. "You're waitin' for us to offer you some money? How about two dollars? A dollar from me and one from Pete. Of course, that means you are going to have to be nice to both of us."

"I asked you to go away. If you don't, I will scream."

Pete took off his bandana and wadded it into a ball. "It's goin' to be hard for you to scream with this bandana in your mouth," he said.

Tom walked down to the scene of the ruckus. "Excuse me, gentlemen, but I do believe I heard the lady ask you to leave her alone," he said.

Tom was six feet two inches tall, with broad shoulders and narrow hips. Ordinarily his size alone would be intimidating, but the way he was dressed made him appear almost foppish. He was wearing a brown tweed suit, complete with vest, tie, and collar. He was also wearing a bowler hat, and he was obviously unarmed. He could not have advertised himself as more of a stranger to the West if he had a sign hanging around his neck proclaiming the same.

19

The two men, itinerant cowboys, were wearing denim trousers and stained shirts. Both were wearing Stetson hats, and both had pistols hanging at their sides. When they saw Tom, they laughed.

"Well now, tell me, Dutch, have you ever seen a prettier boy than this *Eastern* dude?" Pete asked. He slurred the word "Eastern."

"Don't believe I have," Dutch replied. Then to Tom he said, "Go away, pretty boy, unless you want to get hurt."

"Let's hurt him anyway," Pete said, smiling. "Let's hurt him real bad for stickin' his nose in where it don't belong."

"Please, sir," the young woman said to Tom. "Go and summon a policeman. I don't want you to get hurt, and I don't think they will do anything if they know a police officer is coming."

"I think it may be too late for that," Tom replied. "These gentlemen seem rather insistent. I'm afraid I'm going to have to take care of this myself."

"Ha!" Pete shouted. "Take care of this!"

Pete swung hard, but Tom reached up and caught his fist in his open hand. That surprised Pete, but it didn't surprise him as much as what happened next. Tom began to squeeze down on Pete's fist, putting vise-like pressure against it, feeling two of Pete's fingers snap under the squeeze.

"Ahhh!" Pete yelled. "Dutch! Get him off me! Get him off me!"

Dutch swung as well, and Tom caught his fist in his left hand. He repeated the procedure of squeezing down on the fist, and within a moment he had both men on their knees, writhing in pain.

"Let go, let go!" Pete screamed in agony.

Tom let go of both of them, and stepped back as the two men regained their feet.

"Please go away now," Tom said with no more tension in his voice than if he were asking for a cup of coffee.

"You son of a . . ." Pete swore as he started to draw his pistol. But because two of his fingers were broken, he was unable to get a grip on his pistol and it fell from his hand. The young woman grabbed it quickly, then pointed it at both of them.

"This gentleman may be an Eastern dude, but I am not," she said. "I'm a Western girl and I can shoot. I would like nothing better than to put a bullet into both of you, and if the two of you don't start running, right now, I will do just that."

"No, no, don't shoot! Don't shoot!" Pete cried out. "We're goin'! We're goin'!"

The two men ran, and the young woman laughed. To Tom, her laughter sounded like wind chimes. She turned to him with a broad smile spread across her face.

"I want to thank you, sir," she said. She thrust her hand toward him, but when he shied away she looked down and saw that she was still holding the pistol. With another laugh, she tossed the gun away, then again stuck out her hand.

"I'm Rebecca Conyers," she said.

"I'm Tom . . . ," Tom hesitated for a moment before he said, "Whitman."

"You aren't from here, are you, Mr. Whitman?"

Tom chuckled. "How can you tell?"

Rebecca laughed as well.

"What are you doing in Fort Worth?"

"This is where the train stopped," Tom replied.

Rebecca laughed again. "That's reason enough, I suppose. Are you looking for work?"

"Well, yes, I guess I am."

"Meet me in the lobby of the Clark Hotel tomorrow morning," she said. "Someone will be coming to fetch me from my father's ranch. He is always looking for good men. I'm sure he would hire you if you are interested."

"Hire me to do what?"

"Why, to cowboy, of course."

"Oh. Do you think it would matter if I told l him that I have never been a cowboy?"

Rebecca smiled. "Telling him you have never been a cowboy would be like telling him that you have blond hair and blue eyes."

"Oh, yes. I see what you mean," he said.

"It's easy to learn to be a cowboy. Once he hears what you did for me tonight, you won't have any trouble getting on. That is, if you want to."

"Yes," Tom said. "I believe I would want to."

As Rebecca lay in bed in her room at the Clark Hotel half an hour later, she wondered what had possessed her to offer a job to Tom Whitman. She had no authority to offer him a job; her father did the hiring and the firing, and he was very particular about it.

On the other hand, before she left to go to Marshall last week, she heard him tell Clay Ramsey that he might hire someone to replace Tony Peters, a young cowboy who had left for Nevada to try his hand at finding gold or silver. Rebecca had a sudden thought. What if he has already hired someone to replace Peters?

No, she was sure he had not. Her father tended to be much more methodical than to hire someone that quickly. But that same tendency of his to be methodical might also work against her, for he would not be that anxious to hire someone he knew nothing about.

Well, Rebecca would just have to talk him into it, that's all. And surely when her father heard what Tom Whitman had done for her, he would be more than willing.

Rebecca wondered why she was so intent on getting Mr. Whitman hired. Was it because he had been her knight in shining armor, just when she needed such a hero? Or was it because with his muscular build, his blond hair and blue eyes, that he might be one of the most handsome men she had ever seen? In addition to that, though, there was something else about him, something that she sensed more than she saw. He had a sense of poise and self-assuredness that she found most intriguing.

Because it had been unseasonably warm, and because Tom liked to sleep with fresh air, he had raised the window when he went to bed last night. He had taken a room in the same hotel as Rebecca because she had suggested the hotel to him. He was awakened this morning by a combination of things, the sun streaming in through his open window, and the sounds of commerce coming from the street below.

He could hear the sound of the clash of eras, the whir of an electric streetcar, along with the rattle and clatter of a freight wagon. From somewhere he could hear the buzz and squeal of a power saw, and the ring of steel on steel as a blacksmith worked his trade. Newspaper boys were out on the street, hawking their product.

"Paper, get the paper here! Wyoming to be admitted as state! Get your paper here!"

Tom got out of bed, shaved, then got dressed. Catching a glimpse of himself in the mirror, he frowned. He was wearing a three-piece suit, adequate dress if he wanted to apply for a job with a bank. But he was going to apply for a job as a cowboy, and this would never do.

Stepping over to the window, he looked up and down Houston Street and saw, on the opposite side, the Fort Worth Mercantile Store. Leaving his suitcase in his room, he hurried downstairs and then across the street. A tall, thin man with a neatly trimmed moustache and garters around his sleeves stepped up to him.

"Yes, sir, may I help you?"

"I intend to apply for employment at a neighboring ranch," Tom said. "And I will need clothes that are suitable for the position."

"When you say that you are going to apply for employment, do you mean as an accountant, or business manager?" the clerk asked.

"No. As a cowboy."

The expression on the clerk's face registered his surprise. "I beg your pardon, sir. Did you say as a cowboy?"

"Yes," Tom said. "Why, is there a problem?"

"No, sir," the clerk said quickly. "No problem. It is just that, well, sir, you will forgive me, but you don't look like a cowboy."

"Yeah," Tom said. "That's why I'm here. I want you to make me look like a cowboy."

"I can sell you the appropriate attire, sir," the clerk said. "But, in truth, you still won't look like a cowboy."

"Try," Tom said.

"Yes, sir."

It took Tom no more than fifteen minutes to buy three outfits, to include boots and a hat. Paying for his purchases, he returned to the hotel, packed his suit and the two extra jeans and shirts into his suitcase, then went downstairs, checked out, and took a seat in the lobby to wait for the young woman he had met last night.

As he waited for her, he recalled the conversation he had had with his father, just before he left.

"You are making a big mistake by running away," his father had told him. "You will not be able to escape your own devils."

"I can try," Tom said.

"Nobody is holding it against you, Tom. You did what you thought was right."

"I did what I thought was right? I can't even justify what I did to myself by saying that I did what I thought was right. My wife and my child are dead, and I killed them."

"It isn't as if you murdered them."

"It isn't? How is it different? Martha and the child are still dead."

"So you are going to run away. Is that your answer?"

"Yes, that is my answer. I need some time to sort things out. Please try to understand that."

His father changed tactics, from challenging to being persuasive. "Tom, all I am asking is that you think this through. You have more potential than any student I ever taught, and I'm not saying that just because you are my son. I am saying it because it is true. Do you have any idea of the good that someone like you — a person with your skills, your talent,

27

your education, can do?"

"I've seen the evil I can do when I confuse skill, talent, and education with Godlike attributes."

Tom's father sighed in resignation. "What time does your train leave?"

"At nine o'clock tonight."

Tom's father walked over to the bar and poured a glass of Scotch. He held it out toward Tom and, catching a beam of light from the electric chandelier, the amber fluid emitted a burst of gold as if the glass had captured the sun itself. "Then at least have this last, parting drink with me."

Tom waited until his father had poured his own glass, then the two men drank to each other.

"Will you write to let me know where you are and how you are doing?"

"Not for a while," Tom said. "I just need to be away from everything that could remind me of what happened. And that means even my family."

Surprisingly, Tom's father smiled. "In a way, I not only don't blame you, I envy you. I almost ran off myself, once. I was going to sail the seven seas. But my father got wind of it, and talked me out of it. I guess I wasn't as strong as you are."

"Nonsense, you are as strong," Tom said.

"You just never had the same devils chasing you that I do."

Tom glanced over at the big clock. It showed fifteen minutes of nine. Shouldn't she be here by now? Had she changed her mind and already checked out? He walked over to the desk.

"Yes, sir, Mr. Whitman, may I help you?" the hotel desk clerk asked.

"Rebecca Conyers," Tom said. "Has she checked out yet?"

The clerk checked his book. "No, sir. She is still in the hotel. Would you like me to summon her?"

"No, that won't be necessary," Tom said. "I'll just wait here in the lobby for her."

"Very good, sir."

Huh, Tom thought. And here it was my belief that Westerners went to bed and rose with the sun.

As soon he thought that, though, he realized that she had gone to bed quite late, having arrived on the train in the middle of the night. At least his initial fear that she had left without meeting him was alleviated.

When Rebecca awakened that morning she was already having second thoughts about what she had done. Had she actually told a perfect stranger that she could talk her

29

father into hiring him? And, even if she could, should she? She had arisen much later than she normally did, and now, as she dressed, she found herself hoping that he had grown tired of waiting for her and left, without accepting her offer.

However, when she went downstairs she saw him sitting in a chair in the lobby. His suitcase was on the floor beside him, but he wasn't wearing the suit he had been wearing the night before. Instead, he was wearing denims and a blue cotton shirt. If anything, she found him even more attractive, for the denims and cotton shirt took some of the polish off and gave him a more rugged appearance.

Although Tom had gotten an idea last night that the young woman was pretty, it had been too dark to get a really good look at her. In the full light of morning though, he saw her for what she was: tall and willowy, with long, auburn hair and green eyes shaded by long, dark eyelashes. She was wearing a dress that showed off her gentle curves to perfection.

"Mr. Whitman," she said. "How wonderful it is to see you this morning. I see you have decided to take me up on my offer."

"Yes, I have. You *were* serious about it, weren't you?" Tom asked. "I mean, you

30

weren't just making small talk?"

Rebecca paused for a moment before responding. If she wanted to back out of her offer, now was the time to do it.

"I was very serious," she heard herself saying, as if purposely speaking before she could change her mind.

"Do we have time? If so, I would like to take you to breakfast," Tom said.

Rebecca glanced over at the clock. "Yes, I think so," she said. "And I would be glad to have breakfast with you. But you must let me pay for my own."

"Only if it makes you feel more comfortable," Tom said.

"Let's sit by the window," Rebecca suggested when they stepped into the hotel restaurant. "That way we will be able to see when Mo comes for me."

"Mo?"

"He is one of my father's cowboys," Rebecca said. "He is quite young."

Rebecca had a poached egg, toast, and coffee for breakfast. Tom had two waffles, four fried eggs, a rather substantial slab of ham, and more biscuits than Rebecca could count.

"My, you must have been hungry," Rebecca said after Tom pushed away a clean plate. "When is the last time you ate?"

"Not since supper last night," Tom said, as if that explained his prodigious appetite. "Oh, I hope I haven't embarrassed you."

"Not at all," Rebecca said. "Tell me about yourself, Mr. Whitman. Where are you from? What were you doing before you decided to come West?"

"Not much to tell. I'm from Boston," Tom said. "I'm more interested in you telling me about the ranch."

"Oh, there's Mo," Rebecca said. "I won't have to tell you about the ranch, we'll be there in less than an hour."

Tom picked up both his suitcase and Rebecca's, then followed her out to the buckboard.

"Hello, Mo," Rebecca greeted.

Mo was a slender five feet nine, with brown eyes and dark hair which he wore long and straight.

"Hello, Miss Rebecca," Mo said with a broad smile. "It's good to see you back home again. Ever'one at the ranch missed you. Did you have a good visit?"

"Oh, I did indeed," Rebecca answered.

Seeing Tom standing there with the two suitcases, Mo indicated the back of the buckboard. "You can just put them there," he said. Then to Rebecca. "Uh, Miss Rebecca you got a coin? I come into town with no money at all."

"A coin?"

Mo nodded toward Tom. "Yes ma'am, a nickel or a dime of somethin' on account of him carrying your luggage and all."

"Oh, we don't need to tip him, Mo. His name is Tom, and he's with me. He'll be comin' out to the ranch with us."

"He's with you? Good Lord, Miss Rebecca, you didn't go to Marshall and get yourself married up or somethin', did you?" Mo asked.

Rebecca laughed out loud. "No, it's nothing like that," she said.

"Sorry I didn't bring the trap," Mo said to Tom. "This here buckboard only has one seat. That means you'll have to ride in the back."

"That's not a problem," Tom said. "I'll be fine."

"I hope so. It's not all that comfortable back there and we're half an hour from the ranch."

Tom set the luggage down in the back of the buckboard, then put his hand on the side and vaulted over.

"Damn," Mo said. "I haven't ever seen anybody do that. You must be a pretty strong fella."

"You don't know the half of it," Rebecca
said.

CHAPTER TWO

Live Oaks Ranch

Live Oaks Ranch lay just north of Fort Worth. The 120,000 acres of gently rolling grassland and scores of year-round streams and creeks made it ideal for cattle ranching. There were two dozen cowboys who were part-time employees, and another two dozen who were full-time employees. The part-time and full-time employees who weren't married lived in a couple of long, low, bunkhouses, white with red roofs. In addition, there were at least ten permanent employees who were married, and they lived in small houses, all of them painted green, with red roofs. These were adjacent to the bunkhouses. There was also a cookhouse that was large enough to feed all the single men, a barn, a machine shed, a granary, and a large stable. The most dominating feature of the ranch was what the cowboys called "The Big House." The Big House was a stucco-sided example of Spanish Colonial Revival, with an arcaded portico on the southeast corner, stained-glass windows, and an elaborate arched entryway.

Inside the parlor of the Big House, the owner of Live Oaks, Rebecca's father, Benjamin "Big Ben" Conyers, was standing by the fireplace. Big Ben was aptly named, for he was six feet seven inches tall and weighed 330 pounds. Rebecca had just introduced Tom to him, explaining how he had come to her aid last night when she had been accosted by two cowboys.

"I thank you very much for that, Mr. Whitman," Big Ben said, shaking Tom's hand. "There are many who would have just turned away."

"I'm glad I happened to be there at that time," Tom replied.

"Mr. Whitman is looking for a job, Papa," Rebecca said. "I know that Tony Peters left a couple of weeks ago, and when Mo picked me up this morning, he told me that you hadn't replaced him."

"I don't know, honey. Tony was an experienced cowboy," Big Ben said.

"Nobody is experienced when they first start," Rebecca said, and Big Ben laughed.

"I can't deny that," he said. "Where are you from, Mr. Whitman?"

"I'm from Boston, sir."

"Boston, is it? Can you ride a horse?"

For several years Tom had belonged to a fox-hunting club. And unlike the quarter horses, bred for speed in short stretches that were commonly seen out West, fox-hunting thoroughbreds were often crossed with heavier breeds for endurance and solidity. They were taller and more muscular, and were trained to run long distances, since most hunts lasted for an entire day. They were also bred to jump a variety of fences and ditches. Tom was, in fact, a champion when it came to "riding to the hounds."

But he also knew that the sport had mixed reactions, from those who felt sorry for the fox, to those who thought it was a foolish indulgence, to those who did not under-stand the skill and stamina such an endeavor required.

"Yes, sir, I can ride a horse," he said.

"You don't mind if I give you a little test just to see how well you can ride, do you?" Big Ben asked.

"Papa, that's not fair," Rebecca said. "You know that our horses aren't like the ones he is used to riding. At least give him a few days to get used to it."

"I don't have a few days, Rebecca. I have two hundred square miles of ranch to run, and a herd of cattle to manage. I need someone who can go to work immediately. Now, maybe you're right, everyone has to get experience somewhere, so I'm willing to give him time to learn his way around the ranch. But if he can't even ride a horse, I mean a Western horse, then it's going to take more time than I can spare."

"I'm sorry, Mr. Whitman," Rebecca said. "If you don't want to take Papa's test, you don't have to. We'll all understand."

"I'd like to take the test," Tom said.

"Good for you," Big Ben said. "Come on outside, let me see what you can do."

A tall, gangly young man with ash blond hair and a spray of freckles came up to them then.

"Hello, Sis. I heard you were back."

"Did you stay out of trouble while I was gone?" Rebecca asked. Then she introduced the boy. "Mr. Whitman, this is my brother, Dalton."

"Are you going to work for Pa?" Dalton asked.

"I hope to."

"Then I won't be calling you Mr. Whitman. What's your first name?"

"Dalton!" Rebecca said.

"I don't mean nothin' by it," Dalton said.

"I'm just friends with all the cowboys, that's all."

"My name is Tom. And I would be happy to be your friend."

"Yes, well, don't the two of you get to be best friends too fast," Big Ben said. "First I have to know if you can ride well enough to be a cowboy. Clay!" Big Ben called.

A man stepped out of the machine shed. "Yes, sir, Mr. Conyers?"

"Get over here, Clay, I've someone I want you to meet." Then to Tom, Big Ben added, "Clay is the ranch foreman. And I'll leave the final word as to whether or not I hire you up to him."

"Good enough," Tom said.

Clay was Clay Ramsey, who Big Ben introduced as the ranch foreman. Clay was thirty-three years old, with brown hair, a well-trimmed moustache, and blue eyes. About five feet ten, he was wiry and, according to one of the cowboys who worked for him, as tough as a piece of rawhide.

"Saddle Thunder for him," Big Ben said, after he explained what he wanted to do.

"Papa, no!" Rebecca protested vehemently.

"Honey, I'm not just being a horse's rear end. If he can ride Thunder, he can ride any horse on the ranch. There wouldn't be any question about my hiring him."

"I can ride a horse, Mr. Conyers," Tom said. "But I confess that I have never tried to ride a bucking horse. If that is what is required, then I thank you for your time, and I'll be going on."

"He's not a bucking horse," Clay said. "But he is a very strong horse who loves to run and jump. If you ride him, you can't be timid about it; you have to let him know, right away, that you are in control."

"Thank you, Mr. Ramsey. In that case, I will ride him."

"Ha!" Dusty McNally, one of the other cowboys said. "I like it that you said you *will* ride him, rather than you will *try* to ride him. That's the right attitude to have."

Thunder was a big, muscular, black horse who stood eighteen hands at the withers. Although he allowed himself to be saddled, he kept moving his head and lifting first one hoof and then another. He looked like a ball of potential energy.

"Here you are, Mr. Whitman," Clay said, handing the reins to Tom.

"Thank you," Tom said, mounting. He pointed toward an open area on the other side of a fence. "Would it be all right to ride in that field there?"

"Sure, there's nothing there but rangeland," Clay said. "The gate is down there," he pointed.

"Thank you, I won't need a gate," Tom said. He slapped his legs against the side of the horse and it started forward at a gallop. As he approached the fence, he lifted himself slightly from the saddle and leaned forward.

"Come on, Thunder," he said encouragingly. "Let's go see if we can find us a fox."

Thunder galloped toward the fence, then sailed over it as gracefully as a leaping deer. Coming down on the other side Tom saw a ditch about twenty yards beyond the fence, and Thunder took that as well. Horse and rider went through their paces, jumping, making sudden turns, running at a full gallop, then stopping on a dime. After a few minutes he brought Thunder back, returning the same way he left, over the ditch, then over the fence. He slowed him down to a trot once he was back inside the compound, and the horse was at a walk by the time he rode up to dismount in front of a shocked Big Ben, Clay, and Dusty. Rebecca was smiling broadly.

Tom patted Thunder on his neck, then dismounted and handed the reins back to Clay. "He is a very fine horse," Tom said. "Whoever rides him is quite lucky."

"He's yours to ride any time you want him," Big Ben said. "That is, provided you are willing to come work for me."

"I would be very proud to work for you, Mr. Conyers."

"Come with me, Tom, is it?" Clay invited. "I'll get you set up in the bunkhouse and introduce you to the others."

"Tom?" Rebecca called out to him.

Tom looked back toward her.

"I'm glad you are here."

"Thank you, Miss Conyers. I'm glad to be here."

Tom ate his first supper in the cookhouse that evening. Mo introduced him to all the others.

"Where is Mr. Ramsey?" Tom asked. "Does he eat somewhere else?"

"Mr. Ramsey?" Mo asked. Then he smiled. "Oh, you mean Clay. Clay is the foreman of the ranch, but there don't any of us call him Mr. Ramsey. We just call him Clay 'cause that's what he wants us to call him."

"Clay is married," one of the other cowboys said. "He lives in that first cabin you see over there, the only one with a front porch."

"He married a Mexican girl," another said.

"Don't talk about her like that," Mo said. "Maria is as American as you are. Emanuel Bustamante fought with Sam Houston at San Jacinto."

"I didn't mean nothin' by it," the cowboy said. "I think Senor Bustamante is as fine a man as I've ever met, and Mrs. Ramsey is a very good woman. I was just sayin' that she is Mexican is all."

"I assume that none of you are married," Tom said. "Otherwise you wouldn't be eating here in the dining hall."

"Ha! The dining hall. That's sure a fancy name for the cookhouse."

"I don't mean any disrespect for Clay," Mo said. "But it don't make a whole lot of sense for a cowboy to be married. First of all, there don't none of us make enough money to support a family. And second, when we make the long cattle drives, we're gone for near three months at a time."

"And Dodge City is too fun of a town to be in if you are married, if you get my meanin'," one of the other cowboys said, and the others shared a ribald laugh.

A couple of cowboys decided to razz the tenderfoot that first night. Tom had been given a chest for his belongings, and while Tom and the rest of the cowboys were having supper, Dalton and one of the cowboys slipped back into the bunkhouse and nailed the lid shut on his chest.

When Tom and the others returned, Tom tried to open the lid to his footlocker, but he was unable to get it open.

"What's the matter there, Tom? Can't get your chest open?" Dalton asked.

By now Dalton had told the others what he did, and all gathered around to see how Tom was going to react. Would he get angry, and start cursing everyone? Or would he be meek about it?

Tom looked more closely at the lid then, and saw that it had been nailed shut by six nails, two in front and two on either side.

"That's odd," he said. "It seems to have been nailed shut."

The others laughed out loud.

"Nailed shut, is it? Well, I wonder who did that?" Dalton asked.

"Oh, I expect it was a mistake of some sort," Tom said. "I don't really think that anyone would nail the lid shut on my chest as a matter of intent."

"Whoo, do you think that?" Dalton asked, and again, everyone laughed at the joke they were playing on the tenderfoot.

"All right, fellas, you've had your fun," Mo said. "Wait a minute, Tom, I'll get a claw hammer and pull the nails for you so you can get the lid open."

"Thank you, Mo," Tom said. "I don't need the claw hammer to get the lid open."

"What are you talking about? Of course you do. How else are you going to open the lid if you don't pull the nails out first?"

"Oh, it won't be difficult. I'll just open it like this," Tom said. Reaching down with both hands, he used one hand to steady the bottom of the chest and the other to grab the front of the lid. He pulled up on the lid then and, with a terrible screeching noise as the nails lost their purchase, the lid came up. Reaching into the footlocker, Tom removed a pair of socks.

"Ahh," he said. "That's what I was looking for."

"Good God in heaven," someone said, reverently. "Did you see that?"

"Dalton, I don't think you ought to be messin' any more with this one. He's as strong as an ox."

Sugarloaf Ranch, Big Rock, Colorado, May 1
"Did you get a count?" Smoke asked Pearlie.

Pearlie held up the string and counted the knots. There were fourteen knots.

"I make it fourteen hundred in the south pasture," he said.

"I've got another eleven hundred," Cal added.

"And I've got just over fifteen hundred," Smoke said.

"Wow, that's better than four thousand head," Pearlie said. "We've got almost as many back as we had before the big freeze and die-out."

The big die-out Pearlie was talking about happened three years earlier when there had been a huge 72-hour blizzard. After the blizzard, the sun melted the top few inches of snow into slush, which the following day was frozen into solid ice by minus thirty-degree temperatures. Throughout the West, tens of thousands of cattle were found huddled against fences, many frozen to death, partly through and hanging on the wires. The legs of many of the cows that survived were so badly frozen that, when they moved, the skin cracked open and their hoofs dropped off. Hundreds of young steers were wandering aimlessly around on bloody stumps, while their tails froze as if they were icicles to be easily broken off.

Humans died that year too, men who froze to death while searching for cattle, women and children in houses where there was no wood to burn and not enough blankets to hold back the sub-zero temperatures. The only creatures to survive, and not only survive but thrive that winter, were the wolves who feasted upon the carcasses of tens of thousands of dead cattle.

Sugarloaf Ranch had survived, but nearly all the cattle on the ranch had died. Then Smoke heard from his friend, Falcon Mac-Callister. Falcon's cousin, Duff MacCallister, recently arrived from Scotland, was running a new breed of cattle.

Duff MacCallister had been spared the great die-out disaster because his ranch was located in the Chugwater Valley of Wyoming, shielded against the worst of winter's blast by mesas and mountain ranges. Also his ranch, Sky Meadow, had no fences to prevent the cattle from moving to the shelter of these natural barriers, and the breed of cattle Duff MacCallister was raising, Black Angus, were better equipped to withstand the cold weather than were the Longhorns.

Smoke went to Sky Meadow to meet with Duff, and after his visit, agreed to buy one thousand head of Black Angus cattle. That one thousand head had grown into a herd of nearly four thousand in the last four years, and it had been a very good move for Smoke. Whereas the market price for Longhorn had fallen so low that Smoke's neighbors, who were still raising that breed, were doing well to break even on their investment, the market price for Black Angus, which produced a most superior grade of beef, was very high.

"You men take care of things here," Smoke said. "Sally is coming back today, and I'm going to meet her at the train station."

"I'll go get her," Cal volunteered.

Pearlie chuckled. "I'm sure you would, Cal. We've got calves to brand and you'll do anything to get out of a little work."

"It's not that," Cal said. "I was just volunteering, is all."

"Thanks anyway," Smoke said. "But she's been back East for almost a month and I'm sort of anxious to see her again."

When Smoke reached the train depot in Big Rock, he checked the arrival and departure blackboard to see if the train was on time. There was no arrival time listed, so he went inside to talk to the ticket agent. The ticket agent was huddled in a nervous conversation with Sheriff Monte Carson.

"Hello, Monte, good evening, Hodge," Smoke said, greeting the two men. "How are you doing?"

"Smoke, I'm glad you are here," Sheriff

Carson said. "We've got a problem with the train."

"What kind of problem?" Smoke asked. "Sally is on that train."

"Yes, I know she is. We think the train is being robbed."

"Being robbed, or has been robbed?" Smoke replied, confused by the remark.

"Being robbed," Sheriff Carson said. "At least, we think that it what it is. The train is stopped about five miles west of here. There is an obstruction on the track so that it can't go forward, and another on the track to keep it from going back."

"How do you know this?"

"Ollie Cook is the switch operator just this side where the train is. When the train didn't come through his switch on time, he walked down the track to find out why, and that's when he saw the train barricaded like that. He hurried back to his switch shack and called the depot."

"And I called Sheriff Carson," Hodge said.

"I'm about to get a posse together to ride out there and see what it's all about," Sheriff Carson said.

"No need for a posse. Deputize me," Smoke suggested. "Like I said, Sally is on that train."

"You are already a deputy, Smoke, you

know that," Sheriff Carson said.

"Yes, I know," Smoke said. "But I don't want people thinking I've gone off on my own just because Sally is on the train. I need you to authorize this, in front of a witness."

"All right," Sheriff Carson said. "Hodge you are witness to this. Smoke, you are deputized to find out what is happening with that train, and to deal with it as you see best."

"Thanks," Smoke said.

Hurrying back outside, Smoke jumped into the buckboard he had come to town in, and slapping the reins against the back of the team, took the road that ran parallel with the railroad. He left town doing a brisk trot, but once he was out of town, he urged the team into a gallop. Less than fifteen minutes later, he saw the train standing on the railroad. Not wanting to get any closer with the team and buckboard, he stopped, tied the team off to a juniper tree, then, bending to keep a low profile, ran alongside the berm until he reached the front of the train. Hiding in some bushes he looked into the engine cab and saw three men, the fireman and engineer, who he could identify by the pin-stripe coveralls they were wearing, and a third man. The third man had a gun in his hand, and he waved it around every now and then, as if demonstrating his authority over the train crew.

Smoke moved up onto the track, but since he was in the very front of the locomotive, he knew that he couldn't be seen. He climbed up the cow catcher, then up onto the boiler itself, still unseen. He walked along the top of the boiler, then onto the roof of the cab. Lying down on his stomach, he peeked in from the window on the left side of the locomotive.

The man holding the gun had his back to that window so he couldn't see Smoke, but the engineer and the fireman could, and Smoke saw their eyes widen in surprise. He hoped that the gunman didn't notice it.

"You two fellas are doin' just fine," the gunman said. "As soon as we collect our money from all your passengers, why we'll move the stuff off the track and let you go on."

Smoke leaned down far enough to make certain that the cab crew could see him, then he put his finger across his lips as a signal to be quiet.

"You got no right to be collecting money from our passengers," one of the two cab crew said.

"Well, the Denver and Rio Grande collects its fees, and we collect ours," the man said with a cackling laugh.

In mid-cackle, Smoke reached down into the engine cab, grabbed the man by his shirt, pulled him through the window, then let him fall, headfirst, to the ground.

"Hey, what . . ." was as far as the man got, before contact with the ground interrupted his protest. Looking down at him, Smoke could tell by the way the man's head was twisted that his neck was broken, and he was dead.

Smoke swung himself into the engine cab.

"Who are you?" one of the men asked.

"Smoke Jensen, I'm a deputy sheriff," Smoke said. "How many more are there?"

"Four more," one of the men said.

"Five," the other corrected. "I saw five."

"Where are they now?"

"Well, sir, after they found out we wasn't carryin' any money in the express car, they decided to see what they could get from the passengers, and that's what they are doing now."

"How about the two of you going down to move the body of the one who was in here with you? I don't want any of the others to happen to look up this way and see him lying there."

"Yeah, good idea. Come on, Cephus, let's get him moved."

As the two train crewmen climbed down to take care of their job, Smoke crawled across the coal pile on the tender, then up onto the top of the express car. He ran the length of that car, then leaped across to the baggage car and ran its length as well. Climbing down from the back of the baggage car, he let himself into the first passenger car.

"One of your men has already been here," an irate passenger said. "We gave you everything we have."

"Shhh," Smoke said. "I'm on your side. I'm a deputy sheriff. Where are they?"

"There was only one in here, and he went into the next car."

"Thanks," Smoke said. Holding his pistol down by his side, he hurried through the first car and into the second one. He saw a gunman at the other end of the car, holding a pistol in his right hand and an open sack in the other. The passengers were dropping their valuables into the open sack.

"What are you doing in here? You get back in the other car and stay there like you were told!" The gunman said, belligerently.

"I don't think so," Smoke said. He raised his pistol. "Drop your gun."

"The hell I will!"

Instead of dropping his gun, the train robber swung the pistol around and fired at Smoke. His shot went wide and the bullet smashed through the window of the door behind him. Smoke returned fire, and the gunman dropped his pistol and staggered back, his hands to his throat. Blood spilled through his fingers as he hit the front wall of the car, then slid down to the floor in a seated position. His head fell to one side as he died.

During the gunfire women screamed and men shouted. As the car filled with the gun smoke of two discharges, Smoke ran through the car, across the vestibule, and into the next car.

The gunman in the next car, having heard the shot, was looking toward the door as Smoke ran in.

"Red! McDill! Slim, get in here quick!" the gunman called.

Smoke and this gunman exchanged fire as well, with the same result. The gunman went down and Smoke was still standing. When he ran into the next car, he saw the robber dashing out through the back door. He chased him down as well, but he didn't have to shoot him. When the gunman went into the next car, he was brought down by a club wielded by the porter. "Good job," Smoke said.

"The other two has done jumped off the train," the porter said.

Smoke jumped down from the train as well, then he moved away from it to try and get a bead on the two who were running. Smoke snapped off a long shot, but missed. He didn't get a second shot because the outlaws were on horseback and galloping away.

Smoke stood there for a moment, still holding his smoking pistol as he watched the two robbers flee.

"You need to develop a better sense of timing," someone said, and turning, Smoke saw Sally standing there on the ground behind him. He embraced and kissed her, then he pulled his head back.

"What do you mean, a better sense of timing?" he asked.

"If you had been five minutes earlier, the robbers wouldn't have gotten my reticule."

"Sorry. How much did they get?" Smoke asked.

"Just my purse," Sally said with a little laugh. "I had already taken everything out of it."

By now, several others had come down from the train and they were all thanking Smoke for coming to their rescue.

"Look here!" someone shouted. "The two

that got away dropped their sacks!"

"The ones inside never even made it off the train with their sacks," another said. "Ha! Ever'thing they took is still here!"

"Cephus, how long will it take you to get the steam back up?" the conductor asked.

"Fifteen minutes," Cephus said. "Maybe half an hour."

"Do you want to wait until they get the steam back up? Or do you want to come with me now?" Smoke asked. "I left a buckboard just up the track a short distance."

"My luggage is on the train," Sally said.

"Miss, after what your man just did, if you want your luggage, I'll personally open the baggage car and get it," the conductor said.

Mitchell "Red" Coleman and Deekus McDill were the two robbers who got away. They got away from Smoke's avenging guns, but they did not get away with any money.

"Nothin'!" McDill said. "We didn't get a damn thing!"

"Maybe the day ain't goin' to be a total loss," Red said.

"What do you mean, it ain't a total loss?"

"Look over there," Red said.

"What, a store? What good is a store goin'

to do us? We ain't got no money to buy nothin'."

"Who said we were goin' to buy anything?" Red said.

McDill understood what he was talking about then, and he smiled and nodded.

Fifteen minutes later Red and McDill rode away from Doogan's store. Jake Doogan and his wife both lay dead on the floor in the store behind them. Their total take for the robbery was seventy-eight dollars and thirty-five cents.

CHAPTER THREE

Mountain Home, Idaho, May 2

Falcon MacCallister was sitting in a leather chair in the office of Judge Andrew Lathom. The judge was standing at his private bar, pouring brandy into two snuffers. He came back to where Falcon was sitting, and handed one of the brandy snuffers to him.

"You have chased down a lot of bad men since I have known you, Falcon. But I have a feeling that bringing in Amon Deering has given you a distinct sense of satisfaction."

"It has," Falcon answered.

"Why? I mean, after a while, isn't one murderous skunk pretty much like another murderous skunk?" The judge whirled his brandy, then took a sip.

"Because of the girl, Quiet Stream," Falcon said.

"Oh, yes, the Indian girl. But why her, in particular? She was just one of a string of young girls that Deering raped and murdered."

"It was more than that," Falcon added. "I knew the girl. And I knew her father. His name was Bloody Knife, and he was a scout for Custer."

"Yes, I have heard of Bloody Knife. And you knew him, did you?"

"I was with him when he was killed," Falcon said.

"I can see how that would make this more personal," Judge Lathom said. "Well, Falcon, I not only congratulate you, I commend you for not letting your personal feelings get in the way. I know you were tempted to kill Deering yourself, and under the circumstances, if you had done it, there is not a man in the whole country who would have blamed you. I admire your respect for the law."

Falcon smiled, dryly. "Respect for the law has nothing to do with it, Judge," he said. "I never met anyone yet who wouldn't rather be shot than hung."

There was a knock on the door and Judge Lathom yelled for whoever it was to come in. It was his law clerk.

"Judge," the clerk said. "They've got Amon Deering standing on the gallows now. The sheriff is waiting for your signal."

"Thank you, Harry," Judge Lathom said. He finished his brandy, then set his empty snuffer down. "You know, Falcon, I can sentence someone to die . . . and in the case of a person like Deering, after the string of murders he committed, not just Quiet Stream but at least six more that we know about, every one of them a young woman, or worse, a young girl, I can do it with a clear conscience. But when it comes to the part where I actually have to give an order to kill another human being . . . ," Judge Lathom let the sentence hang.

"Who said Deering was a human being?" Falcon asked. "He is a monster masquerading as a human being."

Judge Lathom nodded. "I was going to add that there are exceptions. There are those rare times where I take pleasure in administering the extreme penalty. And this is one of those exceptions. Would you like to come to the window with me and watch? After all, you are the one who brought him in."

"I don't think you could keep me from watching," Falcon said.

Falcon walked over to the window and looked down into the courtyard. There were three or four hundred people gathered around the gallows, including a photographer who had already taken a series of photographs of Deering as he was being prepared for the hanging. Now, the condemned man was in position just under the crossbeam, the noose having already been placed around his neck.

Deering had eschewed the use of a hood, and stood looking out at the crowd, a malevolent smile on his face, as if he actually enjoyed being the central figure in the death drama. His hands were manacled to his belt, so that his arms were stiffly by his sides. His legs were tied together. Any last words he may have had were already spoken at this point and he was quietly counting off the last seconds of his life.

"Roast in hell, you son of a bitch!" A man's voice could be heard. "You raped and murdered my daughter!"

"Did I? Well, I'll see her again in a few minutes," Deering called back. "And after I have another go at her, I'll give her your regards." He laughed a high-pitched cackle and to those who were assembled to witness the hanging, it seemed as if they were hearing laughter from hell.

Even as he was laughing, Judge Lathom nodded his head and, down at the gallows, Sheriff Foley, who had been awaiting the signal, pulled the handle. From his position at the open window in Judge Lathom's office, Falcon could hear the thump of the dropping trap door. Deering's laughter was cut off in mid-cackle.

Elko, Nevada, May 2

Lucas Shelton was not a train robber in the normal sense. That is because he didn't mask himself and stop a train to rob the passengers, or to clean out the safe in the express car. Shelton had been a guard with the Railroad Protective Association, hired by the railroad to guard a money shipment. He had murdered the messenger who trusted him, and stolen the very money shipment he was supposed to protect. The shipment was just over one hundred thousand dollars in cash.

Matt was in for ten percent of the money if he could locate Shelton and bring him in. It took him only two weeks before he found Shelton at a saloon in Elko, Nevada.

"Mr. Shelton, I've come to take you back," Matt said.

"Like hell you will!"

"Look out! Shelton's pulled a gun!" one of the men shouted.

Matt had been expecting this, and when he saw the gun in Shelton's hand he pulled his own, drawing and firing in the same, fluid motion, doing it so quickly that the noise of his shot covered Shelton's so that they sounded as one, even though Shelton had fired a split-second sooner. Shelton's bullet whizzed by harmlessly, burying itself in the wall behind Matt. Matt's bullet caught Shelton right between the eyes, and the one-time President of the Railroad Protective Associates fell back against the bar, then slid down to the floor. Both eyes were open but there was a third opening, a small black hole, right at the bridge of his nose. Actually, only a small amount of blood trickled from the hole, though the bar behind him was already stained red with the blood that had gushed out from the exit wound. The others in the saloon looked at Shelton's body in shock. It had all happened so fast that, for a moment, they could almost believe that it hadn't happened at all. But the drifting cloud of acrid smoke said otherwise.

"Is he dead?" someone asked.

"As a doornail," another answered.

Within moments after the shooting, a couple of deputy city marshals came running in through the front door, guns drawn. Matt's letter of authorization from the Central Pacific Railroad, endorsed by Governor Stevenson, plus the eyewitness accounts from others in the saloon, were all Matt needed to satisfy the deputies.

Two days later, with the money recovered, Matt Jensen was ten thousand dollars richer and moved on.

Fort Worth, May 3

It was a Saturday, and cowboys from several of the area ranches, including Live Oaks, had come into town to enjoy a day off. Clay Ramsey was playing a game of pool in the Trinity Saloon and Billiards Parlor when Tom Whitman came in. Tom had only been at the ranch for just under two months, but in that time he had impressed Clay with his intelligence, his eagerness to learn what he needed to know about ranching, and his willingness to take on any job without complaint. Seeing the strapping young man glance around the saloon as if looking for someone, Clay held up his hand.

"Here, Tom," he called.

Nodding, Tom came toward him.

"Want to play a game?" Clay asked. "I can re-rack them."

"Better not," Tom said. "And you might want to finish this game rather quickly."

"Why? What's up?"

"Dalton is in jail," Tom said.

"Damn." Clay re-racked the balls and put

the cue away. "Please tell me that it isn't something serious."

"I don't know exactly what he did, but I don't think it is anything really serious," Tom said. "And he is in the city jail, not the county jail."

"That's a good thing," Clay said. "Marshal Courtright is a lot easier to deal with than Sheriff Cobb. I'll see what I can do. Have you seen Dalton's horse anywhere?" Clay asked.

"Yes, it's down at the wagon yard."

"Do me a favor, would you, Tom? Get his horse and meet me in front of the jail."

"Do you think you can get him out?"

"I'm going to try," Clay said. "And if it is anything less than murder, I think I can get the job done."

The city jail was on the corner of Second Street and Rusk, about three blocks away from the billiard parlor. It only took Clay a couple of minutes to cover the distance between the two buildings. Then, tying his horse off at the hitching rail in front, he pushed through the front door of the jailhouse.

"Hello, Clay," Marshal Courtright said. "I thought I might be seeing you this afternoon."

"What did he do, Jim?" Clay asked.

"Clay! Clay, is that you?" a voice called from the back. "Get me out of here, Clay!"

"Hold your horses, Dalton," Clay called to him. "Let me figure out what's going on here."

"I'll tell you what's going on here," Dalton said. "They arrested me for no reason at all."

Marshal Courtright walked over to the door that was open onto the jail cells in the back and slammed it shut, effectively silencing Dalton Conyers.

"He tied the back axle of Jack Ebersole's buggy to a lamppost. When Ebersole started out, it jerked the axle out from under the buggy and tossed Ebersole out on his ass."

Clay laughed, and Courtright joined him.

"It was pretty funny," Courtright said. "And Lord knows I can't think of anyone in town I'd more enjoy seeing dumped on his ass than Jack Ebersole. But Ebersole has sworn out a warrant for assault and destruction of private property. And he certainly has every right to do that."

"Can you release the boy to me?" Clay asked. "You know damn well Big Ben will make it right with Ebersole."

Courtright stroked his jaw as he considered Clay's proposition. "You know, Clay, this isn't the first time the boy has been in

66

trouble. If Big Ben don't do somethin' quick, Dalton is going to wind up in real trouble some day."

"I know," Clay agreed. "But Big Ben is just real protective of Dalton."

"I'm just saying, is all," Courtright said. "Look, as far as I'm concerned, Big Ben is as fine a man as you are likely to find in all of Texas. He could have bought himself out of the war, but he went anyway, and was damn near kilt at Gettysburg. As far as I'm concerned, it was men like him that made Texas."

"What about Dalton?" Clay asked. "Are you going to let me take him home?"

"I'm going to let you have him," Marshal Courtright said. "But you tell Big Ben that he is going to have to pay for the damages to Ebersole's buggy. And like as not, Ebersole is goin' to want a bit more soothing money to drop his charges."

"I'm sure Big Ben can work something out with him," Clay said.

"I'll get Dalton."

Clay Ramsey leaned back against the marshal's desk and waited as Courtright went into the back.

"It's about time!" Clay heard Dalton say. He could hear the boy before he saw him. A moment later Dalton came through the door with Marshal Courtright. "Clay, what took you so long to get me out of here? I've been in that jail cell for hours. It stinks in there."

"Dalton, you're lucky I didn't let you stay all night," Clay replied. "You've just cost your Pa a couple of hundred dollars, and I don't think he's going to be all that pleased about it."

"I didn't do it on purpose," Dalton said.

"How can you tie a rope onto the back axle of a buggy, and say you didn't do it on purpose?" Clay asked.

"Well, yeah, I mean, I did that on purpose. But I thought it would just keep him from going, and he would have to get out and untie it. I didn't have any idea that it would actually jerk the axle out." Dalton laughed. "But it was funny, Clay. You should have seen it. Wooee! Ole Ebersole whipped his horse and it dashed out, and the next thing you know, Ebersole is lyin' in the dirt and his horse is galloping off down Main Street, dragging half a buggy behind him."

"Son, you need to grow up," Marshal Courtright said.

"I'm not your son," Dalton said harshly.

"Thank God for that," Marshal Courtright said. "Get him out of here, Clay, before I change my mind."

"Come on, Dalton. Let's go," Clay said.

When they stepped out front, Clay was glad to see that Tom was there with Dalton's horse.

"Does Pa know about it?" Dalton asked as he mounted his horse.

"I don't know if he knows or not," Clay said. "If he does, neither one of us told him."

"Clay, will you go with me when I tell him?" Dalton asked.

"Dalton, if you are man enough to get yourself in trouble, you ought to be man enough to face up to it," Clay said.

"Please? Just this one more time?"

Clay sighed audibly. "All right," he said. "But one of these days, Dalton, I'm not going to be around to bail you out of trouble. You are going to be on your own. What will you do then?"

"Thanks," Dalton said. He slapped his reins against his horse's neck, and the animal burst forward as if being fired from a cannon.

Denver, Colorado, May 5
From the *Rocky Mountain News*

Train Robbery Foiled!

Six desperados made an attempt to rob

69

the Denver and Rio Grande train on Monday, May 1st, attacking it during its transit to Big Rock. Piling stones and other debris on the track, they forced Engineer Green Vaughan to stop his train. Then, constructing another barrier behind the train to prevent any escape by putting the engine in reverse, the robbers accessed the train in order to carry out their nefarious scheme.

Upon learning that the train was not carrying a money shipment, they abandoned the express car and continued their thievery by leaving one of their number in the cab of the engine, and sending the other five through the cars, extracting at the point of their guns the hard-earned money and valuables of the honest passengers, thereon aboard.

Their evil scheme was foiled, however, when Smoke Jensen arrived. Smoke Jensen is a name which most readers will recognize, for he has gained much fame throughout the West, and indeed all of America, by his derring-do in a fight against evil. Activated by his commission as a deputy sheriff, armed by right and a Colt .44, Smoke Jensen single-handedly took on the gang of train robbers, using his pistol with deadly effect.

Porter Jones took care of a fourth robber, but two of the brigands escaped.

They got nothing for their efforts as they abandoned all their booty in their dash for freedom.

After he finished reading the newspaper, Red Coleman put it down with a snort of disgust. The source of Red's nickname was quickly obvious in the shock of red hair that fell to his shoulders. He had a three-corner scar on his left cheek and he rubbed it subconsciously as he read the article.

"What is it? What does the paper say?" McDill asked.

Red slid the paper across the table to him. "Read it for yourself."

"I can't read, Red, you know that," McDill said.

"It says the name of the man who rousted us from the train was Smoke Jensen."

"Smoke Jensen? Yeah, I've heard of him. He is one tough hombre."

"Is he now?" Red asked.

"Yeah, he is. You mean you ain't never heard of him?"

"I've heard of him," Red said. "It's just that this is the first time I've ever run across him."

"Yeah, me too."

"It won't be my last time," Red said.

CHAPTER FOUR

Fort Worth, May 17

The Texas Cattlemen's Association held a dance in Fort Worth, and because there was no single building large enough to hold the event, carpenters had constructed a wooden dance floor near the stockyard in Sundance Square. A band had been hired just for the occasion, coming all the way from San Antonio and arriving by train earlier in the day.

Though most of the other cowboys from Live Oaks were already in town, Tom, Dusty, and Mo waited to ride in alongside the surrey. Clay would be driving the trap, and his wife Maria was already in the surrey, sitting beside him as it waited in front of the big house for Rebecca to join them. Rebecca would ride into town in the back seat.

Like the others, Tom had put on a clean pair of denims and a shirt but then he had second thoughts. While the others were outside with the surrey waiting for Rebecca, Tom went back into the bunkhouse to change clothes. When he came back outside, instead of the denims, Tom was wearing one of the suits he had brought West with him. He chose a dark blue suit with a light blue silk vest and a white shirt. At his collar, he wore a crimson cravat, and as he knew it would, his attire grabbed the attention of all the others when he went outside.

"Whoowee, Tom I'll say this for you. You do know how to turn out," Mo teased.

"Yes, sir, but Tom ain't the only one all fancied up," Dusty said. "Look over there."

The object of Tom's notice was Rebecca. Rebecca, who was walking toward the surrey from the big house, was wearing a bright blue dress trimmed in white faille. A wide white sash was around her waist, beautifully accenting her figure. Tom took in a sharp breath of admiration when he saw her.

Rebecca returned Tom's look with her own appraising stare. She knew that if anyone else had attempted to dress as Tom was dressed, they would have been considered vain and a dandy. But Tom could bring it off because he was handsome enough to do justice to the clothes. In addition, he had already proven to the others by his willingness to work, as well as his brute strength, that any charge of dandyism would be falsely placed.

While Rebecca made her critical appraisal of Tom, she felt a slow-building heat in her body, and she wondered what it would be like to be kissed by him. Embarrassed by what she was thinking, she felt a flushing in her cheeks and she put the thought away as quickly as she could, absolutely certain that someone could read it in her face.

By dusk, the excitement which had been growing for the entire day was full-blown. Several had gathered around to watch the dance, including those who were too young, too old, too uncoordinated, or simply unable to get a partner. Now, as the band warmed up, their music could be heard all over the north end of Fort Worth, adding to the excitement that was already in the air.

Before the dance even began, the band did a few numbers just to warm up the crowd. The dance not being limited to cattlemen only, men and women from the town streamed along the boardwalks toward the dance floor, the women in colorful ginghams, the men in clean blue denims and brightly decorated vests.

To one side of the dance floor a large punch bowl and several glass cups were set on a table, and Rebecca watched as one of the cowboys walked over to the punch bowl to unobtrusively add whiskey from a bottle he had concealed beneath his vest. A moment later another cowboy did the same thing, and Rebecca smiled as she thought of the growing potency of the punch.

The music was playing, but as yet no one was dancing. Then the music stopped, and the caller lifted a megaphone.

"Choose up your squares!" the caller shouted.

The cowboys started toward the young women who, giggling and turning their faces away shyly, accepted their invitations. In a moment there were three squares formed and waiting. As she had hoped he would, Tom asked Rebecca for the first dance, and they were in the square nearest the band.

The music began, with the fiddles loud and clear, the guitars carrying the rhythm, the accordion providing the counterpoint, and a twanging jew's harp heard over everything. The caller began to shout, and he stomped his feet and danced around on the platform in compliance with his own calls. He was the center of fascinated attention from those who weren't dancing, as the caller bowed and whirled just as if he had a girl and was in one of the squares himself. The dancers moved and swirled to the caller's commands.

Around the dance floor sat those who were without partners, looking on wistfully. At the punch bowl table, cowboys continued to add their own ingredients, and though many drank from the punch bowl, the contents of the punch bowl never seemed to diminish.

"Tell me, Tom," Rebecca said after about the fourth dance. "Would an Eastern girl ever ask a man to take her for a walk? Or is that something only a Western girl would do?"

"A gentleman would welcome the invitation whether it came from an Eastern girl or a Western girl," Tom replied. He offered her his arm.

"Thank you for that considerate response, sir," she answered with a smile, putting her hand through his arm.

Leaving the dance floor, they stepped up onto the boardwalk, then walked, arm in arm, south down North Main Street.

Behind them, the lights around the dance floor glittered brightly. The rest of the town was dark, or nearly so. Overhead there was just the barest sliver of a moon, but the sky was filled with stars.

"Have you ever seen anything so beautiful?" Rebecca asked.

"No," Tom replied. "I haven't."

There was something in the tone of Tom's voice that caused Rebecca to look back at him and when she did, she saw that he was staring at her.

"I mean the sky," she said, self consciously.

Tom looked up. "Oh, yes," he said. "That too."

Rebecca smiled. "Maybe we should get back to the dance," she suggested.

"All right. I don't want to make you feel uncomfortable."

Rebecca did feel uncomfortable, but not for the reason Tom was suggesting. She was uncomfortable with herself. She felt a very strong attraction to him, and she knew that it could only lead to a dead end.

When they returned to the dance floor, the dancing had stopped because of some sort of disturbance.

"I wonder what's going on?" Tom asked.

"I don't know, I — oh dear, it's Dalton."

Dalton, Rebecca's younger brother, was her half-brother, actually, since they shared the same father but different mothers.

There were several cowboys gathered

around Dalton, and they were yelling at him.

"What we ought to do is take you over to the stock barn and string you up," one of the cowboys said.

"What's wrong? What did my brother do?" Rebecca said, stepping into the middle of them, putting herself between the angry cowboys and Dalton.

"He, uh, well, I don't want to say it," one of the cowboys said.

"Ask him what he done," one of the other cowboys said. "See if he's man enough to tell you."

Rebecca turned toward Dalton, who was standing there rather sheepishly. "What did you do, Dalton?" she asked.

"It was a joke," Dalton said. "I didn't mean anything by it. It was just a joke, that's all."

"What did you do?" Rebecca asked again.

"I — uh — peed in the punchbowl."

"You did what?" Rebecca shouted at him.

"It was a joke," Dalton said again.

"Dalton, you're my brother, so I'm bound to take your side," Rebecca said. She pointed to the angry cowboys. "But if they beat you to within an inch of your life, I wouldn't blame them one bit. That was a despicable thing to do!"

"I didn't mean anything by it," Dalton said again.

"Dusty?"

"Yes, ma'am?" Dusty replied. Dusty was the oldest of all the cowboys who worked at Live Oaks.

"Please take my brother home."

"I ain't ready to go home yet," Dalton said.

"You aren't ready?"

"No, I'm not. And you can't make me go home."

"I guess you're right. I can't make you go home," Rebecca said. "But I can't protect you either. So if these gentlemen feel they have a score to settle with you, there is nothing I can do to stop them." She turned toward the angry cowboys. "Go ahead, gentlemen," she said. "I'm sorry I interrupted."

"No! Sis! Wait!" Dalton shouted. "No need for that. I'll go home with Dusty."

"I thought you might feel that way," Rebecca said. By now it wasn't just the cowboys, but everyone at the dance who had gathered around to watch the drama play out before them.

"Go on back to enjoy the dance," Rebecca said to the others. "I'll get a new punch bowl and replace the punch."

"Miss Rebecca, how are you goin' to replace the punch? There must've been ten bottles of whiskey in it," one of the others asked.

His question was greeted with laughter which, fortunately, broke the tension.

"Dalton does find ways to get himself into trouble, doesn't he?" Dusty commented that night after they had all returned to the bunkhouse and were getting ready for bed.

"He's a good man," Mo said.

"How can you say that?" One of the other cowboys asked. "Like you say, he's always into first one thing and then another."

"I mean when you consider that me 'n him are good friends, what with him bein' rich and me bein' nothin' but a cowboy."

"Good men don't pee into a punch bowl," Tom said.

"He just needs a little discipline is all," Dusty said. "But I think Mo is right. I think that deep down, he is a good kid. What I don't understand is why he is like he is. I mean, he's got everything anyone his age could possibly want, but somehow it don't seem to be enough for him."

"It isn't a condition that is entirely un-heard of," Tom said.

Tom didn't elaborate, but he could have.

He had seen many a young man, and woman, children of the very wealthy, who for some inexplicable reason were spoiled rotten. Dalton was proof that this particular syndrome was not limited to Boston.

After Tom got to bed he lay there far into the night, thinking of Rebecca. He was sure that if he had wanted to, he could have kissed her that night.

What was he talking about? He did want to kiss her. He wanted to very much. But he knew that if he had, it could open up a can of worms that he wouldn't be able to close again. He was not ready for love — not yet — maybe never again. Not after what happened to Martha. Tom was beginning to think that he should not have gotten off the train in Fort Worth.

Live Oaks, June 1

"Look at that," Mo said, pointing to a broken spoke on the right rear wheel of one of the three heavy freight wagons that belonged to the ranch. "That wheel is going to have to be replaced."

"I'll help you," Tom said.

"Well, the first thing we have to do is get it up on a stand," Mo said. "I'll get the stand and the lever."

A moment later, Mo came back from the

barn with a stand, a long lever, and a block. Putting the block and lever in place, Mo picked up the jack stand.

"I'm smaller than you are, and I can get under the wagon easier," he said. "You lever it up, and I'll get the jack stand set in place."

"All right," Tom agreed.

A moment later, with the right-rear wheel of the wagon levered up from the ground, Mo crawled under the wagon and put the jack in place. Tom lowered the wagon onto the stand, which still kept the wheel clear of the ground.

They pulled the wheel off, took it into the machine shed, and replaced the broken spoke. When they came back, Mo tried to put the wheel back onto the axle, but there was an obstruction underneath that prevented it.

"I'll crawl under there and clear that away," Mo said. "As long as it is on the jack stand, it'll be all right."

It would have been all right, but some of the obstruction was caught under the jack stand itself, and when Mo tried to move it, the jack stand started to fall over.

"It's falling on me!" Mo shouted at the top of his voice.

Acting quickly, and without giving it a second thought, Tom caught the wagon as it was falling. With muscles in his arms and shoulders straining, Tom not only kept the wagon from falling on Mo, he actually lifted it high enough for Mo to get out from under.

"Put the wheel on," Tom said.

"I'll get the lever."

"Put the wheel on," Tom repeated, and quickly Mo slipped the wheel hub back on to the axle. Only then did Tom put the wagon back down.

"Sum'bitch!" Mo said. "I ain't never seen nothin' like that!"

By now the story of Rebecca's initial contact with the two cowboys the night she came back home had made the rounds. The two cowboys, Dutch and Pete, had ridden for several of the ranchers over the last few years, always as part-time riders. When they weren't riding, they performed odd jobs around town. It was said Pete's fingers were still misshapen from his run-in with Tom.

"He may be an Eastern dude, but I tell you true, he ain't someone you want on your bad side," one of the cowboys said, and all the other riders of Live Oaks agreed.

A few days after the incident with the wagon, Rebecca went out on a ride with no particular destination, but with a definite purpose. She needed to sort out her feelings about Tom Whitman. From the very first day, it was clear that Tom wasn't like any cowboy she had ever known, and she had been raised around cowboys.

In fact, Tom was not like any man she had ever known, and in the beginning, her interest in him was curiosity only. That was because she had discovered there was much more to him than met the eye. He was a gentleman of the first order, he could discuss anything, and he was not intimidated by wealth or position. The other cowboys of the ranch sensed the same thing about him, but they harbored no resentment toward him, nor did they ever tease him as they would any other tenderfoot.

As she rode around the ranch that day, she realized that her feelings for Tom had grown beyond curiosity and fascination. She found herself staring at him sometimes, wondering what it would be like to be kissed by him, and more.

She thought back to the dance last month, and the walk they had taken away from the dance. He had not kissed her, though she had the feeling that he very much wanted to kiss her. Why didn't he kiss her? She was certainly letting him know in every way she knew, short of actually coming out and saying it, that she wanted to be kissed.

That night, in bed, she had imagined what it would be like to have him there with her, in bed beside her. Though she was a virgin, she knew what men and women did, and as she lay there, she felt a tingling all over her body as she engaged in thoughts that she dare not share with anyone.

Cresting a small rise in the ground, she saw someone working at a creek just ahead. Then, with a small twinge of excitement, she realized that it was Tom. He was clearing brush from the creek.

She had known this!

She remembered now, hearing her father tell Clay to have Tom clear the brush away from Wahite Creek. She had forgotten that. Or, had she? Had her subconscious mind remembered, and brought her here?

She remained on top of the small hill, sitting her horse for a moment as she looked down at him, wondering if she should turn and ride away before he saw her.

It was too late. He did see her, and he took off his hat, then waved it over his head at her. She felt for a moment as if she were about to jump into a cold pool of water, but taking a deep breath she slapped her legs against the side of her horse and rode down toward him.

"Hello," Tom said cheerfully. "Are you enjoying your ride?"

"Yes," she said. "Are you enjoying your work?" she asked with a little laugh.

"I am enjoying it more now than I was a moment earlier," he said. "Swing down from your saddle and get some circulation going again."

Although she had been mounting and dismounting from the time she was a small girl, she did not decline his offer to help. And that proffer was more than a mere token effort. As she started down, Tom put his hands under her arms and lifted her easily. But he had made a slight miscalculation as he set her down on the ground. The gap between Tom and her horse was such that when he put her into that narrow space it brought their bodies into direct contact. To make matters worse, her horse, almost as if conspiring to do so, moved up against her, pushing her even closer to him. She felt the crush of his chest against her breasts, and the muscles of his legs against hers. She realized then that it was not a miscalculation, but a carefully calculated move.

She shivered, as a thrill, unlike anything she had ever felt before, passed through her.

"I'm on the ground," she said.

"Are you?" Tom asked, his eyes twinkling with great humor. "Because right now, I'm on a cloud."

"What?"

Tom chuckled. "Nothing," he said. "I was just being poetic."

He stepped away, and Rebecca found that she could breathe again. Wanting to change the subject, she walked down to the edge of the creek. "Did you have a lot of brush to clear away? It comes down every spring and starts to clog up the creeks in certain places."

"Choke points," Tom said.

"Choke points, yes."

"It hasn't been too bad," Tom said. "I've nearly gotten it cleared out."

Rebecca reached down to pull a limb from the creek, then tossed it over onto the pile of vegetation Tom had built up by his efforts on the day.

"You trying to take my job away?" Tom asked.

"Ha! I'll just bet that I've cleared out a lot more creeks than you have," Rebecca said.

"Since this is the first time I've ever done this, I wouldn't want to take that bet," Tom said.

"Tom, you never talk about your past," she said.

"What's there to talk about? I'm from Boston, and like many other Easterners, I've come West. I'm glad I did."

"What did you do when you were in Boston?"

"I worked with my father," Tom said.

"What happened? Did you have a falling-out or something?"

"No, not exactly. I just decided that I needed to do something else for a while."

"I can't help but wonder why you left," Rebecca said, pointedly.

"I'm not running away from the law, if that is why you are asking," he added.

"I'm not asking that," Rebecca said, then she amended her comment. "I suppose I am asking it," she added. "Even though it is none of my business, and I have no right to be prying into your private affairs."

He put his fingers on her cheek, and they seemed to have the amazing capability of being both cold and hot at the same time. She could feel a tingling excitement in her body, an exact duplication of the sensations her imagination had generated that night after the dance. The feelings, though, were generated by nothing more than imagination. This time the vibrations in her body were real. She waited, expectantly.

As she knew he would, as she wanted him

89

to, he kissed her, not hard and demanding, but unexpectedly gentle. She was surprised by her reaction to it. The pleasure she felt in her lips spread throughout her body, warming her blood. When he pulled away from her, she reached up to touch her lips and held her fingers there for a long moment as she stared deep into his eyes.

Then Tom kissed her again, but this kiss was not at all like the first kiss — the soft brush of a butterfly wing. This was hard, demanding, almost, but not quite, a bruising kiss. Rebecca was shocked, not by the kiss itself, but by her intense reaction to it. He deepened the kiss, and pulled her against him. As she felt his hard body pressed against hers, Rebecca realized that, though she had been kissed before, they had been the kisses of immature boys, tentative and hesitant. In every previous kiss, Rebecca had been completely in charge.

She wasn't in charge this time, not of him, not even of her own emotions. As her resistance faded she had felt a warmth spreading throughout her body, and she grew limp in his embrace. She lost herself in it as she gave herself into its depths, into him, totally pliant in his hands, subservient to his will, feeling herself spinning into a bottomless vortex. She felt her head spinning and her knees trembling.

Rebecca knew that if he wanted to, he could have his way with her, right now, right here on the banks of the Wahite, in the open, where any cowboy on the ranch, or even her father, could come riding up. And she wouldn't care. She wanted to give herself to him more than she had ever wanted anything in her life, and she waited for him to make the first move, prayed, that he would make the first move.

Tom had tightened his fingers in the silky spill of her auburn hair, then did what Rebecca could not do. He found the strength to gently tug her head back to break the kiss. She stared up at him with eyes that were filled with wonder, and as deep as her soul.

"Tom, I . . . ," she started to say, but she found herself utterly unable to speak. And her knees grew so weak that she could barely stand.

"I'm sorry," Tom said. "I had no right to take advantage of you like that. Clay, or Dusty, or Mo, or any one of the others could have come by," Tom said. "I don't wish to put you in a compromising position. I think it would be better if you continued your ride."

"I — uh — yes, I'm sure you are right,"

Rebecca said. She walked back to her horse and reached up to grab the saddlehorn. "Tom?"

"Yes?"

"You aren't toying with me, are you? I ask, because I am not an experienced woman. I don't know how to judge these things."

"I am not toying with you," Tom said. "I would never do anything like that, Rebecca. I would never do anything to hurt you."

With a warm smile, Rebecca swung into her saddle, then rode away.

Tom cursed himself as he watched her leave. He had no right to intrude upon this innocent young woman's life. Not after what he had done back in Boston. After losing Martha, he didn't think he could or would ever be interested in another woman, nor would he be worthy of another woman's interest.

If he had possessed one ounce of character, he would have left the first moment he realized that he was attracted to Rebecca. No, if he had left the first moment he felt attracted to her, he would have gotten right back onto the train the same night he arrived in Fort Worth.

In the Big House at that exact moment,

Clay Ramsey was visiting with Big Ben. Ranching came easily to Clay Ramsey. He could ride and rope with the best of them, and he could bulldog a calf better than most. He also had a sense of leadership that stood him well with the other cowboys. One would think he had been born and raised on a ranch, but nothing could be further from the truth. His parents had come to Texas even before it was a state, believing it would offer great opportunities for the ambitious and industrious. His father opened a store in Marshall, and though he never realized his goal of being a wealthy merchant, he was able to make a decent living.

Clay had gone to work for his father when he was ten years old, working after school and in the summers. Clay had nothing but respect for his father, but he knew, early in his life, that he had no desire to ever work in a store. When he was sixteen he signed on with a cattle company taking a herd to market in Dodge City. From that day forward he was hooked, and he laid his future out. He wanted to be a cowboy, then trail boss, then the foreman of a great ranch. He had achieved that and was perfectly happy with his life.

He was also happily married, though there

93

were many who had told him that being married wasn't that good of an idea for a cowboy.

"Four dollars and seventy cents a head? Are you sure?" Big Ben said, responding to what Clay had just told him.

"Yes, sir, that was the quote they gave me when I went to Fort Worth this morning," Clay replied.

"That's only a dollar a head more than it costs me to raise them," Big Ben said. "And figuring seventy-five cents a head to drive them up to Dodge City, that means I'd be making a profit of twenty-five cents a head."

"Yes, sir," Clay said. "Well, the plain truth is, Mr. Conyers, folks just don't want Longhorn beef anymore."

"What's wrong with Longhorn beef? I've been eating it for fifty years."

"They say it's tough and stringy."

"It's always been tough and stringy," Big Ben countered.

"Hereford beef isn't tough or stringy," Clay said.

"Yeah, I know," Big Ben said. "Just as a matter of curiosity, what are Herefords bringing?"

"Twelve dollars a head."

"Walter Hannah is running Herefords and has been for the last five years," Big Ben said. "He tried to get me to switch over when he did, but I didn't listen to him. If I were to switch now, it would be the same as admitting that he was right and I was wrong. And if I know Walter, that is something he would never let me live down."

"It isn't my place to say, Mr. Conyers," Clay said. "But is hanging on to your pride worth twenty-five cents a head?"

"You have a point," Big Ben said. "But right now I have to decide what to do about the five thousand head of Longhorn I have. It is barely worth mounting a drive to take them to market, but I don't see as I have any alternative."

"Would you like a suggestion?"

"Yes, by all means."

"I know that Mr. Hurley at the Union Stockyard in Fort Worth is looking to buy cattle."

"Yes, but I understand he is paying a dollar less than they are paying at Kansas City," Big Ben said.

"But consider this," Clay said. "You won't have the expense of driving the herd to Dodge City, and the rail cost of taking them to Kansas City. And, you won't have the risk of losing any of your cattle."

Big Ben stroked his chin. "You may have a point," he said. "I won't make any money, but I won't lose any, either. And if I get rid of this herd, that will leave me the freedom to decide what I need to do next. All right, Clay, I'll ride into town tomorrow and meet with Mr. Hurley. If we can come to some sort of an arrangement, we'll deliver the herd to him at the stockyards."

For the drovers heading Longhorn cattle up the Chisholm Trail to the railheads, Fort Worth was the last major stop for rest and supplies. Beyond Fort Worth they would have to deal with crossing the Red River into Indian Territory. So, because Fort Worth was on the route north, between 1866 and 1890 more than four million head of cattle were trailed through the town.

Then, when the railroad arrived in 1876, Fort Worth became a major shipping point for livestock. This prompted plans in 1887 for the construction of the Union Stockyard Company located about two and one half miles north of the Tarrant County Courthouse. The Union Stockyard Company, was now in full operation.

William Hurley, founder and president of the Union Stockyard Company in Fort Worth, was an average-sized man, though he was dwarfed by Big Ben's towering presence. Hurley, who wore a Vandyke beard, invited Big Ben into his office, offering him a seat across from his desk. A brass locomotive acted as a paperweight for the many pieces of paper that were piled up on this busy man's desk.

"So you want to sell me some cows, do you?" Hurley asked.

"I do."

"Good." Hurley opened a wooden box and handed Big Ben a cigar. "Try this, I think you will like it. It comes from Cuba."

Big Ben nodded as he accepted the cigar. He took a small cutter from his pocket, nipped off the end, then ran his tongue up the side of the cigar. Before he reached for his own matches, Hurly struck a match, let the carbon burn away, then held the flame to the tip of Big Ben's cigar.

"I think," Hurley said as Big Ben puffed on the cigar, securing the light and sending up a white puff of aromatic smoke, "that if a cowman like you, one of the men who made the Texas cattle industry, would start using the stockyard, it would spread to others. And that would be good for Texas."

"And particularly good for you, I would expect," Big Ben replied around the edge of his cigar.

"I'll admit that if I could start a thriving cattle market, right here in Fort Worth, it would be good for me," Hurley said.

"Speaking as a cattleman, I have to tell you that the problem we would have in dealing with you, Will, is the fact that you don't pay enough. It is my understanding that you are paying one dollar a head below the Kansas City market."

"That is true," Hurley admitted. "But, like you, I have to get the cows to Kansas City, and I do that by train, which is quite expensive."

"What you should do is start a meat-processing plant right here in Fort Worth," Big Ben suggested.

Hurley chuckled. "Mr. Conyers, you are a brilliant man, for that is exactly what I plan to do. I have been discussing this very subject with Mr. Phillip Armor, of the Armor Meat Packing Company."

"When you get that done, I think you will have a lot of cattlemen dealing with you. I know that I will."

"I appreciate that," Hurley said. "In fact, to show you how much I appreciate your business, if you will let me use your name in talking to others, I will make you a special deal on your cattle," Hurley said. "Instead of paying one dollar below market price, I will give you ninety cents below market price."

Big Ben was pleased with that proposal, for that wouldn't be much less than he would make if he drove the entire herd to Dodge City, especially considering the fact that he was certain to lose some cattle during the drive. But he knew better than to show how pleased he was with that offer, so he made a counter-bid.

"Suppose I took half a dollar less?"

Hurley shook his head. "I couldn't do that," he said. "But I might be able to go eighty cents below market."

"Make it seventy cents, and you have a deal," Big Ben said.

"Mr. Wiggins," Hurley called through the open door of his office.

A small, bald-headed man stepped into the door. "Yes sir, Mr. Hurley?"

"What is the latest market price for Longhorns in Kansas City?"

"Four dollars and ninety cents."

"Thank you."

Hurley did some figuring, then looked up. "I can give you four dollars and fifteen cents a head. That's seventy five cents below market and quite frankly, Mr. Conyers, this is the best I can do."

Big Ben extended his hand across the desk. "Mr. Hurley, I'll have the cattle here by day after tomorrow," he said.

CHAPTER FIVE

Chugwater, Wyoming, June 27

When Biff Johnson saw a tall man with golden hair, wide shoulders, and muscular arms come into Fiddler's Green, the saloon Biff owned, he reached under the bar to find the special bottle of Scotch that he kept just for his friend, Duff MacCallister. He also poured one for himself, then held his glass up.

"Here's to them that like us, and to them that think us swell," Biff said.

"And to them that hates us, long may they roast in hell," Duff replied, as, with a laugh, the two friends touched their glasses together.

Biff Johnson was a retired U.S. Army sergeant who had been with Benteen's battalion as part of Custer's last scout. When he retired he had built a saloon in Chugwater and named it Fiddler's Green, after an old cavalry legend: Anyone who has ever heard the bugle call Boots and Saddles will, when he dies, go to a cool, shady place by a stream of sweet water. There, he will see all the other cavalrymen who have gone before him, and he will greet those who come after him as he awaits the final judgment. That place is called Fiddler's Green.

In the three years since Duff had come to America, he and Biff had become good friends, partly because Biff was married to a woman from Scotland, and partly because of an incident that had happened shortly after Duff arrived.

"MacCallister!" Malcolm called from the darkness of the saloon. "Why don't you come back out into the street, and I will as well? We can face each other down. What do you say? Just you and I, alone in the street."

"You don't expect me to believe that, do you?" Duff called back.

"Believe what?"

"That it would just be the two of us."

Malcolm laughed. "You think that because I have friends with me, that I may take unfair advantage of you, MacCallister? Alas, that is probably true. Tell me, what does it feel like to know that you won't live long enough to see the sun set tonight?"

All the while Malcolm was talking, Duff was keeping one eye on the mirror and the other on the corner of the watering trough. Then his vigil was rewarded. Duff saw the brim of a hat appear, and he cocked his pistol, aimed, took a breath, and let half of it out. When he saw the man's eye appear, Duff touched the trigger. Looking in the mirror he saw the man's face fall into the dirt, and the gun slip from his hand.

"Carter! Carter!" the man at the end of the trough shouted. Suddenly he stood up. "You son of a bitch! You killed my brother!" He started running across the street, firing wildly. Duff shot one time, and the man running toward him pitched forward in the street.

Duff heard the bark of a rifle, then he saw someone tumbling forward off the roof of the dress shop. The man had had a bead on Duff, and Duff hadn't seen him. Looking toward the sound of the rifle shot, Duff saw Biff Johnson. Smiling, Biff waved at him, then stepped back behind the corner of the Curly Latham's Barber Shop.[1]

"Will you be coming into town for the Fourth of July celebration?" Biff asked.

"When is that?"

"The Fourth of July is on the fourth," Biff answered with a laugh. "Funny thing about that holiday, but it comes on the fourth,

1. *MacCallister: The Eagles Legacy*

every July."

"What day of the week?" Duff asked, laughing with him.

"I know what you meant, I was just teasing you. It's next Friday. Of course, being a Scotsman, our Independence Day holiday won't mean much to you."

"Nae, that's where you're wrong, Laddie," Duff said. "For 'twas on that date that you stole America from the English. And any evil done to the cursed English warms the cockles of any true Scotsman's heart."

"This is sort of a double celebration for us this year. Wyoming is being admitted as a state on the tenth — I don't know why they didn't decide on the fourth. Seems to me like that would be ideal, to celebrate the birth of our country and the birth of our state on the same day," Biff said.

"Maybe they thought Wyoming should have its own birthday," Duff suggested.

"I suppose so. Anyway, there is going to be a dance," Biff said. "And I expect Miss Parker will be wanting you to come. You will be there, won't you?"

"She's my business partner," Duff said. "I have to come."

"Speaking of your business, how big is your herd now?"

"Just over ten thousand head."

103

"I remember when all the other ranchers teased you about raising Black Angus," Biff said. "They weren't hearty enough, some said. Others said it was a temporary thing; that Americans were used to Longhorns and wouldn't take to Angus. Now your herd is the envy of all of Wyoming."

"Not just my herd," Duff said. "Don't forget, Meghan Parker owns one fourth."

"What are Angus bringing at the market now?"

"About fifteen dollars and seventy cents a head."

Biff took a tablet and pencil from under the bar, then did some figuring. "That makes her share worth thirty-nine thousand, two hundred fifty dollars, which is about ten times more that her dress store is worth. She's not only beautiful, she is one smart lady."

"Aye, she is that, all right," Duff said. He tossed down his drink, then with a salute of his empty glass started to the door. "*Slàinte, sonas agus beartas* to ye, m' friend," he called back over his shoulder.

"Health, wealth, and happiness to you as well, Duff," Biff called back.

Chugwater, July 4
There had been a baseball game between

104

the cowboys and the merchants of the town, the game won by the merchants as they had played it much more often. There were also foot races and horse races.

Duff had watched the baseball game, though he had no idea what was going on. He enjoyed the foot racing and horse racing because at least he could understand what it was.

It was Meghan who came up with the William Tell idea. She advanced the proposal that Duff was a good enough shot that she would trust him to shoot an apple off her head from fifty paces. Duff protested and would have absolutely refused, had not Sir Anthony Wellington made his comment.

"I've never yet met a Scotsman who would match his purse with his mouth."

Wellington was an Englishman who had come to America to buy some ranching property, taking advantage of the ill fortunes of those who had lost much during the great freeze and die-out of a few years earlier.

"Mayor Matthews," Duff said. "Did I not hear some discussion as to the cost of building a new school in Chugwater?"

Fred Matthews, who owned the mercantile and was one of Duff's first friends upon moving to Chugwater, was the current mayor of the town.

"It has been discussed, but so far we haven't been able to raise enough money."

"How much do you need?"

"We think twenty-five hundred dollars would be enough to build it," Matthews said.

"Mr. Wellington, would you care to wager?" Duff asked.

"Actually, that would be Lord Wellington," Wellington corrected.

"Nae, not in America. Here, in America, on the day of its celebration of independence from the black-hearted English, here, *Mister* Wellington, there are no Lords." He looked over at Meghan and smiled. "But there are ladies," he said.

"You wish to wager for twenty-five hundred dollars to build the school? How gallant of you, sir. Yes, I shall wager twenty-five hundred dollars. And I will even buy the apple," he said.

Word quickly spread throughout town that Duff MacCallister was going to shoot an apple off Meghan Parker's head, and a crowd gathered on First Street to watch the demonstration.

When Wellington returned with the apple, everyone in the crowd gasped. The apple was no bigger than an average-sized plum.

"That's not fair!" Guthrie shouted. Guthrie, another of Duff's friends, owned a building supply store. "The bet was that he would shoot an apple."

"I bought this in His Honor the mayor's own store," Wellington said. "It was represented to me as an apple. Am I to believe that the mayor is dishonest?"

"You bought the smallest apple you could find, and you know it," Biff said.

"Nevertheless, it is an apple," Wellington said. "And the wager is only that, from fifty paces, he will shoot an apple from the young lady's head. There were no specifications as to how large the apple must be."

"Put the apple on a stake," Duff said. "I will shoot it from fifty paces."

"Oh, no, no, no, my dear sir," Wellington said. "The wager is that you will shoot the apple as it rests upon her head. It is such a pretty head too. It would be a shame to see some injury befall her."

"Give me the apple," Meghan said.

The fifty paces had already been stepped off, and she went to the place marked for her, turned to face Duff, and put the apple on her own head.

"Meghan, I . . . ," Duff started, but Meghan interrupted him.

"Do it, Duff," she said. "Do it, and only

your name will be on my dance card to-night."

Duff nodded, smiled, raised his pistol, aimed, and pulled the trigger. The apple flew into pieces as the bullet penetrated the pulp. The crowd applauded, as much in relief as from appreciation of the marksman-ship.

True to her promise, Duff was the only name on Meghan's dance card that night, though she had confided with her friend that his name already was the only one on her card.

Live Oaks Ranch, July 4
The banner read: "Happy 114th Birthday, America!" In addition to the banner, all the posts and pillars of all the buildings of Live Oaks Ranch were decorated with red, white, and blue bunting. The cowboys, enjoying a rare day of festivities, were laughing and shouting, and running about, setting off fire-crackers.

Two very long tables, each one capable of seating forty diners, had been built by plac-ing planks across several sawhorses. The tables under the spreading live oak trees that gave the ranch its name were filled with cakes, pies, biscuits, potato salad, baked beans, sliced tomatoes and cucumbers.

Early this morning two of the cowboys, Dusty McNally and Mo Coffey, had built a fire of mesquite, then spitted half a steer over the fire. And though only Coleman, the cook for Live Oaks, had the right to apply his "special" barbeque sauce, the rest of the cowboys had taken turns during the day turning the beef slowly over the fires and filling the compound with the delicious aroma of roasting meat.

Everyone on the ranch had eaten beef all their lives, but all agreed that they had never tasted anything this good, and they all complimented Coleman on the wonderful job he did cooking.

"It wasn't nothin' particular I done," Coleman said. "It was the beef. It was Hereford, come over from the Rocking H."

There would be no Live Oaks cattle drive this season because Big Ben had, in accordance with his agreement with William Hurley, sold all his cattle to the Union Stock Exchange in Fort Worth. But Big Ben's friend Walter Hannah, who owned the Rocking H, a neighboring ranch, would be driving his cattle north. In fact, the drive would get underway on the next day after the 4th of July, and because of that, the Rocking H did not celebrate the Fourth. Instead, Hannah presented a side of Hereford beef to Big Ben as his contribution, and he and his cowboys came over to celebrate with the people at Live Oaks.

"What do you think of this beef?" Hannah asked. He and his wife, Louise, were at a table with Big Ben, Julia, and Rebecca. Dalton, by his own request, was sitting at the long table with the cowboys.

"It's good beef," Big Ben said.

"You should have listened to me when I suggested that you switch over to Herefords," Walter said.

"I know."

"Well, now is a good time to do it, seeing as you don't have any cattle."

"I know."

"So are you?"

"Am I what?"

"Are you going to switch over to Hereford cattle?"

"I'm thinking about it," Big Ben said. "I just haven't made up my mind yet."

"Here is a little something to help you make up your mind," Walter said. "Hereford are selling for twelve dollars a head in Kansas City. They cost no more to raise, and they cost no more to drive up to Dodge City, but they are bringing in twelve dollars a head, compared to what? I think Longhorn are now down to about three-fifty a head."

110

"Don't rub it in," Big Ben said.

Walter laughed. "All right, I won't," he said. "I promise, I won't say another word about it. I'll just enjoy the picnic."

After the meal, some of the cowboys performed for the others. One of the performers was Dusty McNally. Dusty, whose real name was Abner Coy McNally, was, fifty-two years old, and looked up to by all the younger cowboys. His hair was gray, his eyes blue, and his skin weathered, with permanent creases around his eyes. He was short, only five feet seven, and he wore a sweeping handlebar moustache that covered his mouth. Born in Tennessee, Dusty was the son of a part-time preacher and full-time farmer. His father had died when he was kicked in the head by a mule. His mother had remarried, but Dusty couldn't stand his stepfather, who abused both him and his mother. When Dusty was fifteen, he had killed his stepfather and ran away. He had been on his own ever since. He met Big Ben during the Civil War. Big Ben was a colonel and Dusty was a private, but when Big Ben lay gravely wounded among the boulders of Devil's Den at Gettysburg, under the observation and in the range of Yankee sharpshooters, no officer or sergeant could find the courage to go to the aid of their fallen commander. It was Private Dusty McNally who braved Yankee fire to drag him back to safety.

The battlefield was a cacophony of sound; from the thunder of cannonading artillery, the loud bang of muskets and pistols, the screams of terror and the cry of the wounded, to the distinctive buzz and whine of Minié balls. Private Dusty McNally was comparatively safe behind a long line of boulders, but he abandoned that safety to dart out into the open field toward his fallen colonel.

"Get him! Get that Reb!" a Union soldier shouted and several of the enemy soldiers fired at Dusty. He could hear the bullets so close to him that they popped as they passed by, then hitting the rocks to ricochet off into the distance with a loud whine.

Dusty was five feet seven inches tall, and Colonel Conyers was almost a foot taller, and twice as heavy. Dusty tried to pick him up, but fell back on his first try.

"Jesus, Colonel, I don't mean nothin' by this, but you are one big sum'bitch," Dusty said as he tried again to pick him up. "Can you sit up?"

"I think so," Colonel Conyers said.

"All right, sit up."

Colonel Conyers sat up, then Dusty squat-

ted down in front of him. "Put your arms around my neck," Dusty said.

The colonel did so, then Dusty put his arms under Colonel Conyer's arms and stood up, lifting the colonel to his feet as he did so. After that he put his shoulder into Conyer's stomach and lifted the colonel so that he was draped across his shoulder. Carrying him in that way, he turned and started back toward the relative safety of the line of boulders.

It wasn't until then that he realized no one was shooting at him, and just as he reached the boulders, he was cheered, not only by the Confederate troops but by the Union soldiers as well.

"Good job, Reb!" one of the Yankee soldiers shouted. "Now, you and that big fella you just hauled off the field, keep your heads down, 'cause we're goin' to commence shootin' again!"

For all intents and purposes, the war ended when Lee surrendered to Grant at Appomattox, Virginia, but for many veterans of that terrible war, the surrender was just the beginning of a much more personal conflict. Young men who had lived their lives on the edge for four years found it nearly impossible to return home and take up the plow, or go back to work in a store, repair wagons, or any of the other things that were the necessary part of becoming whole again.

Some took up the outlaw trail, continuing to practice the skills they had learned during the war. Though few on the ranch knew it, Dusty had taken that path and was, in his own words, on the trail to perdition when he came to Live Oaks and asked for work. Big Ben gave him a job, and Dusty had been with him ever since.

Dusty was a master with ropes, and he gave the others a demonstration which had them all cheering.

Mo Coffey was next. Mo Coffey was about twenty-two years old. He told everyone he was *about* that old, because he had no idea how old he really was. His mother, whom he had never met, had left a newborn infant wrapped in a coffee-bean bag on the doorstep of Our Lady of Mercy orphanage. The sisters at the orphanage named him Coffey after the coffee bag, and Moses because of the story of the baby Moses being left in the bull rushes.

"All right," Mo said. "Now let me show you fellas a thing or two."

He picked up two bottles, gave one to Dalton and one to Dusty.

"Alright, when you are ready, throw the bottles into the air," Mo said.

"You don't have your gun out yet," Dalton said.

"Don't worry about that. Just throw the bottles up into the air."

Mo bent his knees slightly into a crouch, and held his right hand about six inches above his pistol.

"You going to say when?" Dusty asked.

"No, that would be cheating. You throw them when you are ready, then I'll draw."

Dusty threw his bottle up first; then seeing him, Dalton threw his up as well. Mo drew quickly and fired twice, breaking both bottles in the air.

The applause for his feat was even more enthusiastic than it had been for Dusty's roping exhibition.

There were a few other exhibitions as well, including Dusty playing the guitar and Rebecca singing.

When darkness fell, everyone gathered for the fireworks show, which consisted of rockets and aerial bombs.

Rebecca and Tom found themselves together in the darkness and some distance from the others. When Tom put his arm around her and drew her to him, she didn't resist. Nor did she resist when he kissed her.

"Oh, Tom," she said, saying his name even

as they were kissing, so that he felt her lips moving under his. "I love you."

"No!" Tom said. He pulled away from her. "Rebecca, you don't mean that."

"What's wrong? Of course I mean that."

"You can't love me, Rebecca," Tom said. "Because I can't love you. I can't love anyone, ever."

"Tom, what are you saying?"

"You don't understand, Rebecca. I'm not worthy of your love. I'm not worthy of any woman's love, ever again."

Tom turned and walked away from her, quickly blending in with the other celebrants.

Rebecca felt her heart shatter, and crying bitter tears, she turned and ran back into the house.

When Big Ben went into the house after everyone was gone, he saw a lantern burning low in the parlor, and when he went in to extinguish it, he saw Rebecca sitting in the shadows.

"Rebecca, what are you doing here?" he asked.

"Nothing, just sitting here," Rebecca said. "I'll go to bed now."

Rebecca turned her head away, but not before Big Ben saw a tear streak glistening in the lantern light.

"What is it, Rebecca? What is wrong?"

"Oh, Papa, I'm in love," Rebecca said.

"You're in love but you are crying? I may be an old fogey, but I thought people were happy when they were in love."

"I love him, but he doesn't love me," Rebecca said.

"Really. Well, I know it hurts now, darlin', but I reckon there isn't a person in the world who hasn't had the experience of loving someone and not being loved back. I'll say this, though. Anyone who would turn down your love must be an absolute fool. Who is it? George Posey? The banker's son? I know you think that would be a good match, but to tell you the truth, he's always been sort of a weak sister as far as I'm concerned. So if he doesn't love you, then you haven't lost much."

"No, Papa!" Rebecca said, interrupting him with impassioned shout. "It isn't George Posey," she said. "I never even see him except in church from time to time."

"Well then, who is it?" Big Ben asked.

"It's Tom Whitman."

Big Ben blinked a couple of times, as if he didn't understand her.

"Tom Whitman? You mean the cowboy who works for me? What on earth would make you say something like that?"

"I love him, Papa," Rebecca said, fighting hard to keep the words from breaking in her throat.

Big Ben walked over to the front of the fireplace and stood there for a long moment, looking down at the shining brass andirons. Finally, he responded.

"Have you told him this?" Big Ben asked. He did not turn away from the fireplace as he spoke.

"Yes."

"And what did he say?"

"He said he wasn't — worthy of me."

"He's right about that," Big Ben said. "His kind isn't worthy of you."

"What do you mean by 'his kind'?"

"I mean his kind," Big Ben repeated. "Where did he come from? What is he doing here?"

"He came from Boston," Rebecca said. "You know that. He told us that the first day he came here."

"That's the next question. What is he doing here?"

"He said he wanted to see the West."

"How do we know that he isn't running from the law?" Big Ben asked.

"He isn't. I just know he isn't."

"Look here, Rebecca, I don't know how to ask you this but, has he compromised you in any way?"

"Compromised me?"

"You know what I mean."

"No, Papa, he has not compromised me. God help me, I wish that he would."

"You don't mean that."

"Yes, Papa, I do mean it."

"That isn't something you will have to worry about, because you won't be seeing him anymore."

"How can I help seeing him? He works here. He lives here. I see him every day," Rebecca said. "What am I supposed to do? Should I just close my eyes every time he comes into view?"

"Don't be snippy with your father, young lady. You know exactly what I am talking about. When I say you can't see him, I mean you can't — see — him in a . . . ," he rolled his hands as he looked for the right word, "romantic way. He is not for you. I want something much better for you than an ordinary cowboy. Listen to me, girl, because I know what I'm talking about."

"Papa. He is not, in any way you can imagine, an ordinary cowboy. He is so much more than you think he is."

"He could be three times more than I think he is, and still not be worthy of you," Big Ben said. "Rebecca, I know what it is like when a man and a woman of different — well, I don't want to say class, so I'll just say different backgrounds — fall in love. You may think that the love is stronger than any difference, but it isn't. You only wind up getting hurt."

"You mean like with my real mother?"

"I . . . ," Big Ben started. It was obvious that he was surprised by Rebecca's response. "All right, yes, I don't mind saying it, because that is a perfect example of how two people from totally different cultures can destroy each other. That's why I know what I'm talking about when I say that you cannot see him anymore."

"Papa, please," Rebecca said.

"I know you think I'm being unfair, but please understand that your mother and I want only the best for you."

"Which mother would that be?" Rebecca asked bluntly. "Would that be the one you are married to? Or the one who abandoned me?"

"That isn't fair, Rebecca. Julia has been as much a mother to you as she has to Dalton. And you know it."

"I'm sorry. I didn't mean that," Rebecca said. "I call her mother because she has been the only mother I have ever known. I had no right to say such a thing. But, Papa,

I am twenty-one years old. I have feelings and emotions just as any woman has. You have no right to tell me who I can love, and who I can't love."

"That's where you are wrong, Rebecca. As long as you live under my roof, I have every right," Big Ben said. "And you forget, I can fire him, and then it won't be a problem anymore."

"No, I beg of you, don't punish him. He hasn't done anything wrong," Rebecca said. "I — I won't see him anymore."

Big Ben put his arms around his daughter and pulled her to him. "Now you are being reasonable," he said. "Trust me, Rebecca, this is for your own good."

As they stood together in the parlor of the oversized house, Rebecca could see her reflection in the oval mirror that was on the wall above the fireplace behind her father. She closed her eyes to avoid seeing the tears.

That night Rebecca lay in bed replaying the words Tom had said to her.

"You don't understand, Rebecca. I'm not worthy of your love. I'm not worthy of any woman's love, ever again."

Why didn't he consider himself worthy of her love? And what did he mean, when said he was "not worthy of any woman's love ever again?"

Had he been hurt by a woman? He was the strongest man she had ever known. Could he really be so fragile that being spurned by one woman could cause him to never have the courage to love again?

Her father had told her that she couldn't see him again, and she had argued with him, but she knew, down inside, that her father was right. She couldn't see him again but not for the reason her father said. She couldn't see him again because she couldn't trust herself not to debase herself by pleading for his love.

Getting out of bed, Rebecca went over to her vanity and pulled out the letter she had received from her biological mother just before she went to Marshall. Lighting the lantern on her dresser, she re-read the letter that was the only tangible connection between her and the woman who had given her life. She hadn't paid too much attention to the invitation in the letter, because the proposal her mother had made seemed too far-fetched to consider. But now her mother's unexpected offer seemed to offer the best solution to her current problem.

After re-reading that letter, Rebecca knew exactly what she was going to do. Her mother was in Dodge City, and the Rocking

H was driving a herd to Dodge City. She would go with the herd — though she would have to be careful that nobody, especially the Rocking H cowboys, knew about it. When her father discovered her gone, he would check the train depot and the stage-coach station. He would never think that she was going north with a trail drive.

Much later that same night, when she was certain that everyone was asleep, Rebecca cut her hair, which hung down to the middle of her back, to shoulder-length. She gathered the long auburn tresses she sheared off so they wouldn't be found and stuck them in a knapsack, along with two extra changes of clothes she had taken from her brother. Pulling on a pair of denim trousers and an ecru linen shirt, she started down the stairway, walking carefully to avoid any creaking steps. It was dark, but she was able to feel her way by holding carefully to the banister. Also, a full moon sent a splash of muted silver light to form a gleaming pool at the foot of the stairs.

As she reached the bottom step, the grandfather's clock that stood in the foyer suddenly whirred, then came to life with two loud gongs. Although she had grown up listening to the clock, its unexpected loudness made her jump with a quick fear.

Grabbing harder onto the banister, she stood there for a moment until her racing heart stilled again.

Outside, she could still smell the residual aroma of the side of beef that had been cooked that day. She thought of the celebration, the joy shared by everyone, not only those of Live Oaks, but the people from the Rocking H as well. Did she really want to leave this? Couldn't she just stay, and leave things as they were?

No. It was too late for that now. She had made her decision and she wasn't going back on it.

Carrying through with her plan, she saddled her personal horse, then led him away from the barn. She glanced toward the two bunkhouses, their white paint gleaming in the reflection of the moonlight. Tom was in one of them right now, no doubt sleeping the sleep of the innocent, unaware that she was leaving.

What if she went there, right now, awakened him, and asked him to leave with her?

For one insane and wonderful moment, Rebecca considered that. But she knew that he wouldn't agree to it. In his mind he would think that he was the cause of her losing her family and her birthright. And in some sense of "doing the right thing," he would insist that he leave instead, and she stay.

Abandoning that idea, Rebecca walked her horse through the compound of house and outbuildings until she believed she was far enough away to be able to ride without being heard. Mounting her horse, she rode him at a brisk trot over the three miles that separated the two ranches. When she reached the Rocking H Ranch, she dismounted, removed the saddle, then turned her horse loose and smacked it on the rump, knowing it would return home. Then, finding a hay-softened spot in Walter Hannah's barn, she slept.

CHAPTER SIX

"What are you doing here, boy?" a man's gruff voice asked.

Opening her eyes, Rebecca saw that it was daylight.

"I want to go on the trail drive," Rebecca said.

The man who had awakened her was John Cornett, the Rocking H foreman. Cornett had known Rebecca for most of her life, so this would be a really good test as to whether or not her disguise was working.

Cornett chuckled. "Well you damn near slept through it," he said. "Better get on out there, Mr. Hannah is signing on the riders now."

"Thanks," Rebecca said, smiling with relief that she had not been recognized. She picked up the little canvas bag that held her other clothes, then went outside. There were ten or eleven young men standing around a table. Walter Hannah was at the table, signing them up.

"Who's next?" Hannah called.

When nobody else stepped up to the table, Rebecca did. Hannah looked up at her and for a moment, she thought she saw recognition in his eyes. But thankfully, that moment passed.

"How old are you, boy?" he asked.

"I'm sixteen."

"You think you can handle the work?"

Rebecca was an excellent horsewoman, and she had cut cows at her father's ranch many times.

"Yes, sir, I'm certain I can," she replied.

Hannah stared at her for a moment longer, then shrugged and picked up his pen.

"Pay is ten dollars a week, and found," Hannah said. "Figure six weeks there. Is that all right with you?"

"Yes, sir," Rebecca said.

"What's your name?"

Rebecca had already thought this out. Her saddle had the initials RC worked into the side flaps.

"Ron," she answered. "Ron Carmody."

"All right, Carmody. Go see Julius Jackson. He's the wrangler, and he'll help you select your string. You have a saddle?"

"Yes, sir."

"Good."

Julius was a black man, shorter even than Rebecca. He helped her pick out three horses, which she would rotate during the drive. He, on the other hand, as the wrangler, would be responsible for keeping the remuda together for Rebecca and the other cowboys.

"Gracious Lord, boy," Julius said when he saw Rebecca's saddle. "That is one bodacious saddle."

Live Oaks, July 5

"Rebecca hasn't come down for breakfast yet?" Big Ben asked as he split open a biscuit and lathered butter onto it. "That's odd, she's always an early riser."

"Well, we did stay up late last night for the fireworks display," Julia said. "Perhaps she is just tired."

At forty-eight years old, Julia's blonde hair was now showing flashes of gray. She was five feet six inches tall, more than a full foot shorter than her husband. But if they were mismatched in size, they were a perfect match in background, for Julia had come from a very wealthy family. Her father, Justin Caldwell, owned a bank in Fort Worth.

"Go check on her," Big Ben said.

Though Big Ben didn't say anything about

it, he was thinking about the discussion he and Rebecca had had last night, and he had a bad feeling about it.

That feeling was confirmed when Julia came back into the dining room a minute later with a confused and worried look on her face.

"She isn't there," Julia said. "Rebecca isn't in her room."

"I knew it!" Big Ben said, slapping the table. "Damn it, I knew it!"

"You knew what? Ben, what is wrong? Where is Rebecca? What has happened to her?"

"I don't know," Big Ben said. "But I intend to find out."

Big Ben walked out to the cookhouse. He could smell the biscuits and coffee before he got there, and he could hear the conversations and laughter from the cowboys at their breakfast. When he stepped inside the cookhouse most of the conversation stopped, and all the cowboys looked toward the ranch owner, curious as to why he might have come into the building. Though he owned the building and had every right to come into it any time he wanted, the cookhouse, like the bunkhouses, were generally regarded as the private domain of the cowboys.

"Yes, sir, Mr. Conyers," Dusty said. "Do you need something?"

Big Ben looked around the cookhouse and saw Tom Whitman at the table with Dusty, Mo, and a half-dozen other cowboys. Seeing Tom here surprised him, because he was almost certain that Rebecca had run off with him. Big Ben studied Tom's face for a long moment to see if he could detect a look of guilt or nervousness, but he saw nothing.

"Uh, no, nothing," Big Ben said.

Beyond the cookhouse and the two bunkhouses sat a row of ten small, green-painted clapboard houses. Most of them were one-room houses, with the bedroom, kitchen, dining, and sitting rooms combined. But one house, considerably bigger than the others, had three rooms: a bedroom, sitting room, and kitchen-dining room combination. This was the house of Clay Ramsey, the foreman of Live Oaks.

At the moment, Clay was having breakfast with his wife, Maria. Without being asked, she got up from the table and poured a second cup of coffee for Clay.

"Thank you, sweetheart," Clay said.

"I made some cinnamon sopapillas," Maria said. "Would you like one?"

"You are being awfully sweet to me this

morning, Maria, pouring my coffee and offering me sopapillas. Is there something I should know?"

Maria sat down across the table from him and as she looked at him, a huge smile spread across her face.

"*Estoy embarazada*!" Maria was so excited that she spoke the words in Spanish, then translated. "I am with child!" she said.

"What? Are you sure?" Clay asked, his smile now as wide as Maria's.

"Si! I have thought so, but I wasn't sure. I talked to Mama and she said it is so."

Clay walked around the table, and when she started to get up, he put his hand on her shoulder.

"No, you should be careful now," he said. "I will come down to you."

Clay leaned over and embraced his young wife.

"Are you happy, my husband?" Maria asked.

"Happier than I can tell you, Maria," he said. "And I don't care if it is a boy or a girl."

"It will be a boy," Maria said.

"How do you know it will be a boy?"

"Because I had a dream. And in my dream, my *abuelo* came to visit me, and he said it would be a boy."

"Your *abuelo*? Your grandfather?"

"*Si*."

"Your grandfather is dead."

"Even the *muerto* can visit you in your dreams," Maria said as if it were something everyone should know.

"It would be good if it is a boy, but I will be happy no matter what it is," Clay said.

A loud knock on the door interrupted their conversation and Clay went to open it. Big Ben was standing there, and he was obviously agitated.

"Have you seen her?" he asked.

Clay had a confused look on his face. "Have I seen who?"

"Rebecca," Big Ben said, as if it should be obvious. "She's gone. Have you seen her?"

"No, I haven't. When did she leave?"

"She left in the middle of the night," Big Ben said. "Turn out all the men, Clay. We have to find her."

All work stopped while everyone searched for Rebecca. The mystery was deepened when they discovered that, while her saddle was gone, her horse was not, though it wasn't in the corral. They found her horse cropping grass about half a mile from the Big House.

Clay and Tom rode into town to check the

railroad and stagecoach depots, but neither of them reported that Rebecca had bought a ticket.

"Tom, is there something going on that I don't know about?" Clay asked as the two men started back toward Live Oaks.

"What do you mean?"

"You have everyone on the ranch talking about you. None of us have ever known anyone as smart as you are. You are from back East, but you ride a horse like you were born in the saddle. There is something in your past, something that you don't want anyone to know about."

"I'm told there are a lot of men out here who have pasts that they don't want to share," Tom said. "That's one of the reasons I came West."

"So there is something in your past. What is it?"

"You said it yourself, Clay. It is something that I don't want anyone to know about."

"Are you wanted by the law?"

"Is Dusty wanted by the law?" Tom replied.

"Dusty? Well, I — I don't know."

"Why don't you know?"

"Because I've never asked him."

"Then why are you asking me?"

"Because it is different with you," Clay

said. "Maria tells me that Rebecca has set her cap for you. Now, I don't know about such things, but Maria does, and if that's what she says, then that's the way it is. And if that is true, then sure as hell, it's not something that Big Ben would approve of. So I'm going to ask you right out. Is there something going on between the two of you? Do you know where Rebecca is?"

"I don't know where she is," Tom said. "But I think it is my fault that she is gone."

"Why would it be your fault?" Clay asked.

"I'm afraid I hurt her."

"Clay stopped riding and glared at Tom. "Tom, did you hit that girl?"

"What? No, no," Tom said quickly.

"You didn't hit her, or — do anything to her? Because if you did, friendship be damned, I'll have you fired off this place and run out of Texas."

"It was nothing like that, Clay," Tom said. "I promise you. I guess I just told her something she didn't want to hear."

"What did you tell her?"

"I told her that I didn't love her."

Clay was quiet for a long moment. "Yeah," he said. "Yeah, I can see how that could be more than she wants to deal with."

"The thing is, I lied to her," Tom said.

"Why did you lie?"

"Under the circumstances, I thought it might be best," Tom said.

"Yeah, with Big Ben, I see your point," Clay said. "I'm not sure how he would take it, his daughter being in love with one of his hired hands. She's probably hurt now, because she's young, and young people feel this more."

The circumstances Tom was referring to were his own circumstances, not Big Ben's, but it was easier to let Clay think that.

"All right, I believe you. But do me a favor, will you? Don't say anything about this to anyone else. And especially not to Big Ben."

Tom had no intention of talking about it to Big Ben, but as it turned out, he didn't have any choice. When he and Clay returned from town, Big Ben was waiting there for them. And as soon as he learned from them that Rebecca had not taken a train or a stagecoach, he asked Tom to come into his house and talk to him.

Tom glanced over at Clay, but if he was looking for some support from the foreman, he got none, because Clay merely stared down at his own boots.

Tom followed Big Ben into the parlor. This was the first time he had been in the parlor since that first day when Big Ben hired him.

"I'll get right to the point, Whitman," Big Ben said.

Tom flinched at the way Big Ben addressed him. Clay had made it a point to call all of his cowboys by their first name. That he referred to Tom as "Whitman" couldn't be good.

"I want to know what has been going on between you and my daughter."

"Going on? Mr. Conyers, nothing has been going on per se."

"Nothing has been going on per se? That doesn't tell me a damn thing," Big Ben said. "What do you mean per se? That means something has been going on."

"By per se, I mean that your daughter has not been compromised in any way."

"Something is happening," Big Ben insisted. "She told me that she loved you. Is that true?"

"Yes, she told me that."

"And she told me that you said you didn't love her."

"That's not exactly true," Tom said.

"What's not exactly true? Are you calling my daughter a liar?"

"No, I did tell her that. But I was lying, Mr. Conyers. The truth is, I do love your daughter. I love her more than I thought would ever be possible."

"Then why did you tell her that you didn't love her?"

"Because I am not deserving of her love."

Big Ben blinked in surprise, for he had not expected that answer. Then he nodded.

"Do you have any idea where she is, Tom?" This time the words were soft, and non-accusatory. They were pleading. "I'm not asking you this as an angry employer, but as an anguished father. Do you know where she is? Did she say anything to you before she left?"

"No, sir, she said nothing to me before she left, because I didn't know she was going to leave. And I have no idea where she is. Mr. Conyers, if it is your wish, I will leave the ranch."

Big Ben shook his head. "No," he said. "No, there is no need for that. Clay likes you, all the cowboys like you. Damn it, I like you. I just don't think that a marriage between you and Rebecca would be for the best."

"And on that subject, you and I agree," Tom said.

On the trail
For the first several days, the Rocking H

company pushed the cattle hard, not only to get them away from their customary range so as to make them less hesitant to wander away, but also too tired to run at night. By then, the trail was fairly routine with the cattle moving along by habit. The strongest steers had taken their place as leaders; others had positioned themselves somewhere in the long column, and they too, took their places every day, like soldiers with assigned positions.

Because Rebecca was the newest and greenest of the cowboys, she was given the job of riding drag. She came away from the herd each evening with a heavy coating of dust on her hat and eyebrows. That was because the thousands of cattle pulverized the ground into a fine dust.

A typical day began with the last change of guards before breakfast at four o'clock in the morning. Those heading back to their bedrolls for half an hour or so more sleep would awaken the cook, who would build his fire and start breakfast, mostly biscuits and bacon.

Hearing the cook rattling his pots and pans would signal the wrangler to ride out and bring in the remuda. Then, when breakfast was ready, Cornett and the cowboys who would be riding point would rise so they could eat first, then ride out to be with the herd as the cows began rising from their bed ground.

Finally, the cook would start banging on a pot with a large spoon, making a terrible racket as he called out.

"People, people, people! Out of your sacks and into the heat! Off your ass and on your feet! Come and get it, or I'll throw it out!"

"Hey, Bailey, you wouldn't really throw it out, would you?" a young cowboy named Stewart asked.

"You damn right I'd throw it out!" Bailey replied. "I gotta get my wagon ready and move on to the next spot so I can set up for lunch. I don't have time to be lollygaggin' around."

"You better go up there first, kid," Stewart teased. "Because if you don't beat Forney through the chow line, he'll gobble it all up like a pig wallowing through slop."

"What are you calling slop, boy?" Bailey said. "You don't want breakfast, you just say so and I won't even bother to cook it."

"I wasn't talking about your food, Bailey," Stewart said. "I was just funnin' with the kid is all."

By the time breakfast was over, the trail boss and those who rode point had already reached the herd, and the cattle were beginning to leave the bed ground and start their own breakfast, grazing as they started moving north. Those on point positioned themselves well back from the lead steers so the cattle could spread out and graze along at their own pace.

Although Rebecca had been around cowboys for her entire life, she had always observed them from the lofty station of being the daughter of one of the biggest ranchers in Texas. She had thought them to be like children in a way, laughing much, finding fun where they could, but always respectful of her and her parents.

Now she was seeing cowboy life from the other side. The cowboy worked for forty dollars a month and food, and for this the cowboy was prepared to perform labor, no matter how hard it be, fight against Indians or cattle thieves, even to the point of risking his life, put in eighteen hours a day in the saddle, twenty-four in case of an emergency, all the while providing his own clothes, bedding, hat, boots, saddle, bridle, clothes, rope, spurs, pistol, and ammunition. The diet consisted of biscuits, bacon, beef or salt pork, beans, potatoes, dried fruit, and coffee.

Rebecca had not brought a pistol. She didn't own one, and had not thought about it. She took a little ribbing for that.

"Hey, Carmody, what are you going to do if the Injuns decide to attack us? How are you going to fight off the cattle rustlers? What are you going to do, throw rocks at them?"

Rebecca took the teasing good-naturedly, and when the others saw the skill with which she could cut cattle, or run down an errant steer and push him back into the herd, they accepted the new young cowboy as one of them. They even accepted her staying by herself as much as possible, passing it off as being shy.

The storm hit midway through their second week on the trail. Far in the distance, Rebecca could see a line of dark clouds on the horizon. As she stared at the clouds, she saw flashes of light from within. She knew that those were flashes of lightning, but the thunder came so long after the lightning flashes, and was so low, that it was little more than a very distant rumble.

Then the breeze, such as it was, stopped, and it was as if the air itself couldn't move. Sweat began to form on Rebecca's face, actually mixing with the dust to turn into mud. Gradually the flashes became brighter, the thunder closer upon the flashes and louder. In addition, a heavy mist rose from

141

the ground.

Then, as the cloud bank came toward them, it seemed to hang menacingly just overhead. Now it grew dark, almost as dark as nightfall. A sudden, blinding flash of lightning lit up the countryside, followed immediately by a roaring thunderclap. Before the thunder even faded away, the herd was running, and even above the sound of the storm, Rebecca could hear the rumble of hooves and the frightened bellow of the cattle.

Rebecca let go of her reins and squeezed down hard on the saddle horn, hoping that the horse she was riding could keep its feet and stay out of harm's way. Finally the storm abated and the cows stopped running, but the cattle were strung out in one long string and it took until mid-afternoon to get the herd reassembled.

But even though the rain had stopped, their problems weren't over. The rain had turned the prairie into a huge mud bog, making it hard for man and animal to eat. With the cattle, it was because the grass had been pretty much trampled down into the mud, and when the cattle could eat, they wound up consuming as much mud as grass. The cook had a hard time finding dry wood for a meal, and on the night after the big storm, nobody slept due to wet blankets and water on the ground.

It took two more days to dry out, but finally the cowboys were rested because they had been able to sleep dry, and the cattle were content because once more the grass was green and sweet, and the cows were eating well. Then, one week after the great storm, they ran into another problem.

At first, Rebecca didn't believe what she was seeing, but she heard Stewart talking to one of the other cowboys so she knew that she wasn't just imagining things. There, in front of them, far up in the panhandle just west of the Caprock Escarpment and south of the Canadian River breaks —

"What the hell?" Stewart said. "Sheep! Do any of the rest of you see what I'm seeing? Hell, they must be two or three thousand of 'em."

"Where did they come from?" Fowler asked.

"Look at 'em! They're eatin' all the grass," one of the other cowboys complained.

"No problem," a third cowboy said. "All we got to do is start killin' sheep. The rest of 'em will leave."

"Yeah, either that or kill us a few sheep herders," Stewart suggested.

Rebecca listened to the angry comments

of Stewart and the other cowboys and cringed. She wanted no part of killing men or sheep. She breathed a sigh of relief when she heard John Cornett's reply.

"Hold on, let's don't get ahead of ourselves here. Bring the sheep herders to me."

"Be glad to. You want 'em draped over their horses? Or just bound and gagged?" Stewart asked.

"Neither," Cornett replied. "Just bring them here and let me talk to them."

The sheep were being worked by three dogs, so the three shepherds had nothing to do but to stand around and watch the dogs keep the sheep in line. Pierre Dubois was the first to see the rider approaching them, riding fast. He was also the first to see that the rider was holding a pistol in his hand.

"Gaston!" Pierre called to the one that the others recognized as the leader of their little group. *"Quelqu'un vient, et il a une arme à feu!"*

"Yes, Pierre, I see that he has a gun."

Stewart, the rider dispatched by Cornett to summon the shepherds, pulled his horse to an abrupt stop, and shouted angrily.

"Who is in charge? What are these sheep doing here?"

144

"*Comme vous pouvez le voir, les moutons paissent*," Gaston said.

"What? What the hell did you say? What lingo is that?"

Neither Gaston, nor either of the other two, responded.

"All right, come with me," Stewart said. And, making a motioning effort with his pistol, he made it known by sign language that he expected them to follow him, and follow him they did.

Rebecca waited with Cornett and the others, holding The Rockin H herd in place until the shepherds were brought into camp. There were three of them, tall thin men, all with beards and wearing black berets. It was not only their hats that differentiated them from the cowboys. They were wearing short jackets, crimson in color, and dark blue trousers. None were wearing boots.

"Here they are, Boss," Stewart said. "But there ain't none of 'em spoke a word yet that I can understand."

"Spanish?" Cornett asked.

"It ain't Spanish. I don't speak the lingo all that good, but I do recognize Spanish when I hear it. I ain't never heard nothin' like this."

"*Leur dire pas que nous pouvons parler An-*

glais, jusqu'à ce que nous apprenons ce qu'ils veulent," one of them said.

"They're speaking French," Julius Jackson, the black wrangler said. "This one," he pointed to the man who had spoken, "just told the others not to let us know they can speak English until they find out what we want."

"Damn, Julius, are you telling me that you can speak French?" Cornett asked. "I'm impressed."

"No need to be impressed, Mr. Cornett. I'm what you call a Griffe. I'm from New Orleans. My Papa was a colored man, but my Mama was Cajun mulatto and she spoke French."

"What's your name?" Cornett asked the man who had spoken.

"*Pas leur dire quoi que ce soit,*" one of the three said.

"It is too late. They already know we speak English," the shepherd Cornett had addressed said to the others. Then, to Cornett, he said, "My name is Gaston. This is Pierre and this is Andre."

"Well, Gaston, Pierre, and Andre, I have a question for you. Are you just passing through here? And if so, how long to you plan to stay?"

"We are not passing through," Gaston

146

said. "We plan to stay here for the entire summer."

"The hell you will!" Stewart said, angrily.

"Why are you so angry?" Gaston asked. "We mean you no harm."

"Well, maybe you don't mean us any harm, but here is the problem we have," Cornett said. "You see, we have to trail our cattle through here. And our cattle need to graze. Now we've been using this trail for better than twenty years, not only us, but just about every cattle ranch in Texas. This is free range territory, and we depend on grass being available. Our cattle don't eat all the grass, just enough grass to keep us going as we pass through. That way we leave grass for the others who are coming along behind us. And believe me, there will be other herds and thousands more cattle, and they will need grass as well. And, like us, after they pass through, they will leave enough grass for the following herds.

"But your sheep now, they are wiping the prairie clean. They're eating right down to the roots so that there's nothing left. So, here is what I'm going to ask you to do. I'm going to ask you to move your sheep, and I'm asking you nice."

"We can't move our sheep, *Monsieur*. Our employer told us to graze the sheep here,"

Gaston said.

"All right, let's take this to the next step," Cornett said. "Bailey?"

"Yeah, Boss?" the trail cook replied.

"Do you know any recipes for lamb?"

"Oh, yeah, I could make a nice roast of lamb," Bailey said.

"Stewart, go out and kill us a lamb for supper."

"Yes, sir!" Stewart said, pulling his pistol and riding out toward the flock of sheep grazing peacefully nearby.

"*Monsieur, non!*" Gaston cried out.

"Do I have your attention yet, Gaston?" Cornett asked. "If you take your sheep on out of here, it will just end with us having lamb for supper. If you don't, then we'll kill as many as we can. And since cowboys hate sheep, I expect we can kill a hell of a lot of them. And if killin' the sheep don't make you move, well, we might just start havin' to kill a couple of you. Do you understand what I'm saying?"

Even as Cornett was explaining the situation to Gaston, they heard the sound of a gunshot, then Stewart's triumphant yell. Looking over toward the flock, Rebecca saw one of the sheep fall over onto its side, its legs sticking straight out.

"*Oui, monsieur,* I understand."

"Do we need to kill any more of your animals?" Cornett asked.

"*Non, monsier,* please do not kill any more. We will move the flock."

Cornett smiled. "I thought we might be able to come to some sort of an agreement. How much is that one lamb worth?"

"Nine dollars, *monsieur,*" Gaston said.

Cornett took out a ten-dollar bill and gave it to Gaston. "Here," he said. "This is for the lamb we killed, with an extra dollar for your trouble. Now please, move the rest of them as quickly as you can."

Bailey did an excellent job with the lamb, and that night the cowboys enjoyed the best meal they had eaten so far.

"Damn. If I had known that sheep tasted this good, I might 'a become a sheep herder myself," Stewart said as he gnawed the meat away from a small bone.

"Ha! Can you see Stewart wearin' one of them funny-lookin' little hats and that jacket?" one of the other cowboys asked.

"What's the hat got to do with it?" Another cowboy wanted to know.

"Well hell, you seen it, didn't you? All three of them fellers was wearin' those funny hats. You have to wear one of them funny hats to be a sheep herder. That's the law."

"That ain't the law," Stewart insisted.

"Yes it is. If you are goin' to herd sheep, you've got to wear one of them hats and that jacket."

As the others laughed and teased Stewart about the funny hat and jacket he would have to wear, Rebecca walked over to Cornett, who was sitting on the ground, leaning back against the wheel of the chuck wagon.

"That was a very good thing you did," she said.

"What was?"

"Finding a way to resolve this issue without resorting to killing."

"Hell, boy, did you really think I'd kill the sheep herders?"

"I don't know," Rebecca said. "I suppose that I was afraid you might."

Cornett had just taken a bite of meat. He chewed on it for a moment, then sucked his fingers and stared up at Rebecca before he answered. He stared at her for such long time that she became self-conscious. Had he recognized her?

"Yeah, well, that's just what I wanted Gaston to think too," Cornett said. "If I scared him as much as I scared you, then I guess I did my job."

Rebecca's laugh was one of relief.

"I wonder what those people are," Cornett said. "They aren't Mexicans, and they damn sure aren't Americans. They was speakin' French, but it don't seem likely that there would be any Frenchmen over here herdin' sheep."

"I believe they were Basque," Rebecca said.

"They were what?"

"Basque," Rebecca repeated. "It's a group of people who originated in the Pyrenees between France and Spain."

"How do know that?"

"I read about it," Rebecca said. "The Basque have a long history of tending sheep, and a lot of them have come to America for that purpose."

"Carmody, you are a most interesting young man," Cornett said.

Dodge City, Kansas, August 22

It took them forty-two days to reach Dodge City, and Cornett held them just south of the Arkansas River for two days before taking the herd into town. It was another two days before the herd was loaded onto the train and the cowboys were paid out.

Though everyone had missed a lot of sleep while on the trail, the cowboys were more eager to "have fun" than they were to catch up on their sleep. The first stop for most of them was a barbershop, where they had their hair trimmed and got professional shaves. Then they bought new clothes, took baths, dressed, and headed for the nearest saloon, dance hall, gambling establishment or whorehouse.

"Come on, Carmody, let's go get a haircut and shave, then find us some friendly women," Carter invited. "Well, in your case, I guess you're too young to need a shave. But you ain't too young to have yourself some fun."

"Thank you, but I'd rather get a hotel room and catch up on my sleep," Rebecca said.

"Sleep? Hell, why waste time sleepin'? You're goin' to die one of these days, then you can sleep forever. Come on. I'll bet you ain't ever even had a woman, have you?"

"I'd rather not, thank you just the same."

"Leave the boy alone, Stewart," Cornett said to the others. "When we start back he'll still have his pay, and the only thing the rest of you will have will be bruised heads, hangovers, and a couple of cases of the clap."

At the Dodge House Rebecca got a room,

then asked for a key to the washroom.

"The men's washroom is the one in front," the desk clerk said as he handed the key to Rebecca.

For a moment, Rebecca hesitated. Should she take a key to the men's room? She would have to, or she would be found out. On the other hand, what if another man came into the washroom while she was there?

"I, uh, am a very private person," Rebecca said. "How private are the washrooms?"

"Sonny, once you go inside and lock the door, there ain't nobody else goin' to be comin' in on you, if that's what you're worryin' about," the clerk said.

Rebecca smiled in relief. "Thank you," she said.

Half an hour later, Rebecca let herself settle down into a tub full of hot water. It was the first real bath she had had since leaving home, and the sensation was delightful. After washing thoroughly, she just lay in the water for several moments, enjoying it.

Suddenly her moments of reverie were terminated by loud knocking outside.

"How long you goin' to be in there, mister?" an insistent voice called from outside.

"I'm sorry," Rebecca called back. "I'll be right out."

Rebecca got out of the tub, and drying herself as quickly as she could, put her clothes on over a body that was still half wet. Then, wrapping the towel around her head, she left the washroom and hurried down the hall toward her own room without making eye contact with the person who had hurried her so.

During the cattle drive up to Dodge, she had managed to keep one pair of denims and one shirt relatively clean, and that was what she put on now. She did not want to waste any money on buying any more men's clothing, but neither did she want to buy women's clothing, at least not until all the Rocking H cowboys were gone.

August 25
The Rocking H stayed in Dodge for at least two more days with the cowboys boisterous and noisy, sometimes riding at full gallop up and down Front Street, screaming at the top of their lungs, and often augmenting their huzzahs by firing their pistols into the air. Although every ounce of Rebecca's being wanted to go look up her mother, she thought it best not to do so until the others left. And, since she had no intention of

154

"rousting the town" with them, she spent all of her time in the hotel, leaving her room only to go downstairs to take her meals.

Finally, on the morning of the 25th of August, Cornett knocked on the door to her room.

"Carmody? Ron, you in there?"

Recognizing his voice, Rebecca put on her hat, then opened the door. "I'm here," she said.

"We're starting back," he said. "We'll be gathering out in front of the Wright-Beverly and Company General Store in about fifteen more minutes."

"All right, thanks," Rebecca said.

Rebecca closed the door and walked back over to look down onto Front Street from her hotel room window. She could see Julius Jackson standing with Parker and a couple of the others who had made the trip up. She had not yet told Cornett that she wasn't going back, and thought about just not telling him, but was afraid he would come looking for her. So, she decided she would go down to the front of the store to tell him she wouldn't be going back, and to tell everyone else goodbye.

When she got to the store she saw Cornett coming up the walk with Stewart. A deputy marshal was with them.

155

"I want to thank you, Deputy, for releasing Stewart to me," Cornett said.

"Well, it wasn't nothin' but drunk and disorderly, so the marshal said I could let him go when you folks started back," the deputy said.

"I didn't appreciate spendin' the night in jail," Stewart complained. "I didn't appreciate it none at all."

"Son, you ought to be thankful you did wind up in jail," the deputy said. "The way you was goin', you could'a wound up in big trouble."

"I was just tryin' to have a little fun, is all," Stewart said.

"Get on your horse, Stewart," Cornett said. Then, seeing Rebecca standing on the porch, Cornett said, "Boy, you haven't even saddled your horse yet."

"I'll not be going back with you, Mr. Cornett," Rebecca said. "I'm going to stay here in Dodge."

"You sure you won't be goin' back with us, boy?" Cornett asked. "You were a good hand. I could talk Mr. Hannah into takin' you on full time if you wanted."

"Thank you, I appreciate that," Rebecca said. "But I have an older brother who lives here, and he's asked me to come move in with him."

"All right, if that's what you want," Cornett said. He extended his hand. "If you are ever down our way again and looking for a job, look me up."

"Thanks," Rebecca said.

"Dodge ain't as much fun if you live here all the time," one of the cowboys said.

"Hell, that don't make no difference to Carmody," Stewart said. "He didn't leave his hotel room the whole time he was here."

"You men be careful on your way back," Rebecca said, waving goodbye to them as they started back south.

"Carmody," Stewart called. "If you are going to stay in Dodge, you'd better buy yourself a gun. There's some bad people up here."

"I'll consider it," Rebecca replied.

"Yee, hah!" Stewart shouted, and firing their guns into the air, the riders of the Rocking H left the town at a gallop.

CHAPTER SEVEN

Rebecca had not visited the Lucky Chance or any other saloon since arriving in town, but that afternoon she decided that she would go to the Lucky Chance and meet her mother for the first time. She debated as to whether or not she should change into more appropriate garb before she went, but decided that if she went dressed as she is now, she would draw less attention than she would if she went in a dress.

As she got there, she saw a crowd gathering in front of the saloon, and she hurried forward to see what was going on. There were two soldiers standing out in the street in front of the saloon, and another man standing on the saloon porch looking down at the two soldiers. This was a civilian, dressed all in black, with a low-crown black hat, ringed with a silver hatband. He was also wearing a pistol, hanging low in a silver-studded holster. He had close-set, dark beady eyes, and a face that was so drawn it looked as if the skin was stretched over the skull itself, with no cushioning flesh. He was smoking a long, slender cheroot and he took it out; then, as he expelled a long stream of smoke, flipped the cheroot away.

"You soldier boys picked the wrong man to call a cheat," the man in black said.

"You dealt an ace from the bottom of the deck, Mister," one of the soldiers said. "What else would you call someone who does that but a cheat?"

"This is what I want you two soldier boys to do. I want you to say, 'Mr. Lovejoy, we're sorry we called you a cheat. But we are sore losers and lyin' bastards.' You do that, and I might let you live."

"Frank, look at their holsters," a bystander said. "They're army holsters. Both of 'em has got the flap down over their pistols."

"That's right. Makin' them draw wouldn't be fair, would it?" Lovejoy said. "All right, let's make this fair. You two boys draw your pistols and hold them down by your side. I'll leave my gun in my holster. When you see me start my draw, why you can raise your pistols up and shoot."

"What? You're saying draw our pistols first?"

"That's what I'm saying."

"Don't do it, Ernie," one of the soldiers said. "There's somethin' fishy about this."

"Everyone here heard him, Jimmy," Ernie said. "He said we could raise our guns and shoot him soon as we see him startin' his draw. And the way I figure it, we're in too deep now. This here feller ain't goin' to let us go without a fight."

"I don't feel good about it," Jimmy said.

"It's our only chance," Ernie said, opening the flap over his pistol then pulling it, slowly deliberately, so as not to startle Lovejoy. Jimmy pulled his pistol as well.

"You boys ready?" Lovejoy said. "Remember, as soon as you see me start my draw, you can raise your guns and shoot."

Ernie and Jimmy stood there with their pistols in their hands, staring at Lovejoy.

What happened next caught everyone by surprise. In a move as quick as the wink of an eye, Lovejoy drew his pistol and fired twice. Both soldiers went down without so much as a twitch of their gun hands.

Rebecca watched in horror as the drama played out before her. She looked back at the gunman and saw him standing there, holding his still-smoking pistol as he looked at the bodies of the two soldiers that were sprawled out in the street. The look on the

160

gunman's face was one of Satanic glee. He had actually enjoyed the shooting.

"I ain't never seen nothin' like that before in my life!" someone said loudly.

"I'll bet there ain't nobody in all of Kansas who can shoot like that," another said.

"All of Kansas. Not even in all of the country," still another said.

"You folks come on back inside," Lovejoy said, finally putting his pistol back in his holster. "I'll buy a round of drinks."

Nearly everyone who had witnessed the shooting rushed through doors into the Lucky Chance Saloon to take advantage of the free drinks. Rebecca walked out into the street and stared down into the faces of the two dead soldiers. They were both very young, and she wondered about them. Did they have family somewhere, thinking about them? If they did, at this very moment, these two young men would still be alive to them. They would have no idea that their brother, or son, was now lying dead in the dirt and among the horse apples of Front Street in Dodge City, Kansas. Rebecca found the thought that their families, wherever they were, still believed them alive at this moment, to be very disturbing, and she turned away to fight against the tears that had welled so quickly.

When she did so, she saw two women standing on the front porch of Wright's store, both wearing long, gray dresses and cotton bonnets which they had tied down over their ears. They were looking on with as much horror as Rebecca felt, and she wondered if they, like she, had been inadvertent witnesses to the shooting.

She heard loud, boisterous talk coming from inside the saloon, and for a moment she almost changed her mind about going in. But, she had come this far to meet her mother, and she wasn't going to back away now. Gathering herself as best she could, she pushed through the bat-wing doors and went into the saloon.

It wasn't until that very moment that she realized she had never been in a saloon before, and she felt very self-conscious. What would the others think when they saw a woman come in here?

Then she realized that the others wouldn't see a woman. She had passed herself off as a young man for over a month now, spending twenty-four hours a day with a crew of trail cowboys. And in all that time, not one person had ever suspected her to be anything other than what she presented herself to be.

Most of the saloon patrons were standing

at the bar, gathered around the gunman, who was obviously enjoying the accolades being heaped upon him.

There was only one person who was not gathering slavishly around Frank Lovejoy, and he stood at the far end of the bar as if putting as much distance between himself and the others as possible.

"Come on, Billy, come on down here and join the rest of us," someone called. "Didn't you see what your brother just done?"

"I saw him kill a couple of soldiers," Billy said.

"It ain't like he didn't give 'em a chance. He let 'em stand there with their guns already in their hands," someone said, retelling the story to those who, because they had seen it, needed no retelling.

"He pushed the fight," Billy said. "He didn't have to push the fight."

"Pay no attention to my little brother, boys," Frank said. "If it ever comes to a time where he actually has to discover what he is made of, it will like as not be all feathers and shit," he said.

The others laughed.

"Come on, Billy. I would think you would be proud of your brother."

"Why should I be proud of him? Should I be proud because he killed two young men who were serving in the army, protecting the rest of us? No, thank you. That isn't something I care to celebrate."

"I think Frank is right. Forget about Billy. What do you boys think about what we just saw? I mean Frank commenced his draw, even after them two soldier boys already had their guns in their hands. All they had to do was raise up their hands and shoot, but they couldn't do it in time. When we tell folks that, they ain't goin' to believe it. But it just all goes to show how fast Frank Lovejoy really is!"

"I ain't never seen nothin' like it," another said.

"They had their guns in their hands. Can you believe that?"

The accolades dismayed Rebecca, and she found an empty table as far away from the bar as she could. Looking toward the back of the bar, she saw three young women who were dressed rather seductively, and she wondered who and what they were.

Whoever they were, they were obviously as disgusted with the tributes and homage being paid to Frank Lovejoy as was Rebecca herself, because their faces reflected their disapproval. Then one of the young women, seeing Rebecca, came over to the table where she was sitting. Putting her hands down on the table, she leaned forward to show as much décolletage as she could, and Rebecca was surprised by it, until she realized that the young woman thought she was a man.

"Hello, honey," the young woman said. "You are new here, aren't you? I don't believe I've seen you in here before. Come up with one of the trail herds, did you?"

"Yes," Rebecca answered. "I got here a couple of days ago."

"And you're just now getting around to visiting us here at the Lucky Chance? Well now, my feelings are hurt." The young woman effected a pout, and Rebecca smiled.

"What's your name?" Rebecca asked.

"My name is Candy," the young woman said with a flirtatious smile. "So anytime you come in here and you want a girl to have a drink with you, you just ask for Candy. Unless I'm with Billy Lovejoy. Billy is my beau. That's him standing over there." She pointed to the young man who was isolated from those who were gathered around Frank Lovejoy. "He and Frank are brothers, but believe me, they aren't anything alike."

"I would certainly hope not," Rebecca said.

"Honey, you haven't told me your name yet," Candy said.

Rebecca chuckled. "You are going to be awfully embarrassed when you find out who I am," she said.

The young woman looked puzzled. "Well now, honey, who are you?" she said. "I know you are young, but . . ."

"Is there someone here named Janie Davenport?" Rebecca asked.

"Janie Davenport?" Candy answered. "Yes, she is here. She owns the place. That is, she and her husband own the place."

"Would you please tell her I would like to see her?"

"Miss Janie doesn't do any entertaining, if you know what I mean."

"That's all right. I think she'll see me, when she finds out who I am."

"Well that's just it, honey. You haven't told me your name yet."

"My name is . . ." she started to say Rebecca, but remembered that in the letter her mother had referred to her as "Becca."

"My name is Becca," she said.

"Becca?" Candy said. "All right, Mr. Becca, I'll tell her."

Rebecca took off her hat, then let what hair she had left after having cut it, fall to her shoulders.

"And it's not Mister," she said. "It's Miss."

"What?" the bargirl gasped.

Rebecca laughed again. "I told you were going to be embarrassed."

Candy left, and less than a minute later returned with a woman. Rebecca had never seen her mother in her entire life, not even a picture. And other than her father saying, rather vaguely, that "She was pretty," she had never even heard her mother described. But she could tell by the anxious expression on the face of the middle-aged woman, who was now hurrying across the saloon floor toward her table, that this was her mother.

"Becca?" The woman said, hesitantly, hopefully. "Are you my Becca?"

"Yes, Mama," Rebecca said. "I am your Becca."

When the two women embraced, Rebecca did not believe she had ever been squeezed quite so hard.

"What — what are you doing here?" Janie asked.

"I came to visit you, Mama," Rebecca said, the word "Mama" sounding strange to her. "Didn't you ask me to?"

"Oh, child," she said. "Oh, my darling, child. Yes, I did ask, and I hoped and prayed with all my heart that you would do it. But I never thought, I just never thought . . ."

Janie was unable to complete her sentence.

That same day, Rebecca moved in with her mother and stepfather. They had an apartment over the saloon that Oscar Davenport owned. Oscar hung a curtain to separate the alcove from the parlor, and that became Rebecca's bedroom. The alcove was little larger than the bed itself and sometimes, when she felt that it was a little too close, she would think of her spacious bedroom back home and wonder if she had made a mistake.

No. She hadn't made a mistake. It had not been, and was not her intention to permanently absent herself from Live Oaks. This was a temporary arrangement, so she was certain she would be able to stay here for a while.

Shortly after she made her living arrangements, which included working for her mother and Oscar, Rebecca sat down to write two letters, one to Tom and one to her father.

Dear Tom,
    No, I have not dropped off the face of the earth. You won't be able to respond to this letter, because I am not including my return address. I am not sure you would

want to respond to me, anyway.

I am mailing this letter to you in care of Live Oaks, in hopes that you are still in the employ of my father. I am sorry that I told you I loved you on the night of the July 4th celebration. I am not sorry that I love you, but telling you seems to have caused you some discomfort, and that I did not want to do.

I will say nothing more, other than that, while you are much in my thoughts, I do not expect to be in yours.

Fondly,
Rebecca

Since Rebecca knew that her father would be picking up both letters, she had Candy address the one to Tom, so that her father would not recognize the handwriting. Then she made arrangements with someone to mail the letters from two locations other than Dodge City. In that way, she hoped to keep her location a secret, both from her father and from Tom.

Fort Worth, September 10
When Big Ben Conyers picked up the mail at the post office, he found a letter from Rebecca. There was also a letter to Tom, and his first thought was that it, too, would

be from Rebecca, but when he checked the handwriting it was obviously different. Also, the postmark for his letter was New Orleans, whereas the postmark for the letter to Tom was St. Louis.

He stuck both letters in his inside jacket pocket then drove the surrey home. By the time he got home, the letter felt as if it weighed ten pounds, so anxious was he to read it.

When Mo came to take care of the surrey, Big Ben gave him the letter that was for Tom.

"Mo, here is a letter for Tom that I picked up at the post office. Would you give it him, please?"

"Sure thing, Mr. Conyers," Mo said. "Soon as I get this surrey took care of."

"Thanks," Big Ben said. He almost bounded up the stairs, and was calling out loud to Julia even as he opened the front door.

"Julia," he called as soon as he got inside. "Julia, we got a letter from Rebecca!"

Big Ben went into the parlor, then settled into the oversized leather chair that had been built to accommodate his bulk. Then, pulling the letter from his inside jacket pocket he held it until Julia came into the room.

"Oh, thank God, Ben!" Julia said. "That means she's all right. Read it aloud, please."

Big Ben nodded, then taking the letter from the envelope, began to read aloud:

Dear Papa,

I am doing well, so I don't want you and Mama to be worrying about me. I hope everything is going well at the ranch. I won't talk about Tom Whitman because I know that will just make you angry. I hope you did not fire him. He did nothing to warrant being fired. Please believe me, Papa, Tom Whitman was always very much the gentleman around me.

I don't know when I will be coming home. Maybe I will come home by Christmas.

Love,
Rebecca

Big Ben finished reading the letter, then folding it over, he tapped it against his hand.

"This letter was almost more frustrating than it's worth."

"No, don't say that, Ben. You know as well as I do that we have spent the last two months worrying about her, wondering if she was all right. I've had nightmares about what could have happened to her. It is good of her to write to us, to let us know that she

171

is all right," Julia said.

"That's true, I guess. She's been gone for almost three months now, and this is the first letter we have gotten from her. Why did she wait so long? She had to know that we would be worried about her."

"At least she has written. And she did say that she might come home for Christmas."

"I hope I can believe that," Big Ben said.

"Why wouldn't you believe it?"

"She didn't bother to tell us where she was, or how we could even get in touch with her," Big Ben said. He handed the envelope to his wife.

"As you can see, this is postmarked from New Orleans. Is she really in New Orleans? Or did she just give the letter to someone who was going to New Orleans to have them mail it?"

"Why would she do something like that?" Julia said.

"Because she is a very smart girl," Big Ben said. "And if she was serious about keeping us from finding her, this is exactly the kind of thing she would do."

Even though Big Ben had already read the letter to her, Julia re-read it. "Oh," she said. "Ben, do you think she really will be back by Christmas?"

"I don't know," Big Ben said. "Your guess

is as good as mine."

"I know that you are worried about her, as am I," Julia said. "But I have a feeling that all will be well."

"I pray that you are right," Big Ben said.

"Who knows? Maybe she *will* be back home for Christmas," Julia said. "She suggested that."

"What a wonderful Christmas present that would be," Big Ben said.

He walked back to his chair and sat down again and thought about his conversation with Tom Whitman. What if she did marry him? How bad would that be? Tom Whitman was, without a doubt, the most unusual cowboy Big Ben had ever been around.

But that's because he wasn't a cowboy, Big Ben realized. At least he certainly was not a cowboy in the normal sense of the term. But Clay liked him, Dusty liked him, Mo liked him, even Dalton liked him. He was smart as a whip, strong as an ox, and had as even a disposition as anyone Big Ben had ever known.

So why was he here? What was he running from?

That was what bothered Big Ben more than anything else — not just that he wasn't really a cowboy.

■ ■ ■ ■

Back in the bunkhouse, Tom put the letter under the false bottom of his locker, then lay back on his bed with his hands folded behind his head. He stared up at the ceiling, and thought of the letter he had just read. He was the cause of her leaving. He had thought that all along, and this letter confirmed it.

He was glad to have gotten the letter, because he had been feeling very anxious about her. He wished, though, that she had told him where she was.

The last thing he wanted to do was hurt her, and that was exactly why he had reacted as he did. If he could only tell her the truth, tell her how much he loved her. But he couldn't tell her, because he knew that there would be as much pain as joy in such a relationship. And while he could live with it, he had no right to inflict that on anyone else.

"Hey, Tom, did you hear?" Mo asked, stopping by Tom's bunk. "Big Ben heard from Rebecca."

"Did he?" Tom asked.

"Dalton is the one that told me about it, and he said she didn't tell him where she was, just that she was all right."

"I'm glad to hear that she is all right," Tom said.

"Who was your letter from?"

"What?"

"When Big Ben went into town, he picked up a letter for you too. I'm the one who gave it to you, remember?"

"Oh, yes, you did. It wasn't anything, just a letter from someone I used to know."

"Mo!" someone called from the other end of the bunkhouse. "Want to play some cards?"

"I ain't got no money," Mo said.

"That don't matter none. We're playing for matches, tobacco, and cigarette paper and such."

"Yeah," Mo called back. "If that's all we're playin' for, it's fine by me."

Tom thought of the cowboys he was living with now. This was an entirely new experience for him. Never before had he been around men like these, men who fight at the drop of a hat, with fists or guns, men who would gamble for matchsticks with as much intensity as if they were gambling for real money, and men who were loyal to their last breath to the outfit they rode for.

Tom was not a gambler, and because the

ranch provided him with food and a place to sleep, his forty dollars a month was enough for him. Nobody knew, and he had not yet had to touch, the five thousand dollars in cash he had brought with him. That money was hidden in his chest, under the same false bottom where he had put his letter.

He and his father had talked about the money just before he left home.

"If you are going to run away, there is no need for you to wear a hair shirt," his father had told him. "Take some money with you. Take the time to travel, see the country, hell, see the world. It isn't like you can't afford it."

"You don't understand," Tom said. "I need to find out what I'm made of. How am I ever going to find that out if I travel first class, live in the finest hotels, dine at the best restaurants?"

"Do you really want to see what you are made of?" Tom's father had asked. "Take some money with you, say, five thousand dollars, and see if you have the strength of character to have the money, but not use it."

"You think I can't do that?"

"No. I think you can," Tom's father had said. "But I think that you don't believe you can. This would be the ultimate test for you, Tom. If you have the courage to do it."

■ ■ ■ ■

After breakfast the next morning, Big Ben walked around to Julia's side of the table and kissed her. "I'm going to go into town for a while," he said. "Is there anything I can pick up for you? I'm taking the buckboard, so it would be no trouble."

"That's sweet," she said. "But I can't think of anything I might need."

When Dusty saw Big Ben getting a team together to hitch them up to the buckboard, he hurried over to perform the chore for him.

"Thanks, Dusty," Big Ben said as Dusty started attaching the harness. It only took him a couple of minutes until he had the team hitched and ready to go. He indicated that Big Ben could climb into the buckboard.

"Dalton said you got a letter from Miss Rebecca," Dusty said as he handed the reins to Big Ben.

"I did."

"But he said that she didn't tell you where she is?"

"No, she didn't."

"Well, I wouldn't worry about it, Colonel.

177

I expect she'll come back home bye and bye," Dusty said.

"I pray that you are right," Big Ben said. He snapped the lines against the team and clucked to them. The team started forward, pulling the buckboard and Big Ben out of the barn and into the open.

Dusty was the only one who ever called Big Ben "Colonel" because he, alone, of all the hands who worked on the ranch, had served with Big Ben during the war. He had just told Big Ben that he believed Rebecca would come back home bye and bye, but would she?

He certainly hoped that she would. He hoped she would not do as he had done. Because from the time Dusty left home, at the age of fifteen, he never saw his mother again.

Clarksville, Tennessee, 1853
"I'll teach you to damn well do what I tell you to do," Angus Livermore yelled at Dusty. Angus Livermore had married Dusty's mother shortly after Dusty's father died.

Dusty, fifteen at the time, and Livermore were standing in the barn, and Livermore was angry because he didn't think Dusty had done a good enough job in mucking out the stalls. Livermore took a cat-o'-nine-tails that he had constructed from old leather reins, each of the seven leather straps embedded with nails and other sharp bits of metal, and began beating Dusty. He beat Dusty until Dusty was crying for mercy, and when Dusty's mother came out to the barn to beg him to stop, Livermore took the cat-o'-nine-tails to her.

"I'll not have you buttin' in to the way I treat this boy!" Livermore said. Each lash of the cat brought red whelps and blood. "I've told you before, you only got two things to do on this farm. Cook my meals and warm my bed!"

Livermore continued to beat the woman until she was too weak to even cry out anymore. But because he was beating Dusty's mother, he had forgotten, temporarily, about Dusty, and Dusty was able to get away from him.

Dusty didn't go far. He went only as far as the door to the barn, where he saw the axe he had used earlier in the day to chop up firewood. Grabbing the axe, he stepped up behind his stepfather and swung it as hard as he could. The axe opened up the side of Livermore's head, spilling brain, blood, and bone. He was dead before he hit the ground. Dusty left that same day, but not until he wrote a letter explaining that he was the one who had killed Livermore.

In the twelve years after Dusty had left home, he had been a pony express rider, and spent some time at sea before going to war. Not until the war was over did he come back home, and when he did, he found the barn had fallen down and the house nearly so. There was no livestock, not so much as a chicken, and in the fields where cotton and corn had grown before, there was nothing but weeds.

Dusty walked through the house, which had been emptied of anything of any value. When he came back out onto the front porch, he saw Mr. Dement, who he remembered as their next-door neighbor.

"You would be Dusty, wouldn't you?" Dement asked.

"Yes."

"I seen you ride by and thought that might be you. But, bein' as you're all grow'd up now, I wasn't real sure."

"Do you know where my Ma is, Mr. Dement?"

"I sure do." Dement pointed. "She's lyin' over there, next to your Pa. I'm surprised you didn't see that first thing when you come up."

"No, sir, I didn't think to look. I didn't

even know she was dead."

"She's been dead six months now," Dement said. "Had a real nice funeral for her, we did. Nobody in her family come, 'cause she didn't have nobody but you, and most figured you'd been kilt in the war. All the neighbors come, though."

Dusty walked over to the place where his father had been buried. Next to him was a newer gravestone:

EMMA MCNALLY
1821–1865

He was glad to see that Livermore's grave was not there with his parents. He didn't know where it was, nor did he care. As Dusty stood over the graves, looking down at them, Dement walked up to stand alongside him.

"You should have come back," Dement said. "Miz Emma missed you somethin' terrible."

"I always thought that if I came back, I would just cause trouble for her," Dusty said.

"I thought it might be somethin' like that," Dement said. "Then, like I said, awhile ago I seen you ridin' up the lane, and I was pretty sure it might be you." So I brung you this letter which your Ma wrote not long before she died. She wanted me to give it to you. In it, she tells how she told the sheriff that she kilt Mr. Livermore after he beat her real bad. They had a trial and found that she had a good enough reason for killin' him, so they let her go."

"Wasn't her that killed him," Dusty said. "It was me."

"Yep, after all these years, most particular with you not comin' back and all, I sort of figured it might have been you that done it," Dement said. "But I figure that you done it for the same reason your Ma said she done it for, and that makes it all right in my book. It don't matter none now anyhow, seein' as it's all said an' done. Will you be farmin' the place?"

"I don't know, I haven't made up my mind," Dusty said.

"The place is yours now, but I've had the papers all drawed up in case you'd be willin' to sell it."

"How much?"

"Five hundred dollars."

Dusty knew that the farm was worth more than that. But he also knew that he had no wish to stay around. And five hundred dollars was a lot more than he had now.

"I'll take it," he said.

■ ■ ■ ■

Now, a quarter of a century after he sold the farm to Dement, Dusty had no regrets. After a bit of a wild spree where he had actually robbed a couple of stagecoaches and even a train, he had settled down here on Live Oaks, and the people here were the closest thing to a family he had ever had.

He hoped that things could be worked out between Big Ben and Rebecca.

As Dusty started back toward the bunkhouse, Mo and Tom tossed him a wave as they rode out toward the field. With no stock on the range, most of the work being done at the ranch now was maintenance, and he saw that Mo and Tom had wire and pliers with them in order to make some repairs on the fence line.

Nobody had ever said anything directly to him, but Dusty couldn't help but harbor the idea that, somehow, Rebecca's leaving had something to do with Tom.

CHAPTER EIGHT

Union Stockyards, Fort Worth, October 1

"I understand that you have yet to replace your stock," Hurley said. The two men were in William Hurley's office, a place that had almost become Big Ben's home away from home since he sold all his stock.

"I haven't yet, but I'm going to have to do something fairly soon," Big Ben said. "Otherwise I'll be having to let some of my permanent hands go and I would hate to do that. But there is only so much make-work that can done on a ranch that has no cows."

"Are you going to buy Herefords?"

"I suppose I will," Big Ben said. "I certainly see no profit in buying any more Longhorns. I sure hate having to do that though. Walter Hannah is my friend, but if he gets something on you, he never lets go of it. The moment the first Hereford sets foot on my ranch is the moment he will start crowing."

"Maybe you would feel better about it if you knew that Herefords were bringing thirteen dollars a head this morning," Hurley said.

"Yes. Well, that's why I came into town today. I wanted to check the highest price being paid, just to reinforce my decision. So I guess I'll be buying Herefords."

"That's a good move," Hurley said. He chuckled. "Though the truth is, if you were just buying according to the highest price, you wouldn't be buying Herefords."

"I wouldn't?" Big Ben replied, curious by the strange answer. "What would I be buying?"

"Black Angus."

"Black Angus? Yes, I think I have heard of those. I haven't seen any in Texas, though."

"That's because there aren't any Black Angus in Texas," Hurley said.

"Wait. You mean if I brought Black Angus into Texas, I would be first?"

"That's exactly what I mean."

Big Ben laughed, then slapped his hand on his knee. "That would put a sock in Walter Hannah's mouth, once and for all, wouldn't it?" he said. "Tell me, Will, what are Black Angus going for right now?"

Hurley looked at a piece of paper on his desk until he found the figure he was after.

"As of ten o'clock this morning, they were sixteen dollars and thirty cents a head."

"That's even higher than Herefords," Big Ben said. "Now, the next question, is where can I find some to buy?"

"Well, they are my competition," Hurley said. "But setting that aside, my best guess would be the Stock Exchange in Kansas City."

"You wouldn't feel like I'm going behind your back by going there?" Big Ben asked.

"Not if you do business with me once you get your cows."

Big Ben smiled and stuck out his hand. "You've been a good friend to me, Will," he said. "Of course I will be doing business with you."

Stock Exchange, Kansas City, Missouri, October 13

The building was divided into two parts. On one side there was an area that everyone referred to as "the bullpen." It was so called because here, there were six desks crowded rather close together. Behind the desks toiled the inventory clerks, men who came to work and buried their head in endless rows of numbers.

A long counter separated the "bullpen" from the much larger and better decorated director's room where Jay Montgomery had his desk. On the back wall was a large blackboard upon which figures were written, the figures representing the latest quotes from the cattle market. In the corner was a tickertape machine, and at the moment one of the clerks was standing by it, holding the tape in his two hands, reading it as it came from the machine. As soon as he got all the numbers, he would transfer them to the blackboard.

Big Ben, who had left Fort Worth the day before, walked up to the low railing and stood there for a moment, waiting for someone to notice him. One of the clerks who had just finished putting numbers on the blackboard turned, and seeing Big Ben, flinched in surprise. He had never seen a man quite that big.

"Yes, sir, can I help you?"

"My name is Benjamin Conyers. I would like to speak with Mr. Jay Montgomery."

"Just a moment, sir," the clerk said as he hurried out of the bullpen and into an office at the back. A moment later a tall, silver-haired, dignified-looking man came out of the office with the clerk. Smiling, he approached Big Ben with his hand extended.

"Mr. Conyers," he said. "It is so nice to actually meet you, after doing business all

187

these years. Have you come to arrange a cattle sale?"

"No, sir. A cattle buy," Big Ben said.

"A cattle buy? Well, I'm sure we can accommodate you there. What kind of cattle do you want to buy, and how many?"

"I want to buy twenty-five hundred head of Black Angus," Big Ben said.

Montgomery blinked. "Twenty-five hundred head of Angus? That's — uh — quite an order," he said.

"Yes, sir, I suppose it is," Big Ben said. "Can you fill it?"

Montgomery shook his head. "No, sir, I'm afraid I can't. There aren't so many Black Angus in the country for us to have such a large reserve."

"Damn," Big Ben said.

"I understand what you are trying to do, Mr. Conyers," Montgomery said. "All the cattlemen are getting rid of Longhorn now. They simply are no longer profitable. But everyone is going into Herefords, and if you would be interested in that, then we would be able to help you."

"I may have to do that," Big Ben said. "But I don't mind telling you that I was set upon buying Black Angus. How many other places are there like yours? What I mean is, what would be the chances of putting together a herd as large as the one I need?"

"Oh, Mr. Conyers, I don't know," Montgomery said. "I suppose I could check with all the other cattle exchanges in the country, and among those who have any Angus at all, put together a herd for you. But you would have to gather them from all over, and by the time you did that, counting transportation costs and everything, they are likely to cost you thirty dollars a head. That would make them completely cost-prohibitive."

Big Ben breathed out a sigh of disappointment.

"Yes," he said. "I see what you mean."

"Unless . . . ," Montgomery said, brightening, and holding up one finger.

"Unless what?"

"Unless you would be willing to buy them all from a private rancher."

"You know a rancher who has enough Black Angus to be able to sell me two thousand, five hundred head?"

"Yes, I think I do," Montgomery said. "His name is Duff MacCallister, and he lives in Chugwater, Wyoming."

Montgomery walked over to the desk of one of the many clerks and, making a motion for paper and a pen, started writing.

"Here is his name and how to get in touch

with him," Montgomery said. "When you write to him, you can mention my name. It might do you some good. We have done business together quite frequently over the last three years."

"Thank you," Big Ben said. "By the way, what is the market price for Angus, today?"

"Seventeen dollars," Montgomery said without having to check. He smiled. "I just got a quote this morning."

"That's up from the last time I checked," Big Ben said.

"Yes, Black Angus are the most active right now."

"I'll have to keep that in mind when I make my buy," Big Ben said.

Sky Meadow Ranch, Wyoming, October 24
Duff Tavish MacCallister was standing on the front porch of his ranch house at Sky Meadow drinking coffee and watching the light show that the setting sun played upon the long, purple range of mountains called Laramie Ridge. His ranch, Sky Meadow, one of the most productive ranches in all of Wyoming. It was also the location of a producing gold mine. The mine did not produce enough gold to merit full-time operation, but it did produce enough to enable him to build Sky Meadow, and to

190

populate it with Black Angus cattle.

Duff had raised Black Angus back in Scotland; he was well familiar with the breed, and knew of its superiority to Longhorn and even Hereford cattle. He now had the largest Angus herd in the West, and one of the largest herds in the nation.

Earlier in the day, Elmer Gleason, Duff's ranch foreman, had gone into Chugwater. Duff drank his coffee and watched as his foreman rode through the front gate, about fifty yards down the road from the house itself. Elmer was wiry and raw-boned. He had a full head of white hair and a neatly trimmed beard. Duff didn't know exactly how old Elmer was, and Elmer never said. But he knew some of Elmer's past from riding with Quantrill, and later Jesse James, to being a seaman on China Clipper. He knew also that he had never known a man more loyal than Elmer Gleason.

"You got some mail," Elmer said as he dismounted onto the front stoop. He handed the letter to Duff. "But I'd be careful reading that letter if I was you," Gleason said.

"Why is that?"

"Well, sir, because it's postmarked from Texas, and you bein' from Scotland 'n all, like as not you don't know about them

Texans. But they ain't none of 'em to be trusted."

"Sure 'n back in Scotland they say that about the Highlanders," Duff said, chuckling as he opened the letter. "Well now, 'tis a fancy letter on monogrammed stationery it is."

Benjamin Conyers
Live Oaks Ranch, Texas

Dear Mr. MacCallister:

I am informed by Mr. Jay Montgomery that you have the largest and most superior herd of a breed known as Black Angus in the United States. I have been running Longhorns for many years, but as the price of Longhorns at the market has decreased sharply in the last few years, I have sold off my entire herd and now have 120,000 well watered acres, with ample grass, but no cows.

At my last telegraphic query, Black Angus were bringing $17 a head at the Kansas City Market. If you can deliver 2500 head of Black Angus to me here, at Live Oaks, I am prepared to pay you $20 a head, provided there are no steers, but enough bulls and heifers to enable me to increase the size of the herd. However, I shall require delivery before the end of the year. I know that a winter drive may be difficult, but should you make it by Christmas, you will be welcome to celebrate the birthday of our Lord at my ranch. If you agree to these terms, please respond soonest by telegram.

Sincerely,
Benjamin Conyers

"Are you going to do it?" Elmer asked, after reading the letter when Duff showed it to him.

"Aye, that's three dollars a head more than I can get anywhere else," Duff said. "But he is wanting to start a herd so he wants only bulls and heifers, so I've only got about fifteen hundred head that I feel like I can ship."

"You could ask Smoke Jensen to add some of his cattle to the shipment," Elmer said. "You might recall that he started running Black Angus after he lost so much of his cattle in the big freeze and die-out a couple of years ago."

"That's right, he did," Duff said. "I'll ride into town tomorrow and send him a telegram."

"Will you be callin' on Miss Meghan when you go into town?" Elmer asked.

"And why wouldn't I be calling on her, she being my business partner?"

"It ain't just the business that has you sniffin' around her all the time, my friend," Elmer said.

Duff laughed. "Sure, Elmer, 'n you remind me of a Scottish laird, brokerin' a marriage for his tenants. 'Tis no doubt but that I'll be seeing her. But don't be ringing the wedding bells just yet, my friend."

Big Rock, Colorado, October 31
Smoke Jensen was in Longmont's saloon sitting at a table with two of his closest friends in town, Louis Longmont, the owner of the saloon, and Sheriff Monty Carson.

"How long are you going to be in Cheyenne?" Louis asked. "I ask only because I want to know if there will be enough time for me to use my French charm to win the beautiful Madame Sally away from you."

Sheriff Carson laughed. "Louis, if you had until the Second Coming, you couldn't win Sally away from Smoke."

"One can always try," Louis said. Louis winning Sally away from Smoke was a running joke, and everyone knew that it was. But his admiration for her was genuine; aboveboard, but genuine.

"I'm not sure how long I'll be there,"

Smoke said. "Just long enough to conclude some business, or at least, discuss the business if not conclude it."

"Who are you meeting with?" Sheriff Carson asked.

"Duff MacCallister," Smoke said. "He is a cousin of Falcon's, not too long a resident of the U.S. He is the one I bought the Black Angus from, after the great die-out."

"Oh, yes, I remember that," Sheriff Carson said. "How are the cows working out?"

"Great. I've got quite a large herd now. Not as many as I had when I was running Longhorn, but more than I would have thought by now. In fact, I have enough to be able to help Duff out with his project."

The whistle of the approaching train could be heard and Smoke stood, then reached down for his grip. Not until he stood could someone get a good enough look at him to be able to judge the whole of the man. Six feet two inches tall, he had broad shoulders and upper arms so large that even the shirt he wore couldn't hide the bulge of his biceps. His hair, the color of wheat, was kept trimmed, and he was clean-shaven. His hips were narrow, though accented by the gunbelt and holster from which protruded a Colt .44, its wooden handle smooth and unmarked.

Fifteen minutes later, Smoke was on the train, headed for a meeting in Cheyenne with Duff MacCallister.

Dodge City, November 1

As Smoke rode the train through the night toward Cheyenne, 430 miles away, in Dodge City, Kansas, Rebecca Conyers, who was now calling herself Becca Davenport, was sitting in her mother's darkened room over the Lucky Chance Saloon. In the quiet shadows, she listened to her mother's labored breathing.

Rebecca had been in Dodge City for four months now. During that four months she had written three letters to her father just to let him know that she was safe and well. She had not received any replies from him, nor could she, because she had not let him know where she was. And in order to hide her whereabouts from him, she had implored friends who were going to be out of town to post the letters for her from other locations.

"Becca? Honey, are you here?" The voice, weak and strained, brought Rebecca back to the present.

Though Janie had been strong and well when Rebecca first arrived, two months later she had taken ill, and her decline had been very rapid from that time.

"I'm here, Mama," Rebecca said. Her hair, which once fell luxuriously down her back, was just now beginning to grow back. Though much shorter than it had been, it was still long enough come to her shoulders, and to require her to brush some errant tendrils away from her face.

"Move your chair next to the bed," Janie asked.

Rebecca did as asked, then she reached out to take her mother's hand. The hand was small and the grip was weak. Neither Rebecca nor her mother knew when she arrived four months ago that her mother's death warrant had already been signed. She had something that the doctor called cancer, and although he had been treating her illness with compounds of potassium arsenate, the cancer continued to advance, and Rebecca knew now that her mother did not have long to live.

"I want you to know what a joy it has been to have you here," Janie said.

"I am glad that I came," Rebecca said.

"I know you would much rather be back at Live Oaks with your young man, but I'm selfish enough that I will take you any way I can have you."

"Even if I were back home, I wouldn't be

with my young man," Rebecca said. "He has already made it clear that he wants nothing to do with me. And even if he did, Papa wouldn't allow it."

Rebecca had told Janie about Tom, and how she had declared her love for him on the day before she left home, only to have it spurned. She also told Janie about her father's reaction.

"I can't believe that this man, Tom, whom you profess to love, does not love you back. More than likely, he is just unsure of himself, and when he realizes that you are serious, he will have more confidence. And I wouldn't worry about Big Ben either. He is a good man, Becca," Janie said. "If you give him another chance, I'm sure he will come around. He was a good man and I hurt him, just as I have hurt everyone else who has ever been close to me. You are the one I hurt most of all. But I also hurt your Papa, my own parents, and my brother. How sorry I am that I hurt my brother. The two of us share a past that no one else can, and yet, for twenty-five years, we have been strangers to each other."

"You have a brother?" Rebecca reacted in surprise. "I didn't know you had a brother. You have never mentioned him."

"I thought it best not to, but as I think

more about it, you have the right to know about him. He thinks I'm dead," Janie said. "He thinks I died a long time ago."

"And you have never told him otherwise?"

"No, it is much better that he thinks I'm dead. I'm afraid I was quite a disappointment to him," Janie said. "No man wants a whore for a sister."

"Mama!"

"It's true, honey, much as I hate to admit it. During the war, I ran off with a man named Paul Garner. I was young then, younger than you are now. Paul was a gambling man, and he promised me a life of fun and excitement. At the time, anything seemed better than living on a dirt farm in Missouri. We went to Fort Worth and stayed there until the war was over. Then after my gambling man got himself killed, I got a job as bargirl working in one of the saloons in Hell's Half Acre. That was when I met your Papa, fresh back from the war, a wounded hero. Oh, he made quite a presence, Becca. He was a magnificent and kingly-looking man. I fell head over heels in love with him, and one thing led to another, until I became pregnant. I feared that he might run away then, but he didn't. As soon as he learned I was pregnant, he moved me out to Live Oaks. I stayed there until you were born."

"But you and Papa were never married?"

"He asked me to marry him, but I couldn't do it."

"Why not?"

"Honey, your Papa was one of the richest men in Texas. Before I met him I was a gambler's widow, and a part-time soiled dove. Can you imagine what his enemies would have made of that? Someone would have said something and your father would have challenged him. He would have either killed someone, or gotten killed himself. I would not have been able to accept either outcome.

"I didn't fit in his society, Becca. I was a mule in a horse harness. So one morning I just left. I know that sounds harsh, but believe me, it was much better for both of you. And I found out that, within a couple of months after I left, your Papa had married a decent and respectable woman."

"That would be Julia," Rebecca said.

"Has she been good to you, Becca?"

"Oh, yes, she has been a moth . . . ," Rebecca halted in mid-sentence, not wanting to hurt her mother's feelings by comparison.

"You can say it, honey. She has been a mother to you. And judging from the way you turned out, she has been a much better mother to you than I could have ever been."

"But you are my mother," Rebecca said, not exactly knowing where to go with this.

"Yes, I am your mother," Janie said, almost as if apologizing. She was quiet for a long moment. "After I left your father I went farther west, where I whored for quite a number of years, then I met Oscar. Oscar didn't care that I used to be on the line. But I want you to know, Becca, that I have reformed. And you know what they say. No one is more righteous than a reformed whore." Janie chuckled.

"That's why when I learned that Kirby thought I was dead, I decided not to ever tell him any different," she concluded.

"Your brother's name is Kirby?"

"Yes."

"What is Uncle Kirby like?"

"Honey if I told you, you wouldn't believe me. He is a man of legendary accomplishments. Why, did you know that books and plays have actually been written about him?"

"Really? What are some of the things he's done?"

Janie thought for a moment, then she laughed. "I know something he did once that has never been in any book or any play. In fact, I doubt that anyone who knows him knows about this. It happened when we were both very young. But I'll tell you, and then you will know something about your uncle that no one else knows.

"It was back before the war, I was twelve, Kirby was ten. We lived on a farm and Ma and Pa had a couple of milk cows. Kirby and I had the job of milking the cows, and oh how Kirby hated that. Well, the two cows were kept in the same stall, and one morning Kirby got it in mind to tie their tails together. Well of course, you can't tie the tails themselves, but he took the hairy tufts at the end of their tails and tied them together. Then, when the cows were turned out into the pasture, one wanted to go one way and the other wanted go in the opposite direction, so they pulled against each other, and the harder they pulled, the tighter the knot got in their tails."

Janie was laughing now, and so was Rebecca.

"Well, those two cows just kept pulling, and bawling, and pulling and bawling, until finally Pa came out to see what they were bawling about. When he saw those two tails tied together he liked to have had conniptions. Kirby had tied so many of the hairs together that Pa couldn't get them untied, so he finally gave up trying and just cut them apart. Then he asked Kirby what he knew about it.

" 'Well, Pa, the flies were real bad,' Kirby said." By now, Janie was laughing so hard that she was having a hard time telling the story. " 'And those two cows were being tormented something awful by the flies, so they commenced to sweeping their tails at them, trying to keep the flies away, you see. Now I didn't exactly see it happen, but if you was to ask me, I'd say that those cows tied their own tails together while they were trying to swish away those flies.' I think that was the only time I ever saw Kirby get a whipping," Janie concluded.

By the time she finished telling the story, both Janie and Rebecca were laughing hysterically. They were laughing so hard that they didn't even hear the knock on the door. That was when the door was pushed open and a man stuck his head in. "May I come in?"

"Yes, of course," Rebecca said, getting up from her chair.

The door opened, spilling a wedge of light into the room. Janie's husband, Oscar Davenport, stepped into the room.

"Were you two telling jokes up here?" Oscar said.

"No, we were just having girl-talk, that's all," Janie answered.

Oscar was considerably shorter than Rebecca, and nearly bald except for a tuft of hair over each ear. He walked over to the bed, then leaned down and kissed Janie on the forehead.

"How are you feeling, my dear?" he asked, considerately.

"I'm in no pain," Janie answered.

"Good, good. That's good," Oscar said. He turned to Rebecca. "Becca, I was wondering — well, we have a pretty good gathering downstairs, and I thought I might ask you come down and sing a couple of songs. You have such a good voice and everyone seems to enjoy your singing so much. It also helps to keep things calm."

"Mama?" Rebecca asked.

"Go ahead, child," Janie said. "You do sing so beautifully, I just wish I could be down there to hear it."

Rebecca leaned over to kiss her mother, then she followed Oscar downstairs. Oscar was good to her, as he had been to her mother, and he looked out for her.

After coming to Dodge City to join her mother, Rebecca had taken a job working for Oscar in his saloon. Like the other girls who worked in the Lucky Chance, Rebecca would drink with the customers, though with Rebecca the bartender was under strict orders to serve only tea. Unlike the other girls, Rebecca would never visit one of the cribs. Often she would sing for the customers, most of the time the cowboy ballads that they seemed to like. But upon occasion she would sing an operatic aria, doing so with a classically beautiful voice. With her shining auburn hair, full lips, high cheekbones, and dark eyes shaded by long eyelashes, Rebecca was as beautiful as her singing.

Frank Lovejoy stood at the end of the bar watching Rebecca sing. As usual, he was dressed all in black, with a low-crown black hat, ringed with a silver hatband. His ever-present pistol was hanging low in a silver-studded holster on his right side. He was smoking a long, slender cheroot and drinking bourbon.

"Ain't no sense in lookin' at her," Mike Malloy said. "Ever'body knows that she don't do no whorin'."

"Oh yeah, she whores, all right," Lovejoy said confidently. He took a swallow of his bourbon, then wiped his mouth with the back of his hand. "She just don't know it yet, is all."

CHAPTER NINE

Cheyenne, Wyoming, November 1

Duff and Smoke Jensen met in Cheyenne at the Cheyenne Club. Established in 1880 by twelve Wyoming cattlemen, the Cheyenne Club was the place to be for cattlemen from all over Wyoming. At the moment, Duff and Smoke were in one of the club's parlors, enjoying their cigars and drinks, bourbon for Smoke and Scotch for Duff. They were speaking about the letter Duff had received from Benjamin Conyers.

"I met Conyers once," Smoke said.

"Does he measure up to his request?" Duff asked. "What I mean is, do you think he has sufficient funds to pay twenty dollars a head for twenty-five hundred cows? That's fifty thousand dollars."

"It's funny you would ask if he measured up, because measuring is what he does very well."

"I don't understand."

"He is called Big Ben and they call him that for a reason. He stands six feet seven, and weighs in at over 300 pounds."

"Oh, my, that is quite large, isn't it?"

"And don't worry about whether or not he is good for the money. He is one of the most successful cattlemen in Texas. He could buy a herd ten times as large and not strain his resources."

"Good," Duff replied. "I would hate to go to all this trouble, and then not be paid."

"You can come up with what? Fifteen hundred head?" Smoke asked.

"That's about it. I am hoping you could come up with the rest."

"I thought that might be the case. Yes, I can come up with another thousand. That will meet his demand."

"The question now, is how do we get them there?"

"I would suggest that you ship your cattle by train to Denver. I will meet you there with my cattle, and then we'll ship the entire herd by train, or trains in this case, to Dodge City. Once we get to Dodge, we'll have to drive the critters on down to Live Oaks."

"What do you think? About four trains?" Duff asked.

"Let's see, twenty to a car, it would take

125 cars. That would be just over thirty-one cars per train, plus a Pullman car. Yes, four would do it."

"Four trains, but only two of us," Duff said.

"That's no problem," Smoke said. "I know I can get Matt to go with one of the trains. By the way, I hope you don't have any problem with Sally going with us. She's been saying she wanted to take a trip somewhere for Christmas." Smoke laughed out loud. "I'll bet this isn't exactly what she was planning on, though."

"Of course I dinnae have any objections to the fair Sally coming with us. She is not only good company, I've nae doubt but that she can be helpful."

"As for the fourth train, I'll bet you could get Falcon, if you asked," Smoke suggested.

"I'll send him a telegram," Duff said. "Thank you, that's a good idea."

"Yeah, I do get good ideas every now and then."

MacCallister, Colorado, November 3
Falcon MacCallister had received the telegram this morning, but had not yet shared it with anyone. At the moment Falcon, his brothers Jamie, Ian, Morgan, and Matthew, were out at the old MacCallister homestead.

208

Falcon's sisters, Joleen and Kathleen, were there as well. Even the twins, Andrew and Rosanna, were here, and that was rare, for they only managed to show up for family functions about once every five years. Andrew and Rosanna were both famous thespians, their work as well-known in Europe as it was in the United States.

The MacCallister clan was gathering for a family reunion, though, except for Andrew and Rosanna, they didn't have far to go when they held such a gathering. Here, in the MacCallister Valley of Colorado, they were busy ranching, farming, raising kids and grandkids. By now, half of the people in the Valley were MacCallisters. To be precise, there were one hundred and three MacCallisters in MacCallister Valley who were direct descendants of Jamie and Katie MacCallister, who had been barely of age when they settled here considerably more than half a century before.

They had just had their dinner and walked out front to have a moment over the graves of their parents, Jamie and Kate.

"We should have waited to have this reunion at Thanksgiving or Christmas," Ian said.

"Why?" Morgan asked. "This way we get to feast now, and again at Thanksgiving and

209

Christmas."

"Leave it to Morgan to think of food," Kathleen said.

"Well, for my part, it's good that we had it today. I won't be here for Thanksgiving, and probably won't be here for Christmas either. I'm leaving tomorrow morning."

"You're leaving tomorrow? Falcon, what is so important that you can't even stay for a family reunion?" Morgan asked. "You know what Pa and Ma always said. Nothing is more important than family."

"This *is* family," Falcon said. "And it is important."

"How can it be family, when every last one of us are here?" Joleen asked. "Even Andrew and Rosanna."

"I'm talking about Duff MacCallister," Falcon said. "He is our cousin."

"He can't be that close of a cousin," Kathleen said. "I've never even met the man."

"We share a great-great-great-great grand-father," Rosanna said. "Grandfather Falcon MacCallister from the Highlands of Scotland."

"Great, great, great, great grandfather? What is that, fifth cousin?" Jamie asked.

"Technically, I suppose he is, but it feels much closer than that," Andrew said. "Duff

MacCallister is a wonderful man."

"How do you two know him?"

"We were the first ones to meet him," Rosanna said. "We met him in Scotland. Then later, when he came to America, he worked with us in New York for a while. And if Falcon feels that Duff needs him, I don't think we should erect any impediments."

"Erect any impediments," Jolene said with a little chuckle. "Spoken like a true child of the theater," she added, affecting a strong British accent as she teased Rosanna. Then she added in a normal tone of voice. "By all means, Falcon, if you feel that it is important for you to go to the aid of our cousin, Duff, go with our blessings."

"Thanks," Falcon said.

Santa Clara, Colorado, November 5
Matt Jensen had just finished eating his supper, and was leaving the restaurant to go back to the hotel where he had taken a more or less permanent room, when he heard someone call out to him.

"Jensen, look out!"

Concurrent with the shouted warning, Matt felt a blow to the side of his head. Someone had stepped out of the shadows of the narrow space between the restaurant and the leather goods store next door. He saw stars, but even as he was being hit he was reacting to the shout, and that kept him from being knocked down.

When his attacker swung at him a second time, Matt was able to parry the blow; then, with his fists up, he moved quickly out into the middle of the street. He didn't know if there was more than one person hiding in the dark, and he didn't want to take a chance. In the middle of the dirt street, lit by gas streetlamps, he was able to see the man who had attacked him. He was a big man, well over six feet tall with large arms and ham-sized fists. He was an exceptionally ugly man, with a heavy brow ridge and a protruding lower lip. Matt had never seen him before.

"Mister," the man said with a low growl. "You kilt my brother, so now I'm aimin' to take you apart with my bare hands."

This was a change. Most of the men who came after Matt, either for revenge or to settle some personal score, or even to make a name for themselves, came after him with a gun. But this was a big man, and whether it would be a welcome change or not was yet to be seen.

Almost as soon as the fight started, a crowd was gathered around.

"Who's that big man Jensen is fighting with?" someone asked.

"I don't have no idea," another answered.

Matt and the big man dodged and weaved around for a bit, both trying to take the measure of the other, neither of them throwing a punch.

"Who was your brother?" Matt asked. "The one you say I killed."

"Damn, Mister, have you kilt so many you can't keep up with 'em?" the big man asked.

"I've killed a few," Matt said.

"His name was Shelton. Lucas Shelton," the big man said.

"I remember him," Matt said.

"What did you kill him for?"

"He was trying to kill me. I didn't have any choice."

"Yeah, you did. You could'a let him kill you."

"Funny, but I didn't consider that an option," Matt replied.

Shelton swung wildly at Matt, but Matt dodged it easily, then counterpunched with a quick, slashing left to Shelton's face. It was a good, well-hit blow, one that would have dropped the average man, but Shelton just shook it off.

"Damn, did you see that?" one of the spectators asked. "That blow would have pole-axed a steer, but that big sum'bitch acted like he didn't even feel it."

"Five dollars says Jensen gets whupped," someone said.

"I don't know. I've seen Jensen fight before. I'm going with him."

With an angry roar, Shelton rushed Matt again, and Matt stepped aside, avoiding him like a matador sidestepping a charging bull. And, like a charging bull, Shelton slammed into a hitching rail, smashing through it as if it were kindling. He turned and faced Matt again.

There was no more kibbitzing in the crowd now. They grew quiet as they watched the fight, studying it to see whether quickness and agility could overcome brute strength and power.

Shelton swung again, and again Matt avoided the blow. Matt counterpunched and, as before, scored well. But, as before, Shelton merely laughed it off. Matt learned quickly that he could hit Shelton anytime he wanted, and though individually the punches seemed ineffective, Matt saw that there was a cumulative effect to his efforts. Both of Shelton's eyes began to puff up, and there was a nasty cut on his lower protruding lip that started blood flowing down the big man's chin.

Then Matt caught the big man in the nose with a hard right, and he knew that he had broken it. The nose, like the cut lip, began to bleed profusely, and torrents of blood began to flow. Matt looked for another chance to strike his nose, but Shelton started protecting it, and he couldn't get through.

So far, except for the opening blow, not one of Shelton's great swinging blows had landed. Then, Shelton managed to connect with a right which struck Matt on the shoulder. Matt felt as if he had been hit by a club, and he could feel it all through his arm. That single blow had the possibility of ending the fight, for though Matt held his left up, it was for show only. He was, in effect, fighting this big man with only one arm.

Then, when Shelton threw another whistling blow at him, Matt avoided it, counterpunching with a solid right, straight at Shelton's Adam's apple. It had the effect Matt wanted, and the big man grabbed his neck with both hands, then sunk to his knees, gasping for air.

Matt stepped up to him.

"You won't suffocate, but you are going to think that you will, because it is going to swell a lot more and it's going to be even harder to breathe than it is now," he said. "My advice to you is to go lie down somewhere with your head somewhat lower than your neck. Be still for a while. It will take you a few days, but you will recover."

Shelton looked up at Matt and tried to speak, but the only thing to come from his throat was a squeaking rattle.

Matt held up his hand and moved his finger back and forth. "Oh, and don't try to talk, it'll just make matters worse," he said.

As Matt walked away from the kneeling man, listening to the banter of the onlookers as they exchanged the money they had bet on the fight, someone called out to Matt.

"Mr. Jensen, I have a telegram for you."

Matt recognized the telegrapher and walked over toward him.

"I didn't want to bother you during the fight," the small, bespectacled man said as he handed the message to Matt.

"I appreciate that, I guess," Matt said. He gave the telegrapher a half-dollar.

"Thank you, sir," the little man said. "Will you be wanting to reply?"

"Depends on the message," Matt said. He opened the envelope and read the message under the light of a streetlamp.

NEED YOUR HELP FOR A CATTLE DRIVE.

CAN YOU COME? SMOKE.

Matt followed the telegrapher back to the Western Union Office.

YES. I WILL COME TOMORROW. MATT

Chugwater, November 6
Three men; Emerson, Pigg, and Jenks, were sitting together at a table in Fiddler's Green.

"That's him over there, standin' at the bar talkin' to the bartender. His name is Duff MacCallister," Emerson said. Emerson was a particularly ugly man with a drooping eyelid and a mouth full of bad teeth.

"He's a big bastard," Pigg said. Pigg and Jenks were only marginally less ugly than Emerson. Pigg had a beard, not one that he groomed, but one that seemed to have trapped within its unkempt bristles food from his last several meals. Jenks had a long, hooked nose and dark, beady eyes.

"That don't matter. We ain't goin' to rassle him," Emerson said. "We're just goin' to have him tell us where at his gold mine is."

"And you're sure he has a gold mine?"

"That's what ever' one says. It ain't sup- posed to be a very big one, but it's big enough that he's built himself one of the best ranches in Wyoming," Emerson said.

"I hope your plan works," Jenks said.

"Don't worry, it will work," Emerson said resolutely. "Come on, let's go see the lady."

Meghan Parker wasn't all that surprised whenever a man would happen to come into her dress shop. That was because from time to time someone would want to buy a dress for his wife, and he would want it to be a surprise, so he would have Meghan help him. But this time it was three men who came in, and that was unusual. Also, there was something about the three that made her feel a bit uneasy.

Her fear was justified when all three of them pulled guns and pointed them at her.

"Is it true what they say about you?"

"I'm not sure. What do they say about me?"

"They say that you are Duff MacCallister's woman." The man doing the talking had the ugliest teeth Meghan had ever seen; a few were broken so that they were jagged-looking. All of them varied in color from yellow to black.

"Mr. MacCallister is a friend of mine, yes," Meghan said.

"Uh, huh. Well answer me this, Missy. Is he friend enough that more'n likely he wouldn't want to see something happen to you?"

"Mr. MacCallister wouldn't want to see something happen to any innocent person."

"That's good enough for me. Pigg, go on down there to the saloon and tell MacCallister he'd best come out into the street."

"What is all this about?" Meghan asked.

"Gold, Missy. This is about gold," the one with the bad teeth said. "Now, you come with us."

"I can't leave my store," Meghan said.

"Ha! You don't be worryin' none about your store."

"Where are we going?"

"Not far. Just out into the street. Pigg, you go get MacCallister like I told you. Jenks, when we get out there, you run ever'one off the street so there ain't no one out there but us."

Biff Johnson had just said something funny and Duff was laughing when Pigg went back into the saloon, this time holding a pistol in his hand.

"MacCallister!" he called. "We've got your woman out in the middle of the street. If you don't want to see her kilt, best you get on out there."

■ ■ ■ ■

It was very shortly after Pigg summoned Duff that Duff's cousin, Falcon MacCallister, rode into Chugwater in answer to Duff's call for help. Falcon realized at once that something unusual was happening because it was mid-morning, and First Street, a street that should have been busy with commerce, was nearly deserted. He did see people, but they were standing behind the corners of buildings, or looking cautiously through doors and windows at the few people who were on the street. One, he noticed, was Duff. Duff was standing alone, facing three men who were fanned out across the street in front of him. The man in the middle had a beautiful young woman in front of him, and he was holding a gun to her head.

Falcon didn't know any of the three men, but he did recognize the young woman. It was Meghan Parker, the young woman who owned a dress shop and was a one-quarter partner in Duff's ranch. Whether that partnership would ever become anything more, Falcon didn't know, but he was pretty sure it would. That is, he was sure it would, if this situation could be resolved success-fully.

Falcon dismounted, then walked on up the street, staying on the boardwalk very close to the building fronts. Because of his caution, no one noticed him until he had drawn even with Duff. Not until then did he walk out into the street to stand alongside his cousin.

"Hello, Duff," Falcon said. "How soon do you want to get started?"

"Good day to you, Falcon. I thought we might get underway on Saturday. That would put us in Cheyenne by Monday the tenth."

"Good idea."

Duff called out to Meghan. "Meghan, you remember Falcon, don't you? He is going to help me take our cows to Texas."

"You take good care of those cows, Fal-con," Meghan said. "One quarter of them are mine." Unlike most people who would be in her situation right now, amazingly, Meghan's voice showed no fear.

"I'll take good care of them," Falcon promised.

"What the hell are you people gabbing about?" the man behind Meghan shouted. "Don't you understand what's going on here?"

"Do you mind?" Falcon said. "We'll get to you later. Right now, I'm talking to my friends here."

"Yeah, well I was here first," the man behind Meghan said. "And I'm telling you to just back off and let us finish our business."

"If it's all the same to you, I think I'll just stay here."

"All right, but when the shootin' starts, we ain't goin' to be worryin' none about whether or not you are in the way."

"Oh, that's all right, I quite understand," Falcon said.

"Now, seein' as this feller sort of interrupted us, I'll say it again, real plain, so that you understand. I'm told you have a gold mine, so here is what we are goin' to do. You are goin' to show me an' my friends where that gold mine is. 'Cause if you don't, I'm goin' to shoot this here woman. Do you understand that?"

"Oh, I know what you said," Duff replied. "But I don't think you have thought this through."

"What? What are you talking about?"

"Well think about it, Mr. Emerson. That is your name, isn't it? I think I heard one of your friends call you that. If you shoot Miss Parker, you will nae longer have a bargaining position," Duff said.

"Miss Parker?" Meghan said. "Duff Mac-Callister, you mean as close as we are, that you can't call me by my first name?"

"Aye lass, and it is for sure that I can," Duff said. "I just dinnae want to be intimate in front of these men."

"Oh," Meghan said, smiling. "That's real sweet of you."

"What in the hell is wrong with you people?" Emerson asked, the exasperation in his voice increasing. "Are you crazy?"

"Not at all," Duff said. "I'm just pointing out to you the conundrum you have gotten yourself in. It's rather like a dog that sticks its head through a hole in a fence, then can't pull it back out. You see, Miss Parker is valuable to you only as long as she is alive. If you kill her, she is of no value to you whatever."

"Mister, I don't know what the hell you are talking about. Now I'm goin' to ask you again. Are you goin' to lead us to the mine or what?"

"Nae, I don't think that I will," Duff said.

"Duff, it's looks to me like you're dealing with someone who is too ignorant to understand," Falcon said. "It looks to me like the only solution now is for us to just kill all three of them."

"I think you are right," Duff said. "And while I am an accomplished marksman, I am not fast." As Duff was speaking, he was drawing his pistol, very slowly and deliberately. "So if you would be so kind as to help me out with the other two, I'll be for putting a bullet through the eye of that unpleasant gentlemen with the bad teeth."

"I'll be glad to help out," Falcon said.

Duff raised his pistol and aimed.

Despite the peril she was in at the moment, Meghan almost smiled. She recalled the shooting exhibition back in July when Duff had shot the miniature apple off her head. And she knew, now, that Duff had the situation well under control.

"What do you think you are going to do with that gun?" the man behind Meghan asked. "Don't you see that I . . ."

That was as far as he got because Duff pulled the trigger. The man behind Meghan fell to the ground with blood squirting from the eye that the bullet had penetrated. The other two men had been nearly mesmerized by the improbable event they were witnessing. They reacted at the sound of the gunshot, but it was too late. In a lightning draw, Falcon pulled his pistol and firing two shots so quickly that they sounded as one, he killed the other two.

Meghan stood her ground in the middle of the street, looking now at the bodies of the three men who had accosted her.

"Meghan, be ye harmed, lass?" Duff called to her. Even as he called out to her the citizens of the town who had been driven off the street by the unexpected showdown came running out.

"I'm all right," Meghan said.

Duff hurried to her, and they embraced.

After the embrace, Meghan looked down at the body of the man who had been holding his pistol to her head. There was a black, bloody, and seeping hole where his left eye was. His right eye was still open, still registering the shock of what had happened to him.

"That was a perfectly horrid experience," she said.

"You are sure you are all right?" Duff asked again.

"I'm a lot better now than I was a few minutes ago," Meghan said. She shuddered. "You have no idea how bad his breath was."

Duff looked surprised for a moment, then he started laughing and soon the whole town was laughing with him.

Biff Johnson came out into the street then, even as the rest of the town was gathering in morbid curiosity around the bodies of the three men Duff had shot.

"Hello, Falcon," Biff said. "It's good to see you again."

"Hello, Sergeant," Falcon replied. The two men had met first when Falcon had joined Custer's last campaign as a civilian scout. Biff had been a sergeant in D Troop under Benteen. They had gotten reacquainted when Falcon helped Duff locate the land that would become Sky Meadow Ranch.

"Come on over to Fiddler's Green, I'll buy," Biff offered.

"Thanks, but I have to get back to my shop," Meghan said. "Who knows? Something like this might be good for business."

Live Oaks Ranch, November 6
Even though Maria had been pregnant for several months now, no one but her husband and her parents knew about it. Her pregnancy wasn't obvious because of the bulky dresses she wore.

All through supper Clay had been looking at her, and now as they sat in their small sitting room, even though she was knitting, Maria was well aware that she was the subject of his continued scrutiny. Finally she put the knitting down and looked at him.

"Clay, have I suddenly turned green?"

"What?" Clay replied, confused by the strange question.

"Through supper and now, you have been staring at me. I thought perhaps I had turned green."

Clay chuckled. "Can't I stare at my beautiful wife if I want to?"

"Yes, but I think it is not because you think me beautiful," Maria said. Though her English was flawless, there was still a slight, lilting accent to her words, an accent that Clay had always found appealing.

Clay sighed. "You are right," he said. "I have been staring. I have to tell you something, and I have been trying to think of a way to tell you."

"You wish to tell me that you will be going to Dodge City to drive the cattle down here that Senor Big Ben has bought. Yes?"

"Yes," Clay replied, his face registering his surprise at her answer. "How did you know?"

"Clay, this is a big ranch with many tongues that are willing to speak," she said. "I have known for many days that you would be going to Dodge City."

"And you are all right with that?" Clay asked. "I mean, I know that you're pregnant, and I hate to leave you, but I think it will be less than two months."

"I am all right with it, because I am going with you," Maria told him.

"What? Oh, no, I don't know, Maria, I don't think that would be such a good idea," Clay said.

"Please, Clay," Maria said. "I do not want to be here for so long during my time of pregnancy without you. You will need a cook, and you will need someone to drive the chuck wagon. I can drive the chuck wagon, and I can cook your meals. I have done this before."

"Yes, but you weren't pregnant then. Now, you are pregnant."

"Other women have made difficult journeys while pregnant. Think of the women who gave birth on the wagon trains. Think of the women who have given birth on board ship. Think of the Blessed Virgin Mother of our Lord. Did she not make a long and difficult journey while she was with child? Besides, the baby will not come until after we have returned home. And, wouldn't you rather sleep in the wagon with me, than on the ground with the cowboys?"

Clay laughed. "Somehow, you have managed to make sense of that," he said. "All right, I'll clear it with Big Ben, and if he says he has no problem with it, I'll take you with me."

"Oh, thank you!" Maria said, laughing happily. She threw her arms around his neck then squeezed herself so close to him that he could easily feel the baby she was carrying.

CHAPTER TEN

Live Oaks Ranch, November 8

"I received a wire today telling me that the cattle would be in Dodge City on the eighteenth of November," Big Ben said. "How long will it take you to get there to meet them?"

"About eight days, I would think," Clay replied.

"Who will you be taking with you?"

"I've been thinking about it from the time you told me. I believe I'm going to take Tom Whitman, Dusty McNally, and Mo Coffey."

"Yes, they are all good men. Who are you going to have for your Segundo? Dusty?"

"No, it'll be Tom."

"Are you sure about that? He's been here for less than a year. I would think you would want someone like Dusty, or even Mo."

"Dusty and Mo are both good men, that is true. But I want someone who can think on his feet, and Tom is good at that. In fact,

230

he's about the smartest man I've ever met. No, let's make that he *is* the smartest man I have ever met."

"Yes, well, that's what bothers me about him. Why would someone that smart be content to be a cowboy for the rest of his life unless he either has no ambition, or is lazy, or he is hiding something?"

"He isn't lazy, Mr. Conyers, I can attest to that," Clay said. "Why, he works harder than any man on this ranch."

"And it doesn't bother you that a man like that chooses to be a cowboy?"

"I have chosen to be a cowboy, Mr. Conyers," Clay said pointedly.

"Oh, yes, well, I didn't mean it like that," Big Ben said trying to recover. "Who are you taking as your cook? Coleman? It's up to you of course, and I won't interfere. But I think you should know that if you take Coleman, the boys back here won't be all that pleased."

"I'm taking Maria. She'll drive the chuck wagon."

Big Ben looked surprised. "You are taking Maria?"

"Yes. She is a very good cook, as you know. And this won't be the first trail drive she's made. She went with us last year."

"Yes, but that was in the spring," Big Ben

231

said. "In the spring the weather gets better as you go. But this time I'm asking you to drive twenty-five hundred head of cattle through the dead of winter. And these aren't Longhorns, either. They are Black Angus, and Lord only knows how they will take to the trail."

"She wants to go, Mr. Conyers, and I want to take her with me, if you don't mind."

"No, I don't mind. I mean, she is your wife and you will be right there with her. You are also the trail boss, so if you are all right with that, I suppose I can be too. I do have a favor to ask of you though."

"Sure, what would that be?"

"I want you to take Dalton with you."

Clay didn't say anything, but he did suck air in through clenched teeth.

"He's not that bad, is he?"

"He's, uh, a little young for a trip like this, don't you think?"

"Nonsense," Big Ben said. "I've seen many a sixteen-, fifteen-, even fourteen-year-old cowboy on the trail. Hell, you have too."

"Yes, but," Clay started, then he bit off the sentence.

"Look, Clay, I know Dalton can be troublesome," Big Ben said, his words soothing, cajoling. "Lord knows, this business with Ebersole cost me four hundred dollars. It made me want to just take Dalton back into town, throw him into jail and let him live with the consequences of his own actions. But I can't do that. He is, as the Bible says, my only begotten son."

"I understand," Clay said.

"Clay, Dalton needs this. I think a drive like this — a wintertime drive that is going to be two, maybe three times harder than normal, would be just the thing to give the boy some seasoning. And how about this as an inducement? For every cow you get back here, I will give you twenty-five cents a head; half for you, and the other half to be divided out among the other hands."

"Mr. Conyers, are you sure you want to do that? It's going to cost you enough to get that herd down here as it is. You don't need to be spending even more money."

Big Ben put his hand on Clay's shoulder. "I don't need to do it, Clay. I want to do it," he said.

"I appreciate that. But you don't have to pay me extra to take the boy. I will take him just because you ask me to take him."

"This isn't just for taking the boy," Big Ben said. "This is because I want the best personal care given for these cows. They are a very special breed. And once I get the herd

233

established, it will be well worth whatever it cost me to get them here."

"If we are going to get there in time to get back here for Christmas, we need to leave by the day after tomorrow. Right now, I'm going to go gather up Tom, Dusty and Mo. You might ask Dalton to come on over to my place in about half an hour so we can talk about it."

"I will, Clay. And thank you," Big Ben said. "Thank you from the bottom of my heart."

There were two clapboard bunkhouses on the ranch, both painted white. There were twenty bunks in each of the bunkhouses, ten on each side. The inside walls were of wide, rip-sawed, unpainted boards, papered over with newspapers. In the time he had been here, Tom Whitman had read just about every article and every advertisement on every wall. He had committed the one behind his bunk to memory.

W. GLITSCHKA
WHOLESALE AND RETAIL

GROCER
110 Houston St.

FRESH EGGS
GREENS AND VEGETABLES
FRUITS
PROVISIONS OF ALL KINDS

There were two wood-burning stoves in the bunkhouse, one at each end. Though it was cool now in early November, it wasn't cold enough to keep both of them going, so for now only one was being used, and that was as much to keep the pot of coffee warm as it was to heat the bunkhouse.

At the moment, Tom was lying on his bunk with his hands laced behind his head, staring up at the ceiling. At the far end of the bunkhouse, Dusty McNally was playing the guitar and crooning a cowboy song, one that Tom had heard many times being sung to the cattle. Several of the other cowboys were gathered around Dusty.

The memories came back. No, they didn't come back, the memories never left; they were always there, just beneath the surface, a part of him, like an awareness of night and day, heat and cold.

He had a sinking feeling in the pit of his stomach as he walked out onto the balcony. His knees were so weak that he had to grab hold of the banister to keep from falling. He looked down at his hands and saw the blood.

Why did he do it? Why? He could wash his hands, but the blood would not go away. He thought of a scene from Lady MacBeth. "Here's the smell of the blood still: all the perfumes of Arabia will not sweeten this little hand."

Now, as he lay here in his bunk, Tom raised his hands to stare at them.

"Tom! Are you in here?" Clay's shout brought Tom out of his reverie, and he sat up on his bed.

"I'm here," he said.

"Dusty? Mo?" Clay called.

"Yeah, we're here," Dusty answered.

"Put down that guitar, Dusty, and you, Tom, and Mo come on over to my house for a few minutes, will you? We've got a job ahead of us and I'll need to discuss it with you."

Dusty hung his guitar up on a nail above his bunk, and then he, Tom, and Mo followed Clay back to the foreman's house. Maria greeted them warmly when they arrived and, a moment later, all four of them were doing a balancing act with a cup of coffee in one hand and a small plate with a piece of freshly baked apple pie in the other.

There was a knock on the door and when Maria opened it, Dalton stepped in, with a big smile on his face.

"Pa says you're taking me to Dodge to help bring back the herd he's buying," Dalton said.

"That's right," Clay replied.

"Hot dog. I'm going to enjoy this."

"I'm filling the others in on the drive," Clay said. "Get yourself a cup of coffee and a piece of pie and find a place to sit."

"You can sit there, I will bring it to you," Maria said.

"Thank you, Maria," Dalton replied, sitting on the chair she offered.

"We'll get underway day after tomorrow," Clay said. "So get all your gear ready and throw it in the hoodlum wagon. And don't forget to take warm coats and a couple of blankets. It's not that bad now, but it'll be the middle of December before we get back and it's likely to get pretty cold."

"Tom, I'm going to make you my Segundo, my second in command."

"Why me?" Tom asked. "Dusty and Mo have both been here longer."

"I've already spoken with them," Clay said. "And they agree."

"You are smart, like the officers I served under during the war," Dusty said. "I like having someone smart to make the decisions."

"That's right," Mo said. "We both agree."

"Are you all right with that?" Clay asked.

"Yes, I suppose so," Tom said. "I'll try not to let anyone down."

"What about horses?" Dusty asked.

"Pick out three apiece," Clay said. "Get three good ones, you've all been here long enough to know what horses will fare the best. Mo, how about you picking out four mules, two for the chuck wagon and two for the hoodlum wagon?"

"Alright," Mo said. "Who'll be driving those?"

"Maria is going to drive the chuck wagon. She'll be cooking for us."

"All right," Dusty said with a broad smile. He held up what remained of his pie. "If you're goin' to cook like this, then I say it's goin' to be one fine trail drive."

"And Dalton will be driving the hoodlum wagon."

"Wait a minute!" Dalton said sharply. "Who said I would be driving the hoodlum wagon?"

"I said," Clay replied.

"I'm not going to be driving any damn hoodlum wagon, poking along with the chuck wagon while the rest of you gallop all over the country."

"Dalton, your father didn't order me to take you with me. He *asked* me to take you.

238

To my way of thinking, that leaves the choice of taking you or leaving you behind up to me. Now, I'm giving you that choice. You will either drive the wagon, or you will damn sure stay behind. It's up to you, boy, so which will it be?"

Dalton looked at the other three men in the room, but couldn't find any of them who would return his gaze.

"I'm waiting," Clay said.

"All right!" Dalton said, angrily. "I will drive the damn hoodlum wagon."

"I thought you might see it my way," Clay said. He returned to his briefing. "I figure we can make it up there in ten days. It will likely take forty to forty-five days to drive the herd down, but I can't be too sure about that. They are Black Angus, and I've never driven Black Angus before so I don't know how they will handle."

"What is a Black Angus?" Dusty asked.

"It is a black cow," Clay said.

"I can't believe that Big Ben is getting out of the Longhorn business," Dusty said.

"I have read about them," Tom said. "They were developed in the Angus region of Scotland. They are not only black, they are also polled."

"Polled?"

"That means they don't have horns."

239

"The hell you say?" Dusty said. "Are you telling me we are going to drive an entire herd of cows that don't have horns?"

"That's right," Tom said.

"Who would want cattle without horns?"

"The Black Angus make very good beef cattle."

"All right, if you say so, Tom," Dusty said. "No horns, huh? I sure hope none of the boys from over at the Rocking H hear about this. They'll be ridin' us somethin' fierce."

"I want every one of you to take a pistol and a box of fifty rounds. I'll have another five hundred rounds in the hoodlum wagon. Couple of you should also take Winchesters, and maybe a shotgun."

"I'd better take a shotgun," Tom said. "I don't even own a pistol, and I've never become proficient in the use of firearms."

Mo laughed. "Proficient in the use of firearms," he repeated. He slapped his hand on his knee. "Damn, Tom, maybe you can't shoot all that good, but you are the beatinist talker I ever run in to. But don't worry about not having a pistol, I have an extra one, and a holster, that you can take."

"And if you get a pistol from Mo it'll be a good one," Dalton said. "He's the best with a gun there ever was."

Of all the cowboys on the ranch, Mo was

the one that Dalton was closest to, and one of the reasons Clay decided to bring Mo along was his hope that Mo would be an ameliorating influence on Dalton.

"All right, if nobody has any questions, go on back and get your personal gear together. We'll spend tomorrow picking out our remuda and loading on our victuals and gear into the wagons. I plan to get underway Saturday morning."

Sky Meadow Ranch, November 8
The drive from Sky Meadow Ranch to the railhead at Cheyenne would be one tenth as long, and would consist of a herd about two thirds of the number of cattle that would constitute the drive from Dodge City down to Live Oaks Ranch. Duff thought the drive to Cheyenne would be a very good trial run for them.

On the morning they were to leave, the cattle were all bunched up in a long, stretched-out herd, the lead steer was belled, and the chuck wagon was underway. Falcon was one of the cowboys of course, as was Duff. Elmer was there as well, along with two other cowboys from the ranch.

And then there was Meghan, wearing pants and a warm jacket, with a hat that she kept pulled down low. Because of the way

241

she was dressed, and the fact that she was riding straddle, coupled with her riding ability, made it impossible to tell from a distance the difference between Meghan and any of the other cowboys. When one of the cows tended to go astray, Meghan would ride it down and push it back to the herd with as much skill as any cowboy present.

After the chuck wagon started out, Elmer came riding up to Duff, Meghan, and Falcon, who were sitting their horses on top of a gentle rise that allowed them to see the entire herd.

"We're ready to get underway, Duff. Just give us the word."

"All right, get them started," Duff said.

Elmer galloped back down toward the rest of the herd. Taking his hat off, he held it above his head, and shouted out at the top of his voice.

"Yee, haw!"

The other cowboys, whistling and shouting, got the big herd in motion, a few cows in front at first, then, as if picking up momentum, more and more of the herd started moving. Finally, like unraveling a ball of twine, the herd began stringing out until eventually, every cow was in motion.

"Unless you have some other place in mind, I'll take the far side," Falcon said.

"Good enough," Duff replied. "Meghan and I will stay on this side."

"Listen, you two pay attention to the cattle now," Falcon said. "I don't want to look over here and see you sparking."

"Mind your own business," Meghan replied with a little laugh.

Live Oaks Ranch, Saturday, November 8
Two wagons, four riders, and eleven un-saddled horses were lined up on the road in front of the arched gate that led up to Live Oaks Ranch. Big Ben and Julia were there, along with about thirty other ranch hands. Maria was sitting in the driver's seat of the chuck wagon, smiling broadly at the prospect of going with her husband. Dalton was sitting on the driver's seat of the supply wagon, frowning to show his displeasure at having been selected for this job.

For the moment, Clay was alongside Big Ben, getting his last minute instructions.

"I'm sending twenty-five hundred dollars in cash with you, along with my letter of credit," Big Ben said. "That should take care of just about any emergency you might encounter along the way. Send me a wire when you get to Dodge to let me know that you got there all right, and send me another just before you start back with the herd."

"Yes, sir," Clay replied.

"I know Dalton is a little upset now at having to drive the hoodlum wagon, but he'll get over it. I'm reasonably sure he will make a good hand for you."

"I'm sure he will," Clay agreed.

Big Ben stuck his hand out, and Clay took it.

"Good luck," Big Ben said.

"Thank you," Clay replied. Pulling his horse around, Clay galloped back down to where the little party was assembled.

"Let's go!" he shouted.

Maria slapped the reins against the back of her team of mules, and the wagon started forward. Dalton started behind her. The riders held their horses to a slow walk, equal to the speed of the wagons, and with the whistles and cheers of those assembled to watch them depart, the Black Angus retrieval party got underway.

Dodge City, November 8

It was noon, and for the moment there were very few customers in the Lucky Chance. Because of that Rebecca, Candy, and the two other bar girls who worked in the saloon were sharing a table for lunch. Candy was talking about Billy Lovejoy.

"I know he cares for me," Candy said,

wiping away a tear. "He knows what I have been, but he also knows that I would be a good and faithful wife to him. But he is afraid to go against his father."

Rebecca didn't comment, though she knew exactly what Candy was going through. The only difference was that their roles were reversed. Candy was perceived as not good enough for Billy Lovejoy, whereas Rebecca was perceived as too good for Tom Whitman.

"Honey, it's all a dream," Kate said. "Girls like us never leave the line. We never get married."

"Janie did," Candy said. "She told me that she was just like us, once, but she met Oscar."

Suddenly Candy realized that she might have spoken out of turn, and she put her hand on Rebecca's hand. "Becca, I'm sorry, I don't mean any disrespect for your Mama."

"Nor were you disrespectful," Rebecca said. "I know all about my mother's past, and I am proud of her for what she has become."

"Well if you ask me, you don't have any business getting involved with the Lovejoy family in the first place," Rena said. "I know they are rich, but Frank Lovejoy is a horrid person."

"Billy is nothing like Frank," Candy insisted. "Nothing at all."

"I know he's not, honey," Rena said, reaching out to put her hand on Candy's. "It's just that nothing good is going to come of this, and I don't want to see you hurt."

"None of us want to see you hurt," Kate said.

At that moment Rebecca saw Oscar come back down the stairs. He stood at the foot of the stairs for a moment, his head bowed, and his shoulders shaking. Rebecca felt a sudden rush of anxiety, and getting up from the table, she hurried over to him.

"Mama?" she asked, her voice catching on the word.

"She's dead, child," Oscar said, sobbing as he told her. "The light of my life is dead."

Boot Hill Cemetery, November 10
A cold, dry wind whipped through the cemetery as nearly one hundred people gathered for Janie's funeral. The coffin lay on the edge of the already opened grave, and Oscar stood beside it with his hand resting on the gleaming rosewood. His head was bowed, whether in prayer or grief, Rebecca didn't know.

Rebecca had never actually known her

mother until this past few months, and though she had grown close to her, the truth was that, in her mind, Julia was, always had been, and always would be her mother. But she had come to appreciate Janie, even finding it easier than she thought to call her "Mama." She was saddened by Janie's death, but had to confess that her grief didn't match Oscar's.

Most of the mourners were the men who frequented the Lucky Chance Saloon, and they stood in little clumps around the grave, a few of them coming over to mumble something to Rebecca before stepping up to Oscar to reach out and touch him. They were obviously uncomfortable around a weeping man, feeling powerless to help assuage his grief. Candy, Kate, and Rena were there as well, not dressed as they did when they greeted the customers, but as modestly as any schoolmarm.

All three of the girls had been solicitous of Rebecca, but even more so toward Oscar, whose grief was almost inconsolable.

There had not been a church service, but the Reverend T.J. Boyd volunteered to say a few words at the committal. Tall and thin, his nose was red in the cold wind as he stood looking out over the mourners.

"As I look out over those gathered here, I

am reminded that I have never seen any of you in church, and that means that your souls are in peril." He pointed to the coffin. "It is too late for this poor woman, who even now, is writhing in the agony of hell's eternal fire. But it isn't too late for all of you. Leave the saloons, the whorehouses, the dens of iniquity, and repent. Accept our Savior Jesus Christ and be born again, or you, like this poor miserable wretch, will burn in hell for eternity."

The Reverend T.J. Boyd raised his right hand high in the air, his index finger pointed to heaven as his oratory rose to a pitch. "I ask you now to open your heart and accept . . ."

That was as far as he got before Oscar laid him out with a hard uppercut to the preacher's chin. Then something happened at a graveside interment that had never happened before. The mourners broke out into a loud, rousing cheer.

CHAPTER ELEVEN

Denver, November 12

It took three trains of thirty cars each to transport Duff MacCallister's fifteen hundred cows from Cheyenne to Denver. Duff and Meghan were on the lead train, Elmer took the second train, and Falcon had the trailing train.

Smoke, Sally, and Matt had already brought their cattle, and Smoke had made arrangements for holding pens where the cattle would wait until they could be moved to Dodge City.

Smoke, Sally, and Matt were waiting on the platform as the trains arrived.

"Duff, you have met Sally, but I don't think you have met this gentleman. This is Matt Jensen," Smoke said, introducing the young man with him.

Duff shook hands with Matt, who was also greeted by Falcon, who already knew him.

"This is my partner, Meghan Parker,"

Duff said, introducing the attractive young woman who was with him. "And this is my ranch foreman, Elmer Gleason."

"Very good to meet you, Meghan," Sally said. "Will you be coming along on the drive?"

"No," Meghan answered. "I would love to, but I have a dress shop business to run back in Chugwater. And with the approach of the Christmas season, I can't afford to be gone. Elmer and I will be going back tomorrow."

"Oh, that's too bad. I'm going, and it would be nice to have another woman along as company. But at least we will have your company tonight."

"Any trouble with the drive to Cheyenne?" Smoke asked.

"Nae a bit o' trouble," Duff replied. "Sure 'n the cows moved along as if they were the Black Watch on parade."

"If they are like this from Dodge all the way down to Fort Worth, I don't think we'll have a bit of trouble," Falcon added. "They trail as easy as Longhorns, if not easier."

The loading pen manager came up to the group then. "Any of you fellows in charge of the cattle that just came in on this train?"

"Aye, that would be me," Duff said.

"What do you want done with them?"

"Here you go, Mr. Dawes," Smoke said, handing the manager a sheet of paper. "You can put those cattle in with mine. I have the holding pens reserved through Thursday."

Dawes looked at the paper and nodded.

"All right, I'll get them off-loaded."

"Thank you," Smoke said. Then to the others, "I have four trains scheduled. We'll ship the cows to Dodge, then all we have to do is drive the cows from Dodge City down to Fort Worth."

"All we have to do?" Falcon asked with a smile. "You have any idea how far that is?"

"Four hundred and fifty miles," Smoke said. "Figure on making fifteen miles a day, it'll take us just about thirty days. We should be there just before Christmas."

"That's pretty ambitious, considering the weather," Falcon said. "Don't forget, most cattle drives are in the summertime. This is a wintertime drive. We aren't only going to have the weather to worry about, we are going to have to worry about finding enough grass to keep the herd fed."

"I know," Smoke replied. "And I've discovered since I started running them, that Angus eat a lot more grass than Longhorns, or even Herefords."

"We'll do it," Duff said. "We don't have any choice but to do it."

"What do you we say we go to the hotel now, get a good supper and get you checked in."

After taking rooms at the hotel, they met up again in the hotel restaurant. There, they were met by Smoke's two principal hands, Pearlie and Cal. There was a large round table set for nine, eight plates of which were clean. Cal had already started eating, and he stood up with a mouth full of food, chewing it quickly to avoid having to talk with his mouth full.

"Cal, I'm glad you waited on the rest of us," Smoke said, and the others laughed.

"I did wait," Cal said. "I just decided to have a little something to eat while I was waiting to eat."

Smoke chuckled. "Damn, if you all knew Cal the way I do, you would know that, that almost makes sense."

"Duff, this is my foreman Pearlie," Smoke introduced. "And the young man with a face full of food is Cal."

"Pleased to meet you," Cal mumbled around food, not yet swallowed.

When the introductions were completed they sat at the table, and after ordering their meals, began talking about the upcoming adventure.

"So, Sally, is this really the Christmas trip

that Smoke promised you?" Falcon teased.

"I'm looking forward to it," Sally said.

"There you go, Matt," Falcon said. "If you ever get married, you need to find a woman just like Sally."

"There isn't anyone else like Sally," Matt said, "if so, I would have found her and married her long ago."

Sally beamed under the compliment. "Why thank you, Matt. I appreciate that," she said. "But I'm sure that some fine day, someone is going to say the same thing about Meghan."

Everyone around the table looked at Meghan and Duff who smiled, but made no incriminating response.

"Oh, here is something you might appreciate," Smoke said. "I have ordered a private car to be attached to each train," Smoke said. "Since we are going to have a very difficult winter drive, I figure we may as well take what comfort we can, while we can."

"Nobody can find any fault with that," Falcon said.

"Smoke, are you sure you don't want Cal and me to come along?" Pearlie asked. "You're going to have a long drive with just the five of you."

"I've been in touch with Big Ben," Smoke said. "He has promised to send some drovers up to meet us. He will also be furnishing the chuck wagon and a wagon to carry our gear."

"Still, a drive in the wintertime," Pearlie said. "That's going to be rough as a cob. I wish you would let Cal and me help out."

"You and Cal just keep things under control back at the ranch," Smoke said. "That will be help enough."

"All right, if you say so," Pearlie said.

"How have the Angus worked out for you, Smoke?" Duff asked.

"Best decision I've ever made," Smoke said.

"Oh?" Sally asked with an arched eyebrow. "Switching from Longhorns to Black Angus cattle was the best decision you ever made."

"Yes. They are easier to handle, they pay more at the market."

"Smoke, you might want to rethink that 'best move you ever made' comment," Pearlie suggested. "I mean, seeing as you decided to ask Sally here to . . ."

Pearlie didn't have to finish his comment because, belatedly, Smoke caught on.

"Best move I ever made regarding cattle," Smoke said, doing damage control. "Of course, marrying Sally was the best move I ever made."

Sally's laugh told him that she had been

having some fun at his expense, and the others laughed as well.

There was a lot of discussion during the rest of the meal, much of it driven by curiosity as to whether the relationship between Duff and Meghan was more than partnership in a ranch. Neither Duff nor Meghan provided an answer to the speculation.

From the *Colorado Springs Gazette, November 13, 1890*

BIG CATTLE SHIPMENT.

Intelligence has been received of a large rail shipment of cattle which will pass through Colorado Springs on the night of the 14th Instant, for Dodge City, at which point they will be taken from the cars and driven to a ranch near Fort Worth, Texas.

The shipment is the result of a business transaction conducted by Mr. Duff MacCallister of Chugwater Valley, Wyoming and Mr. Smoke Jensen of Big Rock, Colorado with Mr. Benjamin Conyers of Live Oaks Ranch in Tarrant County, Texas. Black Angus Cattle are a much better breed than the Longhorn in that they have more weight, and the

255

beef is said to be of the finest quality. A measure of the animals' superiority can be ascertained by their price at the Kansas Market. The price for Longhorn cattle has fallen precipitously, while the cost for Black Angus remains around $17.00 per head. Two thousand five hundred of these valuable beasts are being shipped, that number being sufficient to require a total of four trains.

Most people who read the article did so with an interest that was generated only by their curiosity in the transaction, or by a bit of pride in the fact that cattle from Wyoming and Colorado were being shipped to Texas.

One of the readers was Red Coleman, and his reaction to the article was considerably different from that of all the other readers. The first thing he noticed was the name Smoke Jensen.

"Lookie here, McDill," he said. "Looks to me like we might be able to square things with Smoke Jensen after all."

"How?" McDill asked. The two men were having a beer at a saloon in the small town of Salcedo.

"It seems that Mr. Smoke Jensen is in the cow business. And not just the Longhorn cow business, but a special kind of cow that's worth seventeen dollars a head. He is puttin' them real valuable cows on four trains that's going to be passing right through here, and we're goin' to steal them cows."

"How we goin' to take four trains?"

"We ain't. We'll only take the first train, and we'll take it when it reaches Lajunta."

"When will it be comin' through?" McDill asked.

"According to the paper, they'll be comin' through tomorrow night."

"How many cows will be on that train?" McDill asked.

"Well, if it is one of four trains, I figure that means that it breaks down to about six hundred and twenty-five," Red replied. "And that's about ten thousand dollars."

"Ten thousand dollars is a lot of money all right, but it's for sure and certain that we ain't goin' to be able to do this alone," McDill said. "We're goin' to need some more folks."

"You don't worry about that. I've got a couple of men in mind," Red said. "I'll gather them up and we'll meet back here this afternoon."

Though it was still mid-afternoon, the saloon was already crowded and noisy with the sounds of idle men and painted women having fun. Near the piano, three men and a couple of women filled the air with their idea of a song, their discordant voices killed whatever melody there might have been, and their interpretation of the lyrics, complete with ribald phrases, would render the song unrecognizable by the composer.

At the moment McDill was standing at the bar, his foot propped up on the rail as he stared into the single beer he was nursing. Every time someone new would come in, he would look over to see if it was Red. After waiting for an hour, all the time nursing a single beer that had grown flat, he saw Red come in with two other men. One, a man named Woodward, McDill recognized. McDill and Woodward had been in jail together back in Denver. But he had no idea who the other man was.

The three men ordered beer at the counter, then started toward an empty table at the back of the place. McDill followed.

"All right," Woodward said. "Now, what's this job you were talkin' about?"

Red told of the four trains that would be going from Denver to Dodge City, Kansas, each one filled with cattle.

"And these ain't your ordinary kind of cows neither," Red said. "They're Black Angus, and Black Angus cows are worth a lot of money."

"How are we going to take four trains?" Woodward asked.

"We ain't," McDill said, speaking up quickly to show that he and Red were the ones who came up with the idea. "We're just goin' to take the first one."

"Still, there's only goin' to be the four of us," Woodward said, keeping up the argument. "You think we can off-load a whole trainload of cows before the next train comes along?"

"We ain't goin' to be off-loadin' 'em," Red said. "We're goin' to leave 'em on the train."

"Leave 'em on the train? Now, that don't make no sense at all," McDill complained. Even McDill had not been filled in on Red's ultimate plan.

Smiling, Red looked around the table at the men he had recruited just for this job. "Burgess, I think it's about time we tell these other two men what you used to do."

"Until I got fired for bein' drunk while workin', I was a railroad engineer," Burgess said.

"Really? You mean you used to drive the trains?" McDill asked, obviously impressed with Burgess's résumé.

"That's what I did, all right."

"And he's going to do it again," Red said. "Burgess, tell them what we have in mind."

"We're goin' to steal the train," Burgess said. "When it gets to Lajunta, we will steal it, then we will leave the Santa Fe tracks," Burgess said.

"What do you mean leave the tracks?" McDill asked. "That don't make no sense a-tall. Hell, even I know you can't drive a train unless it's on tracks."

"We won't be leaving the tracks," Burgess explained patiently. "There is a switch track at Lajunta. When I say we will leave Santa Fe tracks, that's just what I mean. We are going to switch the train off those tracks, and onto the Denver and New Orleans tracks."

"Oh," McDill said, though it was clear that he still didn't fully understand the operation.

"We are going to steal the train," Red continued with the explanation. "Then Burgess is going to drive it. Like he said, we'll leave the Santa Fe track and head south on the Denver and New Orleans. When the other three trains come through, they won't have any idea that anything is wrong with the first train, and by the time they get it figured out, we'll be sitting pretty somewhere with a whole trainload of cattle."

"You make it sound pretty easy," Wood-ward said. "So what are you not sayin'? What do we need to look out for?"

"I don't figure we'll have too much trouble taking the train," Red said, "but Burgess has pointed out what might be a problem."

"Yeah, I thought this was sounding too easy. What is the problem?" Woodward asked.

"On any railroad you've got trains goin' all the time, using the same tracks," Burgess said. "The only way they can keep them from ever runnin' in to each other is by scheduling them so that they know where every train is at all time, and which way it's going. As long as we are on the Santa Fe Tracks, we're on their schedule so there's no problem with other trains. But once we get on the Denver and New Orleans line, they won't have us on their schedule."

"So what you are saying is that another train could run in to us?" Woodward asked.

"Well, it shouldn't be that much of a problem for us," Burgess said. "All we have to do is get clear of the high iron, then we stop somewhere and unload the cattle. But, being as we'll be leaving the train just sittin' there, why, it could be a problem for the next train that comes along. Won't be so bad if the next train to come along is just freight. But if it's varnish, it could wind up killin' a lot of folks."

"Varnish?" McDill asked.

"That means a passenger train," Burgess explained.

"Yeah, but if you think about it, that's not really a problem either," Red said. "If a bunch of folks gets killed and injured, then that will mean that ever' one's goin' to be concentratin' on the train wreck. Like as not, they'll forget all about a few cows."

"What will we do with the cows once we get 'em?" Woodward asked.

"Why, we'll sell 'em of course," Red said.

"To who?" Woodward wanted to know. "It ain't like we can take them cows to market and sell 'em. Bein' a special breed and all, soon as we take 'em, folks are goin' to know about it. And if we show up at some market with the same number and same kind of cows as the ones that was stolen, we'll wind up in prison. And I ain't all that anxious to go back to prison."

"We'll find someone to buy 'em," Red said. "We won't get as much money for 'em by sellin' 'em that way, but we will make enough for this to be worth our time and effort, that's for sure."

In the cab of the 2-4-2 Baldwin locomotive, Engineer Clem Beale and Fireman Jerry Kelly were illuminated by the yellow cabin lights. Beale looked at the steam-pressure gauge, then checked the water level.

"I'm glad we're comin' up on the Lajunta tank," Beale said. "We've been keepin' a lot of pressure and we're using water like it's passin' through a sieve."

"Ahh, we're in good shape to make it to the tank," Kelly said. He opened the door to the firebox then tossed in another few shovelfuls of coal. Slamming the door shut, he leaned back against the side of the cab, pulled out a large red bandana, and wiped the sweat from his face.

"Say, Clem, have you ever heard of Santy Claus?" Kelly asked.

"Of course I've heard of Santa Claus," Beale replied. "Why would you ask a question like that?"

"I wasn't sure whether you had, seein' as you ain't married and don't have any kids or nothin'," Kelly said. "But my two kids is just full of it. I told 'em, it's more than a month 'till Christmas, it ain't time to be worryin' about anything like that yet. But that ain't quietened 'em down any."

263

Beale chuckled. "What are you goin' to do, Jerry? Get yourself one of them red Santa Claus suits?"

"Nah, I'll just wait 'til they're both asleep, then tell 'em they didn't wake up in time to see him."

"Ha, I'm glad I don't have any kids to worry about with Santa Claus and such things," Beale said.

"It ain't really that big a worry when you think about it," Kelly said. "I kind of like it."

Beale smiled and nodded at his friend. "That's because you are a good Pa."

Thirty cars back from the engine, the only other car that was illuminated was the private car owned by the Union Pacific Railroad, but on temporary consignment to Smoke Jensen. Sally was in bed in her nightgown, but not asleep. Smoke, who was not in bed was sitting in a large, overstuffed reclining chair. His feet were propped up on the footrest, and he was looking through the window at the moon-silvered landscape they were passing through.

"Wouldn't it be nice to have our own private car?" Smoke asked. "That way, anytime we wanted to go somewhere, all we would have to do is arrange to have it attached to the end of some train and we could go anywhere we wanted as comfortable as this."

"We can do that anyway," Sally said. "I mean look at us now. We don't own a private car, but we aren't exactly riding in a cattle car either, are we? If we wanted one, we could always rent one."

"Yes, but wouldn't it be neat to sort of drop into a conversation, something like — 'Next week Sally and I will be taking our private car to New York, or Philadelphia, or Madagascar.' "

Sally laughed. "Madagascar is an island. How would we get there?"

"By ship."

"Then we wouldn't need a private car, would we?"

"You are too practical for your own good," Smoke said. He reached for his boots, then set them beside the chair.

"What are you doing?"

"I'm just making my boots handy. I figure we'll be taking on water pretty soon," Smoke said. "When we do, I'm going to take a walk up one side of the train and down the other side, just to make certain everything is all right."

Lajunta, Colorado

It was only a quarter moon, but that was enough to cause the tracks to gleam silver as they stretched out before Red and the three men with him. Far to the west they could see the Rocky Mountains, rising like a huge black slab against a somewhat lighter sky. A few minutes earlier, Burgess had climbed up onto the water tower, and now he climbed back down.

"Did you see it?" Red asked.

"I saw the light."

"How do you know it was the train's light?"

"Because it was in the right place," Burgess replied. "It'll be here in about another ten minutes."

"Remember," Burgess cautioned. "Nobody does anything until after the train has taken on water. We'll be needing that water ourselves."

The men heard a distant whistle.

"I hear it," Woodward said, excitedly.

"We all hear it," McDill said.

"All right, let's get down out of sight," Red Coleman ordered.

CHAPTER TWELVE

The car passed over a rough section of track, then Smoke felt the train beginning to slow.

"We must be coming up on that water tank now," Smoke said. He started pulling on his boots.

"Want me to go check with you?" Sally asked.

"No need for you to get out in the cold," Smoke replied. "You stay inside here, warm and comfortable. I'm just going to walk up to the engine and back and look into all the cars. I'll be back before you know it."

Smoke pulled on his sheepskin coat. He saw his pistol belt hanging from a hook but started toward the door without it. He got as far as the door, then turned around and came back for his pistol. He had no idea why he thought he might need it in the middle of the night, but he just didn't feel dressed without it.

Even above the venting steam and the snap and pop of cooling journals, Smoke could hear the sound of water rushing into the tank, and, in the moonlight, he saw the fireman standing up on the tender, directing the flow of water. Smoke continued to walk down the side of the train, in the shadows of the cattle cars. He could smell and sense the cattle that were packed in the cars and he couldn't help but feel a little sorry for them. Crowded together as they were, they would be unable to rest for the two days of the journey. Also, they would have very little food and water to sustain them for the trip. They would be much better off when they got out on their own with plenty of room to move around, and plenty of grass to eat.

Despite the quarter-moon, Smoke couldn't be seen as he walked along the side of the train, because he was so close to it that he was in the shadow of the cars. He had not detected any problems when he reached the first car, which was the next car behind the tender. There, he turned and started back, but stopped when he heard someone call out.

"Fireman! You, up on the tender! Get your hands up, and climb down here!"

"Who are you?" the fireman asked. "What

are you doing here?"

A gun roared, its muzzle-flash lighting up the night. The fireman slapped his hand over the wound, staggered to the edge of the tender, then pitched forward off the car. He landed hard on his back and Smoke knew that even if the bullet wound hadn't killed him, the fall did.

"Get up there! Get the engineer!" someone yelled from the darkness.

Smoke saw someone put his hand on the mounting ladder, then start to climb up into the engine cab.

"Hold it!" Smoke shouted.

"What the hell! Where did you come from?"

The man who yelled at Smoke fired his pistol at the same time he yelled. Smoke saw the muzzle-flash, and felt the puff of air as the bullet whizzed by his ear. Smoke returned fire and one shot was all it took to drop the man who had been shooting at him.

"Burgess! Burgess!" someone shouted from the dark.

"Burgess has been hit! What'll we do now, Red?"

"Shoot 'im! Shoot 'im!"

At least three pistols began firing from the darkness and Smoke was able to return fire, shooting slightly above and to the right of the flame patterns. Two of the men went down, but the third disappeared. A moment later he heard the thunder of hoofbeats as the last would-be train robber galloped away.

Smoke ran down the berm and, bending over and keeping alert, started toward where he thought the two assailants would be. He found the first one lying on the rocks. His eyes were open and fixed, and a quick look confirmed that he was dead. Smoke heard a low groan from the sagebrush, and holding his pistol at the ready, moved to the sound.

"Where are you?" he called.

"Here," a weak voice replied.

Seeing him then, Smoke realized at once that the man represented no danger. Returning his pistol to his holster, he hurried over to him.

"Who are you?" Smoke asked.

"The name is McDill. I'm gut-shot. Please help me, I'm gut-shot."

Smoke dropped to a knee beside the man, but one look was all it took to tell him that the man was a goner.

"I'm afraid there's not much I can do for you, McDill," Smoke said.

"I'm dyin', ain't I?"

"Yes," Smoke said.

"It wasn't supposed to be like this. Coleman told us it would be easy. We would just take the . . ." the man gasped, then died with a long, life-surrendering rattle.

"Smoke! Smoke, where are you?" It was Sally's voice and there was a worried sound to it.

"I'm all right, Sally, I'm down here," Smoke called back.

"I'll come down," Sally said.

"No need for you to do that. I'm coming up," Smoke replied as he climbed back up the steep slope of the berm.

When he reached the top of the berm he saw that Sally was holding a pistol, and he knew it wasn't a foolish show. Had she been needed, Sally would have acquitted herself well, because she could shoot as well any man, and much better than most.

By now the engineer had climbed down from the cab and stood looking down at the body of the fireman.

"Are you all right?" Smoke asked.

"Yes, sir, I'm fine," the engineer said. "They didn't have no business killin' Jerry. All he was doin' was puttin' water into the tank."

"If you can help me, we'll put him up in the cab until we reach the next town," Smoke said.

"Thanks. We'd better hurry though," the engineer said. He took out his pocketwatch and looked at it. The next train is due within half an hour, we need to be out of the way."

"Where's the nearest sheriff?" Smoke asked.

"Las Animas. It's about fifteen miles farther down the track," the engineer said.

"We'll tell the sheriff about the other three bodies out here. I expect he will want to come out and pick them up."

"Ha!" the engineer said. "I wouldn't doubt but what there's a reward on these galoots, and it'll be owed to you."

"Does your friend have a family?" Smoke asked, indicating the fireman.

"Yes, sir," the fireman said. "Jerry had him a wife and two kids. He was just tellin' me about the kids talkin' about Santa Claus and all."

"If there is any reward, see to it that it goes to her."

The engineer nodded. "Yes, sir, that's mighty kind of you."

Red Coleman had been riding hard since the bungled cattle robbery attempt. He slowed to a walk to give his horse a rest, then looked back over his shoulder. He had come at least two miles, maybe more, from the track and he was sure nobody was after him. He wasn't sure who it was he had tangled with back there, but whoever it was was damn deadly with a pistol. And, as he recalled from the failed bank robbery, Smoke Jensen was deadly with a pistol, so it wouldn't surprise him if it had been Smoke Jensen.

"All right, Mr. Smoke Jensen," Coleman said aloud. "If I can't take a fourth of your cows, I'll figure out a way to take every damn one of them."

Cimarron River, Indian Territory, November 17
Clay Ramsey and his party were camped on the north side of the Cimarron. They had passed through both the Choctaw and Creek nations without any difficulty, and now were in Osage territory. They had no cattle with them so had not experienced any tolls being collected. Clay had brought along three extra horses with him to give to the Indians if that became necessary, but so far he had not had to part with any of them.

They were sitting around a campfire, having had a good supper of chili verde and tortillas. For dessert they had sopapillas with molasses.

"I tell you what," Dusty said. "I been trailin' man and boy for near forty years now, and I've never had trail food like this. Most of the time we have nothin' but beans and chuck wagon chicken."

"Chuck wagon chicken?" Maria repeated with a little chuckle.

"He means bacon, ma'am," Mo said.

"Would you play the guitar for us, Señor Dusty?" Maria asked.

"Yes, ma'am, it would be my privilege," Dusty said. He walked over to the hoodlum wagon and, moving aside some of the gear, pulled out his guitar. Returning to the campfire, he checked the tuning, then pausing for a moment, began to play. The lower strings provided a steady rhythmic beat while the higher strings, plucked by quick and nimble fingers, brought out the melody, like a fine, golden thread woven through a rich piece of tapestry.

Clay wrapped his arm around Maria and she leaned into him as the music lifted from the guitar, as if following the glowing red sparks that danced their way up on the column of heated air until they became lost among the stars.

"Where did you learn to play the guitar like that, Dusty?" Clay asked.

"I spent some time at sea," Dusty said. "Wasn't much to do on board one of those ships, and there was a Spanish fella that could play the guitar. I talked him into teaching me, and I've been playin' it ever since."

"This is by a fella named Bach," Dusty said. "Never learned the name of the piece though," he added.

Dusty began playing and when he was finished Tom complimented him on it. "Beautiful," he said. "And the piece you just played is called *Prelude in D*."

"Damn, I'll have to remember that," Dusty said.

Dusty played a few more songs, then Clay and Maria crawled into the chuck wagon to go to bed. Dusty put away his guitar and threw out his bedroll close to the fire which, though the flames had died down, still retained much of its heat.

Mo and Dalton stayed up talking, long into the night.

"What was it like growing up in an orphanage?" Dalton asked.

"It wasn't just any orphanage," Mo said. "It was an orphanage run by nuns."

"Did you like it?"

"I liked having a place to sleep and food to eat," Mo said. "And I reckon I got more of an education than lots of folks do. But I wasn't that keen on all the praying and Bible reading." Mo chuckled. "I'll bet I know the

Bible better than most preachers."

"Did you ever think of becoming a preacher?"

"Sister Mary Katherine wanted me to become a priest," Mo said.

"Why didn't you?"

"I like drinking, and I like women," Mo said. "Also I never quite got a handle on that turn your other cheek thing. No thank you. I got turned out of the orphanage when I was sixteen, and I've been on my own ever since. And I like it that way."

"Where did you learn to shoot like you do?"

"It was just something I wanted to do," Mo said. "So I practiced a lot. Anybody can get good with practice."

"I've been practicing too," Dalton said. "But I'm not near as good as you are."

"It'll come," Mo said. "Just keep practicing. It'll come."

"I've never been to Dodge City," Dalton said. "They say it's a wild town."

"Oh, it's wild all right," Mo agreed. "But it's the most fun town I've ever been in. I tell you what. When we get to Dodge, you stick with me. I'll show you the town and we'll have us a fine old time."

"Mo?"

"Yeah?"

"You ever wonder who your Ma and Pa is?"

"No."

"Why not?"

"Whoever they was, they didn't care enough about me to keep me, so why should I worry any about them?"

"But don't you ever wish you had a family?"

"I got a family," Mo said. "Clay, Dusty, all the other hands at the ranch. Even you. You're all the family I need."

"I don't have any brothers," Dalton said. "You can be my brother."

"I already am," Mo said.

Dodge City, November 18
Dodge City had holding pens and feeder lots sufficient for 30,000 head of cattle, so Duff, Smoke, and the others had no difficulty in finding accommodations for their herd once they arrived. The last telegram Duff had received from Big Ben said that Clay Ramsey would meet him at the Dodge House.

Duff didn't have to go to the Dodge House because, even as the four trains were off-loading the cattle, a man walked up to him. He had brown hair, a well-trimmed moustache, and blue eyes. About five feet ten, he was thin, but Duff knew better than to mistake his slender form for weakness.

"Would these cattle be bound for the Live Oaks Ranch in Texas?" the man asked.

"Aye, they would be," Duff replied. He stuck out his hand. "I'm Duff MacCallister. You would be Clay Ramsey?"

Clay took Duff's hand. "I am, yes, sir."

Duff waved at Smoke, Matt, and Falcon. "I want you to meet the men who are with me. This is Smoke Jensen, Matt Jensen, and Falcon MacCallister."

As Duff introduced the others, Clay's eyes widened noticeably. "My God," Clay said. "I never thought I would meet any one of you, and now, all three together? I have heard about you — I have read about you. This is quite an honor."

"Don't believe all you read, Mr. Ramsey," Smoke said.

"If I can believe only one tenth of what I have read, I am still honored to meet such genuine American heroes," Clay replied.

"How is Big Ben doing?" Smoke asked. "It's been several years since I've seen him."

"Still big," Clay said, "somewhat ornery, and still honest."

"Honesty is accolade enough for anyone," Smoke said.

Clay glanced toward the holding pen,

which was filling with the introduction of the cattle. "So it's true, Black Angus really don't have horns," he said.

"Nothing to write home about," Smoke said. "Certainly nothing like the magnificent rack Longhorns have."

"They look a lot bigger."

"They are. They'll weigh in anywhere from two to five hundred pounds more than a Longhorn," Smoke said.

"How soon can we start south with them?" he asked.

"We discussed that," Smoke said. "And seeing as these are about to become your beeves, and seeing as you know the area, I reckon that makes you the trail boss. So I figure when we start south is up to you."

"I appreciate the confidence," Clay said. "All right, if I'm to be the trail boss, I would like to start back tomorrow. That is, if you think you and the cows are up to it. If possible, I would like to get back to Live Oaks before Christmas."

"Yes," Duff said. "I believe Big Ben said something about inviting us to a Christmas celebration."

"I'm sure he did. Big Ben has always done Christmas up big. I think you will have a good time."

"We'll be looking forward to it," Matt said.

"Oh, by the way, I should tell you that my wife, Maria, is with us. She signed on to cook for us. I hope you don't have some superstition or something about having a woman on a trail drive."

"I'd be in a fine pickle if I did," Smoke said. "My wife, Sally, is with us."

Clay smiled, broadly. "Really? Why, that's wonderful. Maria will enjoy having another woman along."

"I believe Mr. Conyers said you would have some other drovers with you," Smoke said. "Is that true?"

"Yes, I have four men with me, in addition to my wife."

"Good," Smoke said. "Your four drovers, plus you, make five. We four, plus Sally, make five, so that gives us ten drovers, plus your wife as a cook. I don't think we will have any problem in moving this herd down to Texas. Where would be the best place to take supper, do you think?"

"I imagine it would be the Dodge House," Clay replied.

"Well then, how about you and your men join us for dinner tonight?" Smoke suggested.

"Maria and I would be glad to join you," Clay said. "And I suspect one of my men, an older fella named Dusty, would join us as well. We can invite Tom, Mo, and Dalton, but they have already stated their intention to take in the town."

"Smoke, if you don't mind," Matt said. "I think I'd like to look those fellas up and see the town with them."

"Don't mind at all," Smoke replied.

"I tell you what, Matt," Clay said. "If you'll come with me now, I'll introduce you to them. It will keep you from having to look them up on your own."

"Thanks," Matt said. "I would appreciate that."

With the chuck and hoodlum wagons parked at the wagon park and the horses stabled, the Live Oaks outfit had checked in at the Dodge House. Tom took a room with Dusty, while Mo and Dalton shared another room. Dusty was up in the room taking a nap for, as he said, "When you are cowboyin', you never pass up a chance to get some sleep."

But Tom decided that he wanted to "see the town" with Mo and Dalton, so he was waiting in the lobby for them to come down. As he was waiting, he picked up a copy of the *Dodge City Times* and began to peruse it while waiting for his two young friends to join him.

He was immediately drawn to a story at the top of the page, in the second column from the left.

A SHOOTING INCIDENT.

Last Monday afternoon, one of those little episodes which serve to vary the monotony of frontier existence occurred at the Lucky Chance Saloon. Bob Shaw, the man who started the amusement, accused Frank Lovejoy of having acquired three aces in a game of poker by means other than the luck of the draw. Mr. Lovejoy, our readers will remember, recently dispatched two soldiers from Fort Dodge when they leveled the same accusation. In the case of the shooting of the soldiers, Mr. Lovejoy accorded the soldiers the opportunity to withdraw their pistols from their holsters before opening the ball, the engagement ending in the death of both soldiers.

In the more recent encounter with Bob Shaw, somebody, perhaps in an attempt to prevent further bloodshed, started out in search of a Deputy City Marshal, and finding him, hurried him to the scene of the impending conflict.

When the deputy arrived, he observed

Shaw near the bar with a huge pistol in his hand and a hogshead of blood in his eye, ready to relieve Frank Lovejoy of his existence in this world and send him to those shades where troubles come not, and six-shooters are unknown. Not wishing to hurt Shaw, but anxious to quiet matters and quell the disturbance, the marshal ordered him to give up his gun. Shaw refused to deliver and told the deputy to keep away from him. The deputy then gently tapped belligerent Shaw upon the head with his shooting iron, merely to convince him of the vanities of this frail world. The aforesaid reminder upon the head, however, failed to have the desired effect, and, instead of dropping, as any man of fine sensibilities would have done, Shaw turned his battery upon the officer and let him have it in the right breast. The ball, striking a rib and passing around, came out under the right shoulder blade, paralyzing his right arm so that it was useless, so far as handling a gun was concerned. The deputy fell, and Mr. Lovejoy, perhaps moved by the affront of an attack upon an officer of the law, discharged his pistol, which until that moment had remained in his holster, in the direction of Shaw. The ball, thus energized, struck Shaw with devastating effect, as he quickly expired from the wound.

"Hello, Tom," Mo said, coming into the lobby just as Tom finished reading the newspaper article. "Are you ready to show our young friend here a good time?"

Tom chuckled. "I'm not sure what my position will be here," he said. "I don't know if I am to have a good time with the two of you, or keep you from having such a good time that you get into trouble."

"We aren't looking to get into trouble," Mo said. "But lots of times when you are looking to have fun, well trouble just seems to have a way of finding you."

"That's what I'm afraid of," Tom said.

"There's Clay," Mo said. "I wonder who those people are who are with him . . ."

Clay Ramsey, who had just come into the hotel with four other men, saw Tom, Mo, and Dalton, and he held up his hand.

"Just a minute," he called to them. "I want you to meet these men. They are the ones delivered the herd to us, and they'll be making the drive south with us."

Clay introduced them and there were greetings all around.

"Where is Dusty?" Clay asked.

"He's up in the room asleep," Tom answered. "He said he would join you for dinner, but until then he is going to get as much sleep as he can."

Clay laughed. "He is smarter than all of us," he said. "Tom, how about telling him we are going to dinner now? Oh, and you boys are invited as well."

"We don't need to eat," Mo interrupted quickly. "We can always get pickled pigs' feet and boiled eggs at just about any bar."

"You will still have time to visit the saloons," Smoke said. "But this is a dinner you don't want to miss."

"What's so special about it?" Mo asked.

"We'll be having Angus beef," Smoke said. "We thought you might want to get a taste of what you will be working with."

At dinner, the chef rolled a table on wheels up to the dining table. On the table was a huge piece of beef, its enticing aroma getting the attention of everyone in the dining room.

"Ladies and gentlemen," Duff said. "This is the top blade roast. I believe that you will find it quite tasty."

The chef carved the meat, then served generous portions to all. Smoke, Falcon, Matt, Tom, and Mo asked for seconds.

"Mo, aren't you the one who said that you

could eat pigs' feet and such?" Clay teased.

"Yeah, well, I didn't know we were going to be eating anything this good. You sure this is beef? I've never tasted beef like this before."

" 'Tis Angus beef you are eating," Duff said. "There's no finer beef anywhere in the world."

"Pa's goin' to be pleased with this, that's for sure," Dalton said.

Desert was hot apple pie, topped off by a slice of melted cheese. When the bite was eaten, Mo pushed away from the table.

"I've really enjoyed the supper," he said. "I don't know as I have ever eaten this good, but this is our first night in Dodge, and I don't aim to waste it. So if you good folks will excuse me, I'm going take in some of the sights. Tom, Dalton? You fellas comin' with me."

"I am," Dalton said.

"I'll come as well," Tom said.

"Would you mind if I came along?" Matt asked.

"We don't mind at all," Tom said. "You are very welcome to come."

"Thanks, Tom," Matt said.

CHAPTER THIRTEEN

As Matt, Tom, Mo, and Dalton left the restaurant to take in the sights of the town, Duff, Falcon, Smoke and Sally, and Clay and Maria continued to visit over coffee around the dining table.

"I hope they do not get into any trouble," Maria said. "Dalton is . . ."

"The boss's son," Clay interrupted.

"*Sí*. But he is also — how do you say — *persona enredadora?*"

"Mischief maker," Clay translated for her.

"*Sí*, mischief maker. Evil, no. Mischief, yes."

"Don't worry about it," Clay said. "Tom will look out for him."

"Tell me," Dusty asked. "How is it that you fellas managed to avoid the great freeze and die-out?"

"I didn't avoid it," Smoke said. "Like all the other ranchers around me, I lost a lot of cows. That's why I'm running Angus now. I had to replace my herd anyway, so I figured, why not? I knew that Duff was running Black Angus and had avoided the freeze out, so I got in contact with him and I did the same thing that Big Ben is doing now. I got some cows from Duff."

"What kept you from freezing out?" Clay asked.

"My ranch, Sky Meadow, is in the Chugwater Valley," Duff explained. "I am surrounded by mountain ranges that protect me from the worst of winter's blows. I was very fortunate. While everyone else was losing cattle, my herd was increasing."

"Why did Big Ben decide to get into Angus?" Smoke asked. "I know there was no big freeze-out down in Texas."

"To tell you the truth, I don't know how he got interested in Angus. After the price on Longhorns crashed, I thought for sure he would switch over to Herefords as all the ranchers are. But he's been reading a lot about them lately," Clay said. "And I wouldn't be surprised if he chose Angus because he would be the only one in Tarrant County raising them. Big Ben is nothing if he is not a trailblazer."

All the time they had been talking, Falcon had been studying Dusty McNally.

"Dusty McNally," Falcon finally said.

"Haven't you and I met before?"

"You've got a good memory," Dusty said. "Easy enough for me to remember you, you're a famous man and you don't forget meeting famous men. But I'm not famous, so I don't know how it is that you remember me."

"It was in Tombstone, wasn't it?"

Dusty smiled. "Yes, sir, it was."

"It was outside the Bird Cage Theater. As I recall, you put a load of buckshot into the belly of a man by the name of Otis Jefferson, as Jefferson was about to shoot me in the back."

Dusty smiled. "Yes, sir, I did do that," he said.

"It's not hard to remember someone who once saved your life," Falcon said. "I'm glad that you will be with us."

The men continued their discussion over cigars, and in order to avoid the cigar smoke, Sally and Maria excused themselves. They walked out into the lobby, then found two large overstuffed chairs in front of the fireplace.

"Oh, I'm glad you suggested we leave," Maria said. "The cigar smoke was beginning to make me nauseous."

"Is that the only thing that was making

289

you nauseous?" Sally asked.

"What do you mean?"

Sally smiled, and leaned a bit closer to Maria. "Maria, are you pregnant?"

"Why do you ask that?" Maria asked, anxiously.

"Let's just say that it is something I suspect, woman to woman. No, let me adjust that. It isn't something I suspect, it is something I know. You are pregnant, aren't you?"

Maria blushed, then looked around. "Yes," she said. "But Clay and I have told no one."

"When are you due?"

"In January, I think."

"You are due in January, and you came on this drive? Maria, have you ever been on a cattle drive before? They are not easy. I find it hard to believe that Clay would let you come along, this close to delivery."

"I begged him to bring me," Maria said. "I did not want to take the chance of having this baby at home without him there. He thinks the baby is not due until February. Please do not tell him otherwise."

"Maria, I know you are young and this is all very frightening to you," Sally said. "But it was a very foolish thing for you to do. You have no business being here."

"Perhaps you are right," Maria replied.

"Yes, I am sure you are right. So, I will go back home now. I will leave tomorrow."

Sally laughed. "You've got it all worked out, haven't you?"

"Si, Senora," Maria said.

"I believe Clay said you had come along to cook," Sally said.

"Si. I cook and I drive the chuck wagon."

"Then this is what we will do. On the way down to Texas I will drive the chuck wagon and I will cook," Sally offered.

"Please, I do want to pull my own weight," Maria said.

"As long as the weight you pull does no harm to you or the baby," Sally promised.

"You are a good woman, Senora Jensen."

"My name is Sally."

"You are a good woman, Sally," Maria corrected with a broad smile.

"And we won't tell anyone else that you are pregnant," Sally said. "But Maria, you must promise me, at the first pain, at the very first sign of trouble of any kind, you will tell me immediately."

"I will."

"Is that a promise?"

"Si, Sally, it is a promise."

Rebecca had intended to return to Fort Worth right after Janie died, but when she came to tell Oscar, he was so inconsolable with grief that she decided she would stay just a little longer. And because she was still in Dodge, she was still working at the Lucky Chance Saloon.

Tonight, she was walking through the saloon, stopping at the various tables to chat with the customers.

"Becca, I want you to know how sorry all of us are about your Mama dying," one of the customers said. "She was a good woman."

Rebecca put her hand on the customer's shoulder. "Thank you, Lonnie," she said. "I appreciate that."

Other customers were expressing their own condolences from time to time, but Rebecca, knowing that she had to change the mood — for Oscar if for no other reason — began smiling and joking with the customers until soon the mood had lifted.

Frank Lovejoy was at one of the tables, and as Rebecca stepped up to that table, smiling at the men there, Lovejoy unexpectedly stuck his hand up under her skirt then reached all the way up to grab her by the backside.

"You're right, Doyle," Lovejoy said. "It does feel just like Asa's bald head."

Doyle and the other men at the table

laughed.

"Stop that!" Rebecca said loudly, stepping away from the table as quickly as she could.

"Look who is getting all huffy now," Lovejoy said.

"Mr. Lovejoy, you got no right grabbing her like that," Candy said. "She's not like the rest of us."

"The hell she ain't. Ever' body knows it's only going to be a matter of time until she starts whorin' just like her mama did," Lovejoy said. He looked back at Rebecca. "Honey, if you'd let ole' Frank be first, I could show you what it's supposed to be like."

"Hell, Frank," Doyle said. "What makes you think you would be first?"

Again the men at the table laughed.

With her cheeks burning, Rebecca retreated to the bar and she stood there with her back to the bar, looking at the table where Lovejoy and the others were engaged in animated conversation interspersed with ribald laughter.

"Are you all right?" Stan asked. Stan was the bartender.

"I can't believe he would do something like that and not one person at that table would say a thing to him," Rebecca said.

"Why, Miss Becca, I'm sure you know

how it is. All those men work out at Back Trail for Frank's father. They aren't going to say anything against him. Too bad Frank isn't more like his brother."

"I don't care if his father has all the money in the world, that doesn't give him the right to act like a lout. Well, I just won't make the mistake of going near him again."

"Miss Becca," Lonnie called. "How about if you come over here and play a game of poker with us."

"All right," she said. "But no crying if I win."

There were sixteen saloons in Dodge City, and because Mo and Dalton had announced their intention to visit every one of them, Matt and Tom had no choice but to follow along. The two older men were being very restrained with their drinking, but Mo and Dalton were not, and by the time they stepped into the Lucky Chance, which was only their fifth saloon of the night, Mo and Dalton were already unsteady on their feet.

"Whoa, hold it there, partner," Matt said, reaching out to grab hold of Dalton to keep him from falling when they pushed in through the bat-wing doors.

"This is the first time I've ever been durnk," Dalton said.

"Durnk?" Mo said, and he laughed. "Are you durnk?"

"I guess I am a little," Dalton said. "You won't tell Pa I got durnk — uh — drunk, will you?" Dalton laughed. "I said durnk, didn't I? I said durnk and I meant to say . . . ," Dalton stopped in mid-sentence and stared at one of the tables in the middle of the room. It wasn't the table that got his attention as much as it was the woman sitting at the table.

"What the hell?" Dalton asked. He started across the room toward the table.

"What is it?" Matt asked. "What has he seen?"

"It isn't what, it's who," Tom said.

Tom watched as Dalton approached Rebecca. He could not have been more shocked if he had seen his own mother sitting at that table. What was Rebecca doing here? He knew that she had run away from home to avoid him. But was becoming a prostitute in a place like this really the answer?

He had never heard the exact reason why Rebecca left, he knew only that it had come on the same night that he had told her that he couldn't love her. What an idiot he had been not to have accepted the love she had so innocently given. He did love her, he loved her as he thought he would never be able to love anyone again after Martha, but he had spurned her. Had he driven her to this? Even in the gaudy dress she was wearing now, she was beautiful. But what had she done to her hair? It was much shorter than he remembered.

Tom stepped up to the bar and ordered a whiskey, whereas at the other saloons he had been drinking only beer.

"Who is that woman?" Matt asked. "What's this all about?"

"That woman is his sister," Tom said as he tossed the whiskey down.

"Rebecca!" Dalton said, shouting the word so loudly that it stopped most of the other conversation in the saloon.

Recognizing Dalton's voice, Rebecca gasped, then turned around. "Dalton! What are you doing here?"

"I might ask you the same thing," Dalton replied.

"Please, Dalton, it's not what you think," Rebecca said.

"It's not what I think? What am I supposed to think when I see my sister in a place like this — dressed," he held his hand out then made a dismissive move with it, "like you are dressed."

"Sonny, you need to go on about your

296

business and let her be," Lovejoy said, standing then. "Your sister is a whore, and she don't need your interference."

"I am *not* a whore!" Rebecca said, resolutely.

Lovejoy walked over to Rebecca and put his arm around her, pulling her up against his side as he faced Dalton. "Go on, Sonny. Can't you see you aren't wanted here?" Lovejoy asked.

"Let me go!" Rebecca said, twisting away from him. Lovejoy reached for her again, but this time Dalton stepped up to him and pushed him away.

"Leave my sister alone!" he said.

"Well, now," Lovejoy said. He smiled, but rather than displaying joy or humor, the smile merely stretched his lips and tightened the skin on his face so that it looked just like the skull, in the black "Jolly Roger" flag that pirates once flew.

"You've sort of moved this one up a peg or two, haven't you, sonny? If you had just gone on and minded your own business like I told you to, nothing more would have happened. But that wasn't good enough for you, was it? Well, I see that you are wearing a gun. How about we settle this now? Draw."

"What?" Dalton asked. "Are you crazy? What do you mean, draw? I'm not getting

297

into a gunfight with you."

"You already have, and I'm goin' to kill you for it," Lovejoy said. "Draw."

"If you want my friend you're going to have to come through me!" Mo shouted.

Without another word, or even the hint that he had heard Mo, Lovejoy drew his pistol. Mo was quick, and he prided himself on his fast draw and marksmanship, but his reflexes had been greatly slowed by the whiskey, and he hadn't expected Lovejoy to draw against him without the slightest recognition. By the time he realized Lovejoy was drawing, it was too late. To Mo it looked as if his pistol had just magically appeared in his hand. Mo managed to draw his pistol, but not fast enough. Reflexively, he pulled the trigger on his own pistol, firing a slug into the floor, even as he was falling face down.

"Mo!" Dalton and Rebecca yelled at the same time. Dalton started toward his fallen friend, but Lovejoy called out to him.

"Hold it right there, Sonny," Lovejoy said. His pistol was back in his holster. "Your friend had his chance."

"He wasn't just my friend," Dalton said with tears streaming down his face. "He was my brother."

"Yeah? Well, then when you get to hell,

you can tell him that Frank Lovejoy said hello. 'Cause now it's your turn."

Rebecca stepped in front of Dalton and held her arms out, facing Lovejoy.

"If you shoot him, you are going to have to shoot me first," she said.

"Well, hell, honey. Shootin' you ain't goin' to be all that hard to do. It's not like if I don't shoot you, you are goin' to warm my bed. You've already let me know how you feel. But me and your brother have some unfinished business, so either you step out of the way, or I'll come through you to get to him."

Tom started toward Lovejoy, but Matt reached out toward him and pulled him back.

"No, Tom, wait," Matt said.

"I'm not going to just stand here and watch him kill the woman I love," Tom said with quiet anger.

Matt reached down and snatched Tom's pistol from its holster.

"What are you doing?" Tom asked, angrily.

"Let me take care of this," Matt said. "I expect I've had more experience."

"I'm not going to tell you again, Becca. Get out of the way," Lovejoy said.

"Lovejoy!" Matt called.

"Who the hell are you?" Lovejoy asked.

"Let's say I'm a friend to the boy," Matt said. "And I was a friend to the man you killed."

"And so now, like the avenging angel, you want to take me on," Lovejoy said. "Is that it?"

"Something like that," Matt said.

Lovejoy didn't call the move. Instead, just as he had done with Mo, he made a lightning draw. Only now, by the time Lovejoy's pistol cleared the holster, Matt's gun was already in his hand, and a little finger of flame erupted from the end of the barrel.

Matt's bullet hit Lovejoy in the heart, giving him just enough time before he died to register his shock over having been beaten in a gunfight by a simple cowboy.

Lovejoy wasn't the only one awestruck. Nearly everyone in the saloon had seen Lovejoy in action before. They were convinced that there was no one alive who could beat him, and yet they had just seen it done.

Before the smoke cleared, Sheriff Hamilton Bell was pushing through the front door with pistol in hand. Seeing two men lying on the floor, one of them Lovejoy, he used the barrel of his pistol to push his hat back on his head.

"What happened here?" he asked.

Everyone began to talk and shout at once.

"Hold it, hold it!" Bell said. "One at a time." He pointed to Rebecca. "Becca, did you see this?"

"Yes," Rebecca said in a small, choked voice.

"Tell me what happened."

Rebecca described the events in detail, then Bell looked over at Matt and Dalton.

"What's your name, Mister?"

"Jensen. Matt Jensen."

"I'll be damn. I've heard of you, Mr. Jensen. I reckon if there was anyone who could beat Lovejoy in a fair fight, it would be you. And I've never heard anything that would make me think any the worse of you, so I'm inclined to believe the young lady's report. But just to keep things on the up and up, I'd like to hold a hearing tomorrow morning. Can I have your word that you will be there?"

"I'll be there," Matt promised.

During the entire conversation among the deputy, the witnesses, and the man who had actually shot Frank Lovejoy, Rebecca had been aware of Tom's eyes on her. What did she see in those eyes? Hurt? Anger? Hate? For a moment she was confused by his reaction, then in a moment of clarity she knew exactly what it was.

Frank Lovejoy had called her a whore, and being here, in this place, dressed as she was, interacting with the customers, how could it appear any other way? Rebecca's eyes filled with tears, and she turned her face away. How could this have happened? How? She saw Dalton standing over Mo's body, looking down at him, and saw that, like her, he was crying. And she knew at that moment that she was responsible for Mo's death!

Oh, God help me, the thought. How did I get myself into such a mess?

"Dalton, I'm sorry about Mo," she said. "I'm so sorry."

"Mo was my best friend," Dalton said.

"I know he was, sweetheart. And, it's my fault that he is dead. It is all my fault."

Rebecca was sure that Dalton was going to turn on her, and he had every right to do so. But he didn't.

"Don't be ridiculous, it wasn't your fault," Dalton said. "It just — it just happened, that's all."

"How did you find me? How did you know I was here?"

Dalton shook his head. "I didn't know you were here. We came here to buy a herd of special cattle, and when we came into the saloon, here you were."

"Yes," Rebecca said. "Here I am."

"Come on, sis, we're getting out of here," Dalton said.

"No," Rebecca said, shaking her head.

"Rebecca, I'm not taking no for an answer," Dalton said, showing more maturity and strength than she had ever seen him exhibit before.

"Dalton, I . . ."

"Clay and Dusty are here. So is Maria. You are coming with us," Dalton said.

Rebecca knew that Dalton was right, and she knew, too, that more than anything she wanted to leave this place, once and for all.

She looked over at Tom again, but this time he looked away.

The Dodge House
Clay and the others, having finished dinner, were now sitting in the lobby near the big fireplace, enjoying the warmth as they continued the conversations they had started in the dining room. Dusty is the one who saw her first.

"I'll be damned," Dusty said. Then, with a quick nod of his head to Maria and Sally, he apologized. "Excuse the language, ladies, but I never expected to see her here."

"Who?" Clay asked, turning in his seat to look toward the front door. He saw Tom, Dalton, Matt, and Rebecca coming in. He was so surprised to see Rebecca that he didn't even notice, right away, that Mo wasn't with them.

"Rebecca!" Clay said, standing as she came toward them. The other men stood as well. That was when they noticed that Rebecca was crying. Dalton's eyes were also red. Seeing both of them crying preempted what would normally have been a question as to what she was doing here in Dodge City.

"What's wrong?" he asked. "Why are you crying?"

"It's Mo," Rebecca replied in a choked voice.

"Mo?" Clay noticed then that Mo was not with them. "What about Mo? Where is he?"

"Mo is dead, Clay," Tom said. "He was killed by a man named Frank Lovejoy."

"Lovejoy? Wait, I've heard that name. He's a big rancher up here, isn't he?"

"Yes," Dusty said. "We had a run-in with him a couple of years ago, if you remember. He wasn't going to let any Texas cows come into Dodge because of the Texas fever, even though there weren't any cases that year."

"It wasn't him, it was his son," Rebecca said.

"Well where is Lovejoy now? Has he been arrested?"

"Better than that," Dalton said. "He's been killed. Matt killed him."

"Are you in trouble, Matt?" Smoke asked.

"Not exactly," Matt replied.

"What do you mean, not exactly?"

"The sheriff does want to hold a hearing tomorrow. I promised him I would be there."

"It's all right," Dalton said. "Lovejoy drew first, and everyone in the saloon saw it."

"What happened?" Clay asked. "What I mean is, how did this fracas get started in the first place?"

"It was all my fault," Rebecca said. "Lovejoy tried to force himself on me, Dalton pushed him away, and Lovejoy started demanding that Dalton draw his gun. When he saw what was happening, Mo came over and Lovejoy drew on him and shot him without so much as a fare-thee-well."

"Where is Mo, now?"

"The undertaker called for him," Tom said.

"I expect I had better get my coat on, then go down there and make the arrangements," Clay said.

"Clay?" Rebecca said, calling to Clay as he started toward the stairs to go up to his room.

Clay stopped and turned toward her.

"I would like to go back home with you," she said.

"Yes, ma'am," Clay said. "I expect your Pa is going to be real pleased about that."

"Rebecca," Maria said, going to her and embracing her. "Let me introduce you to a good friend."

Maria introduced Rebecca to Sally Jensen, and then to Smoke, Falcon, and Duff.

As Dalton began to elaborate on the events of the night to Clay, Dusty, Smoke, Falcon, and Duff, Tom leaned up against the marble fireplace with his arms folded across his chest.

He watched Rebecca as she conversed easily with Maria and the others, trying to get out of his mind the thought of that beautiful body pressed up against his.

And how many others, since she came up here?

Back Trail Ranch, Ford County, Kansas
"Boss? Boss?" Doyle was in Seth Lovejoy's bedroom, shaking him awake.

Lovejoy woke up, and startled to see Doyle in his bedroom, sat up quickly.

"What the hell? What are you doing in my bedroom?"

"Sorry, Boss, but I got some bad news for you."

"Bad news? What kind of bad news?"

"Maybe you better come outside. We've got him lyin' on your front porch."

"You've got who lying on my front porch?"

"Frank, Mr. Lovejoy. He got hisself shot tonight. He's dead."

Still in his nightgown, Lovejoy pulled on his boots, then put on his coat and hurried out onto the front porch. Frank was lying on the porch. Someone had folded his arms across his chest.

"The undertaker wanted him, but we figured you'd rather see him first," Doyle said.

"What happened?" Seth asked in a choked voice.

"It was some cowboy by the name of Matt Jensen," Doyle said. "Ain't none of us ever seen him before. He drawed on Frank and kilt him when Frank wasn't expecting it."

"Where is Jensen now?"

"I don't know exactly where he is now, but tomorrow mornin', Sheriff Bell is holdin' a hearing, and this fella Jensen promised the sheriff that he will be there then."

"I want you to make sure that we have that hearing packed with people who will tell the same story you just told me."

"Yes, sir, well, ever'one who was sittin' at

307

the table with us will tell that story," Doyle said. "We've done discussed it."

"What about anyone else in the saloon?"

Doyle cleared his throat. "Well, sir, here's the thing. It could be that the others didn't see it exactly like we seen it."

"It doesn't matter," Seth Lovejoy said. "We need to make sure that our story is told. Morrell?"

"Yeah, Boss?"

"I want you to go back in town, and take at least ten men with you. You'll find all the building materials you need at my building and lumber store. I want you to build something for me, tonight."

"Tonight?"

"Yes, tonight. It has to be finished before the hearing starts tomorrow."

"All right, what do you want built?"

"I'll tell you when you have your men together," Lovejoy said.

The Dodge House

"I know you are planning on starting the drive tomorrow," Matt said. "So you can go ahead if you want to. If I get through this hearing all right, I'll catch up with you."

"We won't be going tomorrow because we need to see to burying Mo. Also, I need to send a telegram to Big Ben to tell him what happened. But, what do you mean if you get through the hearing all right?" Clay asked. "You said the sheriff believed you, didn't you? And didn't all the others in the saloon back you up?"

"Yes," Matt said.

"Don't worry, Matt. We aren't going to leave until this is resolved."

CHAPTER FOURTEEN

When the town of Dodge City awakened the next morning, they were startled to see a fully erected hangman's gallows out on Front Street, right in front of Lovejoy's Building and Lumber Company. There was also a professionally painted sign, sitting on an A-frame in front of the gallows.

**PUBLIC
HANGING
ON THESE GALLOWS
OF MATT JENSEN
THE MAN WHO KILLED
MY SON
FRANK LOVEJOY**

"Look at that!" Dusty said he and everyone else from the cattle drive came out of the hotel the next morning. "I thought this wasn't supposed to be anything but a hearing. Looks like they are ready to hang him."

"I wouldn't read too much into it," Tom said.

"What do you mean? If the town has already built a gallows, they mean to hang him," Dusty said.

Tom pointed to the sign on the store behind the gallows.

DODGE CITY BUILDING AND LUMBER
Seth Lovejoy, *Proprietor*

"I expect Mr. Lovejoy had that built in front of his own property in order to make the others in town think that Matt is guilty."

Everyone from the upcoming cattle drive, Clay, Maria, Dusty, Tom, Dalton, Smoke, Sally, Falcon and Duff were present for the hearing, which was held in the Ford County Courthouse, Judge Anthony Blanton presiding. There was no jury, as this was an inquest only, but the gallery was filled with both witnesses and the curious. And because this was an inquest only, there were no lawyers for the defense. There was, however, a prosecuting attorney who was representing the State of Kansas, and he handled the interrogation.

The first person to testify was Sheriff Bell. Bell testified what had been reported to him

311

by many of the eyewitnesses in the saloon.

"Sheriff Bell," the prosecutor said. "Several weeks ago there was a shooting incident in which Frank Lovejoy killed two men. Do you recall that incident?"

"Yes, of course I recall it," Sheriff Bell said.

"Why is it that Frank Lovejoy wasn't put in jail for that shooting?"

"Because there were enough witnesses who testified that it was a fair fight," Sheriff Bell said.

"In fact, it was more than fair, wasn't it?" the prosecutor continued.

"What do you mean?"

"Is it not true, Sheriff, that Lovejoy allowed the two men to hold the pistols in their hand, telling them they could shoot as soon as they saw him start his own draw?"

"That is true."

"And what was the result of that experiment?"

"Lovejoy killed both of them."

"That being the case, is it reasonable to assume that in a fair fight, another skilled gunman, even someone as skilled as Mr. Matt Jensen obviously is, could beat Lovejoy? And not only beat him, but shoot him before he could even get off one shot?"

"It doesn't seem reasonable, I admit,"

Sheriff Bell said. "But that is exactly what all the witnesses have reported."

"Not all the witnesses, as we shall soon see," the prosecutor said. "Witness is dismissed, Your Honor."

Rebecca was the next person to testify. She explained that she was Dalton's sister, and that while she and Dalton were involved in a family discussion, Frank Lovejoy interfered. She then told how Lovejoy had challenged Dalton to a gunfight, and then killed Moses Coffey when he tried to come to the boy's defense. He again threatened to kill Dalton, but Matt Jensen had stepped up.

"Frank Lovejoy drew first," Rebecca said. "But Mr. Jensen was faster."

Tom, and Dalton also testified in Matt's defense. Their testimonies mirrored Rebecca's, as did those of at least three other witnesses who had no connection to either party, other than being saloon patrons at the time.

Then Tom Whitman was called to testify. His testimony mirrored that of everyone else, but before he was excused, he asked the judge for permission to make an observation for *publici juris*.

Judge Blanton and the prosecutor both,

blinked in surprise at Tom's use of the Latin term.

"Are you a lawyer, Mr. Whitman?" the judge asked.

"No, Your Honor."

"But you wish to make a comment for the public right?"

"For the public's right to know, yes, Your Honor."

"Very well, what comment would you make?"

"Your Honor, with regard to Mr. Lovejoy shooting the two men who were already holding their weapons in their hands, I submit to the court, that rather than being fair with them, Lovejoy, in effect, murdered them."

There were immediate shouts and cries from the court.

"He done it! I seen it myself!" one man yelled. "Them two fellas already had their guns in their hands!"

"Were you a witness to that shooting, Mr. Whitman?" the prosecutor asked.

"No, Your Honor, I was not."

"Then how can you testify *publici juris* on something you know nothing about?"

"I said I did not witness the shooting. I didn't say I didn't know anything about it. But if what everyone who did see it says is

314

true, if Lovejoy told those men not to draw until they saw him start his draw, then I know that it was nothing short of murder."

Again there was a loud outbreak of protests and shouts of surprise from the gallery, and Judge Blanton had to still them with his gavel.

"May I explain?" Tom asked.

"Please do."

"In 1863, a man named Sigmund Exner began a series of experiments with something he calls 'reaction time.' Simply put, reaction time is how long it takes a person from the time their brain tells their muscles to do something, until they actually do it. And in something like drawing your pistol upon response to stimuli, that reaction time constitutes the longest period of time of the maneuver. He told the two men to draw *when they saw him start his draw.*" Tom emphasized that point.

"When Lovejoy started his draw, the longest part of the action, telling his hand to start the draw, had already been accomplished."

"That's preposterous," the prosecutor said.

"Your Honor, if I could have two pistols, and a holster, I could prove this," Tom said. "Empty pistols," he added quickly.

The gallery laughed, nervously.

"All right," the judge agreed. "And I'm doing this more as a matter of curiosity than a matter of law."

Tom strapped a holster on, then, after both pistols were certified as being empty, he put one in his holster, and handed the other one to the prosecutor.

"The witnesses said that the two men were holding their pistols down by their sides, right?"

"That is correct," the prosecutor said.

"Judge, Mr. Prosecutor, I am not a skilled gunman. In fact, I wouldn't even be willing to say that my skills are above average. So I'm going to give this demonstration, then allow the prosecutor to choose anyone from the gallery that he would like to do it a second time to validate this."

"All right, what exactly are you going to do?" Judge Blanton asked.

"The same thing Lovejoy did," Tom said. "I want the prosecutor to hold the pistol down by his side. When he sees me start my draw, I want him to raise his pistol up and pull the trigger."

"Ha!" the prosecutor said. "All right, Mr. Whitman, make a fool out of yourself."

Tom let his hand hover over the pistol, then quickly he drew it and pulled the trigger. He was able to do so before the prosecutor was able to raise his own gun and pull the trigger. The separation of the two snapping triggers was clearly obvious, and the gallery reacted in disbelief.

"Wait, I wasn't ready," the prosecutor protested.

"Shall we do it again?" Tom asked.

"Yes."

"Are you ready?"

"Yes."

Again Tom drew the pistol, and again he clearly beat the reaction time of the prosecutor.

"All right, all right, I want to see someone else do that," the prosecutor said, and he chose two men at random from the gallery. Once the experiment was set up, the man drawing from the holster won every time.

"Thank you, Mr. Whitman, for this — most interesting experiment," Judge Blanton said. "Now, may I ask how this contributes to the *publici juris*?"

"Because, Your Honor, the public has the right to know that Frank Lovejoy's quickness as a pistoleer cannot be validated by the example of his killing the two soldiers in the earlier incident."

"All right, Mr. Whitman, as I decide this, I will take the information you have so

317

pointedly demonstrated into consideration," Judge Blanton said.

"Your Honor, may we get on with the trial?" the prosecutor asked.

"Please do, Counselor," Judge Blanton said.

Marcus Doyle was the next witness. "I don't care what tricks this Whitman fella showed everyone," Doyle said with a sneer. " 'Cause it don't have nothin' to do with the fact that this man," he pointed toward Matt Jensen, "kilt Frank Lovejoy. The way this whore," he pointed to Rebecca, "and the other people been tellin' what happened, ain't what happened at all," Doyle said.

There was a gasp of reproach from most of the gallery, and Judge Blanton banged his gavel.

"Would the court reporter please strike the word whore?" Judge Blanton said. He pointed at Doyle. "Any further comments like that, Mr. Doyle, and I will find you in contempt of court. Do you understand me?"

"Yes, Your Honor."

"You may continue with your testimony."

"Well, sir, Frank was sittin' at the table with some of us riders from the Back Trail Ranch, when we seen what we thought was a fight between the boy there," he pointed to Dalton, "and the — uh — woman named Becca. And Frank, thinkin' the woman might be in danger, went over to help her. I mean that's all it was. Frank was just lookin' out for the girl. Next thing you know, why they was two men a'drawin' on him. Frank managed to kill one of them, but the other one, that one," he pointed to Matt, "kilt Frank."

"Let the record show that the witness pointed to Matt Jensen," the prosecutor said. "Please continue."

"Yes, sir, well, I ain't really got nothin' more to say," Doyle said. "Like I said, both of 'em drawed on Frank, but he was able to fight off only one of 'em."

The next two testimonies were so close, not only to Doyle's but to each other, that it was quickly obvious they had been rehearsed. In addition, they were all employees of Seth Lovejoy.

The last witness for the prosecution was a man named Emerson Morrell. "I don't care what kind of tricks this fella showed you, there wasn't nobody faster than Frank Lovejoy, and ever' one knew that. When this here Matt Jensen fella come up on Frank, he already had his gun in his hand. And there wasn't no waitin' for Frank to draw, like he was showin' us while ago. What he done was just commence shooting without so much as a fare-thee-well."

"Your Honor," Tom called out after the witness named Morrell had been excused. "May I speak?"

"You have already testified, Mr. Whitman," Judge Blanton said. *"Cadit Quaestio."*

"May I take extraordinary exception to the ruling of no further argument, Your Honor?" Tom said. "This man has just perjured himself."

"The fact that his testimony is in direct opposition to the testimony of others is a part of this trial," Judge Blanton said. "It may well be that Mr. Morrell saw things differently. That does not necessarily constitute perjury."

"Emerson Morrell has just testified that the gun was already in Mr. Jensen's hand when he approached Frank Lovejoy, and that Mr. Jensen opened fire without any warning. Mr. Morrell cannot testify to that fact, Your Honor, because he wasn't even in the saloon at the time of the incident."

"How many people were in the saloon at the time of the incident?" the prosecutor asked.

"Twenty-three, counting the bartender."

The prosecutor smiled sarcastically. "Twenty-three? Are you sure? Could it be twenty-two? Twenty-four?"

"Twenty-three," Tom insisted.

"All right, let's assume that there were twenty-three. With that many people there, could it not be possible that Mr. Morrell was there, but you just didn't see him?" the prosecutor asked.

"No. Morrell was not there."

"Mr. Whitman, are you saying that you know everyone who was there?"

"I don't know any of them by name," Tom replied. "But I know who was there and wasn't there."

The prosecutor stepped up to the judge and whispered something to him. The judge nodded affirmatively, then spoke.

"I would like for the entire gallery to leave the courtroom, please," he said.

With protests and grumbling, the gallery, assisted by Sheriff Bell and some of his deputies, left the courtroom. The only ones who remained were those who were directly involved with the proceedings. A moment later, the gallery returned.

"Now, Mr. Whitman, earlier you conducted an experiment for the court, and if you will allow me, I would like to conduct one myself," the prosecutor said. "As you just observed, the judge emptied the courtroom. It is full once more. I wonder if you could look out over the gallery and tell us if there is any difference in their composition."

A murmur of interest and anticipation spread through the gallery as Tom looked out over the men and women who were seated in the courtroom.

"That lady, second from the left in the second row was not here before," Tom said. "The man sitting next to her was here, but he was sitting on the extreme right of the third row." He continued to point. "That man was not here. Neither was he. She was, but was sitting in a different place. There are four people missing, who were here before but are not here now."

The prosecutor stared at Tom with his eyes and mouth open in shock. Then, when Tom was finished, the prosecutor shook his head in wonder, and looked up at the judge.

"Your Honor, Mr. Whitman is correct on every account," he said. "I have no further questions."

The judge did not even have to leave the bench to make his decision. "This court finds no cause to bring charges against Mr. Matt Jensen, and finds him innocent of any wrongdoing in the death of Frank Lovejoy. This hearing is adjourned."

The judge finished his announcement with the slap of his gavel.

■ ■ ■ ■

Later that afternoon, Rebecca found herself standing in Boot Hill Cemetery for the second time within the last two weeks. When Rebecca first saw Dalton and the others, she thought they had come to Dodge City just to find her. She had since learned that they came to Dodge to receive a herd of Black Angus cattle to be driven back to Live Oaks. She learned that from Dalton, who asked her to come to the burial. He was also the one who asked her to come back home.

Rebecca had no reason not to return home now. Her mother was dead, and it was obvious that whatever feelings Tom Whitman might have had for her were gone. He now believed that she had been working as a prostitute in the Lucky Chance, and she had not said anything to him that would disabuse him of that idea. At first, she was hurt that he would even believe such a thing. But as she thought about it, she decided it might be for the best. Her father was determined to prevent any relationship from developing between them, and this would just make it easier to follow her father's wishes.

As the funeral began, Dalton led Mo's

favorite horse, fully saddled, to the side of the grave. There was then, total silence, as the saddle was removed from the off-side, signifying that this horse would never again be ridden by the man whose saddle this was. The horse, almost as if it understood, lowered its head and nodded a few times. Then Dalton led the horse away, and Dusty stepped up beside the open grave. Dusty's father had been a preacher, and Dusty still carried his father's Bible. He opened the Bible to read a few words at Mo's interment.

"I am the resurrection and the life, saith the Lord: he that believeth in me, though he were dead, yet shall he live; and whosoever liveth and believeth in me shall never die.

"We brought nothing into this world, and it is certain we can carry nothing out. The Lord giveth, and the Lord taketh away; blessed be the name of the Lord."

Rebecca listened to Dusty read, and thought how much more comforting these verses were than those hateful words spoken by the Reverend T.J. Boyd at her mother's funeral.

Clay gave the eulogy.

"Mo was raised in an orphanage," Clay said. "He often told me that we were the only family he ever had. And we know that he believed that, from the bottom of his heart, because in defending Dalton, he gave his life for his brother. And now we, his brothers and sisters, are here to commit him to his final resting place." Clay opened his hand to show some dirt. "This is dirt that came from an extra saddlebag that has been lying in a corner of the hoodlum wagon. It is Texas dirt, and that means that even up here in Kansas, our brother Mo, will be buried in Texas soil." He opened his hand and let the dirt stream down onto Mo's coffin. "Be with God, brother."

As Mo's grave was being closed, Rebecca walked over to her mother's grave. There was still a mound of freshly turned dirt over it, not yet having settled. She looked at the tombstone.

JANIE JENSEN DAVENPORT

1846–1890

"A fallen flower has returned to the branch"

"I'm going back home, Mama," Rebecca said quietly. "But I will keep you in my heart, forever."

She stood there looking down at her mother's grave for a long moment, then she turned away. When she did, she saw Tom standing about twenty yards behind her.

"Tom!" she called.

Tom turned quickly, and walked away.

November 20

When Rebecca showed up at the holding pens on the day they were to depart Dodge, she saw the men moving through the holding pens, urging the cows through the long chutes to the open ground, where others were bunching them up into one large, manageable herd. Even as they did this, the leadership among the beeves was being established. Animals that had remained docile while in the pen now began to affirm their authority. The cowboys allowed them to do this because they knew that the herd would be led home, not by them, but by the leadership exhibited by the more assertive cattle.

One of the riders inside the pen pushing the cows out was Tom Whitman. Rebecca stared at him, trying to make eye contact, but he was either too busy to notice her, or he was purposely avoiding looking at her.

"You'll be driving the hoodlum wagon," Dalton said. "I drove it up here, but with Mo gone now, Clay is a man short, and there's no way you could actually ride herd."

Rebecca didn't tell Dalton that she had ridden as a cowboy with Walter Hannah's herd when they came up from the Rocking H Ranch. Along the way she had ridden point, swing, and drag. She had cut cows out of the herd, and she had run down cows who had gotten away.

"You aren't going to have any problem with driving the hoodlum wagon, are you?"

"No. No problem."

"Good. Maria and Mrs. Jensen are driving the chuck wagon, so you won't get lost or anything. All you have to do is follow along behind them."

Rebecca could have told Dalton that she made the trip up here as a cowboy on a cattle drive, and that she wasn't likely to get lost. But she held her tongue.

After settling accounts with the manager of the holding pens, the trail cattle were brought together into one herd, then pushed down to the bank of the Arkansas River. The stage of water in the Arkansas made it easily fordable, so Clay pushed them on across. There was also a bridge available and the bridge was utilized by the two wagons.

Once safely over the river, they made plans to camp at Crooked Creek, which was just about six miles south of the Arkansas. There, they would organize for the 450-mile drive that lay ahead of them.

"I am the foreman and trail boss," Clay said. "But I confess that this is new to me in that I haven't worked Angus cattle before. Duff, you've been around them for a long time. How do they trail?"

"We found out when we trailed down to Cheyenne from Sky Meadow that if you bell one of the leaders, we shouldn't have any trouble," Duff said. "And as long as we can keep that steer going in the right direction, the others will follow along behind."

"With Longhorns we could average about fifteen miles a day. How does that track with the Angus?"

"I think we'll have no trouble in doing that," Duff said.

"If we can do fifteen miles a day that would put us on track to be back home by the middle of December. But with winter coming on, we may not do that well. Still, I think that's what we should shoot for. I would like to be back home by Christmas."

Clay set the watch for the first night, and Sally and Maria served a delicious dinner of fried beef and potatoes.

After dinner, they all sat around the campfire, not only for the warmth but for the camaraderie. Duff played his bagpipes, which was a treat to Clay, Dusty, Dalton, and Maria, who had never heard pipes before. Rebecca had heard them, and enjoyed them immensely. Dusty played the guitar, then both he and Clay prevailed upon Tom to perform.

"What does Tom do?" Smoke asked.

"He calls 'em soliloquies," Dusty said. "They're words from plays, but not just any kind of words and not just any kinds of plays. They are the damndest words and plays you ever heard of, just like the ones in them high-falutin' plays that sometimes comes touring around."

"That ought to be right up your alley, Falcon," Smoke said. Then he went on to explain to the others that Falcon's brother and sister were New York actors.

"Oh, Tom, please do a soliloquy for us," Sally asked. "Do you know Puck's soliloquy from Midsummer Night's Dream? The one that begins, 'Thou speakest aright, I am that merry wanderer of the night'?"

"I know it," Tom said.

"When I was teaching school, the children used to love that one," Sally said. "Please, do it for us."

"Shall I stand and ham it up? Or sit here and just say it?" Tom asked.

"Oh, you must stand. Look at it this way. You aren't here on the barren plains of

Kansas," Falcon said. "You are on stage at the Booth Theater in New York. You wouldn't be sitting cross-legged there, would you?"

Tom smiled, stood up, cleared his throat, then struck a dramatic pose and extending his right arm, palm up, began to speak, rolling his R's and putting emphasis in just the right places.

Thou speakest aright
I am that merry wanderer of the night.
I jest to Oberon and make him smile
When I a fat and bean-fed horse beguile,
Neighing in likeness of a filly foal:
And sometime lurk I in a gossip's bowl,
In very likeness of a roasted crab,
And when she drinks, against her lips I
    bob
And on her wither'd dewlap pour the ale.
The wisest aunt, telling the saddest tale,
Sometime for three-foot stool mistaketh
    me;
Then slip I from her bum, down topples
    she,
And 'tailor' cries, and falls into a cough;
And then the whole quire hold their hips
    and laugh,
And waxen in their mirth and neeze and
    swear

A merrier hour was never wasted there.
But, room, fairy! here comes Oberon.

The others around the fire laughed and applauded. Tom took a good-natured and elaborate bow, smiling as he made eye contact with everyone there.

Including Rebecca.

Rebecca held Tom's eyes for a long moment before she broke away. What did she see in his eyes? Sadness over what might have been between them? Anger at her leaving? Condemnation over how he found her?

It was a long time before Rebecca went to sleep that night. Tom Whitman was less than twenty feet away. What would he do if she moved her bedroll over beside his? Would he welcome her? Would he turn away in disgust?

She lay tossing and turning, sleep evading her, until she heard a voice calling Tom's name.

"Tom. It's your watch."

There was no moon tonight, but there was a single lantern hanging from the elevated tongue of the hoodlum wagon. This served as a beacon for the night riders to find their way back to the camp. It also put out enough illumination to enable Rebecca to watch as Tom sat there pulling on his boots.

He reached for his coat and hat, then walked over to the remuda, pulled out his horse, saddled it, mounted, and rode away.

Tom had relieved Dusty, who was in bed by the time Tom rode out.

Rebecca had watched the interaction between Clay and Maria, and between Smoke and Sally. The love that they shared was obvious, not only in what they said to each other, but the way they touched, and the way they looked at each other.

She lay here in her bedroll, thinking about that as she listened to the soft lolling of the cattle, the sound of wind passing over the wagon, and the hooting of a nearby owl. Rebecca felt the tears welling in her eyes. Was she never to know such love?

She thought of her mother and Oscar. Janie had told her, in no uncertain terms, that she had reached the bottom, with no hope of a future beyond the ever descending rungs on the whore's ladder, from mistress, to brothel, to bargirl, to streetwalker.

"And then I met Oscar," her mother had told her. "I don't know how I happened to wind up in Dodge City, I could just as easily have gone to Denver, or Cheyenne, or San Francisco, or Phoenix. But I got off the train in Dodge City, and of the sixteen saloons here, the Lucky Chance was the first one I walked into. I worked for him for less than a month, then he asked me to marry him.

"I will confess to you, Becca, I married him just to get off the line. But he has been the most wonderful man, and I love him more than I can say. Love came late, but I am just thankful that I lived long enough to experience it."

Would love come to Rebecca?

CHAPTER FIFTEEN

The two night herders rode in a circle about twenty yards outside the sleeping cattle, and by riding in opposite directions were able to keep the cattle under constant observation. The horses caught on quickly to the routine, and would continue their route even if, as often happened, the rider would fall asleep in the saddle. Each time the riders met, they would speak to make certain the other was awake, and also to calm the cows, knowing that they were being protected against any kind of night predators.

If a rider didn't fall asleep, then these long, quiet hours in the middle of the night were perfect for reflection. And that is exactly what Tom was doing.

It had been nine months since he came to work at Live Oaks. At first he intended it to be temporary — just until the scars on his soul were healed. Ranching was certainly unlike anything he had ever experienced before, and while it didn't quite live up to the romanticism of the printed word — he had never read about anyone having to muck out stables, or pull cows from mud bogs — he found the physical labor therapeutic.

He also liked the men that he worked with. What they lacked in education, polish, and sophistication was more than made up for by their sense of honor and horse sense.

He laughed at a definition of horse sense he had heard. "Horse sense means that horses have more sense than to bet on a man."

He wondered what his father would think if he could see him now, riding a horse around a herd of cows in the middle of the night, dressed in denim and sheepskin, wearing a pistol on his hip and carrying a rifle in a saddle-sheath.

"Are you awake, Tom?" Dalton called, as he passed Tom on their circuit.

"How can I sleep with you yelling at me every fifteen minutes?" Tom replied.

Dalton laughed as he rode on by. Tom continued his own circuit.

From the *Dodge City Times*:

REVERSE CATTLE DRIVE.

Our fair city has long been the destination for cattle herds coming north from Texas. But now we are the point of origin for a herd going to Texas. Mr. Benjamin Conyers, a Texas Cowman, has declared his intention to stop raising Longhorns, supplanting those noble creatures with a breed but recently introduced to the United States.

The breed has been raised with some success in Missouri, but this experiment will be new to Texas. The breed is the Black Angus, a cow that is, as its name implies, coal black in color. It is also unique in that it is a cow without horns.

Brought to America from Scotland, the beef it produces is said to be superior in every measure, and they are far more valuable than Longhorns. The Black Angus brings 17 dollars a head in Kansas City, 30 dollars a head in Chicago, and 60 dollars a head in New York.

Mr. Conyers' herd of two thousand five hundred cows is making a rare winter drive from Dodge City to Ft. Worth, Texas. Having gotten underway on the 20th of this month, it is anticipated to reach Ft. Worth before Christmas.

Red Coleman was in the Lucky Chance Saloon in Dodge City. After the failure of his first attempt to steal one fourth of the herd by taking the train the cows were on, he was determined to make another try. And because he knew the herd would be coming to Dodge City, he returned to Lajunta, then took the next train east.

He arrived the day after the herd had departed Dodge City, heading south. The story of the "Reverse Herd," so-called because rather than a herd being brought to Dodge, this herd was leaving Dodge, made the front page of the newspaper. Despite that, the story that was on the lips of everyone in town was about Frank Lovejoy being killed. It was the subject of every discussion in the Lucky Chance.

The man who killed Lovejoy was Matt Jensen. Red didn't know what the relationship was between Matt and Smoke Jensen, but he didn't care. He knew he was on Smoke Jensen's trail.

"I can tell you right now," one of the saloon patrons said. "There ain't no way Seth Lovejoy is goin' to let that feller get away with killin' Frank."

"What's he goin' to do about it? It was a fair fight. Ever' one who saw it says that. Besides which, they done held the trial and found the man that kilt Frank innocent."

"That weren't no trial, that weren't nothin' but an inquiry," the first patron said. "But it don't make no difference anyhow. You mark my words, Seth Lovejoy is goin' to set things right. Leastwise, by his own accounting, he is."

"How is he going to do that? The man that kilt Frank is a cowboy with that herd of cows that just went south. Hell, he ain't even in town no more."

"I don't have any idea how he's goin' to do it. All I'm sayin' is, he's goin' to do it."

That wasn't news that Red Coleman wanted to hear. If this man Lovejoy hit the herd while they were going south, he could mess up the entire deal.

"Who is this fella Lovejoy they are talking about?" Red asked one of the other patrons of the saloon.

"He owns the Back Trail Ranch. He's about the richest man in all of Ford County, and you bein' new here an' all, prob'ly don't know that his boy was kilt here a few days ago by some cowboy that's takin' a herd down to Texas."

"Yes, I read about the trail drive in the

newspaper," Red said. "You think this Lovejoy man might try and rustle their cattle?"

"Rustle their cattle? Nah, why would he want to do that? He's got more money than he can count now. Like as not, all he wants to do is get even with this Matt Jensen fella that kilt his boy."

"Is Matt Jensen fast?" Red asked.

"About as fast as it takes a lightning bolt to get from the sky to the ground," the man said. "Only here's the thing. There's a couple of other men with that herd, Smoke Jensen and Falcon MacCallister, that they say is just as fast, or maybe faster."

Billy Lovejoy was sitting at a table with Candy, having paid enough to buy her company for as long as he wanted it. He had been following the discussion with increasing agitation.

"It is almost like they want Pa to go after that cowboy," Billy said.

"He won't, will he, Billy?" Candy asked.

"I don't know," Billy answered. "I'm afraid he will. He was really upset by the way the hearing turned out."

"But you were here that night," Candy said. "You saw it just like the rest of us did. You know that the hearing did the right thing by saying he was innocent."

"Yes, I saw it," Billy said. "But Pa didn't see it, and Doyle and the others who did see it are telling him just what he wants to hear."

"Why don't you tell him what really happened?"

"I have tried, but he doesn't listen to me," Billy said. "And the truth is, even if he had seen it with his own eyes, he would still believe what he wanted to believe. Frank could do no wrong, as far as Pa was concerned."

Back Trail Ranch

When Billy Lovejoy got home that night, he saw his father sitting in the big leather chair in his parlor and staring at the burning logs in his fireplace. Seth Lovejoy had been drinking, almost non-stop, for the last three days. He was inebriated, but not the kind of staggering, fall-down, speech-slurring drunk one might expect. Instead it was a slow-mounting anger that ate at his soul.

"I see you are home," Seth said. "Have you been with your whore all evening?"

"I've been with Candy," Billy said.

Seth chortled, an evil-sounding cackle. "Hell, boy, I don't mind you being with whores," he said. "I know your brother

340

spent time with whores too. The only thing I mind is you being dumb enough to think that you have fallen in love with one. She is playing you for a fool, thinking that if she could convince you to marry her, she could come out here and live high on the hog on my ranch. Well, she ain't goin' to, 'cause I'm tellin' you right now, if you marry that whore I'm takin' you out of my will. You won't get one red cent."

"Do you think I would let that decide whether or not I marry Candy? Pa, you need to ease up a bit on the drinkin'."

"In case you didn't notice it, I've got a reason to drink. My son, who also happened to be your brother in case you have forgotten, was killed."

"Getting drunk isn't going to bring him back."

"It don't bother you none that Frank was shot down in cold blood?" Seth asked.

"Pa, you heard all the witnesses. Every one of them said that Frank drew first."

"They're lyin', ever' one of 'em," Seth said.

"I was there too, and I saw it. Do you think I'm lying?"

"You are either lying, or you didn't see everything that happened. You know how fast Frank was. There couldn't anybody beat him. Not in a fair fight, they couldn't."

"Face it, Pa. This was goin' to happen to Frank sometime. He was always on the edge, always pushing people, always ready to fight over the least insult, real or imagined."

"Just like you are always ready to run from a fight," Seth said. "You aren't half the man Frank was."

"I'm sorry you feel that way," Billy said.

"What do I have to do, to put a little gumption in you?" Seth asked.

"I'm not sure what you mean by gumption," Billy said. "If you mean how can you turn me into Frank, you can't."

"That's what I'm afraid of. Do you know how much I'm worth, Billy?"

"I have a good idea."

"I'm sure you do," Seth said. He squinted his eyes and looked at Billy accusingly. "And now, with Frank gone, you're thinkin' it's all goin' to come to you, aren't you? Hell, you are probably glad Frank got himself killed so that you don't have to split the inheritance with him."

"I don't think about the inheritance," Billy said. "I wish you were nothing but a store clerk, or a wagon driver or something. If you were, Frank would probably still be alive."

"What do you mean by that?"

"Pa, you not only encouraged Frank to be the way he was, you pushed him into it."

"I did, and why not?" Seth replied. "When you have as much property as I have, you have to be willing to protect it. It's for sure and certain you'll never do anything to protect it."

"And look what it got you," Billy said. "A dead son."

"The wrong dead son," Seth said with a low growl.

"You're drunk, Pa," Billy said. "That's the liquor talking, not you."

"There is a way you can redeem yourself," Seth said.

"How? Not that I feel that I need redemption."

"You can kill the man that killed your brother."

"No," Billy said. "If that's what it takes for redemption in your eyes, I want none of it."

Billy started toward the door.

"You are a coward!" Seth yelled at him. "Do you hear me? You are a coward, and you are no son of mine!"

Billy had been through previous episodes of his father's intransigent anger and irrational behavior, and he knew that he eventually came out of such black moods. He had to admit though that this one was different in that it had been initiated by Frank getting killed, and sustained by heavy drinking. It was also much deeper and darker than it had ever been before. He had no idea how long it would be before his father came out of it this time, but he had no intention of being around until he did. He would stay in Dodge for a while.

The next morning Seth asked Doyle to have breakfast with him. Doyle was the ranch foreman, and had been Frank's closest friend.

"Tell me, Doyle," Seth asked as he buttered a biscuit, "how fast was this man, this Matt Jensen, who shot my boy?"

"He was fast," Doyle answered.

"How fast?"

"Damn fast."

"That's not an answer."

Doyle ran his hand through his hair as he looked across the table at his boss. It was obvious that he wasn't sure how to answer.

"Frank is dead," Seth said. "There's no need to hide the truth from me now. Did Jensen beat Frank fair and square?"

"More than that," Doyle said.

"What do you mean more than that?"

"Frank started his draw first, and Jensen still beat him."

"If that's the case, then I'm not likely to find a gunman who can beat him."

"Maybe Smoke Jensen, or Falcon Mac-Callister could, but you know neither one of them are going to go up against him. And I don't know if they could beat him anyway."

"Then we are going to have to find another way to kill him."

"You won't be able to kill just him," Doyle said. "Smoke Jensen and Falcon MacCallister? They are riding with him right now. Also a fella named Duff MacCallister, and while I don't know much about him, him being a MacCallister is about all I need to know."

"What you are saying is I will have to kill all four of them," Seth said.

"Yes."

"All right, that's what we're going to do."

"Mr. Lovejoy, maybe you ain't listenin' to me," Doyle said. "There's no way we can go up against them fellas."

"We aren't going to go up against them in the way you think," Seth said. "Come in here, let me show you something."

Doyle followed Seth into the study. There, laid out on a table, was a map of Indian

Territory.

"They are taking a herd of twenty-five hundred cows south to Fort Worth, aren't they? Take a look at this map," Seth said. "They are going to have to cross the Cimarron. I know that country, and I know that the only place you can ford the Cimarron with a herd is right a-here." He tapped the location with the end of his index finger.

"They left Dodge City yesterday morning which means they are into their second day. They are driving cattle, so it is going to take at least four more days for them to reach there. But on horseback, we can be there in two days. Now, when they get there, the only thing they are going to have on their minds is pushing the cows across the river. We'll be on the other side, laying low, waiting for them."

"When you say we, Mr. Lovejoy, who are you talking about besides you and me? Even from ambush, I wouldn't want to go after them with just the two of us. It would take an army. We are going to need a lot more people."

"That's right, Doyle, and I'm counting on you to find the people who will go with us," Seth said. "When you recruit them, you can offer them one hundred dollars a man."

"Did I understand you? You are going to

give a hundred dollars to each man who agrees to ride with us?" Doyle asked in surprise.

"I am. I will give one hundred dollars apiece for each man who signs up to go with us," Seth said. "And a hundred dollars for you, plus an extra ten dollars for you for every man you can round up."

Doyle smiled broadly. "Mr. Lovejoy, you will have your army."

"Fine. But get them here quickly, I want to leave today. We need to be there in enough time to make certain we have all the cover and concealment we need."

Lucky Chance Saloon, November 22
When Billy first set foot in the Lucky Chance, he saw that Candy was drinking with someone. Because that was her job, he stayed up at the bar, nursing a beer, until he saw the man she was with leave.

Candy had seen Billy come in, so she came to stand beside him. "Hello, cowboy," she said, smiling at him.

"I don't like it when you do that," Billy replied.

"When I do what?" Candy asked, surprised by his response.

"When you say, 'hello cowboy,' as if I am just another cowboy."

Candy put both her hands around Billy's upper arm, leaned into him, and smiled up at him.

"I mean nothing by it, Billy. As far as I am concerned, you are much more than just another cowboy."

"Can we sit and talk for a while?"

"Sure," Candy said.

Candy led the way to an empty table, one near the stove that was now glowing red as it pumped out enough heat to keep the entire saloon reasonably warm, if not comfortable.

"What is it?" Candy asked. "You look like something is bothering you."

"It *is* bothering me," Billy said. "Pa has rounded up a lot of men and they are going out after the herd that just left here."

"Oh!" Candy said, putting her hand to her mouth. "No, Billy, you have to stop him."

"I tried to stop him," Billy said. "I didn't get very far."

"But you must stop him," Candy insisted. "Becca went with them!"

"Becca went with them? Why would she do that?"

"Don't you know? Her Pa is the one who owns that herd. She is just going back home."

"No, I didn't know that."

"Billy, please try to stop them."

"I'll do what I can," Billy promised.

Live Oaks Ranch, November 22

The Western Union Delivery boy handed Big Ben a telegram.

"Sorry, Mr. Conyers, but this telegram is a couple days late. Mr. Hayward's wife took sick yesterday and he wasn't there to get the telegrams so they was all sent to Dallas. We didn't get them until this morning."

"That's all right," Big Ben said. "I was expecting it anyway." He gave the boy a half-dollar tip.

"Thank you sir," the boy said. Remounting, he rode back to town.

Big Ben took the telegram back inside, sat down in his reinforced chair, then opened it. He was not in any way apprehensive about it. As he had told the messenger boy, he was expecting the telegram, because he had told Clay to telegraph him when they left Dodge City.

The first thing he noticed when he opened the telegram was how long it was. Most telegrams were one or two lines at the most, sometimes three, rarely four, and almost never five. But this telegram had eight lines. This he wasn't expecting.

HERD ARRIVED IN DODGE CITY BY
TRAIN WITH ALL COWS SURVIVING THE
TRANSIT. THERE WERE FOUR MEN WHO
DELIVERED THE HERD AND THEY WILL
ASSIST US IN THE DRIVE BACK TO LIVE
OAKS. WE WILL DEPART DODGE CITY
THIS DAY, NOV 20. REBECCA WILL BE
RETURNING WITH US. THERE WAS A
SHOOTING INCIDENT IN DODGE CITY.
MOSES COFFEY WAS KILLED WHILE DE-
FENDING DALTON. DALTON WAS NOT
HURT.

                              CLAY RAMSEY

After reading the telegram, Big Ben leaned
forward and closed his eyes. Julia came into
the room then and saw him sitting in the
chair, clutching the telegram in his hand,
with his head bowed, his eyes closed.

"Ben?" she said, her voice weak and
frightened. Telegrams always frightened her.
"Ben, what is it?"

Big Ben opened his eyes and looked at
her. He lifted the telegram from his leg and
waved it slightly.

"The herd has left Dodge City," he said.

"Oh," Julia said, relieved. "Oh, is that all?"
She sat on the settee. "Seeing you like that
frightened me."

"There is more," Big Ben said.

"What?" she asked, anxiously.

"Mo was killed."

"Oh, Ben, no. That poor boy. He was such a friend to Dalton. Dalton must be — Dalton!" she suddenly gasped. "Ben, is Dalton all right?"

"Yes," Big Ben said.

"Oh, thank God. Oh, how terrible of me to be thankful that it was Mo instead of Dalton. God, forgive me."

"I'm sure He has already forgiven you, Julia," Big Ben said. He waited for a moment before he added, "There is more."

"More? What more? What more could there be?"

"Rebecca is with them," Big Ben said. "She is coming home."

"Rebecca is coming home?"

"Yes. She must have been in Dodge City."

"Oh, Ben. She will be here for Christmas! Won't that be wonderful?"

"Yes. Wonderful," Big Ben said. There was more anxiety in his voice than there was joy over the return of his daughter.

It was nearly suppertime, so Big Ben walked over to the cookhouse. The cookhouse was a long, narrow building. One third of the building was the kitchen, while two thirds made up the dining area. Here, in the dining area, were three long tables with chairs on either side of the table. Those hands who had not made the drive and who were not married were having their supper now, and there was a lot of talking and laughter going on when Big Ben stepped into the building. For a moment nobody saw him, and he stood quietly, just inside the door, leaning back against the wall. Finally someone saw him, and within less than a minute, all conversation had halted. The eating had stopped as well, and everyone turned their attention toward Big Ben.

"Men," he said. "I have some bad news to report."

The cowboys looked at each other to see if anyone had any advance knowledge as to what Big Ben was about to say. As nobody did, they turned their attention back to him.

"Mo Coffey was killed up in Dodge City."

"How?" someone shouted.

"He was shot," Big Ben said.

"It must have been some kind of shooter who done it," one of the cowboys said. "I've seen Mo shoot, and he was as good as anyone I ever seen or heard about."

There were a few other comments and questions most about what a "good man" Mo was, and how loyal he was to Live Oaks and the others who rode for the ranch. It was during that discussion that Big Ben began to get an idea as to what he wanted to do.

"Do any of you know the name of the orphanage Mo came from?" Big Ben asked.

"Yeah, I know," one of the cowboys said. "It is Our Lady of Mercy. He talks about it all the time."

"What were his feelings about it?" Big Ben asked. "Would you say they were positive or negative?"

"Oh, positive!" someone shouted, then several others threw in their own comments.

CHAPTER SIXTEEN

Cattleman's Bank of Fort Worth,
November 24

"That is a pretty large amount of cash to be carrying around, Mr. Conyers," C.D. Matthews said. "Are you sure you wouldn't rather me issue a bank certificate for the money?"

"No, I want cash," Big Ben said.

"Very well, I'll have the teller make it up and bring it to you. No need for you to have to stand in line with the others."

"Thank you," Big Ben said.

Matthews wrote on a piece of paper, then handed it to a clerk. The clerk nodded, and took off to attend to his errand.

"I hear you are bringing in a herd of Black Angus cattle," Matthews said.

"I am indeed. I have rid myself of every Longhorn."

"Well, that's going to be an interesting experiment," Matthews said. "I'm told that, pound for pound, they are worth much more than Longhorns. What have you heard from the other ranchers for depressing the market even further for them?"

"Mostly they express interest and curiosity," Big Ben replied. "So far there have been no examples of animosity or hostility."

"That is good," Matthews said. At that moment a teller arrived, carrying a bundle of money. Matthews took the money, then counted it out to Big Ben.

"I would ask if you had Christmas in mind for this money, but it isn't even December yet, so it seems a little too early for that," Montgomery said.

"It is not too early for the Christmas I have in mind," Big Ben said.

Our Lady of Mercy Orphanage, Fort Worth
Sister Mary Katherine sat at her desk in Our Lady of Mercy Orphanage, going over the budget. Father Pyron of St. Patrick's Cathedral had just given her the church's orphanage allotment, and it didn't look good. At present there were seventeen children in the orphanage: six girls, from infant to fourteen, and eleven boys, from three to sixteen. The sixteen-year-old would be turned out on his own when he reached seventeen, his birthday being the coming

January.

From time to time the parishioners, and even the people of Fort Worth, would donate money, food, and various items to the orphanage. Thanksgiving was on the 27th, just three more days. She had wanted so, this year, to have enough money to have a big Thanksgiving Day dinner for the children, but it didn't look as if that was going to happen. They would be lucky this Thanksgiving if they had beans and bacon.

Sister Mary Katherine was seventy-three years old. She was the Mother Superior of Our Lady of Mercy Orphanage and had been for thirty years. Before that, she was with the St. Mary's Orphanage in Charleston, South Carolina. She had dedicated her life to serving her Lord by serving His homeless children. She had been through times that were good and times that were bad, and right now it was as bad as it had been since just after the war.

Though Sister Mary Katherine and the other sisters made life as pleasant for the children as they could, life in an institution, even a benevolent institution, could not compare with having a family. The older children did what they could for the younger ones, and already this year some of them, in order to make up for the lack of money for any Christmas gifts, were secretly making wagons, rocking-horses, and other toys.

"Mother Superior?" a nun said, sticking her head in through the open door. Had the door not been open, Sister Dominique would have never presumed to break in on the Mother Superior. She would have knocked, even though Sister Mary Katherine was not that much of a stickler for protocol.

"Yes, Sister Dominique?"

"There is a gentleman to see you."

"Do you know what it is about?"

"I believe he wants to make a gift of some kind."

"A gift is it? Then, by all means, do show him in," Sister Mary Katherine said. She stood and waited for the visitor.

"Right in there, sir," she heard Sister Dominique say.

The man who came into the office was very large, one of the biggest men she had ever seen. He filled the doorway.

"Sister . . . ? Is that the proper way to address you?"

"Yes, Sister Mary Katherine, or Mother Superior. And you are?"

"Benjamin Conyers."

"Please, Mr. Conyers, have a seat," Sister

Mary Katherine invited. "What can I do for you?"

"Do you remember a young man you had here once, named Mo Coffey?"

"Moses Coffey? Of course I remember him," Sister Mary Katherine said. "Why, I remember vividly the night we received him. We found him lying on the front stoop, warmly wrapped on a bag that had been used for coffee. He was with us for sixteen years. A fine young man, and quite intelligent as I recall."

"Yes, ma'am. Mo came to work for me out at Live Oaks. That's my ranch."

"Yes, Mo has dropped by from time to time to visit us and the children we have here now. He did tell us he was working on a ranch, and as I recall, he gave the children a demonstration with the rope. They enjoyed it so much. Please do give Mo my regards," Sister Mary Katherine said, smiling broadly.

"I wish I could do that, ma'am, I truly do," Big Ben said. "But the truth is, I got a telegram from my ranch foreman. Mo went to Dodge City with some of my other hands to pick up a new herd of cows. And while he was there," Big Ben paused, not wanting to drop the news on her, but not knowing any other way to say it, just said it. "Well, I'm afraid, Sister, that Mo was killed."

"Oh!" Sister Mary Katherine gasped. The smile left her face, and her eyes filled with tears. "Oh, dear," she said again. "I am so sorry to hear that." She crossed herself. "God rest his soul."

"I was sorry to hear it as well. And I thought you might want to know."

"Yes, thank you, that was very decent of you to tell us."

"I'm sorry I had to be the one," Big Ben said.

"How did he get along with the others? What I mean is, did he have friends?"

"Oh, yes, ma'am, he had wonderful friends," Big Ben said. "Everyone on the ranch thought the world of him. In fact, he was my own son's best friend."

"I am so heartened by that. I am saddened by the news that Moses was killed, but I am cheered by the fact that he found friends and a purpose for his life."

"Yes, ma'am, he did that, all right," Big Ben said. "I was thinking, Sister Mary Katherine, perhaps there is something I could do for the orphanage, in memory of Mo."

"Oh, we would be most grateful for anything that you might do."

"I thought about a memorial or something like that, then I got to thinking, perhaps it should be more practical. Suppose I just gave you some money, and let you do what you wanted with it."

"Oh, yes, that would be wonderful," Sister Mary Katherine said. She looked down at the budget she had been working with. "In fact, Mr. Conyers, if it would not be too forward of me to ask, if you could find it in your heart to provide a monetary gift large enough for us to have a wonderful Thanksgiving Day dinner for our children. I've been trying to find a way to bring that about."

"You want me to buy Thanksgiving Day dinner for the orphanage?"

"Yes. I know that is very forward of me, Mr. Conyers, and if that is asking too much, please understand that we will be extremely grateful for whatever you can give."

"How about if I buy the Thanksgiving Day dinner, and give you five thousand dollars?" Big Ben said.

Sister Mary Katherine gasped, then stepped back to her chair, falling rather than sitting in it.

"Sister Mary Katherine, are you all right?" Big Ben asked.

The elderly nun looked up at Big Ben and moved her mouth, but no words came out.

"Sister! Sister, come in here quick!" Big Ben called, and a moment later an anxious

Sister Dominique came running into the room.

"What is it? What has happened?" she asked, anxiously.

"I don't know," Big Ben said. "She just suddenly . . . ," he didn't know what to say so he made a motion with his hands toward her.

"Sister Dominique," Sister Mary Katherine said, her voice strong and clear. "Do you have any idea what this — this wonderful gentleman has just done?"

"What?"

"He has just given us five thousand dollars!"

"Oh. God bless you, sir. God bless you!" Sister Dominique said.

Big Ben took the packet of money from his jacket pocket, fifty one-hundred-dollar bills, and put them on the corner of the desk.

"I will stop by Wagner's Grocery Store and tell him to give you whatever you need for your Thanksgiving Day dinner," Big Ben said. "I'll settle with him afterward."

"God, indeed, sent you to us," Sister Mary Katherine said.

"There is something I would like for you to do for me," Big Ben said. "If you would, I would like for you to pray for my daughter.

I mean, I can pray for her myself, and I do, but I have to sort of believe the prayers would mean more coming from you."

"Of course we will pray for her. Is she ill?"

"No. She is — we had a disagreement and she has left home. She is on her way back home now, and I would like you to pray for her safety, and, if it is not too much, for an agreeable reunion between us."

"What is her name?" Sister Mary Katherine asked.

"Her name is Rebecca. Rebecca Jane Conyers."

"We will do a Novena for her," Sister Mary Katherine promised.

"Thank you," Big Ben said.

"No, Mr. Conyers, we thank you. And, God bless you," Sister Mary Katherine said.

The two sisters walked him back out to his surrey. It sagged under his weight, then he reached for the reins, clucked to his horse, and drove off.

"This will be the most wonderful Thanksgiving and Christmas our children have ever known," Sister Dominique said as they walked back into the orphanage. "In fact you might say this is a Christmas miracle."

"It is Moses Coffey's Christmas miracle," Sister Mary Katherine said.

"Moses Coffey?"

"You didn't know Moses," Sister Mary Katherine said. "He left before you arrived. He was one of our young men who left and worked for that wonderful gentlemen who just stopped by to visit. Poor Moses was killed a few days ago, and this money was given us in his honor."

"Then we must remember him in our prayers," Sister Dominique said.

"I will remember him in my prayers for the rest of my life," Sister Mary Katherine said.

On the trail, November 24
With the wagons already gone ahead to find a spot for the noon break, the cows were strung out for three quarters of a mile, heading south. Duff and Clay were riding point, one on each side, Matt and Smoke were on the east side of the herd, while Falcon, Tom, and Dusty were on the west side. Dalton was riding drag.

Duff and Clay rode well back from the lead cattle but moved forward, closing in as the occasion required. That way, they could control the belled steer and set the course. The main body of the herd trailed along behind the leaders as if this were some great army in loose marching order.

The swing men, those riding on either side

of the herd, had the job of seeing that none of the herd wandered away or dropped out. Although it was a cattle drive, there was no real driving to do. Once underway, the cattle moved of their own free will.

"The secret of driving cattle," Dusty had told the others that morning, "is to never let them know they are being drove. From the moment they start out in the morning, you need to let them think they are on their own. Then it becomes just a matter of ridin' along and sort of loafin' in the saddle."

"Hard to loaf when you're eatin' a lot of dust," Dalton said.

"Son, you are the one who didn't want to drive the hoodlum wagon anymore," Clay said. "Now which would you rather do?"

"I'd rather ride point," Dalton said.

"And I'd rather be riding in a fine carriage somewhere, with pretty ladies tendin' to me," Dusty said.

The others, including Dalton, laughed.

They had bacon, beans, and cornbread for lunch.

"I tell you what," Dusty said. "I've been on a lot of cattle drives in my life. But I ain't never ate no better'n what we done comin' up, or goin' back. And I ain't never been on a cattle drive where we had such beautiful ladies to look at. You boys just don't know how lucky you are."

The three women smiled at the compliment.

"Dusty, I hope that compliment wasn't just to get a piece of apple pie," Sally said.

"No, ma'am, it sure wasn't," Dusty said. "But if you happen to have some pie, well, that would be just fine."

"We don't have any pie," Sally said.

"Well, who needs pie with a fine meal like this?"

"But I did make some bear claws," Sally said.

"Wow!" Matt said. "Dusty, you are in for a treat. There is nobody in the world who can make bear claws like Sally."

"Pearlie and Cal should be here," Smoke teased, thinking of how much his two cowboys liked Sally's bear claws.

"If they were here there wouldn't be any left for anyone else," Sally said as she brought a large tin bowl out, filled with the pastries.

After lunch, as the wagons were preparing to move out, Clay came over to Tom.

"Tom, would you take a look at the left rear wheel on the hoodlum wagon? Rebecca says it is squealing something awful, and

Maria says she and Mrs. Jensen can even hear it from their wagon."

Tom looked over toward the wagon and saw Rebecca standing there. He almost asked Clay to ask someone else to do it, but he kept it to himself.

"All right," he said. "I'll see what it needs."

"Probably just needs some grease," Clay said.

There was a bucket of grease hanging from underneath both wagons, and Clay reached under the hoodlum wagon to pull it out.

"I'm sorry," Rebecca said. "It looks like you are going to get your hands all greasy because of me."

"It's not your fault," Tom said. "When a wheel axle has skeins instead of bearings, you are going to get friction. And that friction is going to cause squeaking."

He got down on one knee, then leaned over and studied the wheel hub. "Yes," he said, pointing. "It's nearly dry."

"Tom," Rebecca said. "We have to talk."

"Talk about what?" Tom said. "I was a fool, I know that now. I hurt you deeply. I should have told you that I was married before."

"And she hurt you? Are you divorced?"

"She is dead."

"Oh, Tom, I'm so sorry. I didn't know."

"You couldn't have known. I didn't tell you, because I couldn't tell you."

Tom stuck his hand into the bucket, pulled out a big gob of grease, then started packing it into the hub, working it around the metal extension, or skein, of the axle.

"I didn't leave because you hurt me. At least, not exactly."

"Then why did you leave?" he asked.

"Because father said I could not see you anymore," she said. "He said that he would send you away."

"Send me away where, Rebecca? He could fire me, he could tell me he didn't want me on his land anymore, but that's it. He couldn't send me away."

"I know. I have thought about that a lot over the last four and a half months. I know I made a mistake Tom. All I can say is that I'm sorry."

"What about the saloon?"

"What about it?"

"What were you doing there?"

"Tom, do you think I became a prostitute? Do you think I ran off because I couldn't have you, and became a prostitute in the process?"

Tom shook his head. "No, I don't think you became a prostitute," he said. "I don't know exactly what you were doing in that saloon, or why you were there, but I don't think you became a prostitute."

"Oscar Davenport, the man who runs the saloon, is a wonderful man," Rebecca said.

"I'm sure he is." The tone of Tom's voice was almost sarcastic. "I'm sure all the girls there just loved him. And I'm sure he loved all of them."

"Oscar Davenport was married to my mother," Rebecca said resolutely.

"Your mother? How can that be? Your mother is at Live Oaks."

"Julia Conyers is my stepmother," Rebecca said. "She is the only mother I have ever known, since she and my father were married when I was a baby, but she is my stepmother. My real mother lived in Dodge City, Kansas, and was married to Oscar Davenport. So you see, I didn't just run away, I had a destination in mind when I left."

"What does your mother, your real mother, think about you returning to Live Oaks?" Tom asked.

"My real mother is dead," Rebecca said. "She died two weeks ago."

"I'm sorry," Tom said.

"Did you mean it, Tom?" Rebecca asked. "Did you mean it when you said you couldn't love me?"

"There is more to it than that," Tom said.

"What more is there?"

Tom shook his head. "You don't need to know."

"Yes, I do. Please, Tom, don't you understand? I have laid my heart out for you. I have to know why my love can't be returned. Is it because your wife died? I can understand how that would hurt, but don't you think I could help you heal?"

"You don't understand," Tom said.

"I'm trying to understand," Rebecca said. "Please help me understand."

"My wife is dead, Rebecca, because I killed her," Tom said flatly.

Indian territory, November 25
After breakfast the next morning, the three women washed the dishes, then began loading the wagons, preparing to leave. Two of them were loading the wagons, Rebecca was just finishing with the hoodlum wagon and Sally was closing up the chuck wagon. Maria was standing to one side between the two wagons.

Clay rode over to Maria, then dismounted.

"About ready to go?" he asked.

"Si," Maria replied. "How far do you think you will go before noon?"

369

"I expect we will reach the Cimarron just about noon," Clay answered.

"Do you want to have lunch on this side or the other side of the river?" Maria asked.

"Find a place on this side. We'll cross after we eat," Clay said.

"All right," Maria replied. "Don't be late," she said with a smile.

Clay kissed her, then helped her climb up onto the wagon. It was difficult for her to climb and he noticed it.

"Are you all right?"

"I am fine."

"You just seem to be having a harder time getting around."

"I am pregnant, remember," she said, speaking so quietly that only Clay could hear her.

"I thought you said that wasn't going to be a problem."

"It isn't a problem."

"I shouldn't have let you come."

"You can always send me back home," Maria teased.

"All right, you have made your point. But do be careful. Let the other ladies do all the hard work."

"They are already doing all the hard work," Maria said.

Sally, who had been closing up the back

of the wagon, came up on the other side, then climbed into the driver's seat to pick up the reins.

"I told Maria, I think you should stop just on this side of the river. We'll cross it after lunch," Clay said.

"All right," Sally said. She called back to Rebecca. "Rebecca, are you ready?"

"I'm ready," Rebecca answered.

"Let's move them out," Sally said, slapping the reins against the backs of the team of mules.

Clay watched the two wagons start out, then he mounted his horse and called out to the others.

"Let's get these critters moving!"

His call galvanized the others into action. It was always difficult to get the cows started moving each morning. There were several reasons for that. The campsites were purposely selected for the abundance of grass and water, and an area wide enough to allow the cows to bed down for the night. As a result, the cows were quite comfortable where they were, and that made them reluctant to leave.

Clay and the others would have to shout, poke them in the sides with sticks, and swing ropes at them to get the herd underway. After five or ten minutes of this the cows would eventually begin to move. Then, once the herd was underway, it would change from twenty-five hundred individual creatures into a single entity with a single purpose. The same inertia that had tended to keep the herd at rest now became an asset, as it would keep the cows plodding along for as long as the cowboys wanted to keep them in motion.

A herd this size made its presence known in several ways. It was a black, slow-moving mass, a quarter of a mile long, lifting a cloud of dust that could be seen for many miles. The sound of the hooves and the bawling of the cattle to each other provided a music that quickly became familiar to the cowboys who were working the herd.

But perhaps the most distinctive signature of the herd was its aroma. The smells came from sun on their hides, dust in the air, and especially from the animals' droppings and urine. The odor was pungent and perhaps, to many, unpleasant. To the cowboys who had spent half their lives with cattle, however, it was an aroma as familiar and agreeable as their mothers' home cooking.

As the two wagons moved on ahead of the herd, Rebecca looked toward the western horizon and saw the gray streaks of rain slashing down from the sky, but it didn't look or feel as if the rain would come this way.

What did Tom mean when he said that he had killed his wife? He had not elaborated on the subject. Surely he didn't mean that he had killed her in a fit of jealous rage, did he? She knew that some men did that from time to time.

But Tom?

No, he couldn't have. She could not be that wrong about him.

Still, it was obvious he was running from something. There was so much of his past that she didn't know. And she had never seen a man so out of place as Tom was here. He was obviously educated, extremely educated. It appeared as if money meant little to him. He was silent, but not sullen, a gentleman, but not a weak sister.

No, he wasn't a murderer. She was as sure of that as she had ever been sure of anything in her entire life. If he had killed his wife, it had to have been some sort of tragic accident, something that had scarred his soul. All she had to do was get through that scar tissue.

Cimarron River

Marcus Doyle had rounded up fifteen men. He and Seth Lovejoy brought the number to seventeen, and now they were waiting on the south side of the Cimarron.

Seth Lovejoy had been a Colonel in the Union Army during the war, and he understood the tactics of cover, concealment, and overlapping fields of fire. Because of that, he had his men well-positioned.

"Morrell is coming back," Doyle said, and even as he spoke the others could see a single rider galloping toward them.

Lovejoy and his men had been in position for two days, and he had sent Morrell out both days to keep an early lookout for the approaching herd.

At this point the Cimarron was broad, but only about a foot deep. This was the only ford for several miles in either direction that would accommodate a herd of cattle. Lovejoy knew about it, because it was used in the spring by all the Texas herds that were coming north.

Morrell continued the gallop across the river, his horse's hooves sending up splashes with each footfall. When he reached the south side of the river he dismounted.

"They're comin', Mr. Lovejoy," he said.

"How far back?"

"No more'n three, maybe four miles. I expect they'll be here in an hour or so. The wagons is just over that ridge. They'll be here in about ten minutes or so."

"Do we kill the wagon drivers?" Doyle asked.

"They're women," Morrell replied, answering before Lovejoy could respond to Doyle's question.

"What?" Lovejoy asked.

"The wagon drivers," Lovejoy said. "They're women. Three of 'em."

"Three wagons?"

"No, only two wagons, but one of 'em is bein' drove by two women."

"I ain't goin' to be shootin' no women," one of the men Doyle had recruited said.

"Me neither," another said.

"All right, we'll let the women on through," Lovejoy said. "The only one I'm really wantin' to kill is the one that shot my boy."

"Like I said, Mr. Lovejoy, them wagons will be here any minute now."

"Right. Good job, Morrell. Now, get your horse out of sight and take a position."

"Whoa, mules," Sally said, pulling back on the reins and using her foot to push on the brake.

Sally's wagon and the one behind it squeaked to a stop as the dust trail that had been following now moved up to envelop them.

"The first thing we need to do is get a fire going," Sally said as she climbed down. "Not only for cooking, but for warmth. It's getting cold."

Sally reached up to help Maria climb down, just as Rebecca came up to them.

"Maria, are you all right?" Rebecca asked.

"We may as well tell her," Sally said. "She's going to be with us every day for the next month."

"Si," Maria replied. Then to Rebecca. "I am going to have a baby," she said.

"Maria," Rebecca said with a broad smile. "That is wonderful!"

"Nobody knows except Clay," Sally said. "And Maria would like to keep it that way."

"I won't say a word," Rebecca said. "Why I'll be as quiet as . . ." Rebecca halted in mid-sentence and the expression on her face changed from one of joy for Maria to one of concern as she stared across the river.

"Rebecca what is it?" Sally asked. "You look as if you have seen a ghost."

"I just saw Mr. Lovejoy," Rebecca said. "He's on the other side of the river."

Sally chuckled. "You mean you did see a ghost? Isn't he the one that Matt shot?"

Rebecca shook her head. "No," she said.

"This is Seth Lovejoy. He is the father of the man Matt shot."

Now Sally's face showed concern as well. "That's not good," she said. "It can't just be a coincidence that the father of the man Matt shot is waiting on the other side of the river. If he is over there, he has something in mind." She looked across the river. "I don't see anyone," she said.

"He's —" Rebecca started to raise her hand to point, but Sally reached out to take her hand and prevent her from raising it.

"Don't point," Sally said. "If he is over there, we don't want him to know we have seen him."

"He's not the only one over there," Maria said. "I just saw some more men."

"How many?"

"Three. Maybe four," Maria said.

"Maybe we should leave," Rebecca suggested.

"No, if we try and leave now, he would know we saw him. Chances are he would chase us down to keep us from warning the others," Sally said.

"Then what can we do?" Maria asked.

"We'll start a fire," Sally said. "Rebecca, you start gathering firewood. Keep moving over toward the wood line over there. Once you are far enough inside the wood line to be seen, drop the firewood and start back toward the others, going as fast as you can. Tell them what we have seen."

"I hate leaving the two of you here all alone."

"We'll be all right as long as they don't suspect anything," Sally said. "Now, get going. Maria, we'll start a fire with the wood we've got."

There was a canvas sling beneath the chuck wagon and as Rebecca moved around picking up pieces of wood, Sally and Maria pulled the wood from the canvas sling. They began building a fire.

CHAPTER SEVENTEEN

"What are they doing?" Lovejoy asked.

"Looks like they're getting ready to fix dinner," Doyle said. "Should we stop them?"

"No, let 'em cook," Lovejoy said. "After we take care of the others, we'll be hungry. Might as well let them cook for us."

The others laughed, and Lovejoy put his finger to his lips. "Shhh," he said. "We can't let them know that we are here."

Rebecca moved steadily toward the wood line, picking up a piece of wood here, a stick there, discarding some and keeping others as if she were really gathering wood. She wanted to break and run, and had to fight with every ounce of her being not to do so.

Finally she reached the edge of the woods, went in, came back out, went in, and came back out again as if merely searching for the best pieces. Then, the last time she went in, she continued on until she was sure she was deep enough not to be seen. She dropped the wood she had gathered and began walking rapidly until she reached the top of the hill. Once there, she came out of the woods onto flat ground that was easier, and started running.

Rebecca ran at least two miles before she stopped running, then she walked until she regained her breath. That was when she saw the dust of the approaching herd, and that gave her the energy to run again.

Tom was riding point when he saw a young woman running toward them. Realizing at once that it was Rebecca, he urged his horse into a gallop and closed the gap between them in a few seconds.

"Rebecca, what is it? What is wrong?"

"Ambush," Rebecca said, panting so hard that she could scarcely get the word out.

"My God! You were ambushed?"

"No," Rebecca said. "You will be!"

"Get on," Tom said, reaching down to grab her hand and help her mount the horse behind him.

Tom galloped back toward the herd. By now some of the others had seen what happened, and they were riding out to meet them. Once there, he helped Rebecca down.

"Water," Rebecca said. "Please."

Tom gave Rebecca his canteen and she drank deeply from it. By the time she finished drinking, she had recovered her breath enough to be able to talk.

"Seth Lovejoy is waiting on the other side of the river," Rebecca said. "I know this man. I am sure he is waiting to get revenge."

"Is he all alone?" Clay asked.

"No. He has some men with him, but I don't know how many."

"What about Sally and Maria?" Smoke asked anxiously.

"They are still there, preparing to cook the meal as if nothing is wrong. Sally is the one who sent me to warn you."

"Lovejoy doesn't know he's been seen?" Clay asked.

"I don't think so."

"Did he see you leave?" Duff asked.

"No. I pretended to be collecting firewood until I reached the woods. Then when I was deep enough that I knew I couldn't be seen, I started running."

"Good for you," Falcon said.

"That was Sally's idea," Rebecca said.

"So, what do we do now?" Clay asked.

"Clay, you, Dusty, Tom, Dalton, and Rebecca stay with the herd," Smoke said. "This the kind of thing that Matt, Falcon, Duff and I should handle. We will take care of Lovejoy."

"Besides which, I'm the one he is after anyway," Matt said.

"Are you sure you don't want us to come along?" Clay asked. "You heard Rebecca. He has some men with him."

"And there's no telling how many he has," Dusty added. "Lovejoy is a very rich and very powerful man. He could have thirty or forty men with him. If you ask me, we should all go."

"Suppose he does have thirty men," Matt said. "If all of us go to meet him, that would be his thirty against our seven. What do you think about those odds?"

"Not much," Dusty admitted. "But thirty against seven is better than thirty against four."

"Not necessarily," Tom said. "I can see Matt's point. According to Euripides, ten men wisely led are worth a hundred without a head."

"You rip a what?" Dusty asked.

"Euripides. He was a Greek playwright about four hundred years before the birth of Christ," Tom explained.

Falcon laughed. "Tom, is there anything you don't know?"

"If there is anything Tom doesn't know about, I don't know what it might be," Clay said. "He's like one of those books, what do you call them, that has all the information in them?"

"That would be an encyclopedia," Duff said.

"Yeah, he is like one of them."

"Well, both Tom and Euripides are right," Smoke said. "It would be best for just the four of us to go. Trust me, we've had a lot more experience in this sort of thing than the rest of you."

"I think I should go," Tom said.

"No, you would just . . . ," Smoke started but Tom held up his hand.

"Hear me out. I don't mean go with you. I mean I should go to the wagons, just sort of ride up as if bringing some sort of message from Clay. That will do two things. That will make them think that we aren't on to them, and while they are busy watching me, you four can do whatever it is you have in mind."

"Take me with you," Rebecca said.

"No, there's no sense in putting you in danger again," Tom said.

"They saw me leave," Rebecca said. "If they don't see me come back, but they see you ride up, they may get suspicious."

"I hate to admit it, Tom, but Rebecca has a point," Smoke said.

"All right, I'll take you with me."

"I'll get you another horse," Dalton offered.

"No," Tom said. "If they saw her leave on foot, she needs to return on foot." Tom remounted, then held his hand down to help her up. This time he slid to the back of the saddle and she sat in front.

"We'll start back first," Tom said. "They'll see us and while they are trying to figure out what is going on, you four men will have freedom of movement."

"Clay, you know this river," Smoke said. "Is there another ford close by?"

Clay shook his head. "The nearest ford is about ten miles southeast," he said.

"That ain't entirely true," Dusty offered.

"What do you mean? Do you know a closer ford?" Smoke asked.

"Not one that a herd of cattle can use. But I know one that a man on horseback can cross. Only thing is, even on your horse it's going to get you wet about halfway up to your knees. And that water is going to be really cold right now."

"Never mind that. How far away from the cattle ford is it?"

"It's about a mile downstream."

"That's too close," Matt said. "They could see us."

"No, they can't," Dusty said, smiling.

"What do you mean?"

"Here, let me draw you a map on the ground. This will tell you how to get there. And I can also show you how it is that you won't be seen."

Finding a stick, Dusty scratched a map in the dirt. He drew the river, then showed a bow.

"See here?" he pointed out. "You'll come across the river here. They'll be waiting here. You'll not only be across the river, you'll be behind them because of the way the river bows here."

"Any way to tell where this ford is, exactly?" Falcon asked.

"Yes, right at the edge of the water there are three large rocks, all lined up, flat on top and stair-stepped down from the biggest, to the next biggest. You can't miss it."

When Tom had picked her up the first time, Rebecca had merely ridden bareback behind the saddle. But that was only for a hundred yards or so. This was to be a much longer ride, so she was in the saddle with him, and as she knew it would be, it was a tight fit. She was pressed back against him so close that she could feel the warmth of his body, the hard ripple of his muscles, and the presence of his breath on her neck. He had to put his arms around her to hold the reins, and as she felt his strong arms on either side of her, a warm tingling passed through her.

The rhythmic motion of the horse, the closeness of his body behind her, and something else, the pressure of the saddle-horn against her pelvis, caused ripples of pleasure to move through her body. And yet, the pleasures she felt were bittersweet. Though she had professed her love for him, he had rejected it, and in doing so, rejected her as well.

"Rebecca," Tom said. Her name on his tongue was charged with what? Passion? Remorse?

"Yes, Tom?" Rebecca's voice was expec-tant, hopeful.

"I — uh," he paused for a long time, as if trying to find the words. Then, in what was an obvious retreat from what he was feel-ing, he continued on in an entirely different vein.

"When we get there, I'll let you down just this side of the woods. Then I'll wait until you've come through on the other side before I appear. Don't forget to carry some wood with you when you go back."

"All right," Rebecca replied, swallowing

her disappointment.

Tom felt Rebecca trembling against him — or was he trembling against her? He had not experienced a craving this intense since Martha had died. And yet he dare not give in to it. He had made a commitment once, and what had it gotten him? A lifetime of remorse and pain.

His arms were around her now, holding the reins to be sure, but they were around her, and he could feel her against him, full body-to-body contact. Oh, how he wanted to pull her against him, kiss her neck, taste her lips. It took the last reserve of his strength to fight off that urge. He enjoyed what he could of the connection between them until her voice interrupted the dizzying pleasure he was experiencing.

"Here," Rebecca said.

"What?

"This is the edge of the woods," Rebecca said. "I had better get down here."

"This is the best place?"

"Yes."

Tom put his hands on her sides and lifted her up and out of the saddle. Then, bending over, he set her down on the ground as easily as if she were a child. For a moment she looked up at him, putting her soul into her gaze. He leaned down and the distance between their lips closed. She pursed her lips, waiting for the kiss that was to come.

Suddenly a quail darted up beside them, the whir of his wings startling them both, and the mood was broken.

"You had better hurry," Tom said.

"Yes."

Tom sat his horse as Rebecca disappeared into the woods. He waited a few minutes before he rode ahead. When he crested the hill, he saw that Rebecca had already returned to the encampment, so he knew the others would be expecting him. He rode slowly and steadily toward the camp. Sally came out to greet him when he arrived.

The other side of the river

"Hey, who is that?" Morrell asked.

Doyle moved to where he could look over the berm that was providing them with both cover and concealment.

Doyle chuckled. "You ought to recognize him, Morrell," he said. "He's the one that proved you was lyin' in the hearing. His name is Tom something."

"Yeah," Morrell said. "Yeah, that is him, ain't it? Well, I'll just settle accounts between me an' him right now."

Morrell jacked a round into his Winchester and raised it to his shoulders. Seeing him,

Lovejoy reached out and grabbed the rifle from him.

"What the hell are you doing?" Lovejoy asked.

"That's the son of a bitch that called me a liar in court," Morrell said.

"If you shoot him now it will give us away. I'm only interested in one man, and that's Matt Jensen, the one who killed Frank. Now if you can't go along with that, then you can just leave now. Without the one hundred dollars."

"No, no, that's all right. I reckon there will be plenty of time to kill that fella after we kill Matt Jensen."

"Where are the others?" Doyle asked. "Seems to me like those wagons have been there long enough now."

"Maybe that's what this fella, Tom, come up to tell them," Morrell suggested. "Like as not he come up to tell 'em that the others would be along directly."

Back at the herd, Dusty was the first to see a rider coming toward them.

"Clay, we got a galloper coming in," Dusty called.

Pulling their guns, Clay and Dusty both rode toward the rider. The rider held one hand in the air as he approached.

"Is this the herd Matt Jensen is with?" the rider asked.

"Yeah, it is. What of it?" Clay asked.

"My name is Billy Lovejoy."

"Lovejoy?" Dusty said. "Ain't that the name of the man Matt kilt?"

"Yes," Billy said. "Frank Lovejoy was my brother."

"So what are you doing here? Have you come for revenge?" Clay asked.

"No, on the contrary. I'm here to warn you about my Pa. He is planning to set up an ambush at the Cimarron River."

"We know," Dusty said.

"You know?" Billy asked in surprise. "How do you know?"

"They were spotted on the other side of the river."

"So, what are you going to do now?"

"We are already doing it. We sent someone to deal with it."

"Let me go to my father," Billy said. "Let me see if I can talk him out of it."

"Why didn't you try to talk him out of it before he came down here?" Clay asked.

"I *did* try. He didn't listen to me."

"What makes you think he would listen to you now?"

"I don't know, maybe he won't. But I feel like I have to try."

"What do you think, Dusty?" Clay asked.

"How do we know he isn't comin' to warn his Pa that we are on to him?" Dusty asked.

"I'm not," Billy said. "Please, you must let me go."

"I'm sorry, I can't take the chance," Clay said.

Suddenly, and unexpectedly, Billy urged his horse into a gallop. By the time Clay and Dusty recovered, then got their horses turned around, Billy was sixty feet away. Clay aimed his pistol.

"Better not, Clay!" Dusty shouted. "If this herd gets spooked into a stampede now, with only the three of us, we'll never get it stopped!"

Clay lowered his pistol without firing.

"I think maybe the fella came to do just what he said he came to do," Dusty said. "And if he can get there in time to stop any shootin', well that would be better all around, wouldn't it?"

"Yes," Clay agreed. "But I doubt he will get there in time."

"This looks like the place," Smoke said, pointing to three rocks which, as Dusty had indicated, were stair-stepping down.

Matt walked down to the edge of the water and stuck his hand into it. "Damn, it's cold," he said. "Couldn't we just come back in the summertime?"

"Americans are always complaining about the cold," Duff said. "If you want cold, sure 'n you should come to Scotland." Duff rode down into the water. "Och!! 'Tis cold!" he said, and the others laughed.

All four rode down into the river and, just as Dusty had promised, the water was deep enough to come up on their legs. The water was cold, cold enough that the horses didn't have to be prodded to cross quickly. Fortunately, the ford wasn't too difficult.

When Smoke, Falcon, and Duff got across, they looked around to see Matt coming behind them. Unlike them, Matt had not kept his feet in the stirrups. Instead, he lifted them up and wrapped them around the saddlehorn. As a result, unlike the others, he didn't have cold, wet legs.

"Would you look at that?" Falcon said. "What's the matter, can't take a little cold?"

"You just wish you had thought of it," Matt said. "Let's face it, sometimes being young and innovative counts more than experience."

"Let's find them and get this done," Smoke said.

Deadly serious now, the four men quit teasing and went to work. Because of the way the river made a big U right here, when they crossed they were not only on the same side as the ambushers, they were behind them as well.

Ground-tying the horses, the four men snaked their Winchesters out of their saddle-sheaths then moved quickly, on foot, until they came up behind the would-be ambushers. Smoke counted nineteen of them. All were well-armed, and all were in position behind a berm that would shield them from observation and protect them from return fire.

That is, if the return fire was coming from the other side. In this case, they were on the same side of the river with them, and they were behind them, which meant that the cover and concealment the Back Trail riders had picked for themselves were absolutely useless against Smoke, Matt, Falcon, and Duff.

"Where the hell are they? What's takin' 'em so long?" one of the Back Trail riders asked, his question clearly heard by Smoke and the others as they came up on them.

"Maybe them Black Angus cows just take longer to drive than any other cow," one of the others suggested.

"I don't know, I'm beginnin' to get a bad feeling about this. I think we should just ride across the river, kill them three women and that fella that's with them, then go out and meet the herd."

"No need to go out looking for us. We are right here," Smoke called out to them.

"What the hell?" Seth Lovejoy shouted, whirling around to see Smoke and the others standing about fifty yards behind them. The first thing Seth Lovejoy noticed was that the four men behind them were at the outer edge of pistol range. On the other hand, they were well within rifle range, and all four the men were holding Winchester rifles.

"They're behind us!" Lovejoy shouted. "Shoot them! Kill them!"

Duff raised his rifle and with the first shot took down Morrell, who was the only one of the bunch who had a rifle in his hands.

The others began firing their pistols. Smoke, Matt, Falcon, and Duff could hear the bullets whizzing by. It wasn't that the pistols couldn't shoot that far, it was that it took an extremely skilled marksman to be accurate at that range.

"Lovejoy is mine," Matt said, and even as he spoke, Lovejoy went down.

Birds and animals ran in terror as the gunshots roared. Gunsmoke rolled over the ground between them. Although Smoke and

Matt had been in many gunfights, only Falcon and Duff had actually experienced war, Falcon during the Civil War and again during the Indian campaigns when he was with Custer. Duff had fought in the Battle of Tel-el-Kebir in Egypt as a member of the famed Black Watch Regiment. And the conditions here, with the number of men engaged, the sound of multiple shots being fired, and the billowing cloud of gunsmoke that rolled across the field, gave them both a sense of déjà vu.

Cartridges banged and bullets whizzed as the battle continued. Then Doyle realized that Lovejoy was down. And not only that, the four men shooting at them had cut the number of Back Trail riders in half, without sustaining one casualty. Doyle threw his pistol down and put his hands up.

"Stop shooting!" he called to the others. "Stop shooting and get your hands up in the air!"

"I ain't givin' up to those sons of bitches," one of the others said.

"Yeah, you will," still another said, and this time he was pointing his pistol at the protestor. "Because if you don't, I'll shoot you myself."

"Jensen!" Doyle shouted, for Matt Jensen was the only name he knew. "Jensen! Stop your shootin'! We give up! We give up!"

Matt, Smoke, Falcon, and Duff came walking toward them, all four men holding their rifles at their waists, but pointing toward Doyle and what was left of the Back Trail riders.

"What was this all about?" Smoke asked. "Were you planning on taking our herd?"

"No, no," Doyle said. "We ain't cattle rustlers."

"I see. Just murderers," Smoke said. "Is that it?"

Doyle didn't answer.

"Mr. Lovejoy was wantin' to get revenge for you killin' his boy," one of the others said.

"That's what this was all about? Revenge? For all of you?" Matt asked. "You," he said, pointing to Doyle. "You were there. You saw what happened. I mean, what really happened, didn't you?"

"Yeah, I seen it," Doyle said.

"Whose fault was it?"

"It was Frank's fault," Doyle admitted.

"Did you ever tell Lovejoy the truth?" Matt asked.

"Yeah, I told him. But it didn't make any difference to him. He wanted revenge anyway."

"What about the rest of you? Was Frank

Lovejoy such a friend of yours that you all wanted revenge?"

"I didn't even like the son of a bitch," one of the other men said. "I was doin' it for the money. Lovejoy said he would give us a hunnert dollars apiece if we come with him."

"Did you get your hundred dollars?" Falcon asked.

"No. We was supposed to get it when we went back and the killin' was done."

"So, you didn't get your money and you got ten or more killed. Wasn't such a good bargain, was it?" Duff asked.

At that moment two riders crossed the ford. Neither Smoke nor the others recognized the rider in front, but they all recognized Tom Whitman, who was riding behind. Tom had his pistol drawn, so that it was obvious that the rider in front was his prisoner.

"Who is this?" Falcon asked.

"This is Seth Lovejoy's son," Tom said.

"Billy? What are you doing here?" Doyle asked. "I thought your Pa said you wasn't going to come."

Seeing his father, Billy dismounted and walked over to look down at him. Squatting down, he put his fingers on his father's neck, then shook his head.

"He's dead," Billy said.

"How long is this vengeance trail?" Matt asked.

"What do you mean?"

"Your Pa died avenging his son. Do you have revenge in mind too?"

"No," Billy said. "In fact, when I learned that Pa really had come out here to do this — this foolish thing, I came out here to try and stop him. But I got here too late."

"He's tellin' the truth," Doyle said. "He didn't want none of this from the first."

"Billy, is it?" Smoke asked.

"Yes," Billy replied.

"Take them home," Smoke said. He pointed to Doyle. "What's your name?"

"Doyle. Marcus Doyle."

"Doyle, if we see you again, you will be the first one we kill."

"You ain't goin' to see us again," Doyle promised.

"Take the bodies with you," Smoke said. "As a reminder."

Billy, Doyle, and the others draped the bodies over the backs of their horses and started back. They rode across the ford, then passed the women at their encampment.

"How long before the herd comes up?" Sally asked as they rode past her.

"We'll send them on," Smoke said. "I

think Falcon and I will ride with these scum until they are well clear of the herd."

After the cowboys had their lunch, Clay took the herd on across the river because there was ample water and grass, then made the decision to camp there overnight.

CHAPTER EIGHTEEN

"Rebecca, may I ask you a question?" Sally said as the three women were resting after lunch. "If it is none of my business, and it probably isn't, you can tell me so, and I won't be offended."

"What is the question?"

"Are you in love with Tom Whitman?"

Rebecca didn't answer, but she didn't have to. Immediately after Sally asked the question, Rebecca's eyes filled with tears.

"Oh, my," Sally said. "Me and my big mouth. I didn't intend to open a sore spot. That was very foolish of me, wasn't it? Please forgive me."

Rebecca shook her head and sniffed.

"There is nothing to forgive," she said. "It is a perfectly legitimate question."

"Perhaps, but it is also a loaded and painful question, if one is to gauge by your reaction."

"Yes, I love him," Rebecca said.

"And why is that so painful? Does he not return your love? I can't imagine that he wouldn't. He seems like a very intelligent young man; surely he isn't dumb enough to spurn your love."

"I don't know," Rebecca said. "I think he loves me. He has kissed me as if he loves me." Rebecca felt her face flushing. "But he is bedeviled by something in his past and I think he is afraid to let himself love me. Also, my father does not want me to have anything to do with him. And I don't know if I am strong enough to stand up to him."

"You aren't the first one ever to face that, Rebecca. My father is a banker, back East. The West may as well be a foreign country to him, and when he heard about Smoke, a man who had made a reputation as a gunfighter — even though he had never used his gun for any reason except to right a wrong — well, you can imagine what his reaction was. But Smoke won him over, and, from what I have observed of Tom, I'm sure he could win your father over as well."

"Right now the problem isn't with Tom winning my father over. It is with me winning Tom's love," Rebecca said.

"You will," Sally said. "I know you will. And it will be worth it. I can't imagine my life without Smoke."

401

"Smoke," Rebecca said. "That is such an unusual name."

Sally chuckled. "It's not his real name, of course. It's just a name that was given to him by Preacher, an old mountain man friend who became Smoke's mentor. His real name is Kirby."

"What?" Rebecca gasped. "Kirby Jensen? That's his name?"

Sally was confused and curious by Rebecca's strange reaction. "Yes, Kirby Jensen. Why? Does that name mean something to you?"

"It does if he is from Missouri, and if he had a sister named Janie."

"Oh, my God," Sally said. "Yes, he is from Missouri, and he did have a sister named Janie. But she died a long time ago. What is your connection to this?"

"Janie didn't die a long time ago, though she knew that her brother thought she did. Janie died last month, in Dodge City, only a few days before you got there."

"How do you know?"

"Because Janie Jensen was my mother."

"Janie was your mother?"

"Yes."

"Then that means . . ." Sally stopped in mid-sentence then smiled broadly. "Oh, my, Rebecca! That means Smoke is your uncle."

"And you are my aunt," Rebecca replied, returning Sally's smile.

The two women hugged happily, just as Smoke and Falcon rode up, having returned from escorting the Back Trail riders out of harm's way.

"What are we celebrating?" Smoke asked with a grin as he dismounted.

"Smoke, the most wonderful thing!" Sally said. "You aren't going to believe this."

"What."

"Rebecca is your niece."

"Oh, that's good," Smoke said. "What did you do, adopt her as a niece?"

"No. I mean she really is your niece," Sally said. "Your blood kin, niece."

Smoke shook his head. "That's not possible," he said. "I don't have any brothers or sisters."

"Janie," Sally said.

"Janie? She's dead. She died . . ."

"Two weeks ago," Rebecca said. "My mother, your sister, died two weeks ago in Dodge City, Kansas."

"No, she died a long time ago."

"She knew that you thought she was dead," Rebecca said. "She said that she never told you, because you were better off if you thought she was dead."

"How well did you know your mother?"

"I didn't know her that well," Rebecca answered. "She — abandoned me when I was a baby. I never actually saw her until a few months ago."

"I must confess that abandoning you does sound like something my sister would do. But I just don't believe your mother was my sister. If she had the name I'm sure it was just a coincidence. I imagine there are several Janie Jensens in the country."

"How many of them have a brother who tied two cow's tails together?" Rebecca asked.

"What?" Smoke gasped. He stared at Rebecca with eyes open wide. "How do you know that?"

"She told me," Rebecca said. "Not only that, she also told me that you told your father that the cows had tied themselves together while they were swishing at flies."

"I'll be damn! You *are* my niece!" Smoke said. And, as Sally had before, he welcomed her into his family with arms open wide.

"Smoke! You never told me that story about the cows tying their own tails together," Sally said.

"I've never told that story to a living soul," Smoke said. "Not even Preacher. And there is no way; absolutely no way that Rebecca could know that story unless Janie told her."

Over the next half hour, Smoke questioned Rebecca about his sister. Rebecca told him that Janie admitted to having been a prostitute, but that she had reformed when she met and married Oscar Davenport.

"And when I say reformed, I mean reformed," Rebecca said. "It's as Mama told me, there is nobody more righteous than a reformed whore."

"But, why didn't she tell me?" Smoke asked. "Why didn't she get in touch with me? She knew where I was. I didn't know where she was."

"She said she thought you were better off thinking she was dead. She hurt you, she hurt your father, and she hurt your mother. She was ashamed and contrite, and wanted only to go to her Maker without hurting anyone else. I wish you could have seen her at the end, Uncle Kirby. She was a good woman, and she was a good wife to Oscar. He grieved terribly when Mama died. And, in the few months I was privileged to know her, she was a good mama to me."

"And you say she died just before we got to Dodge City?" Smoke asked.

"Yes."

"What a cruel turn of fate that was," Smoke said. "To think that I came that near to seeing her again."

"Smoke, for years you have resented your sister," Sally said. "Even if you had gotten there in time, I don't know that you could have found it in your heart to forgive her."

"If the wound is deep enough, it takes a while to heal, I'll admit that," Smoke said. "But, still, I wish I had gotten there in time to see her, and to learn what she had become. I wish I had gotten there in time for forgiveness."

"For you to forgive her?" Sally asked.

Smoke shook his head.

"No, Sally. I wish I had gotten there in time for her to forgive me."

"Uncle Kirby, if you had asked Mama, she would tell you that you had done nothing that needed forgiveness. She loved you, I know that she did, I could tell by the way she spoke of you, with such pride, and such emotion."

Smoke took Rebecca in his arms and held her tight. And, for the first time since he had buried his first wife, Nicole, and their baby, Art, he felt his eyes well with tears.

By suppertime, everyone on the trail drive knew that Smoke was Rebecca's Uncle Kirby. Sally told the tale of the time Smoke tied the cow's tails together, to the delight of all the others, and to Smoke's embarrassment.

"How the hell did you do that?" Dusty asked. "I've been around those critters for most of my life and I ain't never seen one with a tail you could tie. That would be like trying to tie two fingers together."

"Look," Smoke said. He took a handful of Sally's hair. "This is the tuft at the end of a cow's tail." He took a hand full of Rebecca's hair. "This is the tuft at the end of another cow's tail." He tied their tresses together.

"Ouch!" Sally said, as she and Rebecca struggled to get untangled.

"Let that be a lesson to the two of you," Smoke said, laughing, "for telling secrets on me like that."

Everyone laughed again.

"Rebecca," Dusty said. "Would you sing for us?"

"What do you want? *Little Joe the Wrangler? Home on the Range? Red River Valley?*"

"No," Dusty said. "I want you to sing one of them real pretty songs I've heard you sing. I don't know the names of any of them, but you know what I'm talking about."

"Rebecca, sing *Panis Angelicus,*" Tom said.

"Do you know the song, Dusty?" Rebecca asked.

"No, ma'am, but once you get into it, I reckon I can strum along."

"I know it," Duff said. "I'll do the intro on the pipes."

Rebecca nodded, and Duff retrieved his bagpipes from the hoodlum wagon, and started the intro, soft, soothing, and beautiful. Then Rebecca began to sing, her voice soaring to the heights and stirring the souls of all around the campfire.

Panis angelicus
Fit panis hominum
Dat panis coelicus
Figuris terminum
O res mirabilis
Manducat Dominum
Paupier, Paupier
Servus et humilis
Paupier, Paupier
Servus et humilis

Then, when Rebecca started through the second time, she was pleasantly shocked to see Tom step up beside her and sing along with her in perfect harmonious rounds.

"Oh, you were wonderful!" Rebecca said, spontaneously hugging Tom as the others applauded.

As Tom lay in his bedroll that night, the lyrics and melody of *Panis Angelicus* played and replayed in his head. He had enjoyed singing it with Rebecca, who had, he believed, the sweetest and purest voice he had ever heard.

And though nobody at the ranch, including Rebecca knew it, Tom had been exposed to such music before. The Harvard Men's Choir, founded in 1858, was one of the best musical ensembles in America, and Tom had sung with the group as 1st tenor.

"Son, you're going to have to make up your mind whether you want to sing or play football," the coach told him. But the other players, having heard Tom sing, told the coach that if Tom couldn't do both, they wouldn't play. The coach acquiesced and a timely tackle by Tom in the 1879 Harvard Yale game preserved a 0-0 tie, the first time in three years that Harvard hadn't been beaten by Yale.

Tom thought of his fellow graduates of the class of 1880. They were all lawyers, professors, politicians, and business leaders now, all of them prominent members of society in their respective home cities. He wondered what they would think about him if they knew he was working as a cowboy for forty dollars and found. The West was wild, there was no denying that. In the last two weeks he had seen twelve men killed by gunfire. Such a thing, he knew, would leave his former acquaintances shocked and mortified, but he had come through it with no damage at all to his psyche.

On the Cimarron, November 27
The next morning during breakfast, Dusty suddenly put his tin plate down and got up and walked several feet away from the wagons and the campfire. He stood there for a long moment looking toward the ragged top of a bluff marking the western boundary of the prairie. He sniffed.

"Say, what's got into Dusty?" Dalton asked.

"I don't know," Clay replied. "But whatever it is, I've got a feeling it's not going to be good."

After a few minutes Dusty came back to the others. "Boss," he said to Clay. "We've got us a fire. I can smell it."

"What? Where?" Clay asked.

"I think it's on this side of the river. And it's west of us, which means it'll be comin' this way."

"He's right," Matt said. "Look." Matt

pointed to the west and there, faintly visible, was a cloud of light brown smoke mixed in with the haze.

"Maybe it's just a morning fog," Dalton suggested.

"It's a fire," Smoke said. "And it's a big one. Look, you can see the smoke from there, all the way down to there."

Smoke pointed out the parameters of the approaching fire.

"We'd better start a back-fire if we want to keep it away from the herd," Falcon said.

Setting a back-fire big enough to stop the oncoming flames would be quite an effort. It might have been easier if everyone could do it, but Clay knew that he would have to hold at least two people back to keep an eye on the herd. He gave that assignment to Matt and Dalton, then told the others to come with him to fight the fire.

"I think we should keep Maria back with the wagons," Sally said.

"No, Maria can do her part," Clay said. "We are going to need every hand."

"Clay, you, more than anyone, should understand why she must stay behind," Sally said.

"Oh," Clay replied, understanding now, what Sally was saying. "Yes, you are right. She should stay behind."

411

"I will stay by the river," Maria offered. "That way, I can keep some sacks wet for you."

"Yeah, that's a good idea," Smoke agreed. "We'll need wet sacks to control the flames of the back-fire, to keep them going in the right direction."

With improvised torches, Clay and the others crossed a shallow coulee and began setting fire to the tangled, brown mat which covered the ground just on the other side.

The men were setting the fires while Sally and Rebecca followed slowly behind them carrying wet sacks, making certain that the flames did not blow back across the ditch. When an errant blaze did attempt to come back, the women would beat it out while it was still small.

They were working under the most difficult of conditions, attempting to set a back-fire with no freshly plowed break of dirt, but only a shallow little dry ditch between the herd and the fire. And even the ditch had dry, tinder-like grass growing so high that it almost met over its top in places. This was anything but an ideal situation, but they had no choice but to try it.

They had barely gotten the back-fire started when a jagged line of fire with an upper wall of tumbling, brown smoke leaped into view at the top of the bluff.

"Smoke!" Sally called pointing to the fire.

"It's closer than I thought it was," Smoke said.

"We've got one thing in our favor," Falcon said. "There is less grass on the hillside than there is down here."

"Aye," Duff said. "And on some places there is nae grass at all." He pointed to a few patches of gray dirt, absolutely bare of vegetation.

When the fire reached those places it would not be able to leap over, but would have to move around. They had one more advantage. The fire was burning noticeably slower coming down a hill than it did while it was on level ground. But even that advantage was somewhat offset by the fact that there were a few long, narrow ditches that ran to the top of the bluff, and they were filled with dry brush. Those long seams would act as flues, drawing the fire down them as easily as flame following a wick.

Because Rebecca was driving a wagon instead of riding a horse, she had been alternating her apparel, wearing pants one day and a dress the next. As luck would have it, she had chosen this day to wear a dress, a choice that turned out to be unfortunate for her.

Maria was keeping the sacks wet, so that not only Rebecca and Sally, but Tom and Dalton also were carrying wet sacks with them. That helped as they beat out the errant little tongues of flame which managed to escape the back-fire line and retreat down one of the seams, or jump across the break to take up new residence.

Rebecca, in turning to extinguish a new outbreak of flames behind her, inadvertently swept her skirt across a clump of burning grass and set it aflame. Because she was intent upon her work, running from one outbreak of flame to another, and with the smoke and smell of fire all about her, she was totally unaware of what had happened.

Tom saw it, and moving quickly, wrapped a wet sack around her. Startled, and still unaware of the flaming skirt, Rebecca called out in shock.

"Tom! What are you doing?"

"Your dress was on fire," Tom said.

Rebecca looked down to inspect the damage done to her dress. When she raised up again, her face was pale.

"Oh, Tom, I . . ."

Tom saw that she was about to faint and he moved toward her quickly, catching her before she fell. She leaned into him, and as he held her, he could feel her heart beating rapidly. He remembered once having picked up a bird with a wounded wing. The little bird's heart was beating rapidly, and it looked at him with eyes full of fear. He had felt nothing but compassion for that bird, and wished with all his heart he could comfort it, let it know that it had nothing to fear from him.

He felt that way now about Rebecca, holding her to him, wishing that he could turn time back a few months and start over with her. He knelt down, bringing her down with him, lying her down on the ground, with her face up. He then positioned her across his lap so that her heart was above her head, and her feet above her heart. After that, he tilted her head to one side to reduce the risk of her swallowing her own tongue.

"Yeah! Oh yeah!" Dusty shouted.

Tom looked to see what Dusty was shouting about, and saw that the back-fire was now well on the way to meeting the approaching fires, leaving behind it a long, very wide strip of black from the charred grass. As the fires met, there would no longer be fuel to sustain them, and they would quickly burn out. The herd was no longer in danger.

"Oh!" Rebecca said, coming to. She looked up at him, suddenly realizing that she was lying, for the most part, on his lap.

"Oh!" she said. "Oh, what happened?"

"You fainted," Tom said.

"I must get up." She struggled to do so, but Tom restrained her. He restrained her gently, but he did restrain her.

"Get up slowly," he said. "Otherwise you could pass out again."

She stopped struggling, then he got up, reached down, and helped her up.

A little unsteady on her feet, she fell into him again, and he held her tightly for a long moment.

"Are you all right?" Tom asked after a moment.

"Yes, I'm fine, thank you," Rebecca said. "You saved my life, didn't you?"

Tom smiled at her. "I wouldn't go that far," he said. "But I might have kept you from getting a painful burn."

Rebecca put her arms around his neck to steady herself. As she did so, their lips came in close proximity as they had before when he set her down from the horse. That time, the unexpected flushing of a quail stopped them. Nothing stopped them this time, and he pulled her to him, crushing his lips against hers.

Rebecca was pleasantly surprised by the kiss, and she reacted to it with a heat that thrilled her to her soul. The kiss went on, much longer than she would have thought, until, finally, it was Tom who broke off the kiss.

Rebecca felt as limp as a rag doll, and she looked at him with her senses reeling.

"I'm sorry," Tom said, self-consciously. "I had no right to do that."

"Oh, Tom," Rebecca said. "You have every right. Don't you know that?"

"We should get back to the camp."

CHAPTER NINETEEN

Indian territory, December 5
The day after the fire, as they were having their breakfast they were surprised to look up and see an Indian, his face lined with age and wizened with experience. The Indian was standing less than ten feet away.

Clay smiled. "Ashki," he said. "I see that you are still able to walk like a bird."

"You did not hear?" Ashki asked.

"I did not."

"You did not see me?"

"I did not."

Ashki smiled. "I am old," he said. "But still I can walk like a warrior."

"Would you like breakfast?" Sally asked.

Ashki made a motion of drinking. "Coffee," he said.

Sally poured a cup of coffee and handed it to him. "Won't you try a biscuit?"

"Biscuit has no taste," Ashki said.

"Sally, offer him a sinker," Smoke said.

Sally gave the Indian a doughnut. He held it to his nose, sniffed, held it out and looked at it for a long moment before he took a tentative taste. At the first taste a huge smile spread across his face, and he nodded.

"It is good, this sinker," he said as he took another bite. "Do you have tobacco?"

"Do you think I would come through Indian Territory without tobacco for my friend?" Clay asked. He walked over to the hoodlum wagon and searched around inside for a moment, then came back with a pouch and an envelope. "This ought to be enough tobacco to last you for a month or two," he said. "And here is another gift for you." Clay handed Ashki the envelope.

Ashki looked inside, then looked up with a puzzled expression on his face.

"Little white papers? Why do you give me little white papers?"

"Let me show you," Clay said.

Clay took one of the little papers, lay it along his forefinger and index finger, curled it, then filled in some tobacco from a small bag. He rolled the paper closed, licked the side, then put it in his mouth and lit it.

"With these you can make a cigarette," he said. "You won't have to use your pipe."

"A pipe you can share with others. How do you share the little papers with others?

419

How do you care for it?"

Clay shook his head. "That's the beauty of it. You don't have to share it with others, because everyone else can have one of their own," he said. "And there is nothing to care for. It burns up as you smoke it. After you smoke it, it's all gone. There is nothing left."

"It is the way of the people to share the pipe with others," Ashki said. He pulled his pipe from a small bag he had hanging from a rawhide cord tied around his waist. "From my father, I got this pipe," he said. "He got it from his father, and from his father before him. To my son I will give this pipe, and to his son and to his son. Can you do this with a paper pipe?"

Smoke laughed. "He's got you there, Clay."

"I can't deny that," Clay said.

Ashki filled his pipe, lit it, then, as his head was wreathed in smoke, he looked out at the herd. He pointed to the cattle.

"Are they buffalo?"

"Buffalo? No, they aren't buffalo," Clay said. "Ashki, you have been around buffalo all your life. You know that isn't buffalo."

"It is being said that you are taking buffalo from our land," Ashki said. "There are many who want to make trouble for you, but I told them that I do not think you are taking buffalo."

"Why would they think we are taking buffalo?" Clay asked.

"Because the cows are black," Smoke said.

"Yeah," Clay said. "I guess you are right. I guess from a distance, someone might think that. But they would have to think that they were awfully small buffalo."

"Dohate thinks you are stealing buffalo," Ashki said. "I told him I do not think so, but he would not listen. He has gathered many. I think he will make war with you soon."

"Make war with us?" Clay replied quickly. "Ashki, are you telling me we are going to be attacked by Indians?"

"I think this is so," Ashki said.

"How many?"

Ashki opened and closed his hand three times.

"Fifteen?"

"Fifteen," Ashki said.

"Where will they be?"

"At the place of the Yellow Hair Fight," Ashki said.

"Do you know where that is?" Smoke asked.

"Yes, he's talking about the Washita River. That's, where Custer and Black Kettle had their fight. That's about five miles south of here," Clay said. "I guess Dohate thinks it would be strong medicine to hit us there."

"Do you know this man, Dohate?" Falcon asked.

"Yeah, I know him. I've had to pay him a toll every time we've come through here. Generally three or four cows is enough. Sometimes a horse or two. Which reminds me, Ashki, do you have a horse?" Clay asked.

"No."

"Dusty, give our friend a horse from Mo's string."

"Come along, Ashki," Dusty said.

As Dusty led Ashki over to the remuda to give him a horse, the others discussed their options.

"How hard would it be to go around the Washita?" Tom asked.

"There are only so many places where you can ford a herd this size," Clay said. "It would add at least two weeks, maybe longer, if we tried to go around."

"They say forewarned is forearmed," Matt said. "Why don't we attack them before they attack us?"

"Why attack him at all?" Tom asked.

"You heard the Indian, Tom," Dalton said. "We don't have any choice."

"Dalton is right," Clay added. "It's either

attack or be attacked, and I'd much rather attack. That way we control when, and where the fight is."

"But you said that you know him, that you have dealt with him before. As I understood Ashki, Dohate's biggest bone of contention with us seems to be that he thinks we are taking buffalo from them. Why don't we leave the herd here and buy him off with a few cows? That way he will know we are not herding buffalo."

"Tom has a point," Smoke said. "If we can show him that we aren't stealing buffalo, then we might be able to get out of this without a fight. I'll cut out three or four cows and go meet him."

"No," Tom said.

The others looked at Tom in surprise.

"What do you mean, no? This was your idea," Clay said.

"I don't think that Smoke, or Falcon, or any of the rest of you should go. I think I should go, and I think I should go alone."

"Why would you say something like that? What if you are wrong? You wouldn't have a chance against them, all by yourself."

"That's exactly why I should be the one to go," Tom said. "If I am wrong, and it comes to an actual armed confrontation, who would you rather have wielding a gun in your defense? Smoke Jensen? Or me?"

"You're not making one lick of sense," Clay said.

"Yes, he is," Dusty said. "And you all know it."

The others looked at each other and, for a long moment, not one person spoke.

"Clay, tell him he is foolish," Rebecca said, a catch of fear in her voice.

"I am not being foolish, Rebecca," Tom said, calmly. "Clearly, I am the most expendable of this group."

"No, you aren't expendable!" Rebecca said. "Not to me, you aren't."

"Rebecca," Tom said. "This has to be done."

"Tom, have you ever had any dealings with Indians?" Smoke asked.

"No. But I have dealt with people in stressful situations. And I'm not one who loses his head easily."

"No, from what I have seen of you, I wouldn't think that you would. Clay, you know Dohate, so why don't you cut out a few cows, how many ever you think it will take? I'll give Tom a quick course on dealing with Indians."

"All right," Clay said. "Dusty, you and Dalton want to cut the cows out? Pick out three."

"Put a bell on the lead cow," Tom said. "And string a rope between them."

"Why do that?" Clay asked. "If you are only taking three cows with you, they won't be that hard to drive."

"If they were buffalo, could you bell the leader and string a line between them?" Tom asked.

"Not unless you wanted to get yourself trampled," Clay said, then, as soon as he answered the question, he realized the point Tom was making, and he smiled. "I see what you mean," he said. "You aren't just book smart, are you? When they see you coming toward them that way, they aren't likely to think you're leading buffalo."

"All right, while they're rounding up the cows for you, let's talk about Indians," Smoke said. "First lesson is, when you are talking to one, look him directly in the eye. If he can't see into your eyes, he won't be able to fathom your medicine. And Indians set a great store by medicine. The stronger your medicine is, the more willing they are to listen to you."

"All right," Tom answered.

"Generally, the first one to talk to you won't be the leader. Pay attention, you'll be able to tell who the leader is, so when you start negotiating, that's the one you want to negotiate with. And, this is important. Don't ask who is the leader, you have to figure that out on your own. If you do that, he will take it as a compliment, meaning that his leadership is so evident that even a stranger can pick it up."

"How will I find them?" Tom asked. "I mean, I know they are at the Washita, but how will I find them?"

"You won't have to find them. They'll find you," Smoke said.

"All right," Tom said again.

"It may be that they will all come toward you, especially since you will be alone, but more than likely, they'll leave a few behind. And, as they come toward you, greet them like this."

Smoke held his arm up, crooked at the elbow, with the palm facing out.

"That will show them that you have come in peace."

"Do you really say 'how', when you meet an Indian?" Tom asked.

Smoke chuckled. "That's close enough," he said. "Actually, the word is 'hau'." Smoke put a guttural phrasing to the word that made it more distinctive, though it was close enough to "how" that Tom could see where that came from.

"Should he take his pistol, or leave it

behind?" Clay asked.

"Well of course he is going to take a pistol," Rebecca said. "You are sending him out to face the Indians alone. Would you send him unarmed as well?"

"I will not take a pistol," Tom said.

"Why not?" Rebecca asked.

"Think about it," Tom said. "If they want to kill me, there is nothing I could do about it, even if I had a pistol, especially considering how many of them there are, and how ineffective I am with such a weapon. On the other if I face them without a weapon, they might perceive that as being without fear."

"Tom does have a point, Rebecca," Smoke said.

"I do have one more question," Tom said.

"What's that?"

"You said I should show them that my medicine is strong. How do I do that?"

Smoke sighed. "Yeah," he said. "That one will be hard, but you are going to have to do it."

"How?"

"It is important, no, let's say it is vital, that you show no fear. No matter what they do, you must not show fear."

"Do you think you can do that, Tom?" Clay asked.

"Nobody can show no fear at all," Rebecca said, anxiously.

"I can do it," Tom said.

"Tom, no, you know you —"

"Rebecca, look at me," Tom said.

Rebecca looked at him.

"I can do it," Tom said resolutely.

Dusty and Dalton returned then with the three cows, tied together by one long rope. And as Tom had requested, a bell had been attached to the lead cow. Tom started toward his horse.

"No," Clay said. "Don't take that horse, take Thunder. I've seen you ride, Tom," Clay said. "Maybe you can't shoot, but I've never seen anyone who could ride better than you, and on Thunder I doubt there is an Indian in the territory who could catch you. If it looks like things aren't going to go the way you think they should, you put spurs in Thunder's side and get the hell out of there."

"Now that is the most intelligent thing I've heard yet," Rebecca said.

"I'll get Thunder saddled for you, Tom," Dalton said.

"Thanks."

"Dalton, wait," Clay called. "I seem to recall that Dohate has a taste for horehound candy. I know you got some while we were in Dodge. Do you have any left?"

Dalton was a little embarrassed by the question. He had bought some, but he wanted to keep it secret, not to prevent any of the others from having any, but because he was afraid they would think it was childish.

"Yeah, I've got some left," he admitted sheepishly.

"After you get Thunder saddled, give some of it to Tom. He might have a use for it."

"All right," Dalton agreed.

"Tom?" Rebecca called.

Rebecca turned and walked toward the wagon, indicating that she wanted him to come to her. He did.

"Rebecca, you aren't going to be able to talk me out of this," Tom said.

"I know," she said. "So I won't even try."

"Good."

"Do you love me, Tom?"

"Rebecca, this hardly seems the time or place for us to discuss something like this."

"I will ask you again, very slowly, and very distinctly. Do — you — love — me — Tom? It's not a hard question."

"Rebecca, there are things about my past that you don't know," Tom said. He held up his hands and looked at them. It was as if he could still see the blood.

"I don't care about your past, Tom. I only care about now," Rebecca said. "I know that you are not who you seem to be. I know you are not a cowboy. I know you are not a Westerner. I know that you have an education, a wonderful education, more than anyone I have ever known. And I know that you must have come from a life that is very different from this one. And whatever it was that made you give up that life must have been something very significant. I don't know what it was and I don't care what it was.

"I only know that here, you have been able to make a new start. Half the men in the West are not that different, Tom. There are many men here, and women too, who are making a new start."

"Tom, we've got the horse here, ready to go," Clay called.

"Do you love me, Tom?"

"This is not good for either one of us, Rebecca."

"I'm only going to ask you this one more time, Tom. This has nothing to do with who you are, what you are, or what you are running from. This has only to do with you and me, right here, and right now. Do you love me, Tom?"

"Yes," Tom said. "For both of our sakes I

wish I could say otherwise, but, God help us, yes, Rebecca, I do love you."

Rebecca smiled, then kissed him, a short, brushing peck only, on the lips.

"Come back to me safely, Tom," she said.

Tom nodded and looked at her, opening himself up to her so that she could look deep into his eyes, all the way to the scars on his soul. Then, turning away from her without speaking another word, he started toward Dalton, who was holding both Thunder, and the string of three cows.

Smoke came over to talk to him.

"Tom," Smoke said. "Even leading the cows, you should be there within an hour. As soon as you give them the cows, turn and start back. Do not break into a gallop. At a gait that is comfortable for the horse, you should be back here within two hours from right now. If you are not back here within two hours, we are coming after you."

"I'll be back," Tom said.

Smoke reached out to shake Tom's hand. "I'm sure you will be," he said.

As Tom rode toward his rendezvous with Dohate and the Indians Dohate had with him, he thought of his conversation with Rebecca. Should he have confessed to her that he did love her? Wouldn't it have been much better to tell her that he didn't, rather

431

than build her up for what could never be?

Or should he tell her of his past? No, he had told her, but it did no good.

Like turning the pages of a book, a part of his past opened up to him.

"I'm telling you now, Tom, don't do this."

"But I can do it, I know I can."

"It is too big a risk."

"I have to do it, don't you understand?"

"Maybe, for one, but not for both of them."

"Are you telling me I must choose?" Tom asked.

"Yes. Choose one, or lose both."

"I can do it. All it takes is a steady hand and self-confidence," Tom said.

"Yes, but there is a difference between self-confidence and arrogance. A big difference. Somehow you don't seem to understand that."

"Arrogance? My God, do you think I'm doing this from a sense of arrogance? This is my wife! This is my child. Now either help me, or get the hell out of the way, because I'm going to do it."

"You are going to have blood on your hands, Tom. Can you live with that?"

Can you live with that? Can you live with that? Can you live with that?

Could he live with it? Tom still didn't

432

know the answer, and now as he continued to ride south, he held up his hands and looked at them. The blood was there still. How could he ask for Rebecca's love?

The Washita River was directly ahead of him now; he could see the long line of trees growing along the banks of the river. Tom remembered crossing it on the way up to Dodge City. He remembered being particularly interested in it, because he had read all about its bloody history. Custer and Black Kettle had fought a battle here. And, because there were several Indian encampments along the river, they had all come to join in the battle, which resulted in over one hundred Indians being killed and fifty-one lodges and their contents burned. In addition, the camp's pony herd of roughly eight hundred horses was killed. The Seventh Cavalry suffered twenty-two men killed, including two officers, Major Elliot and Captain Hamilton. Captain Hamilton was the grandson of Alexander Hamilton.

It had been bitterly cold on the day of the fight, and it was very cold now. Tom couldn't help but relate to the soldiers of the Seventh Cavalry, not only because of the cold, but because he was riding to meet some Indians, and he had not the slightest idea as to what

433

was going to happen.

He knew, though, that he was about to find out, because ahead, emerging from the line of trees, he saw a number of Indians coming toward him. A quick count determined that there were ten of them approaching. If Ashki had been accurate with his own count, that meant that at least five of the Indians were staying out of sight.

As one, all ten started galloping toward him, yipping and yelling at the top of their voices, urging their horses to top speed. Tom was pretty sure, at this point, that he if dropped the rope to the cows, turned around and gave Thunder his head, he could easily outrun them. But that wouldn't accomplish anything. The herd would still have to come through here to cross the Washita, and if this issue wasn't resolved now, the Indians would still be here waiting on them. Because of that, Tom stopped his horse, and simply stood his ground as the ten Indian ponies thundered toward him.

Smoke had told him to crook his arm at the elbow and hold his hand up, palm out, so that is exactly what he did as they approached.

The Indians reined up when they reached him, then looked at each other in surprise. They had expected the lone rider to turn and run.

"How," Tom said. "Good morning."

The Indians began speaking to each other, but as they spoke in their native language, Tom could not understand what they were saying.

"He is a man with powerful medicine. He has no fear."

"He has fear. If I raise my war club over his head, he will show fear."

"No, I think not. I do not see fear in his eyes."

"His medicine is not strong enough to overcome the fear of dying, this I will prove to you. I will raise my war club over his head. If he shows fear, I will kill him. If he shows no fear, I will let him live."

Though Tom had no idea what they were saying, he was certain they were talking about him, and when one of them raised his war club and let out a menacing, blood-curdling yell, he knew they were talking about him.

He also sensed, though he had no idea how he was able to sense this, that the Indian had no real intention of killing him, but was just testing him.

"Show fear, White Man," the Indian said in English. "Show fear, for I am about to kill you!"

Tom remained motionless, staring directly

into the eyes of the club-wielding Indian.

"Show fear!" The Indian shouted again, his voice as loud and menacing as he could make it.

Suddenly, Tom realized that he wasn't going to be killed. He realized too, that he had passed the test, and he smiled.

"Ayiee," one of the warriors said in his own language. "Look at him, how he smiles at death! His medicine is great."

One of the Indians, one who had not spoken before, held his hand out toward the Indian with the war club. Tom knew then that this was the leader. It was as Smoke had told him.

"Put the club away," the leader said in English. Then he spoke to Tom. "My name is . . ."

"I know who you are," Tom said. "You are Dohate."

During the entire confrontation, Tom had not let go of the rope by which he had been leading the three cows. He handed the rope to Dohate.

"How is it that you know my name?" Dohate asked.

"I have heard stories told of Dohate, a brave and fearless warrior," Tom said, playing up to the Indian's ego. He knew that he had scored when he saw the look of pride and satisfaction on Dohate's face.

"Because the cattle we are driving are black, you thought they were buffalo," Tom said. "But as you can see it is only cattle."

"I have never seen cattle such as these."

"They are called Angus," Tom said.

"Angus," Dohate repeated, though when he spoke the word it came out as "Angoose."

"Never have you eaten meat that is better than this," Tom said.

Dohate took the line. "You make gift to Dohate?" he asked.

"Yes," Tom said. "In return, we ask that you let us pass through."

"What is your name?" Dohate asked.

"My name is Tom. I am told, also, that you like this candy." Tom handed a little bag of horehound candy to the Indian and he looked inside, smiled, then took one out and put it in his mouth. He did not offer any of the candy to anyone else.

"Your cattle may pass, Tom."

When the others saw Tom returning, they hurried out to meet him.

"You are here and the cows aren't," Clay said. "I take it that means you and Dohate worked things out?"

"Our cattle may pass," Tom said.

"Good job, Tom!" Clay said.

"Smoke?"

"Yes."

"Thank you for your briefing. It proved to be very helpful," Tom said.

Red River, December 10

They were within sight of Texas now, and though they were still quite a way from their ultimate destination, there was a sense of satisfaction in knowing that they would be back in Texas by the next day. It was bitterly cold, much colder than it had been during any part of the drive, even though they were significantly farther south from where they started.

"As soon as we cross the river, we'll be in Texas," Dusty said.

"But it is later into December than we thought it would be, isn't it?" Sally asked.

"Yes," Clay said. "Later than I would like."

"How long until Christmas?" Dalton asked.

"Fifteen days," Rebecca said. "This is the tenth."

"I wonder what Pa got me for Christmas."

"Why, Dalton," Clay said. "I figured letting you come on this drive was your Christmas present." The others laughed.

"That might be true," Dalton said. "I

know that I've enjoyed this more than anything I've ever done before. It has made me appreciate what cowboys do."

"It's done something else for you, too, Dalton," Clay said. "It has made you a man."

"Clay's right, son," Dusty said. "You've become a man I could work with, and probably some day work for, and be proud to do it."

"Thanks," Dalton said, beaming with pride over the praise. "Dusty, Duff, would you all play some Christmas carols?"

"I'll play them if you folks will sing along," Dusty said.

As the campfire burned brightly, sending sparks high into the night sky, the eight men and three women sat close enough to enjoy its warmth, and filled the night air with their music.

"I wonder which star it was," Dalton said, as he looked into the black vault overhead. The sky was filled with stars, from the brightest ones of the highest magnitude, on down to the smaller and dimmer stars, until finally nothing could be discerned but a fine blue dusting of stars that were just below being visible, except for the blue dust they scattered across the heavens.

"You mean which star led the wise men to

the baby Jesus?" Sally asked.

"Yeah, I wonder which one it was?"

"Maybe it was that one," Dusty suggested, pointing to one particularly bright pin-point of light.

"No, that's Venus," Tom said. "It isn't a star, it's a planet."

"Maybe it was the North Star," Smoke suggested. "It has guided me, many a time," Smoke said. "And there it is."

"That's Polaris," Sally said.

"That's easy to find. All you have to do is line it up with the Big Dipper," Dalton said.

"I wonder if any of the stars in the Big Dipper have a name?" Clay asked.

"They all have names," Tom said. "The first star in the Dipper's handle, is Alkaid. Then comes Mizar and Alioth. The stars in the cup are called Megrez, Phecda, Dubhe, and Merek."

Tom pointed out each of the stars as he named them.

"What is that star?" Dalton asked, pointing to another one.

"I don't know."

"I was beginning to think you knew the names of all the stars."

Tom laughed. "Well, now, there are billions of stars," he said. "So not all of them have names. That means we can name some if we want to. Suppose we name them after the ladies? We can call that one Maria, that one Sally, and that one Rebecca."

"Wow, my sister has her own star," Dalton said.

CHAPTER TWENTY

"That was sweet of you to give me my own star," Rebecca said later that night as Tom got ready to ride on night herd and she got ready to go to bed.

"I can be very generous when it doesn't cost me anything," Tom teased. "If you notice, I even gave one to Maria and Sally."

Both were wearing fur-lined sheepskin coats, and as they breathed and spoke, clouds of vapor filled the air between them.

"Yes, but my star is, by far, the most beautiful," Rebecca said.

Tom smiled. "If you say so." Tom looked around and saw that they were shielded from everyone's view by the hoodlum wagon.

As Tom looked at her, Rebecca saw a smoldering flame in his eyes, and she felt a tingling in the pit of her stomach. He moved toward her, paused for a moment, and encountering no resistance, put his hand behind her head and pulled her lips to his.

It was dark enough here that they could move in to the wagon and no one would ever be the wiser. Why not give in to the need that was clearly driving them both?

"Tom, are you ready?" Dusty called. "Let's get out there."

Tom and Rebecca jerked apart as abruptly as if Dusty had come upon them. Tom pulled his hands back, and Rebecca felt her skirt fall back into place. They stared at each other through the darkness for a long moment, the vapor in the night air almost luminous as it hung between them.

"I must go," Tom said.

"Yes, you must," Rebecca said.

"Tom, come on! You know that Matt and Falcon are getting cold out there!"

"I'll be right there," Tom called back, and with one last long gaze at Rebecca, he hurried out to join Dusty for the night.

Tom realized that he had gone too far now. He couldn't treat Rebecca this way unless he was willing to make a commitment. Could he find the strength to make the commitment? And if he did, would Rebecca be strong enough to stand up to her father?

Red River, December 11

A strong wind came up during the night, making the cold even more difficult. Then, the next morning, as all were gathered around the breakfast fire for its warmth as well as breakfast, Dusty pointed to the west.

"That doesn't look good, Clay," he said.

To the west was a huge reddish-gray wall that, at first glance, looked like nothing more than a building cloud. But closer examination showed that it was an approaching sand storm.

"Get everything in the wagons that we can!" Clay said, and for the next five minutes there was a flurry of activity as everyone worked frantically to make certain that nothing loose was left outside. Then, the sand and dust storm struck them, and it was as if night had fallen again, only worse, for at night they had the moon and stars, and even lanterns to help them. The dust storm blinded them beyond the power of the sun, or of any lantern.

The cattle reacted to the storm, first by lowering their heads and turning their backs to the wind. Then, driven by the wind, they began to drift in one large mass. In the meantime the air was filled with the blowing sand which not only blinded the cowboys, but stung their skin as if they were be-

444

ing rubbed down with sandpaper.

The horses were having a hard time keeping their feet, and they trembled with fear, not quite aware of what was happening to them. Smoke, Falcon, Clay and Dusty managed to make it to the front of the herd, and they started shooting their pistols into the ground, hoping by the noise to check their movement. But so loud was the dust storm, and so abrasive were the wind-tossed granules of sand, that the men on the flank and to the rear of the herd couldn't even hear the gunshots.

Rebecca, Sally and Maria huddled together in the hoodlum wagon listening to the roar of the wind, to the canvas flapping against the wagon bows, and to the rattle of the sand.

"Oh, the poor animals," Maria said. "How awful this must be for them."

"It's not all that good for our men folk either," Sally said.

"Maria, you don't look well," Rebecca said. "Are you ill?"

"I think maybe the baby will come sooner than I thought. I have been having some pains."

"Maria, when you say very soon, you aren't saying — I mean, you don't think that the baby will be born before we get home, do you?" Rebecca asked.

"I don't know," Maria said. "Clay says he thinks we will be home before Christmas, and Mama says the baby will come in January."

"Mrs. Bustamante? Not a doctor?"

"Mama is a *comadrona*," Maria said. "How do you say — she is one who helps women have babies."

"Midwife?" Sally asked.

"Si. *Comadrona*, midwife."

"I hope she is right. I would hate for you to have to have the baby during this drive."

"If she delivers during the drive, we'll just take care of it," Sally said reassuringly. "Hundreds of babies were born on the wagon trains going west."

"That is true, isn't it?" Rebecca said. "Still, I hope the baby doesn't come until we get back to the ranch."

Outside the wagon, the dust storm continued to roar and, even inside the wagon, with the canvas stretched over the bows to protect them against the sharp sting of the sand, the air was so full that they could barely see each other.

The wagon was broadside against the wind, and once or twice the two wheels on the right side of the wagon lifted slightly from the ground.

"We are going to have to turn the wagons into the wind," Sally said. "If we don't, they will surely tip over."

"Not into the wind, away from the wind," Rebecca suggested. "That way the mules will have some protection."

"Yes," Sally agreed.

Even as the men were out with the cattle, the three women, working on their own, managed to prod the mules into turning so that the backsides of the mules, as well as the backsides of the wagons, were into the wind. What normally would have taken no more than a minute or two took at least fifteen minutes because the mules were so hesitant to move.

Now, there was no longer any danger of the wagons tipping over, but without the canvas sides to stop the wind and the blowing sand, they whipped through the wagons at full force.

By the time the dust storm ended, the cattle had drifted more than three miles away. The good thing was that they had stayed together, so it was fairly easy to drive them back to where the wagons were waiting. It was late afternoon, and with the dust gone, the cold winter sky was a clear, bright blue. However it was late enough so that already the sun was sinking in the west. In addition the men, who had been fighting the dust storm for the entire day, were much too exhausted to push the cattle across the river, so they made the decision to spend one more night here.

Sally and the women warmed a big kettle of water and the men washed their faces, which were raw from the cold and the blowing sand. Tom's eyes looked like two glowing embers glaring out from a sheet of parchment. Everyone else's eyes looked the same.

Rebecca handed Tom a warm, wet cloth, and watched as he washed his face and his eyes. Inexplicably, she giggled.

"What is it?" Tom asked, surprised by her laughter.

"It is your eyes," Rebecca said. "They are so red that I wonder if they will glow in the dark."

"I'm Mephistopheles, Rebecca, didn't you know that?" Tom said, making a frightening face.

Rebecca laughed again. "Don't do that," she said. "You'll frighten the others."

Amarillo, Texas, December 11
Lars Prewitt was a slender man with slumped shoulders and long arms. He had sunken cheeks and a Vandyke beard that

was dark in color, contrasting sharply with his gray hair. Prewitt was also the largest cattleman in Potter County, Texas. What nobody in Amarillo or Potter County knew was that Prewitt had help in building his ranch. That help came by way of his providing a ready outlet for stolen stock, and every cattle rustler between Fort Worth and Denver knew that they could sell their stolen beef there.

At the moment, Prewitt was sitting at a table in the White Elephant Saloon, having a drink and a conversation with Red Coleman.

"Why do I need more cattle?" Prewitt asked, in response to a proposal made by Red. "Hell, I damn near have to give away the cows I got now, no more'n they are paying for them at the market."

"What are they paying for Longhorns right now?" Red asked.

"The market opened this morning at four dollars and twenty cents a head," Prewitt said. "I can barely feed them for that."

"Uh, huh," Red said, smiling broadly. "Suppose I told you I could get you two thousand, five hundred head of cattle that are paying seventeen dollars per head?"

"What kind of cattle would that be?" Prewitt asked.

Red reached into his shirt pocket and pulled out the article about the cattle drive he had torn from the Dodge City newspaper. He showed it to Prewitt.

"Yeah, I've read some about these Black Angus cows," Prewitt said shortly after he got into the article. He read for a moment, then slid the article back to Red. "You're right, it says here that they are seventeen dollars a head."

"It might even be more. And those cows could be yours."

"What do you have in mind?" Prewitt asked.

"I have in mind to take that herd when they get into Texas," he said. "After I have the herd, I'll bring 'em to you for four dollars a head."

"You are going to take the herd? Just like that?"

"Just like that."

"You expect the cowboys who are driving the herd to just watch you ride away with the cows, do you?"

"In a manner of speaking, yeah, I do," Red said. "From what I've been able to gather, there are only seven of them. Seven cowboys trying to drive two thousand, five hundred head four hundred fifty miles. That means they are goin' to be all spread out. If I hit them with, oh, say eight men, in the middle of the night, I don't expect any resistance at all."

"This article says the cows are going to Ben Conyers," Prewitt said.

"Yeah, I read that," Red said.

"Conyers. As in Big Ben Conyers," Prewitt said, emphasizing the name. "Don't you know who he is?"

"I've never heard of him before this article," Red said. "Should I have heard of him?"

"Richard King, John Chisolm, Shanghai Pierce, Big Ben Conyers," Prewitt said. "They are the cattle giants of Texas, and there isn't a one of them who would stand by and let their herds be taken."

"It's not his herd yet," Red said easily. "I won't be taking a herd from Conyers. I'll be taking it from Smoke Jensen."

Prewitt's eyes opened wide. "Smoke Jensen? Good God man, that's even worse. Don't you know who Smoke Jensen is?"

"Yeah, I know who the son of a bitch is," Red said. "And I have a score to settle with him."

"Smoke Jensen doesn't scare you off?"

"No," Red said. "Does Conyers scare you off?"

Prewitt paused for a moment before he

answered. "I'll say this. I would like nothing better than to take Big Ben's cows away from him."

"Well, sir, I'm the man that can do it for you," Red said. "All we have to do is come to some agreement on my cut."

"Let's take a walk down to Western Union," Prewitt said.

"Western Union? What for?"

"I know how much Longhorns opened for this morning. I'd like to get a report on these Black Angus."

Lars Prewitt was an average-sized man, but he elevated his height with high-heeled boots and a high-crowned hat. His eyes were such a pale blue that one had to look twice to see any color.

Prewitt was well known in Amarillo, and as he and Red ambled down the boardwalk between the White Elephant Saloon and the Western Union office, several of the citizens spoke to him.

When they stepped into the Western Union office, it smelled of the pipe tobacco the telegrapher was smoking. At the moment, he held the pipe clenched tightly in his teeth as he bent over the clacking telegraph key, writing on a pad the message that was coming in. Prewitt and Red remained quiet until the telegrapher worked the key to sign off. The telegrapher tore the page off the pad, folded it double, then turned in his swivel chair.

"Mr. Prewitt," he said, recognizing one of the county's leading citizens. "What can I do for you?"

"How about getting in touch with the cattle exchange market in Kansas City for me. I want you to check some prices."

"I can save you some money, Mr. Prewitt," the telegrapher said. "I checked on the Longhorns for the newspaper editor, not an hour ago."

"I'm not interested in Longhorns," Prewitt said.

"Oh? What are you interested in?"

"Black Angus."

"Black Angus, you say? Well, now, that's interesting. Who are you checking for? As far as I know, nobody in the whole county has Black Angus."

"I have a chance to buy some Black Angus cattle at, what I think, is a good price. But I want to be certain."

The telegrapher nodded, then bent over his key and gave it a few taps. There was a pause, then a response. The telegrapher responded again, then a moment later the key clacked very quickly as he took the message. When it was finished he swiveled around in his chair again.

"The latest price paid on Black Angus is as of two fifteen this afternoon," automatically, they all looked at the clock, it was two forty-one. "And at that time it was seventeen dollars and seventy-five cents."

"Thank you," Prewitt said, and he gave the telegrapher a dollar.

The two men stepped back out onto the boardwalk in front of the telegrapher's office.

"Do we have a deal?"

"Come out to the ranch," Prewitt said. "This isn't anything I want to talk about in town."

Live Oaks Ranch, December 13
Two of Big Ben Conyers' ranch hands, Roy Baker and Gene Finely, drove a wagon up to the front of the house. There was a coniferous tree in the wagon so large that the top, and fully one third of the tree, extended from the back of the wagon.

"This is about the largest one we could get in the wagon, Mr. Conyers. Fact is, it might be too big to go into your house," Roy said.

"If we can get it in through the door without breaking off too many of the limbs, we can set it up in the parlor," Big Ben said.

"It has a twenty-foot-high ceiling."

"I reckon we can get it in," Gene said. "If we take it in bottom first, it'll cause the limbs to bend up, and that way they won't break off."

"As soon as we get this one up, I want you to find another good tree, and take it in town to the Our Lady of Mercy Orphanage. I told the Sisters there that I'd be bringing them a tree."

"Yes, sir, we got a real nice one picked out," Roy said. "Soon as we get this one up for you, we'll go get that one."

There were at least ten children of the ranch hands, varying in ages from four to twelve. This being Saturday, there was no school, and as the tree was offloaded from the wagon — it took four men — and moved toward the house, the children all gathered around in excitement.

"I'm going to need a lot of help with this tree," Big Ben said. "I just don't know who I can find to help."

"Me, me!" one of the boys shouted, and he was joined by all the others.

"Well, I suppose you can help. Also, Mrs. Conyers made some peppermint candy — way too much for me to eat. I'll need some help with that as well."

Again the response was enthusiastic.

"Well, come on in then, we may as well get started," Big Ben said.

The stand for the tree had been built long ago, a crisscross of boards that not only supplied a receptacle for the base of the tree, but also had long enough arms to hold the tree steady. Roy, Gene, and the other two cowboys got the tree mounted and secured.

"Well, I thank you men, I guess I don't need the boys and girls after all," Big Ben said. "The tree is in, we're all finished."

"No we aren't," a nine-year-old boy said.

"What do you mean, we aren't? The tree is up, isn't it?"

"But it's not decorated," the boy said.

"Oh!" Big Ben said, hitting himself in the forehead. "I *knew* it didn't look right. Mrs. Conyers, do we have any decorations we could put on this tree?"

"How about this?" she asked, putting a box down on the floor.

With shouts of delight, the children opened the box and began applying the decorations.

"Nobody on the ladder unless you are at least twelve years old," Big Ben ordered.

Roy, Gene, and the other two cowboys remained to help the children decorate the tree, especially the upper part of it. Big Ben and Julia stood back, drinking coffee and smiling as they watched.

"I certainly hope that Rebecca and Dalton are back by Christmas," Julia said.

"I think they will be. And if they aren't, well, we'll just have a delayed Christmas, is all."

With the herd

That same night while in camp, Dalton was riding night herd when his horse stepped into a hole, causing the horse and rider to go down. The sleeping herd, disturbed by the unexpected noise, came to their feet as one, and started running.

Dalton got to his feet quickly, but his horse, frightened now by the onrushing herd, ran away, and Dalton suddenly found himself standing in front of the herd with no way to escape.

Tom was the other night rider, and as the entire herd broke into a stampede, he saw at once the danger that Dalton was in. Although the riders rotated their horses from day to day, it was a fortunate turn of events that Tom just happened to be astride Thunder, who was the fastest and strongest horse in the entire remuda.

Tom urged Thunder into a gallop, quickly overtaking the running herd. He dashed across the space in front, and without breaking stride, leaned down from his saddle far enough to wrap his right arm around Dalton's waist. Then, lifting him up from the ground and carrying him with one arm, as if he was a football, he galloped ahead of the herd until he had enough of a lead on them to take an angle to get out of their way. Once he was clear of the running herd, he stopped, then put Dalton down.

"All you all right?" Tom asked.

"Yes, I'm fine," Dalton said, almost too stunned to react.

"There's your horse," Tom said, pointing to the animal that, once out of danger, started back. "I'll get him."

Tom recovered the horse, then brought him back to Dalton.

By now Matt and Dusty, who were already about to come on duty anyway, were in the saddle chasing after the runaway herd. Matt was riding his own horse, Spirit. Spirit was fast, and the ground in front was clear, so he was easily able to overtake and then pass the herd.

Matt pulled his pistol and began firing into the air, hoping that the cattle would be more frightened by the noise in front than the noise in back. The gunfire didn't stop the cattle, but it did have the effect of letting the rest of the outfit know what was going on.

The wagons were about one hundred fifty yards away from where the cattle had been sleeping, so even without Matt's warning shots, there wasn't a man or woman on the drive who didn't know what was going on. Matt knew that the others would come as soon as possible, so he kept Spirit galloping, angling toward the side farthest from the wagon until he was no longer in front of, but even with the leaders. Once in position, he did what he could to keep the herd from splitting.

After a moment he heard gunfire coming from the other side of the herd. He didn't know who was there, but was pleased to know that he was no longer alone in trying to stop the stampede. Unlike for a horse, running is not a natural gait for cattle, so Matt knew that if they could keep them from splitting up, the cattle would quickly tire. Then it would be easier to bring them under control.

Dusty and Falcon came up beside him then.

"We have to turn them!" Falcon shouted.

With the three of them shooting their pistols into the air, and swinging ropes, they managed to deflect the leaders for a few moments, but they had only managed to turn a few hundred head, while the momentum of the main body was such that the rest of the herd continued to bore straight ahead.

Abandoning the animals they had turned, they returned to the herd, once again trying to turn them. The idea was to get the cows running in a huge circle, called milling. Since one cow would follow the cow in front, once you got the herd to milling they would essentially stay in the same place, just running in one huge circle.

But so far they had not been able to do that.

Realizing that the relatively few head of cattle they had turned would have no effect on the rest of the herd, they abandoned the ones they had turned, and returned to the rest of the herd. Those they had turned quickly rejoined the herd as well.

By now every member of the camp except for Maria had joined, and they stretched out their line until there was one rider about every thirty feet. They threw everything against the right point and lead, hoping to gradually swing the entire herd. For a while it looked as if they might be successful, but they were stretched too thin, and the cattle went right between the riders until some found themselves on the opposite side of the herd.

Once more, Clay brought all the riders together with the idea of turning the stampede. Then, as it looked as if they may be achieving some success, they suddenly encountered a mesquite thicket which the lead animals crashed into. Before he knew it, Matt was also in the thicket, and he held on to the saddle-horn to keep his seat as horse and rider tore through the spines, sometimes encountering bushes higher than his head.

When Matt emerged through the other side of the thicket, he found himself in the lead of a long string of cattle. Shortly after that, Smoke came out behind him, then overtook him. Matt started to make another attempt to turn the herd, but Smoke waved him off.

"Let 'em run awhile!" Smoke shouted.

Matt knew that it was Smoke's intention to run them until they were tired, so he ran along with them, his only purpose to keep them from scattering.

There were about sixty big steers in the lead, and Matt and Smoke dashed in front of them, shooting their guns into the ground right in front of them. At that, the lead animals turned and started back the other way. With the rear animals coming up behind them, they were finally able to turn

461

the leaders until, running in a circle, they reentered the herd from the rear. As they were the leaders, it had the effect of creating a mill, and now, giving the horses a much-needed break, the cowboys had an easy time of circling around outside the mill, letting the cows continue in one endless circle until they ran themselves into total exhaustion.

This being December, the nights were long and it was still an hour before daylight. The riders had no idea of the number of cattle they had in the mill, but from the size of the area they covered, and the compactness of the herd, they believed they had captured all twenty-five hundred of them.

By daylight, the cattle had grown quiet and were contentedly grazing, just as if they had just risen. Within a couple of hours after daybreak the wagons came up, Sally and Rebecca having gone back to retrieve them. An hour later they were enjoying breakfast.

"I have something to say," Dalton said, standing up to address the others.

Dalton pointed to Tom. "Tom Whitman saved my life," he said. "I was de-horsed, and standing there watching that whole herd running right at me. There was nowhere for me to go, no way for me to escape them, until Tom come along. He reached down and scooped me up like I was no more than a rag doll, and carried me out of danger."

The others applauded and called out to Tom.

"Good man, Tom," Clay said.

"Anyone else would have done the same thing," Tom said. "I just happened to be in the right place at the right time."

"I doubt that," Matt said. "How many others could ride by at full speed, and reach down and scoop Dalton up like he was nothing more than a sack of potatoes? I think you are a genuine hero, Tom, and you are just going to have to live with that."

The others laughed.

"I'm not finished," Dalton said. "I have something else to say. Tom, I know what you think of my sister, and I know what my sister thinks of you. I know too, what Pa thinks. So what I'm goin' to do when we get back to Live Oaks is talk to Pa. I'm goin' to tell him that if he doesn't get out of the way, he'll have Rebecca and me to deal with."

CHAPTER TWENTY-ONE

Our Lady of Mercy Orphanage, Fort Worth, December 20

It took two wagons and a surrey to bring everyone of Live Oaks Ranch into town to Our Lady of Mercy Orphanage. The Mother Superior had issued the invitation not only to Big Ben, but to all of his employees, to come to the orphanage to see the Christmas pageant.

The pageant was held in the orphanage cafeteria, and it was clear that a great deal of work had been done in preparation. The walls were papered with drawings of the hills of Judea, with a night sky filled with stars. One large star was located over a stable that the older boys had built. All of the children of the orphanage were in period costume.

Big Ben and Julia were provided with comfortable chairs. Because there were more people than chairs, everyone else, children and adults alike, sat on the floor.

"And now," Sister Dominique said, "we'll have a reading from Robert, who is one of our children. As Robert reads from the scripture, the rest of the children will act it out for us."

Robert, a young boy of about fourteen, started the reading.

"And it came to pass in those days, that there went out a decree from Caesar Augustus, that all the world should be taxed."

As Robert read, two boys who were obviously dressed as Roman soldiers went to the others, and pantomimed the orders.

"And all went to be taxed, everyone into his own city."

There were giggles and oohs and ahhs from the audience as, coming in through the back door of the cafeteria, they saw a young boy leading a small donkey. A young girl was riding the donkey.

"And Joseph also went up from Galilee, out of the city of Nazareth into Judea, unto the city of David, which is called Bethlehem: (because he was of the house and lineage of David) to be taxed with Mary, his espoused wife, being great with child."

Mary and Joseph, as portrayed by the two young actors, went from place to place, trying to find a room, but in every case they were turned away.

"*While they were there, the time came for the baby to be born, and she gave birth to her firstborn, a son. She wrapped him in swaddling clothes and placed him in a manger, because there was no room for them in the inn.*"

Three shepherds came onto the stage then, leading three young lambs. Robert continued to read:

"*And there were shepherds living out in the fields nearby, keeping watch over their flocks at night. An angel of the Lord appeared to them, and the glory of the Lord shone around them, and they were terrified. But the angel said to them, 'Do not be afraid. I bring you good news of great joy that will be for all the people. Today in the town of David a Savior has been born to you; he is Christ the Lord. This will be a sign to you: You will find a baby wrapped in cloths and lying in a manger.'*"

The children sang "Away in the Manger."

After the song, Robert read again: "*When the angels had left them and gone into heaven, the shepherds said to one another, 'Let us go to Bethlehem and see this thing that has happened, which the Lord has told us about.' So they hurried off and found Mary and Joseph, and the baby, who was lying in the manger.*"

The three "shepherds" hurried to the crèche where Joseph, Mary, and the Baby Jesus, who was actually an infant girl, the youngest child of the orphanage lay.

"Now when Jesus was born in Bethlehem of Judaea in the days of Herod the king, behold, there came wise men from the east to Jerusalem, Saying, Where is he that is born King of the Jews? For we have seen his star in the east, and are come to worship him."

As Robert read the Christmas story, three of the children, dressed as "wise men," walked solemnly across the cafeteria, each of them bearing gifts. As they did so, the other children sang *We Three Kings.* With great pomp and ceremony they presented their gifts.

The program concluded with everyone singing *Silent Night.*

After the program, Sister Mary Katherine stood to address the visitors.

"We want to thank you very much for attending our Christmas pageant," she said. "And we invite you to join us for cookies and apple cider."

"Ho, ho, ho!"

"It's Santa Claus!" one of the children shouted, and all yelled and cheered with excitement as they hurried toward the man dressed in red, and carrying a huge sack, filled with toys.

"What is this?" Sister Mary Katherine asked in surprise.

"Well, it's like this, Mother Superior," Big Ben said. "Santa Claus stopped by to see me at the ranch and I suggested that since he had gifts for the children there, he may as well stop by the orphanage as well."

As the children all gathered around Santa Claus, who was actually one of the cowboys from Live Oaks, the adults sat to one side of the room, drinking coffee and watching.

"Mr. Conyers," Sister Mary Katherine said. "I have been at this orphanage for thirty years, and this is the most wonderful Christmas ever. I can't thank you enough."

"I'm just sorry that I never thought about doing something like this earlier," Big Ben said. "But I intend to see to it that every Christmas from here on out will be a happy one for the children here."

"Bless you," Sister Mary Katherine said, wiping tears from her eyes. "God bless you, Benjamin Conyers."

Texas Panhandle, December 23
Red Coleman had gathered ten men for the job. He didn't personally know all ten, but he knew several of them, and the ones he didn't know were known by those that he

did know. He was fully confident that the ten of them, choosing the time to make their move, would be able to overcome the seven cowboys who were driving the herd. He had been offered eight dollars a head for every cow he delivered to Prewitt. He had promised five hundred dollars apiece to the men who came with him. That would leave him fifteen thousand dollars' profit from this job.

And, as a bonus, he would take care of Smoke Jensen.

There were also three women with the cattle drive, and Red had thrown them in "as a bonus" for his men. "After we kill the men, you can have your way with the women," he said.

"Where are we going to hit them?"

"At the Canadian."

"Have you seen the Canadian?" Sid Baker asked. "It's higher than I've ever seen it."

"Yes. We will let them cross the Canadian River first, then we will hit them," Red said. "That way we won't have to fool with taking them across ourselves."

"Ha! Good idea!"

"Then, after they cross, while they are still concentrating on that, we'll take their herd."

When he was certain that everyone understood their roles in the operation, he stood in his stirrups, then waved them on.

■ ■ ■ ■

It was a gray and overcast day, with threatening clouds hanging low. Storms upstream had made the Canadian River particularly treacherous, for it had flooded over its banks and was filled with uprooted brush and trees. The river, normally no more than one hundred yards wide, was nearly a quarter of a mile across.

"Whoa," Dusty said. "It sure wasn't like this when we came up."

"Yeah, if were going to cross the river like this, it would have been better doing it on the way up," Clay agreed.

"How deep is it?" Smoke asked.

"This is the ford," Clay replied. "Normally, it's no more than ten to fifteen inches deep here. I have no idea how deep it is now."

"Well, there's only one way to find out," Matt said. He rode down to the river, stopped at the edge for a moment to look at the swiftly flowing water, then urged Spirit ahead.

The water was cold, and Spirit reacted to that, but he went ahead. At no point during the crossing did the water rise higher than about three feet, and that was in the very middle. Once he reached the other side, he turned around and came back, purposely coming back on a different track just to make certain that the bottom was relatively the same.

"I don't think we'll have any problem with the depth of the river," Matt said when he came back. "If we have any problem, it will be with what is floating downstream. A big log piling into the side of the herd as it is midway across could create all kinds of problems for us."

"Suppose we stretched a rope across?" Tom suggested. "That way we could arrest anything big enough to be of danger."

"That would be a good idea if we had a rope a quarter of a mile long," Dusty said.

"It doesn't have to be that long," Tom insisted. "Bernoulli's principle means that the flow will be more rapid in the middle, creating a suction around it which will draw everything toward the middle."

"What principle?" Clay asked. "What are you talking about?"

"Look at the river," Tom said. "Where do you see most of the trash?"

"He's right," Smoke said. "Most of it is in the middle. At least, the bigger pieces."

"All we need to do is stretch a rope across the exact middle of the stream," Tom said.

"I'll be on one end of the rope, and we'll need someone on the other end. We'll hold off anything big while the rest of you get the herd across."

"What do you think, Smoke? Does it make sense to you?" Clay asked.

"I don't know who this Bernoulli fella is," Smoke said. "But if he will keep everything in the middle for us, then I say let's try it."

"Tom, if it's all right with you, I'll take the other end of the rope," Dalton said.

"Fine with me," Tom said.

The two men mounted, then rode out into the river, Dalton taking a position on the far side.

"Dalton!" Tom called. "There's a really big log coming! Let this one go."

"All right," Dalton agreed.

"Clay!" Tom shouted as loudly as he could. When he got Clay's attention, he pointed to the big log coming swiftly downstream.

"We are going to let this one go by! Let it pass before you come into the water!"

"Gotcha!" Clay called back.

Tom waved back at him, and they watched as the object Tom had pointed out floated by them. More than a log, it was a complete tree.

"Damn," Dusty said. "If anything that big

comes floating down the river, they aren't going to be able to hold it back with just a rope."

"True," Clay said. "That's why it is smart to let this one go on by."

"What if another one comes by just as big?"

"We'll just have to hope that it doesn't," Clay said. He looked at the others. "All right," he said. "Let's get these critters across."

There was good grass here, and water, so the cows had been content to stay. Now they were somewhat less content to proceed on, but with Clay and Dusty on one side, Duff and Falcon on the other side, and Matt bringing up the rear, they pushed cattle down into the water. The lead steers formed a rank of eight across, and the rest of the herd, almost as if in military precision, lined up behind them. That stretched the herd out for nearly half a mile, and when the lead steers went into the water, the others followed docilely behind.

The herd was halfway across when another big log came floating swiftly downstream. It wasn't as big as the tree, but it was big.

"Tom!" Dalton shouted. "Look!"

Tom feared that the log might be big enough to jerk Dalton out of the saddle if he tried to hold on to the rope.

"Dalton, wrap your rope around your saddlehorn!" Tom shouted.

"If I do that, I won't be able to maneuver my end!"

"Don't worry about that! Just do as I say!"

Nodding, Dalton wrapped his end of the rope around the saddlehorn, then waited.

Tom was holding onto his end of the rope, and he was able to snag the log as it came by. The log was huge, and when it hit the rope it jerked the line taut, and for a moment, Dalton was afraid his horse might be pulled down. But the horse, after being jerked downriver a few steps, dug his feet in, locked his legs, and stayed up, holding his position.

Tom worked his end of the rope and managed to keep the log captured, and even with the additional items of trash floating downriver, was able to keep all the major pieces away from the herd. Finally, when the last cow had crossed and was climbing out of the water to the bank on the other side, Tom freed the trapped river debris and let it proceed on downstream, now as one great island.

With the herd safely on the other side of the river, it was now time to bring the wagons across. Once again, Tom and Dalton stretched the rope across to catch the debris. Everything was going well until Sally and Maria in the chuck wagon were three quarters of the way across, and Rebecca, following in the hoodlum wagon, was about one quarter of the way across. It was then that another huge tree, at least as big as the first tree to come down the river, came toward them.

The tree was moving downriver faster than a horse could gallop, and looking at it, Tom knew that he and Dalton weren't going to be able to stop it. Glancing back toward Rebecca, he saw that she was directly in the path of the tree. It was too late for her to go back, her only hope was to go forward as fast as she could.

"Rebecca! Hurry!" Tom shouted. "Hurry, get out of the way!"

By now all of the others, including Rebecca, could see the tree coming, and she slapped the reins against the back of the team of mules she was driving, trying to hurry them across. But the mules, whether they perceived the danger and were frightened by it, or just decided to take that time to balk, halted in mid-stream.

"Tom, we aren't going to be able to stop this thing!" Dalton shouted.

Realizing that Dalton was right, Tom

dropped his end of the rope and urged Thunder into a gallop.

At first, the others thought Tom might be trying to escape with his own life, but they saw quickly that he was heading toward the wagon. Rebecca saw him coming toward her, and she stood up on the seat.

"Jump toward me!" Tom yelled, and Rebecca did so. Tom caught her, and managed to barely clear the tree as it slammed into the side of the hoodlum wagon, smashing it into two pieces, and spilling all the contents into the water, to be carried downstream along with the wreckage of the wagon, and the two mules, now braying in terror. Within seconds the mules were quiet, having been swept under the water.

Tom rode up the bank on the other side then turned to look back. Both mules were floating, legs up and silent, until they, what was left of the wagon, and its contents were quickly carried on downstream and out of sight.

"What are we going to do at night, now?" Dalton asked. "Our bedrolls and blankets were in that wagon."

The seven men and three women looked at the raging river with an expression of apprehension on their faces. Dalton had merely vocalized what everyone in the company was thinking. What would they do?

"All right, folks," Clay said. "Looking at the water isn't going to get anything back for us. Let's head 'em up and get 'em out. We need to keep moving, now more than ever before."

Chapter Twenty-Two

On the Canadian River, Texas Panhandle, December 24

It was a cold camp, and because they had lost the hoodlum wagon there were no bedrolls or blankets. In addition, just before sundown, it began to snow. Fortunately it had been cold enough during the day that everyone was wearing their heavy coats, so they didn't lose them when they lost the wagon, and they made use of them by pairing off to put one coat on the ground to sleep on and the other over the top as a blanket. Sleeping in such a way provided both the warmth of the two coats and the body heat, to keep them from freezing. Clay was with Maria, Smoke with Sally, Matt with Dalton, and Falcon with Duff. That left Tom and Rebecca sleeping together. As odd man out, Dusty would be with whoever was left behind when the night guard was posted.

"You know what I think?" Rebecca asked that night as she and Tom bundled up together.

"What do you think?" Tom asked.

"I think you let that tree hit the wagon on purpose, just so we could do this."

There was the suggestion of a laugh in her voice.

"Damn," Tom said. "And here I thought I was being so clever."

The snow continued to fall as Rebecca pushed her body up against his so that they were touching everywhere, from top to bottom.

Duff was riding nighthawk when he heard the sound of a rifle shot. At the sound of the shot, the cattle, which had been bedded down, were up as one, and instantly on the run.

"Dusty!" Duff called to the one who was riding nighthawk with him. "Dusty!"

It just so happened that in their circuitous route around the outside edge of the cattle, Duff was approaching Dusty. Dusty didn't answer Duff's call, and Duff urged his horse into a gallop, reaching Dusty just as he started to reel in his saddle.

"I been shot, Duff," Dusty said. "Damn, I think I've been kilt."

Dusty fell from the saddle, and Duff dismounted quickly to check on him. As it so happened, that dismount saved Duff's life, for a second shot was fired. Duff saw the muzzle-flash, then heard the bullet whiz by, amazingly close, especially for a shot at night.

"Cattle thieves!" Falcon shouted. "Clay, Smoke, Falcon, turn out! Turn out!"

Duff shot back toward where he had seen the muzzle-flash, but had no specific target because he hadn't actually seen anything but the muzzle-flash.

The gunfire startled Tom and Rebecca, and Tom sat up quickly to see what was going on.

By now, rapid fire was coming from the camp itself, as Smoke and the others rolled out of their makeshift bedrolls and into the snow, which was now at least three inches deep. Matt put his pistol away and raised his rifle. He aimed through the falling snow and toward the swirling melee of cattle, waiting for one of the robbers to present a target. A horse appeared, with a rider Matt didn't recognize. The rider was shooting wildly.

Matt fired and the robber tumbled backward. His horse, with its saddle empty now, galloped away.

"Get 'em out of here! Stampede the cattle!" someone shouted.

It wasn't until that moment that Smoke and the others realized how many rustlers there were. There were more rustlers than there were cowboys, and they were able to get the herd running.

"Get mounted!" Clay shouted. "We're going after them!"

Once mounted, they started after the cattle, which now had a good half-mile lead. The cows were running as fast as they could run, which was about three-quarters of the speed of the horses. But what the cattle lacked in speed they made up for with momentum, and that momentum was continued by the shooting and shouting of the rustlers who, as part of their plan, needed the cattle to stampede.

With lowered heads, wild eyes, and flopping tongues, the cattle ran as if there was no tomorrow. More than a million pounds of muscle, bone, and hair, red eyes, running noses, and black hides spotted white with snow. Over twenty-five hundred animals welded together as one gigantic, raging beast. A cloud of white churned up by ten thousand hooves rose up from the herd and billowed high into the air, mixing with the snow that was falling, so thick that within moments it was impossible to see through the blizzard and the dark of the night.

Suddenly a rider appeared out of the swirl just in front of Tom. At first Tom thought it might be Matt, but he realized at once that it wasn't anyone he knew. Then he saw that whoever it was was pointing a pistol at him.

Without thinking, Tom raised his pistol and fired, and he saw the rider reel in his saddle, then turn and try to ride away. He disappeared into the snow and the night, but a moment later, Tom saw him again, this time on the ground, being trampled by the stampeding cattle.

This was the first time he had ever shot anyone, and he felt neither a sense of remorse nor elation. He felt no emotional response at all, and he remembered something his father had told him about his experience in the war.

"I think it is something that God gives us at such terrible times," his father had said. "It is a mechanism that shuts down all emotion such as fear, horror, anger, hate, and love. You can kill if you have to, you can watch your friends be killed, you can wade through a field of bodies and gore without going insane."

Tom was totally disoriented now. He

didn't know where the wagon was, he didn't know where the river was, he had no concept of north, south, east, or west. He knew only where the stampeding cattle were, and he rode alongside them, keeping them to his left.

He knew that if he kept close to the cattle he couldn't get lost, because the others would be in contact with the cattle as well. And he had confidence that at least one among them, Clay, or Smoke, or Dusty, would be able to find their way back. At the moment he was unaware that Dusty was dead.

So far, Tom had seen only one other person since he had left the camp, and that was one of the rustlers. At least, Tom hoped he was one of the rustlers, because Tom had killed him.

The cattle thundered on, a huge, undulating black mass lumbering through snow growing deeper by the minute. Because of the heavy snowfall, the pace slowed more and more. The cattle stopped running, and continued forward in what could only be described as a laboring trot, then a walk, until finally the cattle stopped all together. By now the snow came up almost to Thunder's belly, and the powerful animal was blowing streams of vapor into the air as he labored to keep going.

This wasn't going the way Red Coleman had planned. He had thought that by striking in the middle of the night that they could stampede the cattle away from the drovers who would be asleep, and too confused to be able to react. But two of his men had already been killed, and that left him with only five plus himself. Also, he had not counted on the severity of the snowstorm. Even if he didn't have the cowboys to deal with, he knew now that he would not be able to move the herd. The cattle had come to a complete stop. Clearly, he no longer had the odds strongly enough in his favor to pull this off.

He knew that Smoke Jensen was a deadly shot; he had not only heard of him, he had encountered him before. But it wasn't just Smoke Jensen. There were at least three more with him who were every bit as good as he was. He had run into a hornet's nest!

"Let's get out of here!" he called to the others, then he broke away, moving as rapidly as he could at right angles to the herd. Because of the snow, they were moving only marginally faster than a man on foot would be able to move, had there been no snow. Red's only hope now was that

Jensen and the others would stay with the herd.

"What about the cattle?" one of the others shouted.

"To hell with the cattle!"

At that, all the remaining rustlers broke off to follow Red, leaving the motionless herd behind them.

"They're leaving!" Matt shouted.

"Duff! Stay with Clay and the herd! We're going after them!" Smoke shouted.

Smoke, Matt, and Falcon started toward the outlaws, but they could move no faster than the rustlers could. It made for a most unusual chase, the outlaws urging, unsuccessfully, their exhausted horses to open up more distance between them and those in pursuit of them, and the pursuers urging their horses, with no more success, to close the gap.

Back at the wagon, where the three women were huddled together, the snow was still falling silently and heavily from the night sky. Rebecca, Sally, and Maria had climbed up onto the seat of the chuck wagon so that they were out of the snow, though the snow itself was halfway up the wagon wheels. The three huddled together as best they could for warmth, pulling their heavy, wool-lined coats about them. They were holding a piece of canvas over them to provide them with some protection against the snow, frequently shaking it to keep it somewhat clear.

"I wonder where the men are," Rebecca said.

"And how far did they have to go?" Sally asked.

"Do you think they will be back tonight?" Maria asked.

"I wish I could answer that," Sally said.

In a field about a mile away, the three shepherds who had encountered the Rocking H outfit last summer were huddled around the fire they had managed to get started. The fire reflected from the snow, creating a golden circle around them. Beyond that golden circle, white on white, were the sheep, stilled by the night and the snow still tumbling down.

At first, there were the three of them, Gaston, Pierre, and Andre, trying to keep warm by the fire.

Then there was a fourth. A man whose face was as black as the night, but with skin that was shining in the reflected light of the fire. He was wearing a white buffalo robe, and he held his hands out toward the fire.

"What?" Pierre shouted in a frightened

voice. "Who are you? Where did you come from?"

"My name is Balthazar. I'm sorry if I frightened you," the man said.

"What are you doing out on a night like this?" Gaston asked.

"I am doing the same thing you are," Balthazar said. "I am going about the business of my master."

"The business of your master?" Andre said. "Are you a slave? I thought slavery ended twenty-five years ago."

"I am a slave of no man," Balthazar said.

"What are you doing here, Balthazar? Are you lost?" Gaston asked.

"Tonight, a child is to be born. The mother needs your help."

"Our help? Do you mean to say there is a woman outside, in this blizzard?"

"Yes," Balthazar said. He pointed. "Go for one mile in that direction. You will find her, and with her two more women. You must find shelter for them."

"Where are we going to find shelter?" Pierre asked.

"You know a place," Balthazar said.

"What place would that be?"

"The old barn," Gaston suggested. "Do you remember? It is near here, by the seven trees that form the cross."

"That barn is falling down. There is a hole in the roof," Andre said.

"It is better than leaving the mother outside in this snowstorm," Gaston said. "That is the best we can . . ." he turned toward the fourth man, but Balthazar was gone.

"Where did he go?" Pierre asked, his voice registering his surprise.

"I don't know," Gaston said. "But we don't have time to worry about that now. Come quickly. We must find the woman."

"Do you think there really is such a woman?" Andre asked.

"Why would he tell us there was, if it is not so?" Gaston asked.

"Maybe he didn't tell us," Pierre suggested.

"What do you mean?"

"Maybe he wasn't here."

Back at the wagon Rebecca and Sally had to keep brushing snow away to keep the three of them from being covered. No longer was the trail made by the wagon, horses, and cattle visible. There were no footprints, no signs of encampment.

Suddenly Maria cried out in pain.

"Oh, Maria, no!" Sally said. "Not now!"

"I am sorry," Maria said. She winced

again in pain.

"How long have you been having these pains?" Sally asked.

"All day, but I didn't say anything before. Now they are getting worse, and closer together."

"What are we going to do, Sally?" Rebecca asked, her voice laced with fear and concern.

"Please, come with us," a man's voice said.

The unexpected voice startled the three women and Sally spun around, a pistol already in her hand.

Rebecca saw three tall thin men, all with beards and fur caps heavily dusted by the still-falling snow.

"Sally, no!" Rebecca said. "I know them!"

"You know them?"

"They are shepherds," Rebecca said. "This one is Gaston." Rebecca did not tell the others how she knew them, that these were the same shepherds that the Rocking H had come across during the summer drive up to Dodge City.

"The woman with child, she is about to give birth, yes?" Gaston asked.

"Yes," Sally said.

"Gaston, do you know somewhere we can go to get her out of the cold and the snow?" Rebecca asked.

"Yes, I know a barn that is not far," Gaston said.

"How far?"

"Not far. Maybe one mile."

"Oh," Rebecca said. "In this snow, there is no way Maria could walk a mile. I don't know that she could even do it if there was no snow."

"The mules," Sally said. "We'll put her on one of the mules."

"Yes," Rebecca said. "That is a good idea."

Working quickly, they disconnected one of the two mules that, while out of harness, had been tied to the wagon. There was no saddle for it, but Gaston and one of the other shepherds lifted Maria and sat her on the mule so that both legs were on one side. Maria grabbed onto the mule's mane with one hand, and held Rebecca's hand with the other. Sally walked on the opposite side of the mule to help keep her on, and with two of the three shepherds walking in front to break a path through the snow, Gaston led the mule through the falling snow.

It took them at least forty-five minutes to reach the barn. There was so much snow piled up outside that it took another five minutes to get enough of the snow moved away to enable them to open the door. Inside, they found a stall with straw. Gaston built a fire on the floor of the barn, just outside the stall. There was a hole in the roof, and that plus the open door provided enough of a draft for the smoke to rise.

As Smoke, Matt, and Falcon continued their pursuit of the would-be cattle rustlers, the snowfall stopped, and the clouds rolled away. Oddly, within moments the sky was alive with sparkling stars. A moon that was nearly full, except for a tiny sliver along the left side, bounced its bright light off the new-fallen snow so that, in dramatic contrast to the total lack of visibility earlier, they could now see for great distances. Red and the five riders with him were now quite visible to Smoke, Matt, and Falcon.

"We ain't goin' to get away from 'em!" Red said. "We're goin' to have to fight 'em! Over there, up on them rocks!"

Snaking their rifles from their saddle-sheaths, the six outlaws rode over to the rocky hill that Red had pointed out; then, stepping from their saddles, started a laborious climb up the hill, slipping and sliding as they did so.

"Smoke!" Matt shouted, pointing.

"I see them," Smoke said.

"Once they get into those rocks, they're

going to have cover," Matt said.

"We'll just have to shoot straighter," Falcon quipped.

The three men dismounted, then, as the outlaws had done previously, they pulled their rifles from the saddle-sheaths and levered rounds into the chambers. Bending over at the waist, Smoke, Matt, and Falcon began moving toward the little rock-strewn hill.

"Shoot 'em, shoot 'em!" Red shouted, even as he pulled the trigger on his Henry, and a little flame of fire spit out from the muzzle.

The others with Red began shooting as well, but they had the same disadvantage most marksmen have when shooting up or down at a target. The bullet's flight path depends on the horizontal range to the plane of the target, not the line of sight up or down a hill. In order to hit the target a shooter must aim lower than normal to achieve the desired point of impact.

Smoke knew this, because he had been taught by Preacher. Matt knew it, because he had been taught by Smoke. Falcon knew it, because he had been taught by his father, Jamie Ian MacCallister. But the outlaws did not know this, and though they had the security of the rocks as cover, they would have to raise up to present themselves any time they fired.

Rifles barked, flame-patterns flared, and the bullets fired by the outlaws whizzed by ineffectively, whereas every round fired by Smoke, Matt, and Falcon found its mark. In less than two minutes of fierce engagement, all of the outlaws had come tumbling down the hillside, dead or fatally wounded. Smoke and the others closed in on the fallen rustlers, finding them as black forms in the white snow. Five of them were spread out, lifeless on the ground, but one was still alive, and he was sitting up, holding his hands over a bleeding wound in his stomach.

"Which one of you is Smoke Jensen?" he asked, his voice strained with pain and weakened from loss of blood.

"I am Smoke Jensen."

"I thought it was supposed to be third time is the charm. This is the third time I've gone up ag'in you, and you've won ever' time."

"I don't know you," Smoke said.

"The name is Red Coleman."

"You are the one who tried to hold up the cattle train," Smoke said.

"Yeah, and the train before that," Red said. "Oh, my gut hurts." Red looked down at himself, moved his hands away from the wound and saw the blood, there cupped, spill into the snow. "I reckon I'm a goner, ain't I?"

"I reckon so," Smoke said. Smoke turned and walked back toward his horse.

"Wait a minute, you're walkin' away just like that? Where are you goin'?"

"To get my cows back," Smoke said. He mounted his horse.

"You're just goin' to leave me out here to die?"

"Yeah, I am," Smoke said. He started out after the others, who had already gone in pursuit of the herd.

"You can't leave me here like this you son of a bitch! Come back here! Come back here, do you hear me? Bastard! Bas . . ."

With the cows no longer moving, but standing merely as one black mass against the snow and with the snow fall stopped, Tom was no longer disoriented. He could see Duff, Clay, and Dalton on the opposite side of the herd from him.

"Where are the others?" Tom asked when he rode up to them.

"Smoke, Matt, and Falcon went after the outlaws," Clay said. "Dusty is dead."

"Dusty is dead? Oh," Tom said. "Oh, I

hate that."

When Smoke, Matt, and Falcon returned, they found the cattle standing in place. Clay, Duff, Dalton, and Tom were all together.

"The outlaws?" Clay asked.

"We won't be having any more trouble with them," Falcon said. "Good to see you, Tom, I was afraid we might have lost you as well as Duff."

"I was on the other side of the herd," Tom said.

"The cattle aren't going anywhere," Clay said, "at least, not for the rest of the night. But some of us need to get back to the camp. I don't feel good about leaving the women there alone."

"How far do you think we've come?" Dalton asked.

"Four, maybe five miles," Clay answered.

"Clay, why don't you, Smoke, and maybe Tom, go back to check on the women?" Falcon suggested. "Like you said, these cows aren't going to go anywhere tonight. Duff, Dalton, and I can bring them back in tomorrow morning."

"Good idea," Clay said. "Smoke, Tom, let's go back. That is, if we can find our way back."

CHAPTER TWENTY-THREE

At first, they couldn't even see the wagon when they approached what had been the camp. Then Smoke pointed to a hillock of snow to which a mule was attached. As they drew closer they saw that it was, indeed, a wagon, though the snow completely covered the wheels and the wagon seat. Only the arched canvas protruded from the snow, but the canvas was white so that upon first sight, even it appeared to be snow.

A single mule stood beside it, only the top of its body and its head and neck clear of the snow. As the men approached, the mule turned toward them and began to bray, complaining bitterly about the cold.

"Where are the women?" Clay asked, anxiously. "Maria?" he shouted. "Maria?" he called again.

"One of the mules is gone," Smoke said. "Maybe they went off looking for shelter."

"The baby," Clay said. "I'm worried about

the baby."

"The baby? What baby?" Smoke asked.

"Maria is pregnant," Tom said.

"Wait a minute, how did you know that?" Clay asked. "She has been keeping it covered up."

"I don't mean this as a criticism, Clay, but what is she doing here if she is pregnant?" Smoke asked.

"She didn't want to stay home alone. The baby isn't due until February," Clay said.

"She's much further along than that," Tom said. "I'd say she is due within another week or two at the latest."

"Oh my God! She may be having the baby somewhere right now! We've got to find her! Smoke, I've heard that you are the best tracker there is. Please, find them," Clay begged.

"The snow," Smoke said, shrugging his shoulders. "It has everything covered up, I don't know. It would only be a guess."

At that moment they saw a rider approaching the camp, and Clay, thinking he might be another thief, fired at him, but the rider made no attempt to dodge the bullet. Instead, he kept coming as if nothing had happened.

Clay started to shoot again, but Smoke held out his hand.

"Hold it, Clay," Smoke said. "I don't think he is any danger to us."

When the rider got close enough they saw that he was a black man wearing a white buffalo robe.

"Are you gentlemen looking for three ladies?" he asked.

"Yes," Clay replied quickly. He had started to put his pistol away, but hearing the rider mention the three women, he became suspicious and held the gun in his hand for a while longer. "Do you know where they are?"

"I know where they are. If you will follow me, I can lead you to them."

"Who are you?"

"My name is Balthazar. Follow me. You are needed."

"Is something wrong?" Clay asked anxiously.

"You are needed," Balthazar said again.

Balthazar lead them on, his horse easily breaking a path through the snow so that the others could follow. After no more than fifteen minutes they saw a column of white smoke and rising, glowing, red sparks making a beacon against the dark sky, leading them on until they reached a partially collapsed barn. Three men came out of the barn to meet them.

"Are there women here?" Clay asked.

"Yes. They are in the barn," one of the three said.

"Who are you?" Smoke asked.

"My name is Gaston."

"Clay Ramsey, go inside quickly. Your wife needs you," Balthazar says.

Without stopping to wonder how Balthazar knew his name, or even how he knew that Maria was his wife, Clay hurried inside. In the light of the same fire that had sent up the beacon of sparks, he saw Maria lying on a bed of straw. Sally was on one side of her and Rebecca on the other, both holding her hands, and both with very worried looks on their faces. Maria's face was contorted with pain. The only good thing about the situation was that the small fire inside was keeping the stable warm.

"Maria! Are you all right?" Clay asked.

"She is going to have a baby, but she is having a very hard time," Sally said. "The baby is trying to come out backwards."

"A breech," Tom said.

"The mother and her baby need your help, Doctor Whitman," Balthazar said. He was looking directly at Tom.

The others looked first at Balthazar, then at Tom.

"Tom, why did he call you Doctor Whitman?" Clay asked.

"Because I am — that is, I used to be — a doctor."

"You know what she needs, Doctor," Balthazar said.

"No, I don't."

"Yes, you know," Balthazar said.

"All right, she needs a Caesarian. Are you happy now? She needs a Caesarian, but I can't do it," Tom said. "In a stable? It is impossible."

"Yes, you can. I know that you have the skill that is needed."

"If you know that much about me, then you know what happened, why I can't do this," Tom said.

"You are concerned, Dr. Whitman, because you lost your wife, Martha, and the child. But I say this to you. Have no fear, for you will do this thing, and it will be good."

"No, I will not," Tom said. "I cannot."

"Tom, if you really are a doctor, you can't just turn your back on Maria when she needs you so," Rebecca said.

"You don't understand, Rebecca. I'm not a doctor anymore," Tom said. "Not since I killed my wife and child."

"Tom, please, I beg of you," Clay said. "If you can do something, you must help her!"

"Didn't you hear what I said, Clay? I can't do it! This requires a Caesarian, and I killed my wife and child trying to do a Caesarian. That is a very difficult and invasive operation that fails eighty-five percent of the time. And that is under the very best of conditions. If I were to try such a procedure here, in a barn, in unsterile conditions, and without the proper equipment, it would be little more than murder!"

"Try, Doctor, please try! For God's sake, you must help her!" Clay begged.

"Yes, Doctor," Balthazar says. "For *God's* sake, you must help her."

"I will assist you, Doctor," Rebecca said.

Tom put his hands to his temples and pressed hard, as if by so doing he could make all this go away.

"Tom, you can do it," Rebecca said. She put her fingers on his cheek. "I know you can do it."

Tom lowered his hands and looked at Maria, who was now in great pain. The look on his face evolved through several expressions, from anger at being put in this position, to fear, to remorse, to resignation, and finally, to determination. And once his face showed his determination, he was overtaken by a calm demeanor. As of now, he was obviously in charge.

"I will need a knife," Tom said. "A sharp knife."

"Smoke, you have a knife," Sally said.

"It's a Bowie knife," Smoke said. "Hardly what you would call a surgical instrument."

"I've seen you skin many an animal with that knife," Sally said. "You keep it as sharp as a razor."

Smoke pulled the knife and showed it to Tom. "Will this do, Doctor?" he asked.

"It will have to do," he said. "Take the blade over there and hold it in the fire for about a minute. I'm going to have to sew the wound closed afterward. Clay, do you still have that saddle needle you have for sewing up leather?"

"Yes, but the only thing I have for lacing are rawhide strips."

"The last time I was in town, I picked up some spare guitar strings for Dusty and I never got around to giving them to him. They are gut strings and that will work perfectly. Rebecca, look in my saddle bags. The 'E' string should work. That's the smallest string."

"All right."

"Oh, and you will also find half a bottle of Scotch there. Bring it as well. I'll need an antiseptic," Tom added. He pulled his pistol, emptied all the cartridges, then handed it to

Smoke. "Smoke, put the barrel in the fire, the barrel only. Leave the handle out so you can pick it up when I need it. I will need the barrel to be very hot."

"All right," Smoke said.

"Also, I'll need some hot water," Tom said. We can use snow, but I don't know what to put it in."

"I have a bucket," one of the shepherds said.

"Good, that will work. Fill the bucket with clean snow and start heating water."

"I'll need some rags for cleaning, and something to wrap the baby in when it is born."

"A saddle blanket?" Tom asked.

"Yes, but that won't do for cleaning up the baby. And we'll need some kind of cloth between the baby's skin and the blanket."

"How about petticoats?" Rebecca suggested. "All three of us are wearing petticoats."

"I won't need Maria's. But I will need both of yours."

Nodding, Rebecca and Sally got up, walked into the next stall where, with their action concealed by the wall of the stall, they removed their petticoats and brought them back.

"Rip them up into several strips," Tom

suggested, and the two women did so.

A moment later, Tom had everything he needed, and was ready to begin, and he stood there for a moment, looking at Maria, his face glowing gold in the warming fire. As Rebecca stared at him, she did not see hesitancy, fear, nor doubt. She saw a quiet summoning of resolve.

"Maria, I don't have anything for an anesthetic. I'm sorry, this is going to be very painful. But it has to be done."

"It can't be more painful than it is now," Maria replied through clenched teeth.

"I can help," Balthazar said.

"How can you help?" Tom asked.

"I can help," Balthazar said again, without further explanation. He put his hand on Maria's stomach, and closed his eyes for a moment. His lips moved as if he was speaking, but he wasn't speaking aloud. The others looked at Balthazar in confused curiosity.

"What are you doing?" Tom asked.

"Go ahead, Doctor," Balthazar said. "She does not feel pain now."

"He is right," Maria said. "The pain has stopped."

Tom picked up the knife, then positioned it just over where he was going to make the incision. He held it there for a moment, then he pulled the knife up and looked at Rebecca.

"I can't," he said. "I can't do this. I can't kill Martha all over again."

Rebecca put her hand on Tom's hand. "You can do it, Tom. I know you can," she said. "I don't have the slightest doubt."

"Clay," Tom said. "You do understand the risk, do you not? You are putting a lot of trust in me, and I'm not sure I warrant that trust."

"Tom, in the short time I've known you, I've never known anyone that I trusted more," Clay said. Clay crossed himself and said a quick, silent prayer. The others waited, each of them saying their own prayers.

Tom nodded, then, using Smoke's knife, made the cut. Immediately, blood began to ooze out of the cut.

"Rebecca, pour some whiskey on the wound, and wipe away some of the blood," Tom said. "Smoke, hand me my pistol."

Rebecca did as instructed, and taking the pistol from Smoke, Tom used the hot barrel to cauterize the blood vessels and stop the bleeding. Then he continued with the cut, carving through the fat and muscle, and making an incision in the uterus.

All the while he was operating, Tom

continued to look up at Maria's eyes for any sign of shock, such as a dazed or disoriented look. Amazingly, her eyes were clear and her demeanor calm.

Then, with everything opened up, he reached in to pull the baby out. It was a boy, and, cutting the umbilical cord, he slapped it on the backside.

The baby began to cry.

A broad smile spread across Tom's face. "Welcome to Texas, little fella," he said. He handed the baby to Rebecca.

"If the water is warm enough, clean the baby, but hold back some of the cloth to put between the baby's skin and the saddle blanket."

"All right," Rebecca said.

"I've got the swaddling cloth ready," Sally said.

Tom tied off the umbilical cord then he began sewing up the cuts: first the uterus, then the muscle tissue, and finally the skin. When he was finished, he looked up and saw Rebecca putting the baby, now clean and wrapped in the blanket, in Maria's arms. And while she should be in great pain and near shock, she was anything but. He saw on her face the most angelic smile he had ever seen.

"You did it, Doctor. I knew you could,"

Clay said.

"I'm still Tom," Tom said. He looked at Maria. "Maria, are you not in any discomfort?"

"No, Doctor," Maria answered in a calm and strong voice.

"Did you feel no pain during all that?"

"I felt no pain," Maria said.

Tom looked around for Balthazar. "How did you do that? That's a trick I'd like to . . ."

Balthazar wasn't there.

"What the? What happened to Balthazar?" Tom asked.

"I don't know, I didn't see him go," Smoke said. Smoke walked over to the door of the barn and looked outside. "His horse is gone. Funny he didn't stay around long enough to see that the baby was born."

"I have an idea that he knows," Tom said.

"How?"

"I don't know, how did he do anything?" Tom asked.

"Oh," Rebecca said, as she examined her locket watch by the light of the fire. "It is after midnight. Today is Christmas!"

"Clay," Maria said, holding the baby close. "Isn't it wonderful? Our baby is a Christmas baby. We will name him after my father. We will call him Emanuel."

Big Ben Conyers stood out in the little cemetery that had grown up on his ranch. Behind him, he could hear the music and the celebration of the upcoming wedding. But for now, he was communing with his old friend Dusty.

Here Lies
Dusty McNally
1837–1890
God needed a
Cowboy

"I wish you could be here for this, Dusty," Big Ben said. "You were one of the first people to tell me that Tom Whitman was a good man. I should have listened to you earlier, I would have saved a lot of time, and a lot of heartbreak."

"Pa?" Dalton called to him, and Big Ben turned toward his son.

"Pa, they're goin' to be startin' the weddin' soon."

Big Ben smiled. "Well now, we sure don't want to miss that, do we?"

Dalton returned his smile. "No, sir, we sure don't."

The parlor of The Big House was decorated

with bluebonnets, tulips, jonquils, hyacinth, and greenery. All the furniture had been removed from the parlor so that additional chairs could be brought in. There were several rows of chairs and they were placed in the shape of a fan, with an aisle through the middle. Every ranch hand was present for the wedding, the cowboys pulling at the discomfort of unaccustomed collars and ties. Neighboring ranchers, and friends and business acquaintances from town were there as well. Also present, having come by train from Boston, were Tom's parents, Dr. Thomas Royal Whitman and his wife, Caroline.

Duff MacCallister had come back from Chugwater, bringing Meghan Parker with him this time. Falcon was here as well, and so were Smoke, Sally, and Matt. Duff was wearing the kilt of the Black Watch, complete with a *sgian dubh*, or ceremonial knife, tucked into the right kilt stocking, with only the pommel visible. He was also wearing the Victoria Cross, Great Britain's highest award for bravery. He had his bagpipes, and after all the chairs were filled, he stood at the front of the room, and off to one side. Then, at a signal from the Episcopal priest who would be conducting the wedding ceremony, Duff began to play the haunting strains of Pachelbel's *Canon in D.*

Tom, wearing a tuxedo, stood in front next to the priest as Sally, Maria, Meghan Parker, and Candy processed up the aisle, along with Smoke, Clay, Falcon, and Dalton. Rebecca had asked Candy, her friend from the Lucky Chance in Dodge City, to be her maid of honor, and Tom had asked Dalton to be his best man.

When the bridesmaids and groomsmen were in place, Duff moved from the haunting melody of Pachelbel's *Canon in D* to the stately melody of Wagner's *Wedding March.*

As the music started, everyone turned to see Rebecca, her long auburn hair back to its original length, coming up the aisle on the arm of Big Ben. The train of the wedding gown was such that it was almost as if she were gliding up the aisle, rather than walking.

When Rebecca reached the front, Tom turned, and they both faced the priest. In his opening remarks, the priest issued the charge that if anyone present, or either of them, knew any impediment as to why they may not be married they should confess it now. With no impediment spoken, the priest turned to Tom.

"Wilt thou have this woman to be thy wedded wife, to live together after God's ordinance in the holy estate of matrimony? Wilt thou love her, comfort her, honor, and keep her in sickness and in health; and, forsaking all others, keep thee only unto her, so long as ye both shall live?"

"I will," Tom said.

The priest turned to Rebecca.

"Wilt thou have this man to be thy wedded husband, to live together after God's ordinance in the holy estate of matrimony? Wilt thou obey him, and serve him, love, honor, and keep him in sickness and in health; and, forsaking all others, keep thee only unto him, so long as ye both shall live?"

"I will," Rebecca said.

"Who giveth this woman to be married to this man?"

"I do, with great pride and immense joy!" Big Ben said, his booming voice clearly heard throughout the entire room. With a big, proud smile on his face, he placed Rebecca's hand in Tom's, then he withdrew to sit next to Julia, who was wiping away tears.

Tom and Rebecca then faced each other, and repeating after the priest, declared to take each other as husband and wife according to God's holy ordinance.

"Who has the ring?"

"I do," Dalton said, stepping forward to

hand the ring to Tom.

Tom slipped the ring on to Rebecca's finger. "With this ring, I thee wed," he said.

"For as much as Tom and Rebecca have consented together in holy wedlock, and have witnessed the same before God and this company, I pronounce that they are man and wife. The bride and groom may kiss."

Tom and Rebecca sealed their marriage and their love with a kiss, and then, amidst the applause of those gathered, hurried from the parlor into the living room where the reception was to be held. Here, too, all the furniture had been moved out, and at the back wall was a long table covered with a white linen cloth. A huge wedding cake sat at one end of the table, and a large punch bowl was at the other. Above the table, on the wall, was a long, painted banner.

CONGRATULATIONS TO DOCTOR AND MRS. TOM WHITMAN

Tom and Rebecca cut the cake, then fed each other a piece, then Maria began serving the others.

"Hold off on that punch," one of the cowboys called. "I want to see Dalton drink from it first."

Those who knew of Dalton's "joke" at the town dance last summer laughed, then explained to the others what it was about. Laughing, Dalton strode over to the punch bowl, poured himself a cup, drank it, then held the empty cup.

"Delicious!" he shouted.

As the reception continued, many of the guests came by to talk to the guests of honor.

"I have to tell you, Tom, that when you first showed up, I didn't have any idea what kind of cowboy you would be," Big Ben said. "But you turned out to be as good as any cowhand I've ever been around, and I've been around some good ones, including Dusty. So if you ever get tired of being a doctor and want to ranch again, you will always be welcome at Live Oaks."

"I wish Dusty and Mo could have been here for this," Rebecca said. "Dusty was here from the time I was a very young girl. He was something special."

"Mo was too," Dalton said. "I guess you could say that Mo was my best friend."

"Let's have a drink to them," Clay said. "Wait, I'll get everyone's attention, and we'll all drink to them."

Clay whistled loudly, and all conversation

and laughter stopped as everyone looked over to see what it was about.

"Ladies and gents," Clay said. "As most of you know, we lost two good men bringing the cattle down from Dodge. I'm talking about Dusty McNally and Mo Coffey. I know they would have given anything in the world to be here now, and see these two get married. So, if you don't mind, I'd like you all to raise your cups so we could have a drink to them. Then maybe, take just a minute to think about them.

Everyone raised their cups.

"To Dusty and Mo," Clay said.

"To Dusty and Mo," the others repeated, as one.

From the back of the room, Duff began to play *Amazing Grace.* The first sound was from the drones, then, fingering the chanter, Duff began playing the haunting tune, the steady hum of the drones providing a mournful sound to underscore the high skirling of the melody itself. It was so beautifully played that it took on the aura of a prayer, and when he finished, Father Sharkey, the Episcopal priest who had performed the wedding ceremony said, "Amen."

"Amen," the others said.

■ ■ ■ ■

A while later, Dr. Thomas Doyle Whitman, Tom's father, came over to talk to the bride and groom.

"You're sure now, Tom, that you don't want to come back to Boston to practice? I know the chief of surgeons at Mass General and I'm pretty sure I can get your old position back."

Tom laughed. "Since you are the chief of surgeons there, I'm sure you can," he said. "But I like it here, in Fort Worth. I only hung out my shingle two months ago, and already I have built up a pretty good practice."

"But, son, Texas? You are giving up Boston for Texas?"

Tom recalled something that someone had told him on the train, the first day he came in to Texas.

"Well, Mister, I'll tell you true, you ain't goin' to find any place better than Texas. And any place in Texas you decide to stop, is better than any place else."

"What?" his father asked, confused by the response.

Tom put his arm around Rebecca and pulled her closer to him. "This is where I want to be, Dad. And this is where I intend to stay."

The elder Dr. Whitman chuckled, and shook his head. "Then I won't try and talk you out of it," he said. "But when the children start coming, you won't forget about your mother and me up in Boston, will you?"

"I won't let him forget — Dad," Rebecca said.

"I saw the baby you delivered in the barn on Christmas Eve," Tom's mother said. "What a beautiful child he is."

"It wasn't Christmas Eve, it was Christmas morning," Rebecca corrected. "Emanuel is a true Christmas gift."

"I'm proud of you son. I don't know of another surgeon in the country who could have done that."

"I had help," Tom said.

"I know, you had Rebecca and the others with you."

"No," Tom said. He pointed up. "When I say I had help, I mean I had help."